Sharon Bolton is the author of six critically acclaimed novels: *Sacrifice*, *Awakening*, *Blood Harvest*, *Now You See Me*, *Dead Scared* and *Like This, For Ever*.

Sacrifice was nominated for the International Thriller Writers Award for Best First Novel, and voted Top Debut Thriller in the first ever Amazon Rising Stars. *Awakening* won the Mary Higgins Clark award for Thriller of the Year, and in 2010 *Blood Harvest* was shortlisted for the CWA Gold Dagger for Crime Novel of the Year.

In both 2011 and 2012 Sharon was shortlisted for the CWA Dagger in the Library, an award for an entire body of work.

Sharon lives near Oxford with her husband and young son.

BY

SHARON BOLTON

(PREVIOUSLY PUBLISHED AS S. J. BOLTON)

SACRIFICE

AWAKENING

BLOOD HARVEST

NOW YOU SEE ME

DEAD SCARED

LIKE THIS, FOR EVER

Sacrifice

Sharon Bolton

CORGI BOOKS

TRANSWORLD PUBLISHERS
61–63 Uxbridge Road, London W5 5SA
A Random House Group Company
www.transworldbooks.co.uk

SACRIFICE
A CORGI BOOK: 9780552159753

First published in Great Britain
in 2008 by Bantam Press
an imprint of Transworld Publishers
Corgi edition published 2009

A CIP catalogue record for this book
is available from the British Library.

Addresses for Random House Group Ltd companies outside the UK
can be found at: www.randomhouse.co.uk
The Random House Group Ltd Reg. No. 954009

Penguin Random House is committed to a sustainable future for our business, our readers and our planet. This book is made from Forest Stewardship Council® certified paper.

Typeset in Sabon by
Kestrel Data, Exeter, Devon.

Printed and bound in Great Britain by Clays Ltd, St Ives plc

For Andrew, who makes everything possible;
and for Hal, who makes it worthwhile.

Author's Note

Sacrifice is a work of the imagination, inspired by Shetland legend. Whilst I used common Shetland surnames for authenticity, none of the Shetland characters in my book is based on any real person, living or dead. The Franklin Stone Hospital is not intended to be the Gilbert Bain, and Tronal island, as I have described it, does not exist.

I have no reason to believe that any of the events in my book have ever taken place on Shetland.

'There are nights when the wolves are silent and only the moon howls.'

George Carlin

1

THE CORPSE I COULD COPE WITH. IT WAS THE context that threw me.

We who make our living from the frailties of the human body accept, almost as part of our terms and conditions, an ever-increasing familiarity with death. For most people, an element of mystery shrouds the departure of the soul from its earthly home of bone, muscle, fat and sinew. For us, the business of death and decay is gradually but relentlessly stripped bare, beginning with the introductory anatomy lesson and our first glimpse of human forms draped under white sheets in a room gleaming with clinical steel.

Over the years, I had seen death, dissected death, smelled death, prodded, weighed and probed death, sometimes even heard death (the soft, whispery sounds a corpse can make as fluids settle) more times than I could count. And I'd become perfectly accustomed to death. I just never expected it to jump out and yell 'Boo!'

Someone asked me once, during a pub-lunch debate on the merits of various detective dramas, how I'd react if I came across a real live body. I'd known exactly what he meant and he'd smiled even as the daft words left his mouth. I'd told him I didn't know. But I'd thought about it from time to time. What would I do if Joe Cadaver were to catch me by surprise? Would professional detachment click in, prompting me to check for vitals, make mental notes of condition and surroundings; or would I scream and run?

And then came the day I found out.

It was just starting to rain as I climbed into the mini-excavator I'd hired that morning. The drops were gentle, almost pleasant, but a dark cloud overhead told me not to expect a light spring shower. We might be in early May but, this far north, heavy rain was still an almost daily occurrence. It struck me that digging in wet conditions might be dangerous, but I started the engine even so.

Jamie lay on his side about twenty yards up the hill. Two legs, the right hind and fore, lay along the ground. The left pair stuck out away from his body, each hoof hovering a foot above the turf. Had he been asleep, his pose would have been comic; dead, it was grotesque. Swarms of flies were buzzing around his head and his anus. Decomposition begins at the moment of death and I knew it was already mustering speed inside Jamie. Unseen bacteria would be eating away at his internal organs. Flies would have laid their eggs and within hours the maggots would hatch and start tearing their way through his flesh. To cap it all, a hooded crow perched on the fence near by, his gaze shifting from Jamie to me.

Goddamned bird wants his eyes, I thought, his beautiful, tender brown eyes. I wasn't sure I was up to burying Jamie by myself, but I couldn't just sit by and watch while crows and maggots turned my best friend into a takeaway.

I put my right hand on the throttle and pulled it back to increase the revs. I felt the hydraulics kick in and pushed both steering sticks. The digger lurched forwards and started to climb.

Reaching the steeper part of the hill, I calculated quickly. I would need a big hole, at least six, maybe eight feet deep. Jamie was a fair-sized horse, fifteen hands and long in the back. I would have to dig an eight-foot cube on sloping ground. That was a lot of earth, the conditions were far from ideal and I was no digger driver; a twenty-minute lesson in the plant-hire yard and I was on my own. I expected Duncan home in twenty-four hours and I wondered if it might, after all, be better to wait. On the fence-post the crow smirked and did a cocky little side-step shuffle. I clenched my teeth and pushed the controls forward again.

In the paddock to my right, Charles and Henry watched me, their handsome, sad faces drooping over the fence. Some people will tell you that horses are stupid creatures. Never believe it! These noble animals have souls and those two were sharing my pain as the digger and I rolled our way up towards Jamie.

Two yards away I stopped and jumped down.

Some of the flies had the decency to withdraw to a respectful distance as I knelt down beside Jamie and stroked his black mane. Ten years ago, when he'd been a young horse and I was a house officer at St Mary's, the love of my life – or so I'd thought at the time – had dumped me. I'd driven, heart wrenched in two, to my parents' farm in Wiltshire, where Jamie had been stabled. He'd poked his head out of his box when he heard my car. I'd walked over and stroked him gently on the nose before letting my head fall on to his. Half an hour later, his nose was soaked in my tears and he hadn't moved an inch. Had he been physically capable of holding me in his arms, he would have done.

Jamie, beautiful Jamie, as fast as the wind and as strong as a tiger. His great, kind heart had finally given up and the last thing I was ever going to be able to do for him was dig a bloody great hole.

I climbed back into the digger, raised its arm and lowered the bucket. It came up half-full of earth. Not bad. I swung the digger round, dumped the earth, swung back and performed the same sequence again. This time, the bucket was full of compact, dark-brown soil. When we first came here, Duncan joked that if his new business failed, he could become a peat farmer. Peat covers our land to a depth of between one and three yards and, even with the excavator, it was making the job heavy work.

I carried on digging.

After an hour, the rain-clouds had fulfilled their

promise, the crow had given up and my hole was around six feet deep. I'd lowered the bucket and was scooping forward when I felt it catch on something. I glanced down, trying to see round the arm. It was tricky – there was a lot of mud around by this time. I raised the arm a fraction and looked again. Something down there was getting in the way. I emptied the bucket and lifted the arm high. Then I climbed out of the cabin and walked to the edge of the hole. A large object, wrapped in fabric stained brown by the peat, had been half-pulled out of the ground by the digger. I considered jumping down before realizing that I'd parked very close to the edge and that peat – by this time very wet – was crumbling over the sides of the hole.

Bad idea. I did not want to be trapped in a hole in the ground, in the rain, with a tonne and a half of mini-excavator toppled on top of me. I climbed back into the cab, reversed the digger five yards, got out and returned to the hole for another look.

And I jumped down.

Suddenly the day became quieter and darker. I could no longer feel the wind and even the rain seemed to have slackened – I guessed much of it had been wind-driven. Nor could I hear clearly the crackle of the waves breaking on the nearby bay, or the occasional hum of a car engine. I was in a hole in the ground, cut off from the world, and I didn't like it much.

The fabric was linen. That smooth-rough texture is unmistakeable. Although it was stained the rich, deep brown of the surrounding soil I could make out the weave. From the frayed edges appearing at intervals I could see that it had been cut into twelve-inch-wide strips and wrapped around the object like an oversized bandage. One end of the bundle was relatively wide, but then it narrowed down immediately before becoming wider again. I'd uncovered about three and a half feet but more remained buried.

Crime scene, said a voice in my head; a voice I didn't recognize, never having heard it before. *Don't touch anything, call the authorities.*

Get real, I replied. *You are not calling the police to investigate a bundle of old jumble or the remains of a pet dog.*

I was crouched in about three inches of mud that were rapidly becoming four. Raindrops were running off my hair and into my eyes. Glancing up, I saw that the grey cloud overhead had thickened. At this time of year the sun wouldn't set until at least ten p.m. but I didn't think we were going to see it again today. I looked back down. If it was a dog, it was a big one.

I tried not to think about Egyptian mummies, but what I'd uncovered so far looked distinctly human in shape and someone had wrapped it very carefully. Would anyone go to that much trouble for a bundle of jumble? Maybe for a well-loved dog. Except it didn't seem to be dog-shaped. I tried to run my finger in between the bandages. They weren't shifting and I knew I couldn't loosen them without a knife. That meant a trip back to the house.

Climbing out of the hole proved to be a lot harder

than jumping in and I felt a flash of panic when my third attempt sent me tumbling back down again. The idea that I'd dug my own grave and found it occupied sprang into my head like a punch-line missing a joke. On my fourth attempt I cleared the edge and jogged back down to the house. At the back door I realized my wellington boots were covered with wet, black peat and I knew I wouldn't be in the mood for washing the kitchen floor later that evening. We have a small shed at the back of our property. I went in, pulled off my boots, replaced them with a pair of old trainers, found a small gardening trowel and returned to the house.

The telephone in the kitchen glared at me. I turned my back on it and took a serrated vegetable knife from the cutlery drawer. Then I walked back to the . . . my mind kept saying *grave site*.

Hole, I told myself firmly. *It's just a hole*.

Back in it I crouched down, staring at my unusual find, for what felt like a long time. I had an odd feeling that I was about to set off along a hitherto untrodden path and that, once I took the first step, my life would change completely and not necessarily for the better. I even considered climbing out and filling in the hole again, digging another grave for Jamie and never telling anyone what I'd seen. I crouched there, thinking, until I was so stiff and cold I had to move. Then I picked up the trowel.

The earth was soft and I didn't have to dig for long before I'd uncovered another ten inches of the bundle. I took hold of it round the widest part and pulled gently. With a soft slurping noise the last of it came free.

I reached for the end of the bundle I'd uncovered first and tugged at the linen to loosen it. Then I inserted the tip of the knife and, holding tight with my left hand, drew the knife upwards.

I saw a human foot.

I didn't scream. In fact, I smiled. Because my first feeling as the linen fell away was enormous relief: I must have dug up some sort of tailor's dummy, because human skin is never the colour of the foot I was looking at. I let out a huge breath and started to laugh.

Then stopped.

Because the skin was the exact same colour as the linen that had covered it and the peat it had lain in. I reached out. Indescribably cold: undoubtedly organic. Moving my fingers gently I could feel the bone structure beneath the skin, a callus on the little toe and a patch of rough skin under the heel. Real after all, but stained a rich, dark brown by the peat.

The foot was a little smaller than my own and the nails had been manicured. The ankle was slender. I'd found a woman. I guessed she would have been young, in her twenties or early thirties.

I looked up at the rest of the linen-wrapped body. At the spot where I knew the chest would be was a large patch, roughly circular in shape and about fourteen inches in diameter, where the linen changed colour, becoming darker, almost black. Either something peculiar in the soil had affected this patch of linen or it had been stained before she'd been buried.

I really didn't want to see any more; I knew I had to call the authorities, let them deal with it. But somehow, I couldn't stop myself from taking hold of the darker linen and making another cut. Three inches, four, six. I pulled the cloth apart to see what was beneath.

Even then I didn't scream. On legs that didn't feel like my own I stood up and backed away until I came up against the side of the pit. Then I turned and leaped as if for my life. Clambering out, I was surprised by the sight of the dead horse just yards away. I had forgotten Jamie. But the crow had not. He was perched on Jamie's head, digging furiously. He looked up, guiltily; then, I swear, he smirked at me. A lump of shiny tissue, dripping blood, bulged from his beak: Jamie's eye.

That was when I screamed.

I sat by Jamie, waiting. It was still raining and I was soaked to the skin but I no longer cared. In one of our sheds I'd found an old green canvas tent and laid it over Jamie's body, leaving just his head exposed. My poor old horse was not going to be buried today. I stroked his lovely bright coat and twisted show plaits into his mane as I kept silent vigil by my two deceased friends.

When I could no longer bear to look at Jamie, I raised my head and looked out across the inlet of sea water known as Tresta Voe. Voes, or drowned valleys, are a common feature of this part of the world, dozens of them fraying the coastline like fragile silk. It is impossible to describe accurately the twisting, fractured shapes they make, but from the hill above our house I could see land, then the water of the voe as it formed a narrow, sand-rimmed bay, then a narrow strip of hill, then water again. If I were high enough and had good enough vision, I would be able to see it go on, striping alternately, land and sea, land and sea, until my eyes reached the Atlantic and the rock finally gave up the fight.

I was on the Shetland Islands, probably the most remote and least known part of the British Isles. About a hundred miles from the north-eastern tip of Scotland, Shetland is a group of around a hundred islands. Fifteen are inhabited by people; all of them by puffins, kittiwakes, bonxies and other assorted wildlife.

Socially, economically and historically, the islands are unusual; geographically, they verge on the bizarre. When we first stood together on this spot, Duncan wrapped his arms around me and whispered that, long ago, a terrible battle was fought between massive icebergs and ancient granite rocks. Shetland – a land of sea caves, voes and storm-washed cliffs – was its aftermath. At the time, I liked the story, but now I think he was wrong; I think the battle goes on. In fact, sometimes I think that Shetland and its people have spent centuries fighting the wind and the sea . . . and losing.

* * *

It took them twenty minutes. The white car with its distinctive blue stripe and Celtic symbol on the front wing was the first to pull into our yard. *Dion is Cuidich, Protect and Serve,* said the slogan. The police car was followed by a large, black, four-wheel-drive vehicle and a new, very clean, silver Mercedes sports car. Two uniformed constables got out of the police car, but it was the occupants of the other cars that I watched as the group headed towards me.

The Mercedes driver looked far too tiny to be a policewoman. Her hair was very dark, brushing her shoulders and layered around her face. As she drew closer I saw that she had fine, small features and hazel-green eyes. Her skin was perfect, lightly freckled across her nose and the colour of caffe latte. She wore new, green Hunter boots, a spotless Barbour coat and crimson wool trousers. There were gold knots in her ears and several rings on her right hand.

Beside her the man from the four-wheel-drive looked enormous, at least six two, possibly three, and broad across the shoulders. He too wore a Barbour and green wellingtons but his were scuffed, shiny and looked a dozen years old. His hair was thick and gingery-blond and he had the high-coloured, broken-capillaried complexion of a fair-skinned person who spends a lot of time outdoors. His hands were huge and callused. He looked like a farmer. I stood up when they approached and dropped a piece of canvas over Jamie's head. You can say what you like, but in my book even horses have a right to privacy.

'Tora Guthrie?' he asked, stopping two yards away and looking down at the huge, canvas-covered form at my feet.

'Yes,' I said, when he'd looked up at me once more. 'And I think you might be more interested in that one.' I indicated the hole. The woman was already standing on the edge, staring down. Behind her I watched two more police cars pull into my yard.

The policeman-farmer took two strides to bring himself to the edge of my pit. He looked in and then turned back to me.

'I'm Detective Inspector Andy Dunn of the Northern Constabulary,' he said. 'This is Detective Sergeant Dana Tulloch. She'll take you inside now.'

'About six months,' I said, wondering when I was going to stop shivering.

We were in the kitchen, Detective Sergeant Tulloch and I sitting at the pine table, a WPC standing in the corner of the room. Normally, our kitchen is the warmest room in the house, but it didn't feel so today. The sergeant had unbuttoned the neck of her coat but hadn't removed it. I could hardly blame her, but seeing her all bundled up wasn't exactly making me feel any warmer. The constable, too, had kept her outdoor coat on, but at least she'd made us coffee and the hot mug between my hands helped a little.

Without asking, DS Tulloch had plugged a tiny notebook computer into a socket on the wall and, in between shooting questions at me, had been typing away at a speed that would have impressed a 1950s typing pool.

We'd been inside about thirty minutes. I'd been allowed to change out of my wet clothes. Actually, they'd insisted. Everything I'd been wearing had been taken from me, bagged and carried out to one of the waiting cars. I hadn't been given a chance to shower, though, and I was very conscious of peat stains on my hands and dark-brown earth under my fingernails. I couldn't see the field from where I sat but I'd heard several more vehicles pull into the yard.

Three times already, in increasingly tiresome detail, I'd described the events of the last hour. Now, it seemed, it was time for a different line of questioning. 'Five or six months,' I repeated. 'We moved here at the beginning of December last year.'

'Why?' she asked. I'd already noticed her soft, sweet east-coast accent. She wasn't from Shetland.

'Beautiful scenery and a good quality of life,' I replied, wondering what it was about her that was annoying me. Nothing specifically to complain of: she had been polite, if a little detached; professional, if a little cold. She was particularly economical with language, not a word escaping her lips that wasn't strictly necessary. I, on the other hand, was talking too much and getting edgier by the minute. This tiny, pretty woman was making me feel oversized, badly dressed, dirty and – of all things – guilty.

'And it's one of the safest places to live in the UK,'

I added, with a mirthless smile. 'At least, that's what it said on the job ad.' I leaned towards her across the table. She just looked at me.

'I remember thinking it a bit odd,' I gabbled on. 'I mean, when you apply for a new job, what are the questions you like to ask? Does it pay well, how many days' holiday do I get, what are the hours like, how expensive are the local houses and are there good schools in the area? But "Is it safe?" How many people ask that? Almost makes me think you have something to prove up here.'

Detective Sergeant Tulloch had the sort of self-possession I could only dream of. She broke eye contact and looked down at her mug, so far untouched. Then she raised it and sipped carefully before putting it down again. Her lipstick left a faint pink smudge. I never wear lipstick myself and hate to see lipstick stains. They look too personal, somehow, to be left behind like litter; a bit like dropping a tampon wrapper on someone's lounge carpet.

DS Tulloch was looking at me. There was a glint in her eyes that I couldn't identify. She was either pissed off or amused.

'My husband is a ship-broker,' I said. 'He used to work at the Baltic Exchange in London. Around the middle of last year he was offered a senior partnership in a business up here. It was too good a deal to turn down.'

'Bit of an upheaval for you. Long way from the south of England.'

I bowed my head, acknowledging the truth of what

she said. I was a long way from the gentle, fertile hills of the English county where I'd grown up; a long way from the dusty, noisy streets of London, where Duncan and I had lived and worked for the past five years; a long way from parents, brothers, friends – if you didn't count the equine kind. Yes, I was a very long way from home.

'For me, perhaps,' I said at last. 'Duncan is an islander. He was brought up on Unst.'

'Beautiful island. Do you own this house?'

I nodded. Duncan had found the house and put in an offer on one of several visits he'd made last year to sort out the details of his new business. Thanks to a trust fund he'd come into on his thirtieth birthday, we hadn't even needed to apply for a mortgage. The first time I'd seen our new home was when it was already ours and we'd followed the removal vans along the A971. I'd seen a large, stone-built house, about a hundred years old. Large sash windows looked out over Tresta Voe at the front and the hills of Weisdale at the back. When the sun shone (which, I grant you, it sometimes did), the views were stunning. There was plenty of land outside for our horses; plenty of room inside for the two of us and anyone else who might happen to come along.

'Who did you buy it from?'

Realizing the significance of the question, I came out of my little daydream. 'I'm not really sure,' I admitted.

She said nothing, just raised her eyebrows. It wasn't the first time she'd done so. I wondered if it was an interrogation technique: say the minimum yourself and let the suspect gabble. That's when I realized I was a suspect in a murder investigation; and also that it's possible to feel scared, angry and amused, all at the same time.

'My husband handled it,' I said.

Her eyebrows stayed up.

'I was working out my notice in London,' I added, not wanting her to think me one of those women who leave all the financial stuff to the menfolk, even though I am. 'But I do know that no one had lived here for quite some time. The place was in pretty bad shape when we moved in.'

She glanced around my none-too-tidy kitchen, then looked back at me.

'And the previous owners were some sort of trust. Something to do with the church, I think.' I'd taken so little interest. I'd been busy at work, completely unenthusiastic about the move and preoccupied with . . . stuff. I'd just nodded at what Duncan told me and signed where he'd asked me.

'Yes, definitely something to do with the church,' I said, 'because we had to sign an undertaking that we'd behave appropriately.'

Her eyes seemed to get darker. 'Meaning?'

'Well, daft things, really. We had to promise that we wouldn't use it as a place of worship of any kind; that we wouldn't turn it into a drinking or gambling house; and that we wouldn't practise witchcraft.'

I was used to people being amused when I told

them that. DS Tulloch looked bored. 'Would such a contract be enforceable, legally?' she asked.

'Probably not. But as we don't practise witchcraft, it's never really been an issue.'

'I'm glad to hear it,' she said, without a smile. I wondered if I'd offended her and decided I didn't care. If her sensitivities were that delicate she should have chosen a different profession. The room seemed to be getting colder and my limbs were stiffening up. I stretched, stood up and turned to the window.

Behold the crime scene: more police had arrived, including several wearing jumpsuits that appeared to have been made from white plastic bin-liners. A tent had been erected over my excavations. Red-and-white-striped tape stretched the length of our barbed-wire fence and marked out a narrow pathway from the yard. A uniformed policeman was standing just a little too close to Jamie. As I watched, he flicked cigarette ash on to the canvas that covered him. I turned back.

'But given the state of the corpse out there, maybe someone around here dabbles in the black arts.'

She sat up, lost her bored look.

'What do you mean?'

'You should wait for the post-mortem. I could be wrong. The pelvic region is my specialty, not the chest. Oh, and could you ask your colleagues to be careful? I was fond of that horse.'

'I think they have more on their minds than your horse right now, Dr Guthrie.'

'It's Miss Hamilton. And they can show some respect.'

'What do you mean?

'Respect for my property, my land and my animals. Even the dead ones.'

'No, what do you mean, "It's Miss Hamilton"?'

I sighed. 'I'm a consultant surgeon. We are addressed as Mr or Miss. Not Dr. And Guthrie is my husband's name. I'm registered under my own.'

'I'll try to remember that. In the meantime, we need to do something about that horse.'

She stood up. My heart quickened.

'We'll need to get rid of the carcass,' she went on. 'As quickly as possible.'

I stared at her.

'Today,' she emphasized, when I hadn't responded.

'I'll bury him myself just as soon as you're done,' I said, as firmly as I knew how.

She shook her head. 'I'm afraid that won't be possible. The Scientific Support Unit from the mainland will be arriving soon. They'll need to sweep the entire area. We may be here for weeks. We can't work around a rotting horse.'

I think it was her choice of words, accurate but insensitive, that caused the tight ball to materialize in my chest, the one that tells me I'm mad as hell and I really, really need to take care what I say for the next few minutes.

'And, as I'm sure you're aware, burying your own horse has been illegal for several years,' she continued. I glared back at her. Of course I was bloody aware: my mother had been running a riding school for the last thirty years. But I was not about to argue with Sergeant Tulloch about the prohibitive cost of having a horse taken away on Shetland. Nor was I going to tell her about my (admittedly very sentimental) need to keep Jamie close.

Tulloch stood up and looked round. She spotted the wall-mounted telephone above the fridge and walked over to it.

'Would you like to make the arrangements,' she said, 'or should I?'

I honestly think I might have hit her at that point; I even started to stride towards her and, out of the corner of my eye, I saw the WPC step forward too. Fortunately for us both, before Tulloch could lift the receiver, the phone rang. To my increasing annoyance, she answered it, then held it out. 'For you,' she said.

'You don't say!' I made no move to take it from her.

She withdrew her hand. 'Do you want to take the call or not? Sounds important.'

Giving her my best glare, I grabbed the phone and turned my back on her. A voice I'd never heard before started talking.

'Miss Hamilton, Kenn Gifford here. We have a twenty-eight-year-old patient. Thirty-six weeks pregnant. She arrived about fifteen minutes ago, haemorrhaging badly. Foetus showing signs of mild distress.'

I willed myself to focus. Who the hell was Kenn

Gifford? Couldn't place him at all; one of the house officers, maybe, or a locum?

'Who is she?' I said.

Gifford paused. I could hear paper being shuffled. 'Janet Kennedy.'

I swore under my breath. I'd been keeping a close eye on Janet. She was about three stone overweight, had a placenta praevia and, to cap it all, was a rhesus negative blood group. She was booked in for a Caesarean six days from now but had gone into labour early. I looked at the clock. It was five-fifteen. I thought for a second.

Placenta praevia means that the placenta has implanted in the lower, rather than the upper, part of the uterus. It blocks the baby's exit, meaning the little tyke is either stuck where it is – not a good situation – or is forced to dislodge the placenta and interrupt its own blood supply – an even worse situation. Placenta praevia is a major cause of bleeding in the second and third trimesters and of haemorrhage in the final two months.

I took a deep breath. 'Get her into theatre. We need to anticipate intra-operative bleeding so let the blood bank know. I'll be twenty minutes.'

The line went dead, just as I remembered that Kenn Gifford was the Chief Consultant Surgeon and Medical Director at the Franklin Stone Hospital, Lerwick. In other words, my boss. He'd been on sabbatical for the past six months, his departure pretty much coinciding with my arrival on Shetland. Although he'd approved my appointment, we'd never met. Now he was about to watch me perform a difficult procedure with a serious possibility the patient might die.

And there I'd been, thinking the day couldn't possibly get any worse.

2

TWENTY-FIVE MINUTES LATER I WAS GOWNED UP, scrubbed and heading for Theatre 2 when a house officer stopped me.

'What?'

'We don't have any blood,' the young Scotsman replied. 'The bank's out of AB negative.'

I stared at him. What the hell else was going to go wrong? 'You're kidding me,' I managed.

He wasn't kidding. 'It's a rare group. We had an RTA two days ago. We have one unit, that's all.'

'Well, get some more, for God's sake!' On top of everything I'd been through already that day, I was sick with nerves about the coming procedure. I'm afraid I don't do polite in those circumstances.

'I'm not an idiot, you know. We've ordered it. But the helicopter can't take off at the moment. The wind's too strong.'

I glared at him and then pushed my way into theatre just as a huge man in airforce-blue cotton scrubs made the final incision into Janet's uterus.

'Suction,' he said. He took a tube from the attendant scrub nurse and inserted it to drain off the amniotic fluid.

In spite of the mask and theatre hat he wore, I could see at once that Kenn Gifford was exceptional-looking; not handsome, quite the opposite in fact, but striking all the same. The skin I could see above the mask was fair, the type that reveals the blood vessels beneath it and looks permanently pink after a certain age. He hadn't reached that age yet, but the theatre was hot and his colour was high. His eyes were small and deep set, hardly visible from a distance and of an indeterminate colour, even close up. They weren't blue or brown or green or hazel. Dark rather than light; grey perhaps came the closest, and yet I didn't look at him and think, grey eyes. Large, half-moon shadows lay beneath them.

He saw me and stepped back, holding his hands at shoulder height and, with his head, gestured me forward. A screen had been set up to shield Janet and her husband from the gorier aspects of the operation. I looked down, determined to think about nothing but the job in hand; certainly not of Gifford, who was standing, uncomfortably close, just behind my left shoulder.

'I'll need some fundal pressure,' I said, and Gifford moved round to face me.

I went through the usual checklist in my head, noting the position of the baby, location of the umbilical cord. I put my hand under the baby's shoulder and eased gently. Gifford began to push on

Janet's abdomen as my other hand slipped in around the baby's bottom. My left hand moved upwards to cup the head and neck and then gently, forcing myself to go slowly, I lifted the mucus-covered, blood-smeared little body out of his mother and into his life. I felt that second of sheer emotion – of triumph, elation and misery all at once – that makes my face sting, my eyes water and my voice tremble. It passes quickly. Maybe one day it won't happen at all; maybe I'll get so used to bringing new life into the world that it will cease to affect me. I hope not.

The baby began to scream and I allowed myself to smile, to relax for a second, before I handed him to Gifford – who had been watching me very closely – and turned back to Janet to clamp and cut the cord.

'What is it? It is all right?' came her voice from behind the screen.

Gifford took the baby to the Kennedys, allowing them a few moments to cuddle and greet their son before the weighing and testing would begin. My job was to take care of the mother.

Over at the paediatrician's table, Gifford was calling out numbers to the midwife, who was recording them on a chart.

'Two, two, two, one, two.'

He was checking the baby against the Apgar score, a test devised to check the health and fitness of the newborn. Baby Kennedy had scored nine; the test would be repeated twice more but I didn't need the results. I knew he was pretty much perfect.

I couldn't say the same for the mother. She'd lost

a lot of blood, more than we were able to replace and the bleeding was continuing. Immediately after delivery the anaesthetist had given her Syntocinon, the drug routinely administered to prevent post-partum haemorrhage. In most cases it worked. In a very few it didn't. This was going to be one of the few. I delivered the placenta and then called my boss over.

'Mr Gifford.'

He crossed the room and we stood a little back from the Kennedys.

'How much blood would you say she's lost?' I asked. Glancing to the left, my eyes were on a level with his shoulder.

'Couple of units, maybe more.'

'We have exactly one unit in stock.'

He cursed under his breath.

'She's still haemorrhaging,' I said. 'She can't lose any more.'

He stepped closer to Janet and looked at her. Then at me. He nodded. We walked round the screen and stood facing the Kennedys. John was holding his son, joy beaming out of every muscle in his face. His wife, on the other hand, did not look well.

'Janet, can you hear me?'

She turned and made eye contact.

'Janet, you're losing too much blood. The drug we've given you to stop the bleeding hasn't worked and you're getting very weak. I need to perform a hysterectomy.'

Her eyes widened in shock.

'Now?' her husband said, his face draining pale.

I nodded. 'Yes, now. As soon as possible.'

He looked at Gifford. 'Do you agree with this?'

'Yes,' said Gifford. 'I think your wife will die if we don't.'

Pretty blunt, even by my standards, but I couldn't argue with him.

The Kennedys looked at each other. Then John spoke to Gifford again. 'Can you do it?'

'No,' he said. 'Miss Hamilton will do it better than I can.'

I somehow doubted that, but it wasn't the place to argue. I looked over at the anaesthetist. She nodded at me, already set up to administer the general anaesthetic that would be needed for the procedure. A nurse arrived with the consent forms and John Kennedy and his son left the theatre. I shut my eyes briefly, took a deep breath and got to work.

Two hours later, Janet Kennedy was weak but stable, the wind had dropped and the blood she badly needed was on its way. She was probably going to be OK. Baby Kennedy, now named Tamary, was fine and dandy and John was dozing in the chair by his wife's bed. I'd showered and changed, but felt the need to stay at the hospital until the blood arrived. I phoned home to check messages but Duncan hadn't called. I had no idea if the police were still there or not.

Gifford had stayed in theatre throughout the hysterectomy. He might have pretended absolute confidence when speaking to the Kennedys but he'd kept a pretty close eye on me throughout. Only once had he spoken: a sharp 'Check your clamps, Miss Hamilton' when my concentration had slipped a fraction. He'd left the theatre without a word when the operation was over, at least trusting me to close by myself.

I really wasn't sure whether he'd been satisfied with me or not. It had all gone pretty smoothly, but there'd been nothing slick, certainly nothing polished about what I'd done. I'd looked like what I was: a newly qualified and very nervous consultant, desperate not to put a foot wrong.

And now I was annoyed with him. He should have said something; even criticism would have been better than just leaving. I may not have been brilliant but I'd done OK and now I was tired, a bit weepy and rather in need of an encouraging word and a pat on the back. It's a part of myself that I really don't like, this constant need for approval. When I was younger, I assumed it was something I'd eventually grow out of; that self-assurance would come with greater experience and maturity. Just lately, though, I've started to have doubts about that, to wonder if maybe I'll always need the reassurance of others.

I was standing at my office window, watching people and vehicles move around in the car park below. I jumped as the phone rang and rushed back over to my desk, thinking the blood had arrived sooner than expected.

'Miss Hamilton, this is Stephen Renney.'

'Hello,' I said, stalling for time, thinking, *Renney, Renney, I should know that name.*

'I heard you'd been called in. If you're not too busy, there's something you can help me with. Any chance of you popping down?'

'Of course,' I said. 'Anything I need to bring?'

'No, no, just your expertise. Call it professional pride, even professional conceit, if you like, but I do want to hand over a complete report when the big boys get here. I've got a suspicion that could be important and I don't want a couple of smart-arses from the mainland waving it in my face tomorrow morning like some big discovery.'

I had no idea what he was talking about but I'd heard it all before. So reluctant were the islanders to be thought in any way inferior to their mainland counterparts that they created a climate of excellence, even over-achievement, as the norm. Sometimes it actually got in the way of doing the job; sometimes *good enough* was really, honestly, all you needed. When I was in a bad mood and some bolshie registrar was giving me a hard time, I called it the Collective Chip on the Shetland Shoulder.

'I'm on my way,' I said. 'What room are you in?'

'103,' he replied. A room on the ground floor. I put the phone down and left the office. I made my way along the corridor and down the stairs, past radiology, paediatrics and accident & emergency. I followed the corridor, counting off room numbers as I went. I couldn't place room 103 and had no idea of

Stephen Renney's field. I saw the number and pushed open the door.

On the other side, totally blocking the corridor were DI Dunn, DS Tulloch and Kenn Gifford, still in scrubs but having lost the mask and hat. Also a small, bespectacled man with thinning hair who I knew I'd seen before. I guessed he was Stephen Renney and, feeling like a complete idiot, I finally remembered that he was the hospital's locum pathologist.

Room 103 was the morgue.

3

THE SMALL MAN CAME FORWARD, HOLDING OUT a bony hand. There were traces of eczema around his wrist. I took it, trying not to shiver at how cold it felt.

'Miss Hamilton, Stephen Renney. I'm so grateful. I've just been explaining to the detectives that, in the interests of completeness, I really do need—'

The doors opened again and a porter wheeled in a trolley. We all had to stand back against the wall to let him past. Gifford spoke and, away from the tension of theatre, I realized he had one of those deep, educated Highland voices that, prior to my moving here and hearing them on a regular basis, had been guaranteed to put a tickle behind my knees and a smile on my face. One of those 'oh, just keep talking' voices.

'Why don't we go into your office for a moment, Stephen?'

Stephen Renney's office was small, windowless and absurdly tidy. Several pen-and-ink drawings hung on the walls. Two orange plastic chairs were placed, too close together, in front of his desk. He waved his hand at them, glancing from DS Tulloch to me, then back to the detective sergeant. She shook her head. I remained standing too. With a tight smile, Renney lowered himself into his own chair behind the desk.

'This is entirely inappropriate,' Tulloch said to her inspector, gesturing towards me. She was probably right, but I don't like being described as inappropriate; it tends to put my back up.

'Miss Hamilton isn't under suspicion, surely?' said Gifford, smiling down at me. I was surprised and intrigued to see that he wore his hair unusually long for a man, especially a senior surgeon. As he leaned under the powerful electric light above Stephen Renney's desk it shone golden-blond, as I imagined it would do in the sun. His eyebrows and lashes were the same pale colour as his hair, destroying in one fell swoop any claim he might otherwise have had to conventional attractiveness.

'She's only been here six months,' he went on. 'From what you tell me, our friend next door is headed for the British Museum. What's your best guess, Andy? Bronze Age? Iron Age?' He was smiling, not quite pleasantly, as he spoke. I had the feeling Andy Dunn wouldn't know his Bronze Age from his Iron from his Stone, and that Gifford knew it.

'Well, actually . . .' said Stephen Renney, rather quietly, as if afraid of Gifford.

'Something like that,' agreed Dunn, and I was

struck by how alike he and Gifford were – huge, fair-skinned, rather ugly blond men – and also by how many island men I could think of who resembled them. It was as though the islands' gene pool had been pretty much undisturbed since the time of the Norwegian invasions.

'Wouldn't be the first to be found up here,' Dunn was saying. 'Peat bogs are notorious. I remember one in Manchester in the eighties. Police identified it as a woman they suspected of being murdered by her husband twenty years earlier. They brought him in and he confessed. Only it turned out the body was two thousand years old. And a bloke at that.'

Sergeant Tulloch's eyes were darting from one man to the next.

'But if I can—' tried Renney.

'We saw Tollund man once,' said Gifford. 'Do you remember that trip to Denmark in the lower sixth, Andy? Absolutely incredible. Came from the Pre-Roman Iron Age but you could see the stubble on his chin, wrinkles on his face, everything. Perfect preservation. Even the contents of his stomach were still there.'

I wasn't remotely surprised to hear that Gifford and Dunn had been high-school contemporaries. Shetland was a small place. I'd long since got used to everyone knowing everyone else.

'Exactly,' replied Dunn. 'We've got a forensic anthropologist coming over. Maybe we can hang on to it. Be good for tourism.'

'Sir . . .' said Tulloch.

'I really think . . .' said Renney.

'Oh, for God's sake!' I snapped. 'She isn't from the Pre-Roman Iron Age.'

Dunn turned to me as if only just remembering I was there. 'With all due respect—' he began.

'Correct me if I'm wrong,' I interrupted. 'But as far as I'm aware, women in the Pre-Roman Iron Age didn't paint their toenails.'

Dunn looked as though I'd slapped him. Tulloch's mouth twitched briefly, before she pulled it straight again. Gifford stiffened but I couldn't read his expression. Stephen Renney just seemed relieved.

'That's what I've been trying to tell you. This is not an archaeological find. Absolutely not. Peat is confusing. You're right about it having remarkable preservative properties but there are traces of nail varnish on her toenails and her fingernails. Plus some very modern dental work.'

Beside me I heard Gifford take a deep sigh.

'OK, what can you tell us, Stephen?' he asked.

Dr Renney opened the one file that lay on top of his desk. He looked up. I wondered if he felt uncomfortable, staring up at the four of us, but he was such a tiny man he was probably used to it.

'You understand the subject was only brought in just under three hours ago. This is very much an initial report.'

'Of course,' said Gifford, sounding impatient. 'What have you got so far?'

I saw Dunn glance sharply at Gifford; technically, the police inspector was in charge, but the hospital was Gifford's patch. I wondered if we were going to see a clash of the titans.

Stephen Renney cleared his throat. 'What we have,' he began, 'are the remains of a female, aged between twenty-five and thirty-five. The peat has tanned her skin but I've had a good look at her face, her bone structure and her skull and I'm pretty certain she was Caucasian. I'm also as certain as it's possible to be that death wasn't due to natural causes.'

Well, there was an understatement if ever I'd heard one.

'What then?' asked Gifford.

I turned to look at him, wanting to see how he took the news.

Dr Renney cleared his throat. Out of the corner of my eye I saw him glance at me.

'The victim died from massive haemorrhage when her heart was cut out of her body.'

Gifford's head jerked; his face blanched. 'Jesus!' he said.

The two officers didn't react. Like me, they'd already seen the body.

Having got the worst over, Renney seemed to relax a little. 'A series of slashes, some ten, possibly twelve, in all, with a very sharp instrument,' he said. 'I'd say a surgical instrument, or maybe a butcher's knife.'

'Through the ribcage?' said Gifford. It was a surgeon's question. I could think of no common surgical instrument that would cut straight through a ribcage. Neither could he, judging by the way his eyebrows had knit themselves together.

Renney shook his head. 'The ribcage was opened first,' he said. 'Forced open with some sort of blunt instrument, I'd say.'

Saliva was building at the back of my mouth. The orange plastic chair in front of me started to look very inviting.

'Could the heart have been used again?' asked Dana Tulloch. 'Could she have been killed because someone needed her heart?'

I watched DS Tulloch, following her train of thought. One heard of such things: of people being abducted and their organs forcibly removed; of covert, evil operations, organized and funded by people with poor health but heavy wallets. It happened, but in far-away countries with strange-sounding names, where human life, especially that of the poor, was cheap. Not here. Not in Britain and certainly not in Shetland, the safest place to live and work in the UK.

Renney paused before replying and studied his notes for a moment.

'My guess is not,' he said. 'The inferior vena cava was quite neatly removed. As were the pulmonary veins. But the pulmonary trunk and the ascending aorta were quite badly hacked about. As though someone had made several failed attempts. This was no harvest. I'd say someone with a rudimentary knowledge of anatomy, but not a surgeon.'

'I'm off the hook then,' quipped Gifford.

Tulloch glared at him. I bit the inside of my lip to stop the giggle slipping out. I was nervous, that's all; it was really no joking matter.

'I've done a few quick tests and there are very high levels of Propofol in her blood,' continued Renney. He looked at DI Dunn. 'She was almost certainly very heavily anaesthetized when it happened.'

'Thank goodness for that,' said DS Tulloch, still shooting daggers at Gifford.

'How easy is it to get hold of Pro . . .' she began.

'Propofol,' said Renney. 'Well, you can't buy it at the chemist but it's a pretty common intravenous induction agent. Anyone with access to a hospital wouldn't have too much trouble. Maybe someone who worked at a drug company.'

'You can buy just about anything on the black market these days,' said Dunn. He looked at Tulloch. 'Let's not go chasing any red herrings.'

'I also found evidence of trauma around her wrists, upper arms and ankles,' continued Renney. 'I'd say she was restrained for quite some period before death.'

I'd done with being macho. I stepped forward and sat down. Renney caught my eye and smiled. I tried to reciprocate but couldn't quite manage it.

'OK, so we know the how,' said Gifford. 'Any thoughts on the when?'

I leaned forward in my seat. This had been exercising my mind, whenever it hadn't been totally focused on other things, for the whole afternoon. I should explain that, before choosing obstetrics, I'd toyed with the idea of making a career in pathology and had done some rudimentary training. That was before realizing that the moment of life, rather than that of death, held infinitely more appeal. Typical

Tora, my mum had said, always swinging from one extreme to the other. Actually, she'd been hugely relieved. Anyway, thanks to the preliminary training, I had a slightly better than average idea of the decomposition process.

First, the golden rule: decomposition begins at the moment of death. After that, it all depends: on the condition of the body – its size, weight, any wounds or traumas; on its location – indoors or out, warm or cool conditions, exposed to weather or sheltered; on the presence of scavengers or insects; on whether burial or embalming has taken place.

For example, take a corpse abandoned in woodland in a temperate climate such as that of the British Isles. Upon death, the body's internal chemicals and enzymes will combine with bacteria to begin breaking down tissue.

Between four and ten days after death, the body will start to putrefy. Fluid is released into body cavities and various gases – foul-smelling to humans but as tempting as a gourmet dinner to insects – are produced. Gas pressure inflates the body whilst young maggots rampage their way through, spreading bacteria and tearing through tissue.

Between ten and twenty days after death, a corpse reaches the stage of black putrefaction. The bloated body collapses, its exposed parts turn black and it gives off a strong smell of decay. Body fluids will drain into the surrounding soil and, by this stage, several generations of maggots and other larvae will have enjoyed a spell of residence.

By fifty days, most of the remaining flesh will have been removed, the body will have dried out and butyric acid will give it a cheesy smell. Parts in contact with the ground will ferment and grow mould. Beetles will replace maggots as the primary predator and the cheese fly makes a late arrival to finish off any remnants of moist flesh.

A year after death, the body will have reached the stage of dry decay, with only bones and hair remaining. Eventually, the hair too will disappear, eaten by moths and bacteria, leaving only the skeleton.

That's one example. A body frozen in Alpine ice, neither exposed to sunlight nor torn apart by glacier movement, might remain perfect for hundreds of years. On the other hand, one placed in an above-ground vault during a New Orleans summer would be expected to disappear almost completely within three months.

And then you have peat.

Stephen Renney was talking. 'Yes, exactly: when? When did she die? When was she buried? Million-dollar questions, I expect.'

Behind me I heard a sharp intake of breath and felt a stab of sympathy with the detective sergeant. Stephen Renney seemed to be enjoying himself just a little too much. I didn't like it and neither, I guessed, did she.

'Very interesting questions, anyway, because the normal process of decay is completely thrown into the air when you bring peat into the equation. You see, in a typical peat bog – especially one on these islands – you have the combination of cold temperature, the absence of oxygen – which, as we know, is essential for most bacteria to grow – and we also have the antibiotic properties of organic materials, including humic acids, in the bog water.'

'I'm not sure I'm following you, Mr Renney,' said DS Tulloch. 'How can organic materials slow down decomposition?'

Renney beamed at her. 'Well, take sphagnum moss, for example. When the putrefactive bacteria secrete digestive enzymes, the sphagnum reacts with the enzymes and immobilizes them in the peat. The process is brought to an abrupt halt.'

'You're very well informed, Stephen,' said Gifford.

I swear I saw Stephen Renney blush at that point.

'Well, the thing is, I'm a bit of an archaeologist in my spare time. Sort of an amateur Indiana Jones. Part of the reason why I took this job. The wealth of sites on these islands is, well . . . anyway, I've had to learn quite a bit about the nature of peat bogs. Did a bit of reading up when I first came here. Every time there's a dig I go along and volunteer.'

I'd risked a sneaky glance back at DS Tulloch, wanting to see how she took the comparison of the mouse-like Stephen Renney with Harrison Ford. There was no hint of amusement on her face.

'I'm sure Miss Hamilton will correct me if I step out of line,' said DI Dunn, making me jump, 'but nail varnish was around for most of the last century. She could still have been down there for decades?'

Tulloch threw a quick glance at her boss, three tiny frown lines creasing the skin between her eyebrows.

'Well, no, I don't think so,' said Renney, for all the world as though he were apologizing. 'You see, although soft tissue can be very well preserved by acid peat bogs, the same thing just doesn't apply to bone or teeth. In a peat bog, the inorganic component of the bone, the hydroxyapatite, is dissolved away by the humic acids. What's left behind is the bone collagen, which then shrinks into itself and deforms the original outline of the bone. Another thing that happens is that the finger- and toenails,' he glanced at me, 'although preserved in themselves can separate from the body. I've taken bone samples and examined her teeth and I can say with some confidence that there is no trace of this process happening. Her nails are all intact. On the strength of that alone, I'd say she can't have been buried for more than a decade, probably fewer than five years.'

'Looks like you could be a suspect after all, Miss Hamilton,' drawled Gifford, behind me. I decided to ignore that.

Renney looked up at him in alarm. 'No, no, I really don't think so.' He looked down again and shuffled through his notes. 'There's a bit more I have to tell you. Ah yes, when I heard the body was coming I ran a quick Internet check on Miss Hamilton's village. Tresta, I think it's called?'

He waited for confirmation. I nodded.

'Right. Well, I wanted to find out if the area has a history of bog finds. It hasn't, as a matter of fact, but I did find something very interesting.'

He waited for us to respond. I wondered which of us would. I really didn't feel like talking myself.

'What would that be?' asked Gifford, impatient now.

'A massive sea storm took place in the area in January 2005. Severe gale-force winds and three very high tides. The tidal defences – such as they are – were breached and the whole area was flooded for several days. The village had to be evacuated and dozens of livestock were lost.'

I nodded. Duncan and I had been told about it when we bought the house. It had been described as a one-in-a-thousand-year event and we hadn't let it worry us.

'How would that be relevant?' I asked.

'If a bog gets flooded,' replied Renney, 'by either sea water or very heavy rain, its tissue-preserving abilities become impaired. Soft tissue, flesh, internal organs start to deteriorate and skeletonization kicks in. If our subject was in the ground when that storm occurred, I would expect her to be in a much poorer condition than she is.'

'Two and a half years,' mused Gifford. 'Starting to narrow the field down.'

'This will all have to be confirmed,' said Dunn.

'Of course, of course,' gushed Renney. 'I also had a look at her stomach contents. She'd eaten, a couple of hours before she died. There were traces of meat and cheese, some possible remains of grains, maybe from wholemeal bread. Also, something else, that took me a while to identify.'

He paused; no one spoke but this time our unwavering attention must have been enough for him.

'I'm pretty certain they're strawberry seeds. I couldn't find any actual berries, they're very quickly digested, but I'm pretty sure about the seeds. Which would suggest to me a death in early summer.'

'Strawberries are available all year round,' I said.

'Exactly,' snapped Renney, looking delighted. 'But these seeds are unusually small. Less than a quarter the size of normal strawberry seeds. Which suggests . . .'

He was looking at me. I looked back, stupidly, with no idea what he was driving at.

'Wild strawberries,' said Gifford quietly.

'Exactly,' said Renney again. 'Tiny wild strawberries. They can be found all over the islands but have a very short season. Less than four weeks.'

'Late June, early July,' said Gifford.

'Early summer 2005,' I said, thinking I'd misjudged Stephen Renney. He was self-important and irritating but a very clever man nonetheless.

'Or early summer 2006,' said DS Tulloch. 'She could have been in there just a year.'

'Yes, possibly. The key will lie in the tanning process. Matter doesn't tan instantly when it's put in peat; the whole process will take some time. But our subject was completely coloured, meaning the acids had time to seep through the linen and stain the corpse. The time all that takes will be pretty crucial. I intend to get on to it this evening.'

'Thank you,' said Tulloch, sounding as though she meant it.

Wild strawberries. As a last meal I could think of worse. She had eaten wild strawberries and then, a few hours later, someone had cut out her heart. I started to feel sick. Ghoulish curiosity had been satisfied and I wanted to go. Unfortunately, I'd yet to play my part.

'What do you need me for, Dr Renney?' I asked.

'Stephen,' he corrected. 'I need to check something with you. Something in your area.'

'Was she pregnant?' asked Tulloch quickly.

Stephen shook his head. 'No; that I could have spotted for myself. A foetus in the uterus, even a tiny one, is pretty much unmistakable.' He seemed to be waiting for me to speak.

'How big is it?' I said.

'About fifteen centimetres across the diameter.'

I nodded. 'Probably,' I said. 'I'd need to see it to be sure, but maybe . . .' I turned to Inspector Dunn.

'What?' he said, eyes flicking from me to Stephen Renney.

'Our victim had given birth,' said Renney. 'What I can't tell you, and I'm hoping Miss Hamilton can, is how shortly before death it occurred.'

'The uterus swells during pregnancy,' I explained, 'and then starts to contract again immediately after delivery. It usually takes between one week and three. Generally, the younger and healthier the woman, the quicker it happens. If the swelling is still in evidence, it means she gave birth within a couple of weeks of her death.'

'Are you happy for Miss Hamilton to examine the body?' asked Stephen.

DS Tulloch's eyes shot to her boss. He raised his wrist, checked the time and then glanced at Gifford.

'Is Superintendent Harris coming over to take charge?' asked Gifford.

Andy Dunn frowned and nodded. 'For the next couple of days,' he said.

Of course, I had no idea who Superintendent Harris was, but I assumed some bigwig from the mainland. I guessed, from the speed at which they'd arrived at my house earlier, that DI Dunn and DS Tulloch were local and were shortly to find themselves sidelined. Given the rarity of serious crime on Shetland, that had to be incredibly frustrating for them and one look at Tulloch's face told me I was right. Dunn, I was less sure about. He looked troubled.

'Can't hurt to know,' said Gifford. 'Are you OK to do this, Tora?'

I had never felt less OK in my life.

I nodded. 'Of course. Let's get on with it.'

We gowned and scrubbed up, the five of us, each witnessing that the others had totally followed procedure. We put on gloves, masks and hats and followed Stephen Renney into the examination room. It took about fifteen minutes and I had an absurd sense of urgency; of time running out; of needing to make haste, get it done before the grown-ups arrived and put an end to our games.

She lay on a steel trolley in the centre of a white-tiled room. Her linen shroud had been cut clean away, leaving her naked. She looked like a statue, a beautiful brown statue; almost like a bronze carving that had lost some of its lustre. I found myself wandering up towards her head.

She'd been pretty, I thought, but it was hard to be sure. Her features were small and dainty, close to perfect in their regularity. But beauty is so much more than perfection of feature; the particular mix of colour, light and warmth that gives a face beauty are totally lacking in a corpse.

She had very long hair; so long it trailed over the sides of the trolley. It twisted in long spirals; it was the sort of hair I'd dreamed of having as a child. I started to find it hard to look at her face and moved down the body.

Although I'd attended post-mortems in the past – an essential part of training – I'd never seen a murder victim before. Even if I had, I don't think anything could have prepared me for the damage I was looking at.

On her abdomen Dr Renney had made a Y-shaped incision to enable examination of her internal organs. It had been crudely sewn up; an ugly, disfiguring wound. The damage to her chest area was even more extensive but, in this case, Dr Renney carried no responsibility. There was a deep wound between her breasts, roughly oval in shape and about two inches long, where I guessed the blunt instrument had been inserted. I tried to imagine the force needed to inflict such a blow and was glad Dr Renney had told us what he had about Propofol. A jagged tear stretched vertically from the wound in both directions, reaching close to her neck and down almost to her waist, where the forcing open of the ribcage had torn her skin. I had a sudden vision of hands, red with blood, plunging themselves into her and of large, scarred knuckles tensing white with strain as the rib bones started to crack under the force. I swallowed hard.

When I'd found her, the ribcage hadn't been properly closed. I'd seen something of the damage inflicted inside and the missing organ had been conspicuous by its absence. I was inclined to agree with Renney. A heart removed in such a fashion couldn't have been used again.

The room had fallen silent. I realized everyone was waiting for me.

'It's here,' said Renney, from behind me. He was holding a steel dish. He carried it over to the worktop that ran along three walls of the room and I followed. Tulloch stood to my left, Gifford slightly behind. I could hear his breathing above my right ear. Dunn kept his distance.

Bracing myself, I lifted the uterus. It was heavier and larger than you would expect in a woman of her size. I put it on the scales. Fifty-three grams. Dr Renney offered me a ruler. I measured the length and the breadth at its widest, superior level. An incision had already been made and I opened it. The cavity was large and the muscular layers thicker and more defined than you would find in a woman who had never gone to full-term pregnancy. The whole process took about three minutes. When I was satisfied I turned to Stephen Renney.

'Yes,' I said. 'She gave birth between a week and ten days before death. Difficult to be more precise.'

'Will you have a look at her breasts for me?' he asked, smiling, delighted to have been proved right. I swallowed my irritation. This was his job; naturally he wanted to do it thoroughly.

I walked back to the trolley. Our victim was slim, but now I knew what I was looking for, I could see a few rolls of pregnancy fat around her midriff. The flesh around her abdomen looked slack and her breasts seemed large on a small frame. I went closer and ran my hands around the right one; the left was too badly damaged. The lactiferous ducts were swollen and her nipples were large and had cracked in places.

I nodded.

'She'd been feeding,' I said, hearing my voice tremble and not caring. I couldn't look at any of the others. 'Are we done?' I said.

Renney hesitated. 'Well, I was wondering . . .' He glanced down the body. Oh no, I was not examining this woman's vagina. I knew what I would find.

'Perhaps we should leave it for the others now,' I said.

He paused for a moment. 'There is one other thing the officers should see. Will you help me turn her?'

Gifford caught my eye. 'I'll do it,' he said, stepping forward. He walked to the head of the trolley and slid his gloved hands beneath her shoulders. Stephen Renney held her around the hips, counted down, 'Three, two, one, turn,' and she was lifted up and turned. We could see her slender back, freckled shoulders, long slim legs and curved buttocks. No one spoke. The two police officers stepped closer to the trolley and – I couldn't help it – I did too.

'What the hell are they?' asked Gifford at last.

Symbols, three of them, had been carved into the victim's back: the first between her shoulder blades, the second across her waist and the third along her lower back. All three symbols were angular, made up of entirely straight lines; two of them were vertically symmetrical, the third was not. The first, the one between her shoulder blades, reminded me a little of the Christian fish symbol:

ᛟ

The second, across her waist, consisted of two triangles lying on their sides with their apexes touching; how a child might draw an angular bow on a kite string:

ᛞ

The third was just two straight lines, the longest running diagonally from just above the right hip bone to the cleft of her buttocks and the second crossing it diagonally:

Each one measured about six inches at its longest dimension.

'Very shallow wounds,' said Renney, the only one of us not transfixed by what we were looking at. 'Painful, but not life-threatening in themselves. Made with an extremely sharp knife. Again, a scalpel springs to mind.' He glanced at Gifford. So did I. Gifford was still staring at the woman's back.

'While she was alive?' asked Tulloch.

Renney nodded. 'Oh yes. They bled a little, then had time to heal partly. I'd say a day or two before she died.'

'Which would explain the need for restraint,' said Dunn.

Tulloch glanced down and then up at the ceiling, her hands clenched into fists.

'But what are they?' asked Gifford again.

'They're runes,' I said.

Everyone turned to me. Gifford screwed up his already deep-set eyes and twisted his head as if to say, *Come again*.

'Viking runes,' I elaborated. 'I have them in my cellar at home. Carved into some stone. My father-in-law identified them. He knows a lot about local history.'

'Do you know what they mean?' asked Tulloch.

'Haven't a clue,' I confessed. 'Just that they're some sort of ancient script brought over by the Norwegians. You see them quite a lot around the islands. Once you know what you're looking for.'

'Would your father-in-law know what they mean?' asked Tulloch.

I nodded. 'Probably. I'll give you his number.'

'Fascinating,' said Gifford, seemingly unable to take his eyes off the woman.

I peeled off my gloves and was the first to leave the room. Tulloch followed close on my tail.

'So, what happens next?' Kenn Gifford asked, as the four of us walked back down the corridor towards the hospital entrance.

'We start combing through the missing-persons lists,' replied Dunn. 'We get the nail varnish tested, find out what make it is, maybe even what batch, where it was sold. Same with the linen she was wrapped in.'

'With DNA and dental records, and what we know about her pregnancy, it shouldn't take long to find out who she is,' said Tulloch. 'Fortunately, we have a relatively small population up here to work with.'

'Of course, she might not be from the islands at all,' said Inspector Dunn. 'We might be just a convenient dumping ground for a body. We may never know who she was.'

My stomach twisted and I realized how totally unacceptable that possibility was. There would be no closure for me until I knew who she was and how the hell she'd got into my field.

'With respect, sir, I'm sure she was local,' said Tulloch, surprise clear on her face. 'Why would anyone travel out here to bury a body when there are miles of ocean between us and the nearest mainland? Why not just dump her at sea?'

It occurred to me that, had I murdered anyone, I'd have done that anyway. The Shetland Islands have an estimated coastline of around 1,450 kilometres, but a land mass of just 1,468 square kilometres: a very uncommon ratio. Nowhere on Shetland is more than about five miles from the coast and nothing could be simpler than accessing a boat. A weighted body flung overboard a mile or so out to sea would stand a much smaller chance of being discovered than one buried in a field.

At that moment, my pager and Gifford's went off simultaneously. Janet Kennedy's blood had arrived. The two officers thanked us and left, heading for the airport to meet the mainland team.

An hour later, all had gone well and I was back in my office, trying to summon up enough energy to go home. I was standing at the window, watching the day growing dimmer as banks of cloud rolled in from the sea. I could just about make out my reflection in the glass. Normally I change before going home but I was still dressed in surgical trousers and one of the tight vests I always wear under my coat in theatre. I had a sharp, almost stabbing muscle pain between my shoulder blades and I reached back with both hands to massage it.

Two hands, warm and large, dropped on to my shoulders. Instead of nearly jumping out of my skin, I relaxed and allowed my hands to slide out from underneath them.

'Stretch your arms up, high as you can,' commanded a familiar voice. I did what I was told. Gifford pushed down on my shoulders, rotating backwards and down. It was almost painful. Actually, it was very painful. I felt the urge to protest, as much at the impropriety as at the physical discomfort. I said nothing.

'Now, out to the sides,' he said. I reached out, as instructed. Gifford wrapped his hands around my neck and pulled upwards. I wanted to object but found I couldn't speak. Then he twisted, just once, to the right and released me.

I spun round. The pain was gone, my shoulders were tingling and I felt great; as though I'd slept for twelve hours.

'How'd you do that?' I was barefoot and he towered above me. I took a step back, came up sharp against the window ledge.

He grinned. 'I'm a doctor. Drink?'

I felt myself blush. Suddenly unsure of myself, I looked down at my watch: six forty-five p.m.

'There are things I need to talk to you about,' said Gifford, 'and I'm going to be snowed under for the next few days. Besides, you look as though you need one.'

'You got that right.' I found my coat and shoes and

followed him out. As I locked my office I wondered how he'd managed to open the door and cross an uncarpeted room without my hearing him. Come to think of it, how come I hadn't noticed his reflection in the window? I must have been deep, deep in a daydream.

Twenty minutes later we'd found a window seat in the inn at Weisdale. The view of the voe was grey: grey sea, grey sky, grey hills. I turned my back and looked at the fire instead. At home, in London, the blossom would be out in the parks, tourists starting to crowd the streets, pubs dusting off their outdoor furniture. On Shetland, spring arrives late and sulking, like a teenager forced to attend church.

'I'd heard you didn't drink,' said Gifford, as he put a large glass of red wine down in front of me. He sat and ran his fingers through his hair, sweeping it up and back, away from his face. Allowed to fall, it just brushed his shoulders. It was fringeless and layered, a style you sometimes see on men who've never quite got over the rebellion of their youth. On a member of the Royal College it seemed ridiculously out of place and I wondered what he was trying to prove.

'I didn't,' I replied, picking up the glass. 'That is, I don't. Not much. Not usually.' Truth was, I used to drink as much as anyone, more than many, until Duncan and I started trying for a family. Then I'd taken the pledge, and tried to persuade Duncan to do the same. But my resolution had been increasingly weakened of late. It's just so easy to tell yourself that one small glass won't hurt and then, before you know it, one glass becomes half a bottle and another developing follicle is seriously compromised. Sometimes I wish I didn't know quite so much about how the body works.

'I think you have a pretty good excuse,' said Gifford. 'Have you read Walter Scott's *Ivanhoe*?'

I shook my head. The classics had never really been my thing. I'd struggled with, and eventually despaired of, *Bleak House* whilst studying for O-level English. After that, I'd concentrated on the sciences.

Gifford picked up his drink, a large malt whisky. At least that's what it looked like, but for all I knew, it could have been apple juice. Whilst his attention was elsewhere I allowed myself to stare. His face was a strong oval, the dominant feature being his nose, which was long and thick, but perfectly straight and regular. He had a generous mouth, rather well drawn, plump and curved with a perfect Cupid's bow; one could almost say a woman's mouth were it not far too wide to suit a woman's face. That evening it sat in a half smile and deep indentations ran from the corners of his nose to its edges. Gifford was not a good-looking man by any standards. He certainly couldn't measure up to Duncan, but there was something about him all the same.

He turned back to me. 'Pretty nasty thing to happen,' he said. 'Are you OK?'

He'd lost me. 'Umm, finding the body, getting dragged into the post-mortem, or being deprived of *Ivanhoe*?' I queried.

Around us the pub was getting busy; mainly men, mainly young: oil workers, without families, seeking company more than drink.

Gifford laughed. He had large teeth, white but irregular, his incisors particularly prominent. 'You remind me of one of the characters,' he said. 'How are you settling in?'

'OK, thanks. Everyone's been very helpful.' They hadn't, but this didn't seem like the time to grouse. 'I saw the film,' I said.

'There've been several. That yacht's in very shallow water.'

He was looking over my shoulder out of the window. I turned round. A thirty-foot Westerly was sailing close to the shore. It was keeled over hard and if the skipper wasn't careful he'd end up scraping his hull. 'He has too much main up,' I said. 'Do you mean the woman played by Elizabeth Taylor?'

'You're thinking of Rebecca. No, I meant the other one, Rowena the Saxon.'

'Oh,' I said, waiting for him to elaborate. He didn't. In the voe the Westerly crash-tacked and sped off at an obtuse angle to its original course. Then someone on board released the halyard and the mainsail collapsed. The jib started flapping and a rush of movement in the water behind the stern told us he'd started his engine. The boat was under control and heading towards a mooring but it had been a close shave.

'Gets them every time,' said Gifford, looking

pleased. 'Wind pushes them too far to the western shore.' He turned back to me. 'Quite an experience you've had.'

'Can't argue with that.'

'It's over now.'

'Tell that to the army digging up my field.'

He smiled, showing his prominent incisors again. He was making me incredibly nervous. It wasn't just his size; I am tall myself and have always sought the company of big men. There was something about him that was just so *there*. 'I stand corrected. It'll be over soon.' He drank. 'What made you go into obstetrics?'

When I got to know Kenn Gifford better, I realized that his brain works twice as fast as most people's. In his head, he flits from one topic to another with absurd speed, like a humming bird dipping into this flower, then that, then back to the first; and his speech follows suit. I got used to it after a while but at this first meeting, especially in my keyed-up state, it was disorientating. Impossible for me to relax. Although, come to think of it, I don't think I ever relaxed when Kenn was around.

'I thought the field needed more women,' I said, sipping my drink again. I was drinking far too quickly.

'How horribly predictable. You're not going to give me that tired old cliché about women being gentler and more sympathetic, are you?'

'No, I was going to use the one about them being less arrogant, less bossy and less likely to jump on their dictatorial high horse about feelings they will never personally experience.'

'You've never had a baby. What makes you so different?'

I made myself put my drink down. 'OK, I'll tell you what did it for me. In my third year I read a book by some chap called Tailor or Tyler – some big obstetrical cheese at one of the Manchester hospitals.'

'I think I know who you mean. Go on.'

'There was a whole load of bunkum in it, mainly about how all the problems women experience during pregnancy are due to their own small brains and inability to take care of themselves.'

Gifford was smiling. 'Yes, I wrote a paper along those lines myself once.'

I ignored that. 'But the bit that really got me was his dictum that new mothers should wash their breasts before and after each feed.'

Enjoying himself now, Gifford leaned back in his chair. 'And that is a problem because . . .'

'Do you have any idea how difficult it is to wash your breasts?' From the corner of my eye, I saw someone glance in our direction. My voice had risen, as it always does when I'm sounding off. 'New mothers can feed their babies ten times or more in twenty-four hours. So, twenty times a day, they're going to strip to the waist, lean over a basin of warm water, give them a good lather, grit their teeth when the soap stings the cracked nipples, dry off and then get dressed again. And all this when the baby is screaming with hunger. The man is out of his tree!'

'Clearly.' Gifford's eyes flicked round the room. Several people were listening to us now.

'And I just thought, "I don't care how technically brilliant this man is, he should not be in contact with stressed and vulnerable women."'

'I completely agree. I'll have breast-washing taken off the post-natal protocols.'

'Thank you,' I said, feeling myself starting to smile in response.

'Everyone I've spoken to seems highly impressed with you,' he said, leaning closer.

'Thank you,' I said again. It was news to me, but nice news all the same.

'Be a shame for you to be thrown off course so early.'

And the smile died. 'What do you mean?'

'Finding a body like that would unsettle anyone. Do you need to take a few days off? Go visit your parents, maybe?'

Time off hadn't even occurred to me. 'No, why should I?'

'You're traumatized. You're handling it well, but you have to be. You need to get it out of your system.'

'I know. I will.'

'If you need to talk about it, it's better that you do so away from the islands. Actually, much better if you don't do it at all.'

'Better for whom?' I said, understanding, at last,

the real reason for our cosy little chat down the pub.

Gifford leaned back in his chair and closed his eyes. For several seconds he didn't move; I even started to wonder if he'd fallen asleep. As I watched, his mouth, not his nose, became the most prominent feature of his face. It almost became a beautiful mouth. I found myself thinking about stretching out a finger, gently tracing its outline.

He sat up, startling me, and glanced around. Our audience had all returned to their own conversations but he lowered his voice all the same.

'Tora, think about what we saw in there. This is no ordinary murder. If you just want someone dead, you slit their throat or put a pillow over their face. Maybe you blow their brains out with a shotgun. You don't do what was done to that poor lass. Now, I'm no policeman but the whole business smacks of some sort of weird ceremonial killing.'

'Some sort of cult thing?' I asked, remembering my taunts to Dana Tulloch about witchcraft.

'Who knows? It's not my place to speculate. Do you remember the child abuse scandal on the Orkneys some years ago?'

I nodded. 'Vaguely. Satanism and some stuff.'

'Satanism codswallop! No evidence of wrongdoing or abuse was ever discovered. Yet we had family homes broken into at dawn and young children dragged screaming out of their parents' arms. Have you any idea what the impact of all that was on the islands and the island people? Of the impact it's still having? I've seen what happens on remote islands when rumour and hysteria get out of hand. I don't want a repeat of that here.'

I stiffened. Put my drink down. 'Is that really what's important right now?'

Gifford leaned towards me until I could smell the alcohol on his breath. 'Too right it's important,' he said. 'The woman in Dr Renney's tender care is none of our concern. Let the police do their job. Andy Dunn is no fool and DS Tulloch is the brightest button I've seen in the local police for a long time. My job, on the other hand, and yours, is to make sure the hospital continues to function calmly and that a ridiculous panic does not get a hold on these islands.'

I could see the first prickles of a beard jutting through his chin. The hairs were mostly fair but some were red, some grey. I made myself look back up into his eyes, but looking directly at him was making me uncomfortable; his stare was just a little too intense. Green, his eyes were, a deep, olive-green.

'You've had a terrible experience, but I need you to put it behind you now. Can you do that?'

'Of course,' I said, because I didn't have a choice. He was my boss, after all, and it was hardly a request. I knew, though, that it wasn't going to be that easy.

He sat back in his chair and I felt a sense of relief, although he hadn't been anywhere close to touching me. 'Tora,' he said. 'Unusual name. Sounds like it should be an island name, but I can't say I've heard it before.'

'I was christened Thora,' I said, telling the truth for the first time in years. 'As in Thora Hird. When I got brave enough I dropped the H.'

'Damnedest thing I ever saw,' he said. 'I wonder what happened to the heart.'

I sat back too. 'Damnedest thing I ever saw,' I muttered. 'I wonder what happened to the baby.'

4

'Tora, what the hell were you thinking of?'

Our sitting room was gloomy. The sun appeared to have called it a day and Duncan hadn't bothered with the light switch. He was sitting in a battered old leather chair, one of our 'finds' from our bargain-hunting days around Camden market when we were first married. I stood in the doorway, looking at his outline, not seeing his face properly in the shadows.

'Trying to bury a horse by yourself,' he went on. 'Do you know how much those animals weigh? You could have been killed.'

I'd already thought of that. A moment's carelessness, a tumbling earth-mover and I could have become the body in the peat. It could have been me lying on the steel trolley today, being probed and measured and weighed by the good Dr Renney.

'And it's illegal,' he added.

Oh, give me a break. It had been illegal in Wiltshire too, but when had that ever stopped a Hamilton woman? Mum and I had buried dozens of horses over the years. I wasn't about to stop now.

'You're home early,' I said, pointing out the obvious.

'Andy Dunn phoned me. Thought I should get back here. Jesus! Have you seen the state of the field?'

I turned my back on Duncan and walked through to the kitchen. I tested the weight of the kettle and flicked the switch. Beside it stood our bottle of Talisker. The level seemed to have gone down considerably. But then again, I'd just come from the pub myself, hadn't I? Who was I to get preachy?

A movement behind me made me jump. Duncan had followed me into the kitchen.

'Sorry,' he said, putting his arms around me. 'It was a bit of a shock. Not quite the welcome home I'd expected.'

Suddenly, it all seemed more manageable. Duncan, after all, was supposed to be on my side. I turned round so that I could put my arms around his waist and drop my head against his chest. The skin of his neck smelled warm, musty; like paper fresh off the mill.

'I tried to phone,' I said lamely.

He let his chin drop so that it rested on the top of my head. It was our favourite hug pose, familiar, comforting.

'I'm sorry about Jamie,' he said.

'You hated Jamie,' I replied, nuzzling into his neck and thinking that one of the best things about Duncan was that he was so much taller than I. (One of the worst was that his jeans were two sizes smaller than mine.)

'Did not.'

'Did too. You called him the Horse from Hades.'

'Only because he repeatedly tried to bring about my demise.'

I leaned back to look him in the face and was struck, for the millionth time, by how bright blue his eyes were. And by how gorgeous a contrast they made with his pale skin and spiky black hair. 'What are you talking about?'

'Well, let me think. How about the time he got spooked by some cyclists on Hazledown Hill, leaped into the air, spun a 180-degree turn, shot across the road in front of the vicar's new convertible, and took off down the hill with you yelling "Pull him up, pull the fucker up!" at the top of your voice.'

'He didn't like bikes.'

'Wasn't too keen on them myself after that.'

I laughed, something I couldn't have imagined myself doing just half an hour earlier. Nobody, my whole life, has ever been able to make me laugh the way Duncan can. I fell in love with Duncan for a whole host of reasons: the way his grin seems just a little too wide for his face; the speed at which he can run; his complete refusal to take himself seriously; the fact that everyone likes him and he likes everyone, but me most of all. As I say, there were a whole load of reasons why it all started, but it was the laughing that kept me in there.

'And what about that time we were crossing the Kennet and he decided to roll?'

'He was hot.'

'So he gave me a cold bath. Oh, and—'

'OK, OK, you've made your point.'

He tightened his arms around me. 'I'm still sorry.'

'I know. Thanks.'

He pushed me away from him and we made eye contact. He ran the side of his hand down my cheek.

'Are you OK?' He wasn't talking about Jamie any more.

I nodded. 'I think so.'

'Want to talk about it?'

'I don't think I can. What they did to her, Dunc . . . I can't.' I couldn't go on, couldn't talk about what I'd seen. But that didn't mean I could stop thinking about it. I wasn't sure I would ever be able to stop thinking about it.

Women in the first few days after childbirth – especially their first childbirth – are intensely vulnerable, often physical and emotional wrecks. Their bodies are weakened, thrown into confusion by the trauma of delivery and by rampant hormones, racing round all over the place. Feeding at all hours, they soon become exhausted. Plus, they're often reeling from the shock of the overwhelming connection they feel to the tiny life they've just produced.

There are good reasons why new mothers look and act like zombies, why they burst into tears at the drop of a hat, why they so often think normal life will be, for ever more, beyond them. To take a woman in this state, pin her down and carve up her flesh was the most unspeakable act of callousness I'd ever imagined.

He shushed me and held me close again. We stood, not talking, for what felt like a long time. Then, almost out of habit, I raised one finger to stroke the hair at the nape of his neck. It had been cut recently and was very short. It felt like silk.

He shivered. Well, he had been away for four days.

'The police will want to talk to you,' I said, straightening up. I was hungry and needed a bath.

Duncan's arms dropped to his side. 'They already have.' He walked over to the fridge and opened the door. He squatted down, peering inside, more in hope than expectation.

'When?' I asked.

'Did it all over the phone,' he said. 'Dunn said he shouldn't need to bother me again. She was almost certainly buried before we came here.'

'They were asking about the previous owners.'

'Yeah, I know. I said I'd drop the deeds off at the station tomorrow.' Duncan stood up again. He carried a plate on which sat a half-eaten chicken carcass. He crossed to the table, put it down and returned to the fridge. 'Tor, we need to try and forget about it now.'

Twice in two hours someone had told me that. Forget about the fact that you dug up a corpse – minus heart, minus newborn baby – in your back field this afternoon.

'Dunc, they're digging up the field. They're looking for more bodies. I don't know about you, but I'm going to find that a bit difficult to ignore.'

Duncan shook his head, the way a fond parent does when his child has become over-excited about something. He was preparing salad and I didn't like the way his knife was slicing into a red pepper.

'There aren't any more bodies and they'll be finished by the end of tomorrow.'

'How can they possibly know that?'

'They have instruments that can tell. Don't ask me exactly how it works. You probably understand it better than I do. Apparently, decomposing flesh gives off heat and these gizmos can pick it up. Like metal detectors.'

Except any bodies out there were buried in peat. They weren't decomposing. 'I thought they'd have to dig up the whole field.'

'Apparently not. The wonders of modern technology. They've already done one sweep and found nothing. Not even a dead rabbit. They'll do another tomorrow, just to be sure, then they're out of here. Do you want something to drink?'

I filled a jug with water from the tap and added ice from the freezer. One benefit of living on Shetland was that we were saving a fortune on bottled water. Oh, and the local smoked salmon was pretty good. Apart from that, I was struggling.

'That wasn't the impression Detective Sergeant Tulloch gave me. She thought they'd be here for some time.'

'Yes, well, reading between the lines, I think the sergeant has a tendency to get a touch over-enthusiastic. Bit too anxious to make her mark and not afraid to set a few hares running in the meantime.'

Which hadn't been the impression I'd had of Dana Tulloch. She'd struck me as someone who played her cards quite close to her chest.

'You seem to have got very chummy with DI Dunn on the strength of one phone call.'

'Oh, we know each other from way back.'

I should have known. I felt a touch of annoyance that Duncan, who'd played no part in the discovery of the body, should have been given far more information than I had, purely on the strength of being a fellow islander.

We sat down. I buttered some bread. Duncan served himself a large helping of cold chicken. Some of the flesh was still pink and jelly had congealed around it. At the sight of it, the nausea I'd been fighting in the post-mortem room reared up again. Great, after nearly fifteen years in medicine, I was getting squeamish. I helped myself to salad and a piece of cheese.

'Were there any reporters when you got home?' I asked. By the time I'd arrived, just before nine, the place had been deserted apart from one solitary copper standing guard. I'd braced myself to run the gauntlet of press questioning and been pleasantly surprised.

Duncan shook his head. 'Nope. Dunn's trying

to keep a lid on the whole thing. Apparently under pressure from his Super. Thinks it might be bad for business, just as the summer tourist season starts.'

'Jesus, not again. I had the same thing from Gifford just now. Bad for hospital PR. I think you people need to get your priorities sorted out. This is not the people's republic of Shetland. You are remotely answerable to the outside world.'

Duncan had stopped eating. He was looking at me, but I didn't think he was still listening.

'What?' I said.

'Gifford,' he replied. The shine had gone from his eyes.

'My new boss. He's back. I met him just now.' Mentioning the drink didn't seem like a terribly good idea.

Duncan stood up, emptied his glass of pure Shetland water into the sink and poured an inch of neat Talisker into it. He drank, looking out of the window, his back to me.

'Can't help thinking there's a story here,' I said.

Duncan didn't answer.

'Anything I need to know?' I tried again.

Duncan muttered something that included more than one expletive and the phrase 'should have known'. Unlike me, he doesn't normally swear much. By this stage I was shamefully, gleefully curious.

He turned. 'I'm going for a bath,' he said as he left the room.

I made myself wait ten minutes before I followed him. I wandered back into our sitting room. There was one bookcase, its contents somewhat sparse. I'm really not much of a reader. Duncan tells anyone who'll listen that I won't consider a novel not written by someone called Francis (Dick or Claire – take your pick). Duncan is marginally better, but not exactly one for the classics. He had, however, inherited his grandfather's library and there were a few volumes by Dickens, Trollope, Austen and Hawthorne on the top shelf. I looked closely. Nothing by Walter Scott.

So I switched on the TV just as the late news was starting. If I'd been hoping for a starring role I'd have been disappointed. The last item was a twenty-second piece about the discovery of a corpse in some peat land several miles outside Lerwick. The location hadn't been specified, nor had there been any footage of our home. Instead, DI Andy Dunn, standing outside Lerwick police headquarters, had said the minimum possible whilst still using words. He did, though, finish with a speculative comment about the possibility of an archaeological find – I guessed the recording had been made before we'd met Stephen Renney. It was an obvious attempt to play down the situation but I assumed he knew what he was doing.

When I judged I'd left enough time I went upstairs. Duncan was in the bath with his eyes closed. He'd filled the tub so full that water was trickling down the overflow pipe. I knew from experience that the temperature would be pretty close to forty degrees. Duncan and I never shared a bath. About a year ago, before the sperm tests, I'd wondered if Duncan's hot baths were behind our failure to conceive. The effect of hot water on sperm is well known and I'd suggested he might try soaking his testicles in ice water for five minutes a day. He'd looked me straight in the eye and asked, 'How?' I was still thinking about it. Maybe one day I'd invent a device for the convenient cold soaking of the male genitalia. Western fertility levels would soar and I'd make my fortune.

I leaned against the sink. Duncan made no sign of knowing I was there.

'You can't just leave it at that, you know. I have to work with the man. We're probably expected to entertain him and his wife for dinner over the next couple of months.'

'Gifford isn't married.'

I felt a jolt of something like relief mixed with alarm. Had I been hinting? And if I had, had Duncan spotted it?

'What is it?' I tried again.

Duncan opened his eyes but didn't look at me. 'We were at school together. I didn't like him. The feeling was mutual.'

'He's from Unst?'

Duncan shook his head. 'No, I'm talking about secondary school.' That made more sense. On Shetland, children from the more remote islands often attend secondary school in Lerwick, either boarding during the week or staying with relatives.

'Is that it?' I said.

Duncan sat up. He looked me up and down. 'You coming in?'

I leaned across, dipped my hand in the water and took it out again quickly. 'No,' I said.

Duncan picked up the loofah and held it out to me. It looked like some sort of kinky invitation. If I picked it up, we would have sex. If I didn't, I was rejecting him and would have to deal with sulks for the next couple of days. I thought for a second. My period was due any day but you can never be sure about these things. It was worth a try. I reached out for the loofah. Duncan leaned forward towards the tap, exposing his sleek, strong back.

'I prefer my handmaidens naked,' he said.

With one hand, I started to rub the loofah up and down his back. With the other, I unfastened the buttons of my shirt.

5

AFTER DUNCAN AND I HAD MADE LOVE I SLEPT deeply. Until something woke me. I lay in the half light of our bedroom, listening to Duncan's steady breathing beside me. Otherwise silence. Yet I'd heard something. People don't wake suddenly from deep sleep for no reason. I listened hard. Nothing.

I turned to look at the clock: three-fifteen a.m., and about as dark as it ever got on Shetland during the summer, which wasn't very. I could see everything in the room: cherry-wood furniture, lilac light-shades, free-standing mirror, clothes slung over the back of a chair. A pale glow like early dawn shone around the blind.

I got up. The rhythm of Duncan's breathing changed and I froze. After a few seconds I walked to the window. Slowly, trying not to make a sound, I pulled up the blind.

It wasn't the brightest of Shetland nights; it still appeared to be raining softly, but I could make out just about everything: white police tent; red-and-white-striped tape; sheep in the neighbouring field; the solitary spruce tree that grew at the bottom of what passed for our garden; Charles and Henry, wide awake, with their noses poking over the fence, the way they do when someone appears in the next field. Horses are friendly – and nosy. If they see someone close by, they hurry over for a better look. So who were they looking at?

Then I saw the light.

It appeared inside the police tent, a faint brightness shining briefly behind the white canvas; flashing quickly then disappearing; then again. Flash, sweep, flicker.

Something stroked my bare hip. Then Duncan's warm body pressed against me from behind. He swept my hair up, pushed it over one shoulder and bent down to kiss my neck.

'There's someone in the field,' I said. His hands slid around my waist and moved higher.

'Where?' he asked, nuzzling the place behind my ear.

'In the tent. There's a torch. There.'

'Can't see anything,' he said as his hands found my breasts.

'Well, you won't. You're not looking.' I pushed his hands away and they dropped down to the window ledge.

'It'll be the police,' he said. 'Dunn said they'd be leaving someone here overnight.'

'I suppose.'

We stood staring out into the darkness, waiting, but the light didn't appear again.

'Did they hurt her?' asked Duncan after a minute or two, so quietly I could barely hear him.

I turned in surprise, glared at him. 'They cut out her heart.'

Duncan's pale face drained. He stood back, arms falling to his sides. Instantly I regretted being so brutal. 'Dunn didn't tell you that? I'm sorry . . .' I began.

He shushed me. 'It's OK. Did they . . . he . . . was he cruel?'

'No,' I said, remembering everything Dr Renney had told us about the strawberries, the anaesthetic. 'That's the strangest thing. He . . . they . . . they fed her, gave her pain relief. They almost seemed to . . . care for her.' They cared for her. Before they tied her up and carved Nordic symbols into her skin, of course. What kind of sense did that make? I shut my eyes, but the image was still there.

Duncan rubbed his hands over his face. 'Jesus, what a mess.'

There didn't seem an immediate answer to that, so I said nothing. Duncan made no move to go back to bed and neither did I. After a while I started to feel the chill. I closed my eyes and leaned against him, seeking warmth rather than intimacy, but he wrapped his arms around me and his hands started to move down my back. Then stopped. 'Tor, would you consider adoption?' he said.

I opened my eyes. 'You mean a baby?' I asked.

He squeezed one buttock. 'No, a walrus. Of course I mean a baby.'

Well, he'd certainly taken me by surprise. I hadn't thought about adoption, hadn't considered we were anywhere near that stage. We had any number of boxes to tick first. Adoption was the last resort, wasn't it?

'It's just there's a good programme on the islands. Or, at least, there always used to be. It's not difficult to adopt here. A newborn, I mean. Not an emotionally screwed-up teenager.'

'How can that be?' I said, thinking that the adoption laws here were surely the same as for the rest of the UK. 'How can Shetland have more babies than anywhere else?'

'I don't know. I just remember it being discussed when I lived here before. Maybe we're more old-fashioned about single mothers.'

It was possible. Churches were better attended here than on the mainland and, on the whole, moral standards seemed comparable with what they'd been in the rest of the UK some twenty or thirty years ago. In Shetland, teenagers stand up on buses to let old ladies sit down. On the roads, drivers wait by passing spaces instead of racing to beat the oncoming car. Maybe this was a real possibility that I hadn't considered.

Then Duncan took hold of me round the waist and lifted. He put me down on the window ledge. The glass was cold and slightly damp against my back. He lifted my legs and wrapped them around his waist. I knew exactly what was coming. The ledge was just the right height and we'd done this before.

'Of course,' he said, 'we could just keep trying.'

'For a little while longer maybe,' I whispered, watching him lower the blind.

And we kept on trying.

6

SARAH SAT ON THE EDGE OF HER CHAIR. SHE had the *look* in her eye: angry, ashamed, impatient; the one that would increase in intensity month by month, anger gradually giving way to despair as the arrival of each menstrual period signalled a fresh failure. Of course, it could also disappear, completely and for ever, the second she knew she was pregnant. I knew that look so well. I saw it all the time. And not just on the faces of patients.

Robert's expression, on the other hand, I couldn't read. He had still to look me in the eye.

Although this was their first meeting with me, Sarah and Robert Tully had already run the gauntlet of tests, examinations and interviews with counsellors. They were running out of patience. He wanted the pats on the back down the local and the weekends browsing through model-train brochures. She wanted her feet up in stirrups and a good dose of artificial hormone coursing round her veins.

'We were hoping you'd put us on the IVF programme,' she said. 'We know there's a waiting list for NHS treatment but we have some money saved up. We want to start right away.'

I nodded. 'Of course. I understand.' Oh, how well did I understand: *Get me pregnant. I don't care how you do it. I don't even want to think about everything that comes after – the nausea, exhaustion, backache, stretch marks, total lack of privacy, and then pain beyond anything I could ever have imagined. Just wave your magical, medical wand and make it OK for me too.*

What I was about to suggest they would find incredibly hard to accept; patience and the biological urge to reproduce don't make comfortable bedfellows. 'There is another way forward that I'd like you to think about.'

'We've been trying for three years.' With something between a hiccup and a sob she started to cry. Robert glared at me as though their failure to conceive was entirely my doing and gave his wife the handkerchief he'd had ready in his hand.

I decided to give them a moment. I stood and walked to the window.

It had been raining as I'd driven into Lerwick that morning and the clouds above were low and heavy, the town dark and damp.

Lerwick is a grey stone town on the eastern coast of the main island, a short channel hop from the island of Bressay. Like the rest of the islands' townships, it isn't noted for its architecture: the buildings are simple and functional but rarely beautiful. The traditional choice of building material is local granite with a slate roof. For the most part, two storeys are thought ample by the practical islanders – maybe they worry about high winds blowing roofs away – but in the older parts of town and around the harbour a few three-storey, even four-storey houses can be seen. They seem to represent a rare flash of ambition, or defiance, on the part of the islanders.

Gazing at a rain-washed Lerwick did nothing to improve my mood.

I found myself stifling a yawn. I hadn't slept well. Even when I hadn't been fully awake and out of bed, I'd been restless, my head full of the woman I'd found. I'd seen her, touched her, knew something of what had happened to her. It was appalling . . . I should be appalled, and I was . . . but I was angry too. Because I'd wanted to plant snowdrops on Jamie's grave to remind me of the time he tried to eat some. I'd gone out one evening to call him in and found a tiny white flower sticking out of his mouth. He'd looked like an equine flamenco dancer. But now I'd never be able to do that because some sick bastard had chosen our land to bury his dirty work on. And Jamie had been carted off to the knackers' yard.

There was a movement behind me; a fidget. Sarah had stopped crying. I sat down again and turned to her.

'You're only thirty-one. You have a long way to go before you need worry about time running out.' I, on the other hand, was thirty-three. 'There's no guarantee of a baby using IVF. The clinic I'd refer you to has an average success rate of 27 per cent per treatment and, frankly, you're likely to have a below-average expectation of success.'

'Why?' said Robert.

I glanced down at the file again, although I already knew what it said.

'Between you, you're dealing with sub-quality sperm and highly irregular periods. The tests you had on your last visit and the lifestyle questionnaire you filled in suggest some reasons why that might be.'

Both looked defensive, as though I was about to tell them it was their fault. Well, in a way it was.

'Go on,' said Robert.

'Both of you show deficiencies in certain minerals that are very useful to conception. Sarah, your levels of zinc, selenium and magnesium are very low. You also have a lot of aluminium in your body. Robert, you have low zinc levels too, but what worries me more is a very high level of cadmium.' I paused. 'That's a toxin present in tobacco smoke. You smoke about twenty cigarettes a day. And you drink alcohol most days. You too, Sarah.'

'My father smoked forty a day and drank whisky just about every day of his adult life,' said Robert. 'He had five kids before he was thirty.'

I was losing this couple; but I wasn't about to compromise everything I believed in just to give them some false hope today. On the other hand, they might just get pregnant on their first IVF attempt. It was a huge lottery and I could be doing them a great disservice by persuading them to wait.

'What I'd like to suggest is that you forget all about getting pregnant for the next six months and concentrate on becoming as healthy as you possibly can.' I could see Robert about to interrupt. 'Healthy people have the best chance of conceiving, Robert. I'd like to see you give up smoking and both of you to cut out alcohol completely.'

Robert shook his head, as though despairing of my idiocy.

'I know it will be hard,' I went on, 'but if you want a baby, you'll try. Even cutting down will help. Also, I'm going to prescribe a course of supplements to eliminate the various deficiencies you have and I want you both to be tested for a number of infections.'

They weren't going to buy it. They'd come here for sophisticated medical intervention and I was offering them vitamin C.

'Do you really think just that will make much difference?' asked Sarah.

I nodded. 'Yes, I do. I've written everything down.' I handed over a typed sheet to Sarah. 'If you follow this plan, at the end of six months, you'll be much healthier than you are now and the chances of IVF being successful will have substantially increased.' I tried to smile. 'Who knows, you may not even need IVF.'

They stood up, sullenly, like children denied a treat. I wondered if they'd try the plan or just travel to a clinic on the Scottish mainland, where they'd almost certainly be guaranteed a more sympathetic response. Not everyone shared my conviction about the importance of health and nutrition when trying to conceive.

Sarah turned at the door. 'I know you mean well,' she said, 'but we just want a baby so much.'

The sound of their footsteps along the corridor faded away. I opened my top drawer and took out an orange file. The first sheet was the result of a sperm test taken in London twelve months earlier.

Total number of spermatozoa present: 60 million per ml – normal
Percentage of sperm alive at one hour: 65% – normal
Morphology level: 55% – normal
Antibody levels: 22% – normal

And so on, down to the bottom of the page. Everything normal. The name on the top was Duncan Guthrie, my totally normal husband. It was the third test he'd had. The results of the previous two were practically identical. Whatever our problem, it didn't lie with him.

My own notes were underneath. FSH, LH, oestrogen and progesterone levels were all well within the normal ranges. My hormones were OK and, as far as I could tell via a slightly awkward self-examination, everything appeared to be in place.

The Tullys had been my last appointment but I had a ward round in twenty minutes. Immediately afterwards I had to drive north and catch a ferry to the island of Yell for my monthly visit. I'd meet with the island's midwife and hold a clinic for the eight women currently pregnant there.

Getting up, I wandered back over to my office window. The car park was immediately below. Without really thinking I found myself searching for Gifford's silver BMW. Let it go now, he'd said, let the police do their job. He was right, of course. But I still had eighteen minutes to kill.

Back at my desk I accessed the hospital's intranet site. I clicked on a few icons, thought a bit, then clicked on a couple more. For a hospital website it was surprisingly easy to navigate. It wasn't long before I had the file I wanted: a list of every baby born on the islands since records had been computerized.

Stephen Renney believed the woman in my field had been dead for around two years, meaning her baby had to have been born sometime during 2005. If he was right about the strawberry seeds, the birth would most likely have taken place in summer. I highlighted the section between March and August and pressed print, then collected five printed sheets of A4 and spread them out on my desk.

If she was a local woman and if her labour had been medically managed, then my friend from the field was one of the names in front of me. It would just be a matter of going through the list, checking if each woman were still alive and well.

A normal year on Shetland sees between 200 and 250 births and 2005 had been pretty typical with

227. Of these, 140 had been delivered between March and August. I turned back to my screen and opened up a few individual files, looking for a Caucasian woman between twenty-five and thirty-five years of age. Just about every file I opened fitted the bill. There were a few teenage mothers, one or two older ones who could probably be discounted, two Indian women and one Chinese. Most of the women I was looking at would remain potentials until the patient graft of someone like DS Tulloch proved otherwise.

I wondered how she was getting on. Before leaving home that morning, I'd caught a few minutes of the Scottish news on TV. There had been no mention of my discovery. On Shetland, one hears frequent grumbles about events on the islands not being considered important enough to make the national Scottish news. I'd always thought it more likely to be a matter of economics than anything else; it would be expensive to fly a TV crew out to Shetland. Even so, you'd think they'd make a bit more effort for a murder.

I stared up and down the list: 140 women, 140 babies.

My mind started wandering, in the way minds do when they come up against a brick wall and are not quite sure how to get around it. Out of nowhere, I heard Duncan talking about more babies being available for adoption on Shetland than in other parts of the UK. I thought for a moment, wondering how I could check quickly. What sort of mother typically puts her baby up for adoption? Almost invariably, it's the young, unmarried ones.

I left the hospital's intranet site and accessed the Internet, typing 'General Register Office for Scotland' into the search engine. The site appeared immediately and I called up the latest annual report. Table 3.3 offered details of live births outside marriage, together with the age of the mother, in Scotland. I'm not great with stats, but even for me it was pretty clear. Teenage pregnancy rates were quite low on the islands. In fact, for the year I was looking at, they had been nearly 40 per cent lower than in the rest of Scotland. Wherever Duncan's glut of babies was coming from, it wasn't from our teenage mothers.

I went back to my list of 2005 babies. How could 140 names be narrowed down? If DS Tulloch's theory about the body being a local woman was correct – on the grounds that no sensible murderer would transport a body across water just to bury her on my land – then our friend had probably gone into labour here at the Franklin Stone Hospital.

Unfortunately, that didn't help much. Most Shetlanders live on the main island and consequently most births take place here at the hospital. As I went down the list, I saw the occasional appearance of one or other of the smaller islands – Yell, Unst, Bressay, Fair Isle, Tronal, Unst again, Papa Stour. Too few for ruling them out to make a real difference.

Tronal? Now that was a new one on me. All the other islands I knew. They all had medical centres, resident midwives and regular antenatal clinics, presided over by yours truly. But Tronal I'd never even heard of, let alone visited. And yet it seemed to play host to several deliveries each year. I counted. Tronal appeared four times. That probably meant between six and eight births a year, more than some of the other smaller islands. I made a mental note to find out about Tronal as soon as I could.

Forcing myself back to the task in hand, I looked at the list again. It was giving me the name and age of the mother; the date, time and place of delivery; the sex, weight and condition (i.e. live or still birth) of the baby. And something else. The initials KT appeared at the end of one entry. I tried to think of any condition or obstetric outcome that might be abbreviated to KT and couldn't. I glanced up and down the list. There it was again. KT, at the end of an entry recording the birth of a baby boy born in May on Yell. And again; a home birth here in Lerwick in July.

I glanced at my watch. Time up. I was gathering up my things when there was a knock on the door.

'Yes, hello!' I called out. The door opened and I looked up to see Bossy Tulloch. Her trouser suit was slate-grey in a crisp, smooth fabric. Not a crease in sight.

'Good morning,' she said, giving me the once-over and making me feel grubby, at least two seasons out of fashion and as oversized as a carthorse next to a prize-winning Arabian filly. 'Got a minute?' she added, still waiting in the doorway.

‘I have a ward round,’ I said. ‘But we’re supposed to run at least ten minutes late.’

She raised her eyebrows. I was starting to hate it when she did that.

‘It’s written into our contract,’ I went on. ‘Creates the impression of being busy and important; gives the patients a sense of proportion; stops them getting too demanding.’

She didn’t smile.

‘I understand my field will be cleared today after all,’ I said.

‘Yes, I understand that too,’ she replied, walking over to my desk. She picked up the list. I strode over, meaning to take it back, even if it made me look childish.

‘I came for this,’ she said.

I held out my hand. ‘I can’t just hand over patient information. I have to ask you to put it down.’

She looked at me, put the papers back down on my desk, tucked her hands behind her back and carried on reading them. I reached out. She held up a hand to stop me.

‘From what I’ve seen already, most of this is a matter of public record. I can get it elsewhere. It just seemed quicker to come to you. I thought you might want to help.’

Well, she had a point. Personal dislikes aside, she and I were supposed to be on the same side. I picked up the list anyway. We stood, looking at each other. She was a good four inches shorter than I but, somehow, I didn't think height alone was going to intimidate her.

'How many?' she asked.

'Hundred and forty,' I replied.

'All of them healthy Caucasian women in their twenties and thirties?'

'Pretty much.'

'No big deal. It's what we do all the time. Should only take a few days. But if you make me go elsewhere or get a court order, it could waste a day or more.'

'I really should check before I—'

'Tora,' she said, using my name for the first time. 'I've spent ten years in the police force, a good part of that in the inner cities. But nothing could have prepared me for what we saw on the autopsy table last night. I want to go back to my office and get my team making phone calls to check these women are alive and busy looking after their two-year-old children. And I really want to do that now.'

I handed her the list. Something in her face softened as she took it from me.

'You can discount the ones who had Caesarean sections,' I said, wondering why I hadn't thought of it before. 'She didn't have a scar.' Well, not that sort of scar anyway.

'Anything else?' she asked.

I shook my head. 'Not immediately. Have the Inverness pathologists finished yet?'

She didn't reply and I looked pointedly at the list in her hand.

'Pretty much,' she said. 'We've also spoken to some experts on the impact of peat on organic material like linen. Dr Renney was spot on about spring or summer 2005 being the time she died. This list is important.'

She thanked me and made for the door. 'Can I pop round to your house later?' she asked, glancing back. 'I need to see your runes.'

I suppressed a smile and nodded. I told her I'd be home about six and she left. I was logging off my computer when I noticed I had new mail. It was from Kenn Gifford.

To all staff.

Following the commencement of the murder inquiry by the Northern Constabulary, all staff are reminded not to give interviews to either police or media, or to release any hospital information without prior approval from me.

In the words of the immortal bard – oh shit.

My ward rounds were soon over and I collected my coat and grabbed a sandwich from the cafeteria. On the way to the lift I sensed someone behind me and turned. It was Kenn Gifford. He nodded at me but didn't speak. The lift arrived and we walked in. The doors closed. Still he said nothing.

There are some people, I've noticed, who are totally unselfconscious, able to remain silent in company without showing the slightest sign of embarrassment. Gifford was one of them. He didn't even look at me as the lift went down, just gazed at the lift buttons, seemingly lost in thought. It was one of the big, hospital lifts, designed to take trolleys, but there were just the two of us inside. Now, I get nervous in confined spaces with just one other person; I feel the need to make conversation, even with a perfect stranger. Three people is fine, I can leave the other two to talk, but when it's just me and one other I have to say something. Which is probably why I chose that moment to 'fess up.

'I gave DS Tulloch some information this morning. Before I got your email.'

He didn't turn. 'I know. Try not to do it again. Do you get headaches a lot?'

Oh great, we were off again.

'A few,' I admitted. 'It was a list of births here on the islands,' I went on. 'Women who were delivered during spring and summer 2005. She said it was all a matter of public record anyway.'

The moment I said that I regretted it. It sounded like I was making excuses. He turned to look at me. 'Is that why you did it?' God, what colour were those eyes? Gunmetal?

'No. I gave her the information because I wanted to help.'

He moved closer. 'Thought so. What did we talk about last night?'

That annoyed me. He was my boss, not my father.

'Umm, *Ivanhoe*, sailing . . .' The lift door opened. '. . . child sex abuse on the Orkneys and the difficulties of washing breasts,' I said, considerably louder than necessary, as we walked out and two house officers moved in to take our place. Both doctors shot curious glances, first at me, then at Gifford.

I risked one myself. He was smiling.

'You're ridiculously tense in theatre,' he said. 'Have you tried yoga? Or t'ai chi?'

I thought about telling him I wasn't nearly so tense when he wasn't breathing down my neck but it didn't seem a good idea. Or entirely true. He was right, I was tense in theatre, but being told so, even by my boss, seemed patronizing. And I had a feeling he was laughing at me.

'Why do you and my husband dislike each other?'

His smile didn't falter. 'Does he dislike me? Poor Duncan.'

He held the outer door open and I walked outside, feeling very relieved to have somewhere else to go.

My clinic on Yell overran and there was a queue for the return ferry. When I finally arrived home, several hours later, Dana Tulloch's sports car was parked in my yard. I'd totally forgotten she was coming. I glanced at my watch. If she'd been on time, I'd kept her waiting for nearly three hours. Damn! After rudeness of that magnitude, I was going to have to be nice. I got out of the car just as she climbed out of hers.

'I'm so sorry,' I said, 'I should have phoned. Have you been here all this time?'

'Course not,' she said. 'When you didn't arrive at six I started making phone calls. I came back about ten minutes ago.'

I was starving and desperate for a coffee but didn't think I could keep her waiting any longer. She followed me inside and we went straight to the cellar, accessed via eight stone steps leading down from the kitchen.

'Good lord,' she said, as we reached the bottom and I turned on the solitary and completely inadequate light bulb. 'You'd never dream all this was beneath your house, would you?' She pulled a torch out of her bag and walked forward, shining it all around.

Our cellar is probably the single most interesting feature of our property. It's older than the house, for a start. In places it shows the remains of fire damage so we can only surmise that the original house was destroyed some time ago. It's also much larger than the house, indicating the previous building to have been considerably grander than our own. Divided into low rooms, accessible by stone archways, it looks like a smaller version of the cavernous wine cellars you see beneath French chateaux. I led Dana into the biggest room and stopped just in front of the north-facing wall.

'A fireplace?' she said. 'In a cellar?'

It had puzzled us too, but there it was. A fully functional fireplace with stone grate and chimney flue leading up to our chimney stack on the roof.

A stone lintel had been fixed into the wall above the hearth and it was on this that the runes had been carved. Five symbols. None of which I recognized.

'All different,' she said, more to herself than to me. With a small digital camera she took several photographs.

'Did you phone my father-in-law?' I asked.

She shook her head. 'Haven't needed to yet,' she replied. 'Found a book.'

She finished her photographs and looked towards the stone archway that led to the rest of the cellars.

'Mind if I look around?' she asked.

'Be my guest,' I said. 'Mind if I go and get something to eat?'

She shook her head and turned away. I made for the steps. On the second one, I called after her.

'Oh, Sergeant, if you find anything . . . organic, don't tell me about it tonight. I'm all done in!'

She didn't reply. I already suspected she found me childish.

When she appeared ten minutes later, I was tucking into a microwaved portion of pasta with cream and ham. I pointed to the chair opposite mine. 'I made you a cup of tea.' Guessing she hadn't eaten either, I'd put some local shortbread on the table. I wanted her to tell me about the runes.

She glanced at the biscuits, then at her watch; looked uncertain for a second and then sat down. She picked up the tea, cradling it with one hand, and then gulped down a piece of shortbread in two bites.

I continued eating, silently. The tactics worked; she spoke first.

'What do you know about the history of this property?'

I shrugged. 'Very little. My husband handled the purchase. I really wasn't that interested.'

'When does he get home?'

I shrugged again. 'I never really know these days.'

Her face clouded over.

'We can phone him,' I added, in a belated attempt to seem helpful.

She shook her head. 'I'd like to bring a team down here tomorrow, though. It can't be coincidence that similar runes appear both in your house and on a body found on your property.'

'Guess not,' I agreed, not sure where she was going but definitely not liking the implications. 'You mean she was probably killed in the house? Maybe the cellar?'

Now it was her turn to shrug. 'We do need to find out who owned this house before you.'

'I thought Duncan brought the deeds over to the station this morning.'

'He did. But they don't tell us much. Some sort of church or religious building used to be here but it was derelict for years before it was demolished to make way for this house. There were trustees named on the document but, so far, most of them seem to be dead.'

'Dead?'

She shook her head. 'Old age, nothing significant.'

I finished my supper. I was no longer starving but

hardly satisfied; it hadn't exactly been a relaxing meal. I stood up and took the plate and cutlery to the dishwasher.

'So what about the runes?' I asked.

She looked at me, bit on another piece of shortbread, seemed to make up her mind. She leaned down and pulled her camera, a notebook and a small, blue leather-bound book from her bag. There was a runic script printed in gold ink on the front of the book and, although she'd laid it upside-down, I could read the title, *Runes and Viking Script*. The print was too small for me to make out the name of the author.

'You say your husband's father is into all this?' she asked.

I nodded. 'Very much so. I doubt there are many people who know more about the history of these islands than he does.'

She turned the book round for me. On the inside front cover were pictured twenty-five runes: each a simple, mainly angular symbol. They all had descriptive names, like Disruption, Standstill, Gateway, but when Richard, my father-in-law, had referred to them, he'd used their Viking names.

'I don't get it,' she said. 'There are only twenty-five. Each one appears to have a distinct meaning of its own. How can it form any sort of alphabet and make words? There just aren't enough characters.'

I started to flip through the book. 'I think it works a bit like the Chinese alphabet,' I said. 'Each character has a principal meaning but also several sub-meanings. And when you use two or more together, each one impacts slightly upon the others to create a meaning unique to that combination: a bit like a word. Does that make any sort of sense?'

'Yes,' she said. 'But I think there are over two thousand Chinese characters.'

'Maybe the Vikings didn't talk much.'

She opened her notebook and turned it to face me. The page I was looking at had a reproduction of the three runes we'd seen in the morgue the day before. 'So what we have here,' she went on, 'are the runes for Separation, Breakthrough and Constraint, inscribed on the body of our victim. What's that all about then?'

I looked from her notes to the textbook. On the next page the runes were reproduced again, this time with their Viking names. The fish-like symbol was called Othila, meaning Separation; the kite-bow was Dagaz, meaning Breakthrough, and the diagonal, sword-like rune was Nauthiz, meaning Constraint. I looked up at her. She was watching me carefully.

'What about the sub-meanings?' I asked.

'Go ahead,' she encouraged.

On the page opposite, lesser meanings for each rune were listed. Othila also meant Property or Inherited Possessions, Native Land and Home; Dagaz meant Day, God's Light, Prosperity and Fruitfulness; Nauthiz meant Need, Necessity, Cause of Human Sorrow, Lessons, Hardship.

'Separation of significant internal organ from rest of body?' I suggested, not entirely seriously. She gave me an encouraging nod. I looked down at the book.

'Breakthrough . . . umm, breaking through the chest wall to reach the heart? Constraint . . . well, she was constrained, wasn't she? The bruises around her ankles and wrists . . . And she certainly suffered hardship . . .' I tailed off and looked at Dana.

'Seem good enough to you?' she asked.

I shook my head. 'No,' I said. 'Seems like bollocks.'

'Like meaningless doodles?' she suggested.

'Much more elegant way of putting it,' I agreed. 'What about the ones downstairs?'

She pressed a button on her camera and pulled up the photograph she'd taken just ten minutes ago. There were five symbols inscribed along the lintel.

'An arrow pointing upwards,' I said.

Dana flicked to the back page of the book. 'Teiwaz,' she said, 'meaning Warrior and Victory in battle.'

I looked at her. We both made mystified faces.

'Next up looks like a slanted letter F.' I reached over and indicated it on the page. 'There, what does it say?'

'Ansuz,' she replied, 'meaning Signals, God and River Mouth.'

'Our third symbol of the evening is a flash of lightning.'

'Sowelu. Wholeness, the Sun.' She looked up again.

'This is just more bo— meaningless doodles,' I said.

'Certainly looks that way,' she agreed. 'What about the last two?'

'We have an upturned table called Perth, meaning . . . aah!'

'What?'

'Initiation.'

She frowned. 'I always worry when I hear that word.'

'Know what you mean. And, finally, a crooked letter H, called Hagalaz, meaning Disruption and Natural Forces.'

'Warrior, Signals, Wholeness, Initiation and Disruption,' Dana summarized.

I held up my hands. 'Meaningless—'

'Bollocks,' she said. And smiled. It was a pretty smile.

I laughed. 'You need to talk to Duncan's dad. Maybe it's a question of context.'

'Who needs to talk to my dad?' said a voice from the doorway. Duncan had crept up on us. He stood there, grinning, looking from Dana to me, and I felt my stomach tensing the way it always did when Duncan was in the presence of a pretty woman who wasn't me. They had a way of softening, somehow, around him: their skin would blush, eyes shine, bodies instinctively lean towards him. I braced myself for Dana to respond in the time-honoured way and, to my surprise, she didn't. Dana, that night, gave me the totally new experience of watching my gorgeous husband and an equally gorgeous babe and feeling no jealousy whatsoever. They exchanged a few pleasantries, she ascertained that he knew nothing more about runes than I did, and then she left. She didn't promise to keep in touch.

7

'GO ON, GO,' I URGED, AS HENRY MOVED INTO top gear. I rose out of the saddle and leaned forward, balancing over his neck as he pounded along the beach.

My favourite place to ride on Shetland was a half-moon beach, where dusky pink, grass-tufted cliffs rose like the sides of a pudding basin around a bay of deepest turquoise. As I thundered along, spray blurred my vision and all I could see was colour: emerald grass, turquoise sea, pink sand and the soft, robin's-egg blue of the distant ocean. There are times on the islands when flowers seem superfluous.

The wind is rarely still on Shetland but it seemed content, that morning, just to whisper its presence, and the ocean was smooth but for small bubbles of white foam at the water's edge.

I turned Henry and we walked back through the surf. Both of us were panting. Blissful emptiness of mind disappeared and reality came tumbling back.

Thursday was my regular day off. I was expected

to stay near a phone and respond to any emergency but otherwise I was free to relax. Some hope. I was having a period of what Duncan called 'the stressies'. I was finding it hard to get to sleep at night, waking up much too early in the morning and spending the day exhausted. For much of the time, I was grinding my teeth and clenching my fists without realizing it. A permanent headache nagged just shy of the point of being disabling and I was loaded up with aspirin and paracetamol twenty-four hours a day.

What was my problem?

Well, for a start, something was worrying Duncan but he wasn't telling me about it. We were hardly communicating at all; except in bed, if the non-verbal kind was allowed to count. His new business was proving harder to settle into than he'd expected and the hours he was working were as long as mine, but he was doing it six, sometimes seven days a week. The couple of times I'd mentioned babies his face had tightened and he'd changed the subject just as soon as he could. He hadn't spoken about adoption again. That morning, he'd left the islands on a three-day trip back to London for meetings with clients and I was finding it almost a relief to have the house to myself for a few days, not to have to pretend that everything was fine.

Second, I wasn't performing well at work. Nothing had gone wrong yet, all my babies had been successfully delivered and were doing well. With the help of the team I'd probably saved Janet Kennedy's life the other day. But somehow it just wasn't coming together. I was awkward, clumsy both in theatre and in the delivery room. I was pretty certain that no one, either on the medical team or among the patients, actually liked me. And it was my fault. I couldn't relax and be natural. Either I was stiff and cold or I tried too hard in the other direction, making inappropriate jokes and getting glassy-eyed stares in response.

Third, I was itching to know what was happening in the murder investigation. The day after DS Tulloch visited me at home I'd been interviewed again by a DCI from Inverness. He'd done nothing but reiterate the questions Tulloch had already asked me and, to my surprise, he'd even nodded sagely when I'd repeated DI Dunn's theory about the murdered woman being an islander. Since then, I'd heard from Duncan that most of the mainland team had been called home and that Dunn and Tulloch were, once again, in charge, although Dunn, Duncan told me, wasn't normally based on Shetland but at Wick on the mainland.

I'd thought about calling Dana Tulloch but didn't much fancy the inevitable rebuff I'd get. I'd made a point of catching the main news each evening for the last few days but had learned nothing. There had been some coverage in the local press and on Shetland TV, but far less than I'd expected. Nobody from the media had tried to interview me. Nobody at work had bothered to ask about it, although I was sure I'd caught one or two suspicious-looking glances. Neither had any of our neighbours been round in a spirit of friendly nosiness.

Sharing a table in the hospital canteen with some other members of staff, I'd found myself incredibly frustrated that the topics of conversation had ranged from school sports days to rising prices on the buses and road works on the A970. For God's sake, I'd wanted to yell, we dug up a body four days ago, not ten miles from here. She's in the morgue right now. Does nobody care? I hadn't, of course. But I had wondered if Gifford's oblique warning to me in the pub that night had been repeated across the hospital: don't discuss the particularly grizzly murder that has taken place amongst us, because that will be bad for the social and economic health of the islands; don't talk about it and it might just go away.

And then there was Kenn Gifford.

I'd met him just four days ago, and during those four days he'd been on my mind an awful lot more than he had any business to be. I'd even gone so far as to buy Walter Scott's *Ivanhoe*, drinking in greedily any descriptions of the character he'd likened me to and finding myself absurdly flattered by references to '*superior height*', '*exquisitely fair complexion*' and '*profuse hair of a colour betwixt brown and flaxen*'.

I've been married for five years and of course Gifford wasn't the first man I'd found attractive during that time. I'd also met quite a few who had found me . . . interesting. It had never really been a problem. I have this simple test, you see; I say to myself, 'Tora, however amiable, however pleasing to the eye he may be, can he really, honestly measure up to Duncan?' And the answer has always been the same: never in a million years. But with Gifford the answer wasn't quite so clear-cut.

All in all, I had quite a lot to think about.

Henry, perhaps picking up on my mood, started to jump and skitter about. Then a guillemot flew close and he shied, backing into the water. Henry had ridden through waves, not to mention rivers, streams and ponds many times and there was absolutely no reason why the feel of water around his hoofs should bother him, but for some reason it did. He started to buck and kick, spinning in the water and going in deeper. He was in danger of slipping and I of losing my seat. I tightened the reins and pulled him up sharply.

'Pack it in!' I snarled, pulling him round so that he was facing up the beach and out of the sea. He side-stepped and backed up further.

Mildly concerned now, I kicked him forward, re-gretting not having brought a whip with me. I raised his head and kicked again. He shot forward, just as I saw a man standing on the cliff top, staring down at us.

Gifford, was my first thought, but it was im-possible to be sure. The cliffs were to the east of us, the sun was still low and the man was little more than a shadow blocking out a fraction of the early-morning light. He was tall and broad and his hair, long and loose, seemed to gleam like gold. The sun was hurting my eyes and I looked away for a second, screwing them closed to shut out the brightness. When I opened them again the man was gone.

I urged Henry away from the surf and put him into an active walk along the beach. It was two miles to home and I still had Charles to ride.

Charles was in no state to be ridden.

Missing Henry and with no Jamie to keep him calm, he'd panicked, jumped a fence into the next field, stumbled on the uneven ground and fallen into the stream that runs down our land. That, in itself, wouldn't have been too bad, but in slipping he'd dislodged an old barbed-wire fence and wrapped it around his left hind leg. The least sensible of my horses was trapped in a stream, with several razor-sharp points digging into his flesh. Not surprisingly, he was seriously distressed. His eyes were rolling and his grey coat was dark with sweat.

I untacked Henry as fast as I could and pushed him into the field. Hearing Charles's panic he rushed up to the fence and started calling out to him. Horses have a particular whinnying cry when they're hurt or distressed. It's a sound you rarely hear, fortunately, because it pierces your heart the way I imagine the screams of a terrified child would. Charles's cries doubled in volume and he started to struggle and kick.

I knew I'd never get the wire off Charles without some sort of wire-cutter so I turned and ran back into the house. I was wearing an ancient pair of green Hunter wellingtons and they were caked in mud from the last time I'd worn them – Jamie's aborted burial day. The mud had dried and started to flake off over the carpet as I rushed upstairs to the spare room where Duncan kept his tools. I found a pair of pliers, then grabbed another, stronger pair just for good measure and raced back downstairs again. On the fourth stair from the bottom I slipped and went down, banging my coccyx badly on the stairs. It hurt but I forced myself to stand up and get moving.

Running outside, I found Charles and Henry winding each other up and Henry prepared to jump the fence and join Charles in the stream. He needed to be tied up but the time it would take me to find a head-collar and catch him just couldn't be spared. Blood was running down Charles's leg. Even if I did manage to get him free – and from the state of him that was looking increasingly unlikely – he'd probably done irreparable damage to his leg. Surely I wasn't about to lose a second horse in as many weeks?

Forcing myself to move slowly, I approached Charles. The stream is a narrow one, at times barely visible under rushes and long grass. In summer it doesn't carry much water but the gully is deep. Charles was using his front legs in a scrambling motion to propel himself out but, fastened as he was by his hind leg, it was impossible. Plus, every effort he made sapped his energy, increased his panic and pushed the sharp prongs of the wire deeper into his flesh. I hadn't faced a situation remotely like it before and for a second I was tempted to just throw back my head and scream for help. Except I knew none would come.

I stood just out of reach of Charles's hoofs and tried to calm him. If he would let me touch his head I was in with a chance.

'Steady, steady, steady, whoa now, steady.' I reached towards him. He tossed his head up and towards me, grabbing with his teeth. Then he spun round, trying to scramble away. I'd known this horse since he was two years old; he'd come to my mother's farm to be broken in and I was the only regular rider he'd known, but pain and fear had turned me into the enemy. I looked down. The left hind leg was pretty well immobilized and there appeared to be two – no, three – strands of wire connecting Charles to the fence. If he let me approach, I might be able to cut through the wire, enabling him to climb out of the ditch.

I jumped down into the gully and Charles glared, swinging round to face me. A kick from a big horse can seriously injure, if not kill – and yet without getting close, I could do nothing to help him. Talking gently, wishing my voice sounded calmer, I moved forward. He was panting heavily and his eyes were rolling. If he sprang, I could be pinioned beneath two very powerful forelegs; if he fell, I'd be crushed. It all looked impossible and for a moment I was tempted to give up and ring the vet. Yet I knew the chances of him being able to come straight away were slim and if there were to be any possibility of saving Charles I had to get him loose from the wire-fence pretty much immediately.

I moved forward again as Charles reared, balancing precariously on his trapped rear limbs. He fell forward and I moved again before he had chance to recover. I was no longer talking to him, my voice just wouldn't work any more. Crouching down in the ditch, I willed myself to ignore the half-ton of muscle and bone poised above me as I squeezed the pliers around the first thick strand of wire. It snapped in two and Charles chose that moment to kick out with both hind legs. The remaining wire dug deep into his fetlock and he screamed out loud with the pain. He reared again and this time those murderous forelegs were directly above me and coming down fast. I had to move!

'Stay where you are,' said a voice.

I froze.

Above me I could see clear blue sky; soft, white clouds; and the imminent prospect of a violent death.

Charles's forelegs came down with a thud on the bank and he sobbed. I know, you've never heard of a horse sobbing and doubt it's even possible, but believe me, that's what he did. A tanned, freckled arm covered in fine golden hairs was wrapped around his neck and two enormous hands were gripping his mane, holding him still. It was impossible. No man is strong enough to hold a panicking horse, without reins or even a head collar, but Gifford was doing it.

As I lay half in and half out of the ditch, unable to

move a muscle, I watched Gifford stroke Charles's mane. Gifford's head was pressed against Charles's nose and I could hear his voice, whispering softly in words I couldn't understand. Gaelic, possibly, or some obscure Shetland dialect. Charles was trembling, still visibly distressed, but otherwise perfectly still. This was my chance. If I moved quickly I'd be able to cut the two remaining strands of wire. I had to do it now because Gifford would not be able to hold Charles for long. Yet I must have been in shock because I still didn't move.

'The pliers are behind your head, slightly to your left,' said Gifford, without moving from his close embrace of the horse. His left hand was still clutching Charles's mane, his right was stroking his neck; short, quick, firm strokes. There was something slightly hypnotic about the movement. 'Get them now,' he said, and I turned. Lying on my stomach, I reached out for the pliers and then pushed myself forward, closer to Charles's hind leg. Charles shuddered and Gifford resumed his low Gaelic chanting. Shutting my mind to what could, at any moment, come slamming down on top of me, breaking my back and rendering me crippled at the very least, I reached forward with both hands, clamped the pliers around the closest piece of wire and cut it. Without stopping to think I reached for the second wire and squeezed. It broke with a high-pitched zinging sound that seemed to echo around the voe.

'Get out of there,' called Gifford and I rolled, over and over, until I judged I was far enough away to be safe. I looked back to see that Gifford had pulled Charles out of the ditch and was struggling to hold him still. Free at last of the painful brace, Charles just wanted to bolt, but Gifford was having none of it. He hung close around Charles's neck, being tossed this way and that by the superior strength of the horse, muttering in his ear all the while. After a minute or two, Charles admitted defeat. He drooped, seeming to lean against Gifford.

It was, quite simply, incredible. I'd heard, of course, of people with uncanny abilities to calm animals. I'd seen the film *The Horse Whisperer*, and had even gone so far as to read half the book, but I'd never seen anything like it in real life.

'Tora, will you get over here?' said Gifford, sounding half exasperated, half amused. I struggled to my feet and looked round for the pliers I'd dropped when I rolled out of the ditch. They were nowhere to be seen but the other, smaller pair lay close by. I picked them up and, glancing nervously at Gifford – I wasn't sure how long this mojo of his was going to last – approached Charles. He gave me his leg quite easily, as though it was any normal day at the blacksmith's.

Carefully, slowly, I snipped at the wire around Charles's leg. Five snips and the wire fell away. I picked it up, stepped back and Gifford let go. Charles reared and bucked and then cantered off towards the fence, where Henry had been watching the whole incident with increasing impatience. After a few paces Charles slowed to a walk. He was lame but still able to put weight on the damaged limb. I started to hope that it wasn't going to be too bad after all.

'How'd you do that?' I asked, without taking my eyes off Charles. 'He wouldn't let me near him.'

'You were more afraid than he was,' replied Gifford. 'He could sense that and it made him worse. I wasn't scared and I wasn't standing for any nonsense.'

It made sense. Horses are herd animals, following without question a strong leader – equine or human. Horses like to know who is boss.

'And I used a bit of hypnosis. Just to calm him down.'

That made no sense. I turned to look at Gifford.

'Animals are very susceptible to hypnosis,' he said. 'Especially horses and dogs.'

'You're kidding me,' I said, although I wasn't sure. He looked perfectly serious.

'You're right, I'm kidding you. Now, painkillers and a tetanus jab. Possibly antibiotics.'

'I'll call the vet,' I said, watching Charles and Henry nuzzle each other over the fence.

'I'm talking about you,' said Gifford, running his hand up my right arm towards the shoulder. The pain was as sharp as it was surprising; either Charles had kicked me after all, without my noticing, or I'd fallen on a pretty sharp stone. I turned towards Gifford and – oh shit – the pain disappeared beneath a stab of lust so unexpected it made me want to run for cover. I swear he'd grown two inches since

I'd last seen him and in jeans and a T-shirt he was definitely not dressed for work. He was gleaming with sweat.

'Let's go in,' he said. 'I'll see what I've got in my bag.'

Gifford's car was parked in our yard and he took his bag from the boot as we walked past. In the kitchen I took off my riding helmet and sat down at the table, acutely conscious of the debris from breakfast, my red, sweaty face and hair that badly needed washing. I probably didn't smell too good either. Gifford turned on the tap and let it run till the water steamed.

'I can take you into the hospital where we can be properly chaperoned or you can have my word that I'm not about to behave inappropriately.'

I'm sure I blushed at that but my face was so red to start with he couldn't have noticed. I unbuttoned my shirt – an old one of Duncan's – and wriggled out of the sleeve. I held the fabric close to me, less out of modesty, if I'm honest, than because my bra was not the pure-white lacy one I'd probably have chosen for the occasion.

Gifford started to bathe my arm and I turned my head to assess the damage. Most of my upper arm was already starting to bruise. There was a nasty scratch, which was bleeding, but I didn't think it looked too deep. I had no recollection of it happening but, now that I was no longer running on adrenaline, it was hurting like hell.

Gifford dressed the wound and gave me a tetanus

jab. Finally, he offered me two small, white tablets. They were painkillers, stronger than the sort you can buy over the counter, and I took them gratefully.

He looked at his watch. 'I have surgery in twenty minutes.' He started to pack away his things.

'What are you doing here?'

He laughed. 'Thank you, Mr Gifford, for saving my life, not to mention that of my horse, and offering immediate and highly efficient first aid.' He closed his bag. 'I was planning to ring the vet for you but I guess I won't bother now.'

'Put my bad manners down to shock. Why are you here?'

'I wanted to talk to you away from the hospital.'

And there was my heartbeat, skipping away on a roller-coaster ride of its own again. I just knew there was bad news coming.

'Oh?'

'There've been complaints.'

'About me?'

He nodded.

'From whom?'

'Does it matter?'

'Does to me.'

'I told them I'm highly impressed with what I've seen so far, that you're doing a perfectly acceptable job and that I have every intention of keeping you on the team. But that you are in a very new environment, things will seem strange for a while and they need to cut you some slack.'

'Thank you,' I said, feeling no better. Having one

friend is never enough; not if everyone else hates you.

'Don't mention it.' He closed his bag and lifted it.

'Why are you telling me?'

'Because you need to know. You need to make the effort, too. Your technical skills are all there but you don't handle people that well.'

That pissed me off, big time. Probably because I knew he was telling the truth. I stood up. 'If you have a problem with my performance at work there are procedures you need to follow. You don't need me to tell you that.'

Gifford wasn't remotely intimidated. 'Oh, get over yourself. We can do it by the book if you want. It will take an immense amount of time that neither of us can spare and the end result will be no different, except there'll be a cumbersome and potentially damaging paper trail on your file. I'll see you tomorrow.'

He turned and was gone, leaving me alone with a very sore arm and my self-esteem in tatters.

8

TEN MINUTES LATER THE VET HAD BEEN summoned and the pain in my arm had faded to an ache. I sat on the fence, watching Charles hobble around, knowing there was nothing more I could do for him but reluctant to leave him by himself. I found both pairs of pliers and used the stronger pair to cut several strands of wire from the broken fence posts. Then I gathered it up and carried it back to the yard.

Goddamned Gifford for a patronizing, manipulative bastard. I knew exactly what he was up to. I'd come across those exact tactics before, the first time in the primary-school playground. Sally Carter had taken me gently to one side and told me that none of the other girls in our class liked me. They thought I was stuck up and bossy and a know-it-all. But I wasn't to worry because she, Sally Carter, thought I was nice and had stuck up for me. To this day I can remember the bewildering mix of emotions that hit me at that moment: misery at my recently discovered unpopularity; a sort of pathetic gratitude for having at least one friend; fury at the said friend for telling me all this and ruining my day; and, at the bottom of it all, a sneaking, half-formed suspicion that she wasn't much of a friend anyway, if she could make me feel this bad. I'd met other Sally Carters over the years and learned to recognize this crude but highly effective piece of professional one-upmanship.

I took the pliers back inside. Duncan was fussy about his tools and took a dim view of my using and abusing them.

Of course, recognizing the tactic was a long way from being able to deal with it. I could (and was frequently tempted to) dismiss it as a bit of obnoxious power play. On the other hand, I've always known I'm not popular: I don't have the gift of making small talk and I'm uncomfortable in large groups; I know I don't smile easily and I have quite a way with the clumsy remark and the ill-timed joke. Much of the time I try, unsuccessfully, to be different; but sometimes I just want to scream at the people around me to grow up. I am a perfectly competent doctor; I work hard, commit no crimes, never knowingly carry out a mean or dishonourable act. I'm one of the bloody good guys, but because of a lack of surface charm, I'm doomed to be disliked by those around me. Well, fuck that for a game of soldiers!

On the third stair up there was a gold ring.

I stood, staring at it. It was a wide band, with some sort of pattern etched around the upper and lower circumferences. Gifford, I wondered briefly, but Gifford hadn't left the kitchen all the time he'd been here. In any case, this ring hadn't been worn for some time; it was caked in dried mud.

I bent down to pick it up. Some of the mud flaked away, a sizeable piece with a definite indentation down one side. I sat down and took off one of my boots. Hunter boots have a distinctive pattern on the underside and the piece of mud that had fallen away from the ring seemed a pretty good match. The ring must have spent the last few days stuck to the underside of my boot. My running up the stairs earlier or, more likely, my falling down them had dislodged it.

I felt a bolt of panic. I'd been wearing these boots when I'd found the body last Sunday but had taken them off before entering the house to get a knife. The police forensics team had taken away the trainers I'd replaced them with, but I'd forgotten all about the boots. I'd seriously fucked up a major investigation.

It's her ring. That's what they were looking for in the field the other night.

I sat there, thinking hard. I really didn't want this ring to be connected in any way to my lady from the field. For one thing, I found it highly disturbing that I'd been walking round with a piece of her jewellery stuck to the underside of my foot. For another, if someone had been looking for it, then whoever killed her was, without question, still on the islands.

Suddenly, I was nervous. I stood up, listening for sounds in the house, as though someone might be creeping up on me even now. Then I walked back into the kitchen and closed the back door. I even considered locking it. Instead I went to the kitchen sink and ran about two inches of lukewarm water. I dropped the ring into it, waited a few seconds then rubbed it between my palms. I dried it on a tea towel and held it up to the light. Without really thinking, I slipped it on to the third finger of my left hand. It wouldn't go past the knuckle; it had been made for slim fingers.

The body I'd seen on the morgue trolley was that of a slim woman. Was I now looking at her ring? When I'd cut open her linen shroud, pretty much all my attention had been on the horrific chest wound. If a ring had fallen off her left hand, I could have stood on it without noticing.

Well, her ring or not, I had to let Bossy Tulloch know immediately. Naturally, she'd be furious with me. Not only had I been responsible for carrying a crucial piece of evidence away from a crime scene and delaying its discovery by several days, but I'd even gone as far as to wash away the surrounding mud. I'd pretty much driven a cart and horses through the forensic evidence.

I put the ring down on the kitchen worktop and crossed to the phone. As I started to dial the sun flashed in through the window, making the ring gleam. I put the phone down and picked up the ring again. There was an inscription inside.

Too easy, I thought, too, too easy. I glanced round at the door again. This time I did move to lock it before holding the ring up to the light. The inscription was hard to read, written in that pretty but virtually indecipherable script that I think is called italic calligraphy. A period in the peat hadn't helped much.

The first letter was J, the second H or maybe N. Then there was a K followed by what could have been a C or a G. Then there were four numbers: a four, a five, a zero and a two. If they were the initials of the marrying couple and the wedding date and if – big *if*, this – the ring had come from my friend, then we'd done it. We'd identified her.

I turned round to look at the phone. *Over here, now!* it barked. I turned my back on it and found the phone book. There were twenty registration districts on Shetland. I dialled the number for the Lerwick office. It was answered immediately. I took a deep breath, heart pounding, feeling ridiculously, inexplicably guilty, and then told the woman who I was, stressing my position of seniority at the hospital. As usual, it worked; she became interested, eager to help.

'We've found a piece of jewellery,' I explained. 'I think you may be able to help trace its owner.'

'Of course, what can we do, Miss Hamilton?'

'I think it's a wedding ring. It has an inscription that looks like a wedding date and some initials. You keep records of weddings, don't you?'

'All weddings in Lerwick, yes. Did the wedding take place in the town?'

'I'm not sure; I think so. I don't have a name, though. Can your records be searched just with a date?'

'Well, you could look up all the weddings that took place on that particular day and see if your initials matched any of them.'

Was it really going to be that simple?

'Can I do that? Can a member of the public just come along and search the records?'

'Absolutely. We normally charge £10 for an hour's search but I'm sure in your case we could . . .' She left the offer hanging.

'Do I need to make an appointment?

'No, just come along. Our hours are 10 a.m. till 1 p.m. and then 2 p.m. until 4 p.m.'

I glanced at the clock. The vet was due any second and I had nothing planned for the rest of the day that couldn't wait.

I knew I should hand the ring over to DS Tulloch and let her get on with it.

'Thank you,' I said. 'I'll be along this afternoon.'

Two hours later I arrived at the register office in Lerwick. The vet had been and gone. Charles was going to be fine: lame for a few days, but then good as new. The news had softened, a little, my fury with Gifford. He might have given my fragile professional confidence a kicking but at least he'd saved my horse.

Before leaving home I'd phoned DS Tulloch and left a brief message on her voicemail, telling her I'd found something that might be connected to the murder and that I'd drop it by the station on my way into town. I hadn't been specific. I'd put the ring in a sterile bag and enclosed it, with a brief note, inside a large brown envelope. When I'd arrived at the station, Dana was still out so I left it, marked for her attention, at the front desk. I felt like I'd just lit the blue touch-paper on a firework and needed to stand well back.

Marion, the woman I'd spoken to on the phone, led me to a computer screen. I checked my watch. Twelve-thirty. I had half an hour before the office closed for lunch. Taking a folded Post-it note out of my bag I double-checked the date I'd noted before handing the ring in: 4.5.02, 4 May 2002. I found the right year and scrolled down until I came to the May weddings. It was a popular month for tying the knot. There had been four Saturdays in that particular May and several weddings on each; also a few mid-week ceremonies. Twenty-two weddings in all. I scanned down the list until I found the fourth of the month and immediately spotted a definite possibility. Kyle Griffiths married Janet Hammond at St Margaret's Church. I scribbled down all the details before checking the rest of the list. Nothing else.

'Found anything?'

I jumped before I could help it, then took a deep breath and told myself that I was not going to look guilty, apologize or ramble on mindlessly. I turned round.

Dana Tulloch, as usual, was immaculately dressed, in black trousers, simple red top and an obviously expensive black, red and white plaid jacket. I found myself wondering how she managed to be so well dressed on a police sergeant's salary.

'You look nice,' I said, without thinking.

She gave me a surprised look and pulled up a chair beside me. I showed her my scribble. She nodded.

'I'll get it checked,' she said. 'Anything else?'

I shook my head. She reached into her bag and pulled out the clear plastic wallet I'd left at the station earlier. The ring gleamed inside it. My note had been removed.

'When did you find it?' she asked, looking at the ring, not at me.

'This morning,' I said. 'Late morning.'

She nodded. 'How sure can you be that it came out of the same patch of ground?'

'I can't,' I said. 'But I'm pretty certain I haven't worn those wellingtons since Sunday.'

'They should have been given to the SSU.'

I couldn't remember what the SSU was, but I knew I was in trouble.

'Slipped my mind,' I said truthfully. 'I was traumatized.'

'You washed it,' she said, in an *I-really-do-give-up* sort of voice.

'Didn't wash the wellington,' I offered.

She shook her head. 'It's all far from ideal.'

Behind her, Marion was making herself conspicuous. She wanted to close for lunch. I lowered my voice. 'I'm sure the woman missing her heart would agree with you.'

Dana sighed and leaned back in her chair. 'You really shouldn't be here.'

I looked her straight in the eye. 'What can I say? I dug her up. I have an interest.'

'I know. But you should let us do our job.' She broke eye contact, looked down at her nails. Of course, they were perfect. Then she stood up. 'I spoke to your father-in-law,' she went on. 'He said the book I had was as good an authority as I was going to get. He was sorry he couldn't be more help.'

I stood too. 'There are eight more registration districts on the southern part of the mainland,' I said.

She looked at me. 'And?'

'I have no plans for the rest of the day.'

She shook her head. 'It's not a good idea.'

Something not quite resolved in her voice told me the argument wasn't over yet. I showed her the page I'd torn out of the phone book.

'From here, I'm going to Walls, then to Tingwall. I expect to be done by about five and I'll probably be in the mood for a drink in the Douglas Arms. Tomorrow I'm back at work and no longer available to act as your unpaid personal assistant. If I were you, I'd make the most of it.'

I walked out of the offices, wondering if she'd try to stop me, not sure if she even could and feeling rather spitefully pleased at doing something of which I knew the police and my boss – especially my boss – would disapprove.

* * *

By five fifteen I was back in Lerwick. I walked into the dim interior of the Douglas Arms and spotted Dana sitting alone at a table in one of the darker corners, gazing at the screen of her notebook computer. I bought myself a drink and sat down beside her.

'Come here often?' I asked.

She looked up and frowned. 'Anything?' she said, looking seriously pissed off. Just when I'd thought the ice queen was melting.

I opened my notebook. 'Two more possibilities,' I said. 'A Kirsten Georgeson, aged twenty-six, married a Joss Hawick at St Magnus's Church in Lerwick. Also, a Karl Gevvons married Julie Howard, aged twenty-five. Registry-office wedding. Both women are the right age.'

Without asking, she ripped out the page.

'How about you?' I asked.

'Three districts, no matches,' she said. 'And I checked out the one you found earlier. Janet Hammond is divorced, living in Aberdeen and very much alive.'

'Well, good for her.'

'Quite. I think this may have been a waste of time.'

'Why?'

She wiggled the mouse around on the table and a new screen appeared: the list of births on the islands I'd given her three days earlier. 'The team have almost finished checking this,' she said.

I leaned closer; the screen was absurdly tiny and,

if not at the right angle, pretty much unreadable. 'Yeah,' I prompted.

'The ones in the right age and ethnic groups are almost all accounted for. It looks as though she wasn't a local woman, after all.'

I thought about that for a moment. 'That throws it wide open.'

'Oh yes.'

I now understood why she looked annoyed. Her boss was about to be proved right and she wrong.

There was a rush of cold air as the door opened and a group of men from one of the rigs came in. Noise levels in the pub leaped up. One or two of them glanced towards us and I looked away quickly; Dana hadn't even noticed them.

'What do you know about Tronal?' she asked.

I had to think for a second. According to my list, several babies had been born on Tronal during 2005. I'd made a mental note to ask Gifford about it.

'An island,' I said. 'Four women on the list gave birth there.'

Dana nodded. 'Two of whom we haven't been able to trace yet. So yesterday, DI Dunn and I took a trip. It's about half a mile off the coast of Unst. Privately owned. They sent a boat to meet us.'

'Is there a medical centre there?' I asked.

'There's a state-of-the-art private maternity hospital, run by a charitable trust, with links to the local adoption agency,' said Dana, appearing to enjoy the look of amazement on my face. 'They offer, and

I'm quoting now, a "sensitive solution to unfortunate and ill-timed pregnancies".'

'Hang on . . . but . . . where do these women come from?'

She shook her head. 'All over the UK, even overseas. Typically, they're young career women, not ready to be tied down.'

'Don't such women just have terminations?'

'Tronal does those as well. But they say some women have ethical difficulties with abortion, even in this day and age. They didn't say as much, but I guess they get some of their custom from the nearby Catholic countries.'

I was still struggling with the idea of a maternity facility I knew nothing about. 'Who provides obstetric support?'

'They have a resident obstetrician. A Mr Mortensen. Fellow of your – what do you call it – Royal College?'

I nodded, but was far from happy. A Fellow of the Royal College of Obstetrics and Gynaecology? For fewer than a dozen births a year?

'Nice man, I thought,' continued Dana. 'He has two fully qualified midwives working with him.'

'What happens to the babies?' I asked, thinking that perhaps I already knew, that Duncan had been thinking about Tronal when we'd talked about adoption the other night.

'Most of them are adopted here on the islands,' said Dana, confirming my guess.

'And you think the woman in my field could have been a Tronal woman? Maybe a mother who changed her mind about giving up her baby?'

'It's possible. The only women outstanding from your list gave birth there.'

I fell silent then, wondering about Tronal, why I'd been told nothing about it. It was a few seconds before I realized Dana was talking to me and I had to ask her to repeat herself.

'What does KT mean?'

'Sorry?'

'KT. I assume it's an abbreviation. It appeared on your list seven times. What does it mean?'

I'd forgotten about that too. I was beginning to realize that, for all my enthusiasm, I'd make a pretty poor detective. 'I don't know,' I had to confess. 'I'll check it out tomorrow.'

She fell silent again. I realized I needed the loo.

When I returned, she was miles away, so lost in thought I don't think she noticed my sitting down beside her. She was staring at the computer again, at what appeared to be an online telephone directory.

'What's up?' I said.

She looked up, startled, then back down at her screen. 'I've been trying to track down the two women you found today, the ones who got married on 4 May 2002. Julie Howard would be Julie Gevvons now. If she's still alive, that is.' She flicked down a few screens, then stopped for a second. 'There's a Gevvons family living in town. It's on my way back to the station. Want to stop by and check out how healthy Mrs Gevvons is looking?'

'Absolutely.'

* * *

We drove for ten minutes then pulled up outside a semi-detached house in a pleasant, modern cul-de-sac; the sort you see all over the UK, built with first-time buyers and young families in mind. I always think of them as happy, hopeful sorts of places, filled with boxed-up wedding presents and plans for the future. They make me feel both cosy and sad at the same time. A small tricycle lay on its side on the grass in front of the house.

Dana knocked. I stood slightly behind her. The door was opened by a young woman who looked around five months pregnant. A toddler in lilac pyjamas clutched her leg and played peek-a-boo at us. Something tense inside me released and I found myself grinning at the child.

'Mrs Gevvons?' Dana held up her ID.

The woman looked puzzled, then alarmed.

'Yes,' she said, looking nervously from Dana to me.

'I'm sorry to disturb you so late in the day, but we've found a wedding ring with initials inside that match yours and your husband's. Have you lost a ring? With an inscription inside?'

As Dana was speaking I caught a glimpse of Julie Gevvons's left hand. It was bare, but I thought I knew why.

Mrs Gevvons looked down at her own hand. 'I don't think so,' she said. 'I haven't been wearing it for a few weeks. My hands have swollen.' She looked uncertain.

‘Is it possible you could check you still have it?’ asked Dana.

Mrs Gevvons nodded and then backed into the house, pushing the toddler along with her. The door closed.

Dana and I waited. After a minute or two Julie Gevvons returned. In her hand she held a thin, gold band, not dissimilar to my own. As we left, I saw her trying to push it past the swollen knuckle of her third finger.

9

WHEN SHE REACHED HER CAR DANA STOPPED. She stared at the lock on the driver's door but made no attempt to open it. I stood watching her for a second or two, feeling foolish. She seemed to have forgotten I was there.

'Ahem,' I said theatrically.

She looked up. 'Sorry.' She pressed the unlock button on her keypad and the vehicle beeped at her cheerfully.

'I'll come by your house later,' she said. 'On my way back to the station.'

'You're not going straight back?'

She frowned, as though my curiosity was misplaced, impertinent somehow. We might have reached an uneasy truce today but this was her business and, no two ways about it, I was interfering.

'I need to check out the Hawicks,' she said. 'I think this ring could be a red herring. I want to get it out of the equation.'

'Want some company?' I ventured, not expecting

for a moment that she would say yes.

She frowned again, then nodded. 'Yes, thank you,' she said. 'That would be good.'

We took her car. There were two Hawick families to check out; the first lived just off the A970 on the outskirts of Lerwick. One look at Kathleen Hawick and we knew we could cross her off the list. She was in her fifties, plump, and that worn, gold wedding band, barely visible beneath the folds of flesh, was not coming off her finger before she died. When we thanked her and left she went happily back to the game show we could hear playing inside the house.

The other Hawick family lived at Scalloway, the old capital of Shetland, a much smaller town about six miles due west of Lerwick. The road was quiet and we arrived in just over fifteen minutes.

Dana pulled over and took out her computer. She tapped away for a few seconds and then we were looking at a map of Scalloway.

'You're pretty handy with this thing,' I said, as she passed it on to my lap and we set off again. 'Left at the bottom. Whatever happened to the old notebook and pencil?'

'Still the weapons of choice at Lerwick nick.'

'Second on the right,' I instructed. We slowed and turned into the street where a J. Hawick lived. It ran directly along the coastline on the south side of the town. The Hawicks had a great view but little protection from the elements and the moment we left the car, the wind raced towards us like a battle charge. As we waited on the doorstep of the house, both Dana's hair and my own were whipped up and tangled together. Mr Hawick, when he opened the door, must have thought two dishevelled mermaids had come to pay him a visit.

From his physique and his hair colour, I guessed Joss Hawick to be in his mid to late thirties, but his face suggested someone a good decade older. He had the appearance of someone suffering from insomnia or maybe long-term stress. His white work shirt was slightly grey and hadn't been particularly well ironed.

Dana went through the routine of showing her ID and introducing herself and me. Hawick looked only mildly interested and not remotely concerned: like a man with nothing left to lose.

'What can I do for you?' he asked. He was Scottish but not an islander. From some way south, I thought; Dundee maybe, or Edinburgh.

Dana explained about the ring and its engraving. Before she'd even finished speaking he was shaking his head.

'Sorry, Sergeant, wasted trip. Now if you'll excuse me.'

He began to back away; the door started to close on us.

Dana was having none of that. 'Sir, this is important. Are you certain that your wife is not missing a ring? Could we just check with her?'

'Sergeant, my wife is dead.'

Dana flinched, but I wasn't remotely surprised.

The drawn, empty look that Joss Hawick wore so prominently is invariably seen on the faces of the bereaved. This man had been in mourning. Still was.

'I'm so sorry.' I spoke for the first time. 'Did she pass away recently?'

'Three years this summer.' Longer than I'd have guessed; this man wasn't easily coming to terms with his loss.

'Had you been married long?' I could sense Dana making impatient movements by my side. I ignored her.

'Just two years,' he said. 'Last Friday would have been our anniversary.'

I thought quickly. Today was Wednesday, the ninth of May. Friday, five days ago, had been the fourth of May. But the year didn't fit. This man's wife had died in 2004, not 2005. Because of the sea flood, Stephen Renney had been certain our victim hadn't been in the ground longer than two years and the Inverness team had backed him up.

'Mr Hawick.' It was Dana this time. 'The inscription on the ring refers to the fourth of May 2002. Was that your wedding day?'

Angry now, he looked from Dana to me. We were raking open wounds that hadn't even begun to heal properly.

'What is this about?' he demanded.

We were inside. His house, brightly coloured and trendily furnished, still looked like the home of a young, affluent couple but it smelled stale, the way houses of old people smell, how old people themselves sometimes smell. Layers of dust lay on the mantelpiece and on the window-sill behind us. He'd offered us a drink, which we'd declined, and had left the room to get himself one. Glancing round, I noticed two dirty glasses on the floor by my end of the yellow sofa and an ashtray full of cigarette stubs. The rug covering most of the wooden floor hadn't been vacuumed any time recently.

On the mantelpiece were several pewter figures of animals and a large photograph in a pewter frame. A younger, happier Joss Hawick beamed at the camera. At his side, white veil billowing around her head, was his wife. Kirsten Hawick had been a tall, attractive woman – with long red hair, falling in ringlets almost to her waist. I looked quickly at Dana. She'd seen the photograph already. She frowned at me, her unspoken instruction clear: keep quiet!

Hawick came back and sat down on a chair opposite us. That was one large Scotch he carried and it didn't look diluted. I realized my hands were shaking. I tucked them under my thighs, glad that Dana would be doing the talking. I felt an overwhelming urge to turn and look at the photograph again, but knew that would be the worst thing I could do.

'I'm sorry for your loss, sir,' she began.

He turned to me and I felt a stab of alarm.

'Why are you here? Are you about to tell me the hospital did something wrong?'

Dana spoke quickly, as though afraid the situation was getting out of control.

'Miss Hamilton has only been at the hospital six months. She knows nothing about the manner of your wife's death. May I ask you some questions?'

He nodded. And drank.

'Could you just confirm your wife's maiden name?'

'Georgeson,' he said. 'Kirsten Georgeson.' He drank again. More than a sip.

I glanced again at Dana. Her face was giving nothing away but she had to have registered that the names fitted. KG and JH. The date was right, too. I forced myself to look down at the carpet, worried my face would give me away. I'd watched enough detective programmes to know that the first suspect in a murder case is always the spouse. What I'd taken for grief on Joss Hawick's face might actually be guilt, not to mention fear of being found out. Dana and I could be alone in a house with a murderer. I looked at Dana again. If she was as worried as I, she wasn't showing it.

There was still, of course, the discrepancy of the year. The woman in my field had died sometime during 2005. Hawick claimed his wife had died in 2004.

'May I ask how and where she died?' Dana said, not taking her eyes off Hawick for a moment.

He looked at me again. 'In hospital,' he said. 'In your hospital.' He made it sound like an accusation. 'She'd been in a riding accident. Her horse was hit by a lorry just a couple of miles north of here. She was still alive when they got her to hospital but with very severe brain damage and a broken neck. We switched the machines off after three hours.'

'Who treated her?' I asked.

'I can't recall his name,' he replied. 'But he said he was the senior registrar. He said she had absolutely no chance of recovery. Are you about to tell me he was wrong?'

'No, no,' I said hurriedly, 'nothing like that. I do need to ask you something else, though; and I am truly sorry to add to your grief. Did your wife have a baby shortly before she died?'

He flinched. 'No,' he said. 'We were planning a family, but Kirsten was a good rider. She wanted to compete for a few years before giving up.'

Joss Hawick was pretty convincing. But he had to know I could check his story out in minutes.

Dana stood up. It was crunch time. I stood too.

'Tora,' said Dana, gesturing towards the door. I went quickly, almost jogging along the corridor, and grabbed at the front door, half expecting to find it locked. It opened and I stood there, allowing the wind from the voe to sweep into the house, making sure Dana joined me.

'One thing puzzles me,' he said as Dana and I stood in the doorway, she outwardly calm, I ready to bolt at any second.

'What's that, sir?'

'You said you'd found a ring. May I see it?'

Dana was a good liar. 'I'm sorry, sir, the ring is

still at the station. But if your wife's ring is missing I can bring it round for you to identify. The inscription inside should make it very easy.'

Hawick shook his head. 'That's what I've been trying to tell you. It can't be Kirsten's.'

'Why not?'

'It was inscribed, but I knew it was tight on her finger and I didn't want it forced off. I asked that she be buried wearing it.'

I couldn't help it. 'Where?' I said. 'Where was she buried?'

He looked surprised and a little disgusted, as though the question was in poor taste. Which it was – but hell, I had an excuse.

'St Magnus's Church,' he said. 'Where we were married.'

'We should have brought two cars,' said Dana. 'Damn!' She started the engine and drove five hundred yards down the road, until we were just out of sight.

I fumbled in my bag and found my cell phone. Within minutes a local taxi was on its way to us. Dana pulled out a notebook and started scribbling.

'He's lying,' I said.

'I know.' She carried on writing. I glanced down at the page. She'd written *Kirsten Hawick, née Georgeson. Died summer 2004. Head injury. Franklin Stone Hospital. Senior Registrar in attendance.*

'It's her,' I said.

'Possibly.'

'You saw the photograph. How many women have hair that long? It's got to be her.' I couldn't stop talking.

'Tora, calm down. It was a small photograph. We can't be sure.' She scribbled something else. A number.

'This is my mobile,' she said, tearing the page out and handing it to me. 'Get to the hospital as soon as you can and check it. Don't speak to anyone else. I'll stay here until I hear from you.'

I nodded. 'Will you be OK?'

'Of course. I'm just going to sit in my car and watch.'

'Can you radio for back-up?'

She smiled. I was using language straight from a cop show.

'As soon as I hear from you. Let's just keep this to ourselves until we're sure.'

The taxi arrived shortly afterwards and I was off.

Fifty minutes later I called her mobile. She answered on the first ring.

'It's me,' I said. 'Can you talk?'

'Go ahead.'

I took a deep breath. 'Everything he told us is true.'

Silence. I thought I could hear the wind whistling around Scalloway Voe.

'What now?' I said.

She thought for a moment. 'I need to drop by the station,' she said. 'Go home. I'll see you there.'

* * *

Just after eight in the evening and the Franklin Stone was still busy. I hoped I wouldn't bump into anyone I knew as I left the building. I was seriously disturbed and I'm not a good liar at the best of times.

Kirsten Hawick had to be the woman I'd dug up in my field. Death hadn't changed her much. That delicate, white skin, with just a faint scattering of freckles, the type you only see on Scottish women, had been tanned by the peat, but her face had still been the perfect oval that I'd seen in the photograph.

Yet I'd just called up her hospital medical records. She had indeed been admitted on 18 August 2004 (the better part of a year before the woman in the peat was supposed to have been killed), presenting with severe head trauma and multiple fractures of her upper spine. She'd been pronounced dead at 7.16 p.m. and her body released for burial two days later. There had even been a post mortem.

I stopped at the front desk. At six in the evening the receptionist is replaced by a night porter. He was reading a newspaper and clutching a half-empty coffee mug.

'Hi!' I said, a lot more cheerfully than I felt.

He glanced up, didn't think much of what he saw and went back to his paper.

'Do you by any chance have a street map of the town that I could look at?' I asked.

He shook his head and carried on reading.

I fumbled in my bag, found my hospital ID card

and placed it carefully on his newspaper. He looked up then.

'A map,' I said. 'The front desk needs to have one, or you can't do your job properly. If you don't have one, I'll make a complaint on your behalf, through the formal channels, that you're not being kept properly supplied.'

He glared at me. Then he got up, walked to a filing cabinet at the back of the room and searched inside. It took thirty seconds. He brought the map back and opened it.

'What would ye be looking for?'

'St Magnus's Church.'

With a tobacco-stained finger he pointed to a spot on the map.

I looked carefully, trying to memorize the place. It wasn't far from the hospital.

'Thanks,' I said.

He pushed it over towards me. 'Take it,' he offered.

'No thanks,' I said. 'Someone else might need it.'

I turned and left, feeling all warm and cosy inside at having made yet another friend at the hospital.

I was glad it was still light when I arrived at St Magnus's. I had to park on the main road and walk down the short, narrow street, and after dark I'm not sure I'd have found the courage to do so. The area was deserted. Tall, granite buildings towered overhead. Converted to offices, they were empty for the evening, but I had the sense of dozens of windows from which I could be watched.

Opposite the church was a large, old house set in a walled garden. Trees, the like of which I'd never seen before, grew along the cobbled driveway. They looked like some sort of willow, but were a far cry from the tall, graceful trees that line English rivers. None of them was more than about twelve feet high and none had a central trunk. Instead, thick, gnarled branches sprang from the ground, twisting and knotting as they reached upwards. Leaves hadn't started to open and the bare branches reminded me of an enchanted forest in one of the scarier fairy stories.

There was no easy way into the small, walled churchyard. I guessed official visitors had to go through the church. I spent a few seconds plucking up courage and then I leaped over the wall. None of the headstones near by carried dates later than the nineteenth century so I followed the narrow, overgrown path around to the back. The rear left corner looked promising. There were patches of bare ground, the graves were better tended and one grave even had a raised mound and some remains of funeral flowers.

It took me five minutes to find it. A large, rectangular headstone, the granite dark and glossy, the carving simple:

Kirsten Hawick
1975–2004
A most beloved wife.

The mound of earth had been flattened and planted with spring bulbs. Some of the daffodils were still in bloom; others had dried, their petals shrivelled and orange. They needed to be deadheaded, tied in neat bunches and replaced with summer bedding plants but I had the feeling that Joss Hawick probably didn't come here too much. I suppose it's a very individual thing, one's relationship with the grave of a loved one. Some people seem to need the close personal connection they feel with the deceased and can spend hours just standing or sitting by a grave. For others, I guess, a grave is a rather dreadful reminder of the physical process of decay taking place beneath their feet.

I knelt down and, because I really couldn't think of anything else to do, I started knotting the stalks. When I'd finished the grave looked neater, apart from the weeds. After all the rain we'd had recently they came out pretty easily, but my hands were soon filthy.

'Touching,' said a voice.

I spun round to see two men standing over me. Two tall men. The setting sun was directly behind them and for a second I wasn't sure who they were. Then, with a sinking heart, I recognized both. I stood up, determined to brazen it out, and looked down at the grave. 'So, who do you reckon is down here?' I said.

Andy Dunn looked back at me as though I was a difficult child in whom he'd invested an enormous amount of time and energy and who had just let him down, again.

'Kirsten Hawick is buried here,' he said. 'Joss Hawick is extremely distressed. He'll probably make a formal complaint.'

Well, I may not be the sharpest knife in the box but I know bullshit when I hear it.

'I can't imagine what about,' I snapped. 'He was handled with extreme sensitivity and the visit was perfectly legitimate. There was every chance the ring – and I'm referring to the one that *I* found, by the way, on *my* land – was his wife's.'

'How's your horse?' asked Gifford, successfully interrupting my train of thought. Christ, had that really only been this morning?

'Please, Kenn,' said Dunn, sounding tired.

I decided to ignore Gifford. Well, at least try. Looking directly at Andy Dunn I said, 'I saw her photograph this evening. It's the same woman. How else do you explain the fact that a ring, bearing the exact date of their wedding and their initials, could be found in my field. In the hole I dug her out of, for God's sake?'

'Tora,' it was Gifford again, 'you saw the corpse only twice. The first time it was covered in peat and you were understandably in shock. The second time was on an autopsy table and, frankly, you didn't look at her face that much.'

I looked at Gifford. His eyes seemed larger and brighter than I remembered. For the first time that evening I started to have doubts.

'Lots of women on these islands look like she did,' he said. 'Red hair, fair skin and small features are typically Scottish. But I knew Kirsten Hawick. For one thing, she was nearly your height. A good five inches taller than the corpse you found.'

I shook my head, but what he was saying was plausible.

He reached out and put a hand on my shoulder, speaking quietly, as though he didn't want Dunn to hear. 'Two doctors, a nurse and her husband were present when the machines were turned off. Kirsten Hawick died in our hospital.'

I wasn't giving in easily. 'Then her body was stolen. Probably from the hospital morgue. Someone stole the body because they wanted her heart.'

They looked at me like I was deranged.

'Don't ask me why they wanted it, but someone did. They stole the body, took out the heart and dumped her in my field.'

'The woman in your field had just had a baby. Kirsten Hawick had never been pregnant.'

Well, I had to admit, he had me there. Plus, according to Dr Renney, the heart had been removed while the victim was still alive, not post mortem.

'And the timing just doesn't fit,' added Dunn, imitating Gifford's gentle tones. 'I've checked with Stephen Renney and the Inverness pathology team. They've had a chance to examine the body extensively and to carry out all sorts of tests on the peat around her. The woman from your field could not have been dead since 2004.'

I looked down at the grave. 'There's one way to know for sure.'

Well, that at least dented Dunn's annoying self-control. He flushed and glared at me. 'Don't even think about it. We are not about to start exhuming graves. Do you have any idea how much distress that causes? To the whole community, not just the family concerned.'

Gifford's hand left my shoulder and slid down my arm, my sore arm. He squeezed gently and I had to grit my teeth not to flinch. 'This is exactly what I was afraid of. Tora, I don't blame you, but this has all become too personal. I want you to think again about taking some time off.'

At least he wasn't firing me yet. But I wasn't about to take time off. There were some difficult deliveries coming up and the hospital needed me. I shook my head.

'OK.' He glanced at Andy Dunn, as if to say, *I've done my best. You see what I have to deal with*?

Maybe he was right, maybe I did need to detach at bit. Forget about the murder, just concentrate on doing my job and let the police do theirs.

'You have a clinic in the morning, don't you?' Gifford was saying.

I nodded.

'I'd like to see you just before. Can you be in by eight?'

I nodded again, feeling like a delinquent teenager whose parents were being just too understanding.

Gifford smiled at me. He laid his arm along my shoulders and pushed me gently down the path.

'Come on, I'll walk you to your car.'

Andy Dunn followed us in silence as we walked down the path and left the churchyard. As I drove away, I could see them both, in the rear-view mirror, standing in the road and watching me.

When I arrived home a shadowy figure was huddled on my doorstep. I shrieked as it moved towards me.

'It's OK, it's only me.' Dana stepped out into the light. The body is slow to catch up with the brain on these occasions. Even as I knew there was nothing to worry about, my nerve endings felt as though someone had administered a thousand tiny electric shocks. I looked round.

'Where's your car?'

'Down the road.'

I stared at her stupidly. 'Why?' I managed.

'I don't want anyone seeing it outside your house. We arranged to meet here, remember?' she prompted.

'Yes, but . . . you obviously haven't seen your DI this evening.'

'Of course I've seen him. Why, have you?'

I nodded. 'He found me in St Magnus's churchyard. At Kirsten's grave.'

Her eyebrows shot up. 'Did he now?'

'He explained everything. He and Kenn Gifford.'

She looked at me with both amusement and pity on her face. 'And you fell for it? Tora Hamilton, you are not the woman I took you for.'

10

'I SAW HER GRAVE, DANA. IT'S JUST NOT POSSIBLE.'

We were sitting at my kitchen table, doors locked, blinds drawn. I was tired and had an uncomfortable sense of being drawn back into something I'd been happy to leave behind just half an hour ago. We were drinking hot, strong coffee. I'd offered red wine but Dana had shaken her head. 'We need to think,' she'd said. Scary word: *we*. Suddenly, we were accomplices, working against clear instructions from our superiors. We were arguably being foolish, possibly about to do considerable harm and definitely in for a whole heap of trouble when – not if – we were found out.

I'd also offered food and Dana had given me a vague look. I wasn't sure if it meant yes or no. I was hungry and acutely conscious of cold ham in the fridge and fresh bread in the larder.

'Everything is possible. I just can't see how they did it.'

'Who exactly are *they*? You're talking about my

boss. He's a fellow of the Royal College of Surgeons, for heaven's sake. There were other people in the room with her when the machines were turned off. Kirsten Hawick died. Nearly a year before our victim did.'

Dana clicked her tongue. 'Yeah, yeah . . . I've heard all that too. But – just to put it another way – you find a wedding ring on the same patch of ground you found a corpse; the inscription inside suggests it belongs to a dead woman, one Mrs Hawick, who not only fits the age and ethnic group of our victim, but also, judging by her wedding photos, bears a reasonable resemblance to her. And we're being told it's just coincidence. How likely does that seem to you?'

Not remotely, was the honest answer. But the evidence for Kirsten's death had been pretty convincing. I stood up. I was not going to be intimidated out of making a sandwich in my own home. I got out the ham, butter and bread.

'I felt such an idiot,' I said. 'God knows what they thought when they saw me digging up weeds on her grave.'

'Does it strike you as odd that the two of them should follow you to the churchyard? How did they even know you'd gone there? And why would it bother them?' Dana stopped, thought for a second, then said, 'Do I sound paranoid?'

I glanced over my shoulder. 'Only totally.'

'Thanks.' To her credit, she managed a smile.

'Welcome.' I bent down again, fumbling in the

back of the fridge for the mayonnaise. When I straightened up she was serious again.

'There's something I want you to do,' she said.

Just when I'd thought it was safe. 'What?'

She reached into a briefcase and pulled out a folder of thin, green cardboard. From inside she removed a sheet of black and white transparent film.

'This is a dental X-ray that was taken of our corpse. My team have been checking it against records of women on the missing-persons list. No matches so far, although obviously not all records are available to us.'

I brought the food back to the table and went to get cutlery. 'What do you want me to do?'

'I have nagged and pleaded and begged, but DI Dunn will not even consider asking Joss Hawick to release his wife's dental records for comparison.'

I really couldn't see where she was going with this. 'So . . .'

'You should be able to find them.'

Back at the table, I started buttering bread. I shook my head. 'Most dentists work privately. No one else can access their records. Even if we knew who Kirsten's dentist was, he couldn't release them to me without Joss Hawick's permission.'

'Tora, you're thinking of England. It's different up here. Most people use an NHS dentist. Plus, there was an IT pilot scheme carried out here a year ago. All the islands' dental records were computerized and made centrally available.'

'I still don't see . . .'

'There's a dental unit attached to your hospital. Kirsten's records will be on the hospital computer system. You can access them.'

She was probably right.

'I'm not a dentist,' I said lamely.

'You've studied anatomy. You know how to read X-rays. You'd have a better chance of seeing a match than I would.'

Following a hunch was one thing, asking someone you barely knew to carry out an illegal search was another. What wasn't she telling me?

'Will you do it?' she asked.

I didn't know.

'If there's no match, that's it. The ring is a red herring and we waste no more time on it.'

It was worth it, surely, to be able to close the chapter. I could prove to Dana that the corpse was not Kirsten and that would be the end of it.

'OK, I'll do it tomorrow.'

I indicated the food. 'Help yourself.' Dana ignored the ham and took a slice of bread and butter.

I, on the other hand, was no longer hungry.

11

I'M NOT SURE AT WHAT POINT IN THE NIGHT I STARTED to suspect that there was someone in the room with me. Sometime around two a.m., I guess, because that, typically, is when I'm in my deepest sleep and find it hardest to wake up. Ten years of being on call through the night and you get to know your sleep rhythms.

So there I was, two a.m. or thereabouts, alone, because Duncan was not expected back before Saturday morning, with a glimmer of consciousness returning and a niggling fear that all was not as it should be. Because someone had entered my bedroom.

I can't really explain how I knew; I just did. When you habitually sleep with a partner, you develop a sense of the closeness of the other and, upon waking, a dozen different triggers will remind you in an instant that he (or she) is still there: the scent of skin, the sound of breathing, the extra warmth another body creates. You settle back down reassured: you are not alone and the otherness beside you is comfort and familiarity.

This was neither comfortable nor familiar. The presence I could sense was far from the cosy warmth of a sleeping husband; it was alien, intrusive, predatory.

As always, I was huddled well down in the bed, covers drawn up around my face, and, like a child hiding from the bogeyman, I felt a sense of the quilt's protection; that if I lay still, pretending all was well, then maybe – just maybe – it would be; that whatever was in the room with me – quite close now, I could sense it – would just fade away into the realm of forgotten dreams. The drowsy side of me just wanted to slip back into oblivion and take the chance.

At the same time, the part of me that was trying desperately to wake up properly knew this wasn't just another night-time jelly-wobble, the kind of thing that occasionally happens when you sleep alone. This wasn't a random creaking floorboard or the wind rattling next door's dustbins. For one thing, I couldn't hear anything: the wind had dropped, the house's water-heating system had finally settled down for the night and even the night birds – often so loquacious on the Shetlands – were taking a break. Dead silence. A deep, dark, impenetrable silence.

I braced myself to move, to jump up, startle whoever it was and give myself a fighting chance. And found that I didn't dare. I lay there, totally exposed to the threat beside me and unable to move a muscle. I couldn't even open my eyes. I'm not sure how much time passed: it felt like for ever; realistically it was probably only a minute or two. Then the lightest movement of air passed across my cheek, the atmosphere in the room changed and I found myself sitting up.

The room was dark, much darker than normal. Light never really disappears during the Shetland summer, but this was as dark a night as I could remember. I looked all around, struggling to make everything out, to see into the deepest shadows. There was nothing and no one in the room that shouldn't be there. Except the smell.

I was breathing too fast – shallow, rapid, panicky breaths – and I made myself slow down, breathe in properly through my nose, be sure I wasn't imagining it. Like a perfumier testing a new fragrance, I explored the air around me: sweat, ever so faint but unmistakeable; and the softest hint of cigarette smoke, not the smell of a smoker, but of someone who might have passed briefly through a smoke-filled room; something else too, faintest of all, something that made me think of my mother's spice cupboard: cinnamon maybe, or ginger. It was a smell you might experience twenty times a day and think nothing of: passing someone in a corridor, getting on to a train, shaking hands with a stranger. Just the normal, everyday aroma of a normal, everyday male.

So what the hell was it doing in my bedroom in the middle of the night?

That's when I noticed something else that wasn't right. The bedroom door was slightly ajar. Strange though it may seem, I cannot sleep when there are doors open around me. The door to the corridor, to our en-suite bathroom, even those on the wardrobes have to be closed. Duncan laughs at me, I even laugh at myself, but before I go to sleep, without fail, I close all the doors.

I remained frozen on the bed, listening as hard as I'd ever listened in my life before. Nothing. There was a phone on my bedside cabinet and I was pretty certain the police, Dana at least, would come straight over. But what, exactly, was I going to report? A smell? A door not properly closed?

I made myself climb out of bed as I tried to remember what we are supposed to do in these situations. Make a noise or be silent? Pick up the phone and loudly pretend to be calling the police? I walked to the door and eased it open. The corridor was empty. Four more doors led off it, three to spare bedrooms, one to the main bathroom. Downstairs something scraped along a wooden floorboard.

I ran back into the bedroom, pulled open the wardrobe door and reached up to the top shelf. My fingers touched what I was searching for and I pulled it down. I checked the bolt was set and held it out in front of me, the way I'd seen people do on television. Then I crossed the room, stepped out along the corridor and paused at the top of the stairs. I was carrying a humane horse-killer, fifty years old if it was a day, a crude, inefficient weapon of iron and copper. It had belonged to my grandfather and had been designed to put down injured or very old horses by firing a four-inch iron bolt directly into their brains. Duncan had begged me many times to get rid of it. I'd always resisted and now I was glad I had. It was completely ineffective unless the target was close enough to touch, but most people probably wouldn't know that. Having a weapon, even this one, gave me the courage to walk down the stairs.

Our front door was at the bottom. I checked quickly: still closed and locked. I pushed open the door to the dining room and looked round. Nothing that I could see. Our sitting room, on the other side of the hall, was a much bigger room; three large sofas for people to hide behind. I took a step inside. And another.

Down the hall came the sound of something breaking, footsteps running, a door being pulled open. I ran from the room and into the kitchen, fumbling for the light-switch as I went. A large glass vase, which I'd left too close to the edge of the worktop, had smashed into a thousand pieces on the slate floor. The back door was open and the cold night air was pushing its way into the room. I ran across, slammed it shut, turned the key and pulled both bolts into place.

As I turned to the phone I noticed the door to the cellar was open and the light on. Three paces took me to the top of the steps.

I had no intention whatsoever of going into the cellar. The area beneath our house is spooky enough at the best of times. But something lay at the bottom of the steps; something that most definitely should not be there.

It was a piece of fabric wrapped around an object the size of a grapefruit. I was still some distance away and the light in the cellar wasn't good. I was pretty certain, though, that the fabric was linen, ivory in colour – except where its contents were staining it a bright scarlet.

My brain was telling me to call the police; they'd deal with it, whatever it was. But first one foot and then the other took me down. There were only eight steps and I was soon at the bottom, close enough to touch. I crouched down beside it.

The stain was still wet. Red liquid was oozing out, seeping on to the stone floor of the cellar. I reached out, expecting to feel warmth beneath my hand. The package was cold and smelled of something that was . . . a total surprise. I picked it up. Pulled the linen apart. Some of the contents spilled over on to the floor. The rest lay in my hands.

I was looking at strawberries.

Not wild – it wasn't the season for them – just common or garden strawberries, found in supermarkets and greengrocers the length and breadth of the land. Most of them had been crushed, hence the red liquid seeping through the linen and the sweet summery smell. As I knelt in the poor light of the cellar, I found that I was mad as holy hell that I'd been scared so much for this. Not remotely frightened any more, but seething with rage, I scooped up the berries that had fallen and climbed the steps to the kitchen, the horse gun tucked under one arm. I reached the top, shut the door behind me and was about to head for the phone.

I stopped moving, even stopped breathing. The kitchen started to go dark around me but I absolutely could not take my eyes off what lay in front of me. For a second or two I even thought I'd lost my mind. What I was looking at was impossible. I'd been in this room not two minutes earlier and there was no way I could have missed seeing . . . *that* . . . on the kitchen table.

The strawberries fell to the floor and the gun nearly did likewise but I managed to catch it. I turned, almost fell over and grabbed the phone. Then I ran, out of the kitchen, across the hall and into the downstairs lavatory. I slammed the door behind me, pulled the ridiculously inadequate bolt and sank to the floor. I pushed my back up against the door and wedged my feet against the opposite wall. Fighting back nausea, I phoned the police.

12

FOR THE TWENTY MINUTES IT TOOK THEM TO arrive, I barely moved. I grew cold, but didn't think that was the only reason I couldn't stop shaking. Every few minutes nausea reared up but thankfully always stopped short of making me chuck. I phoned Duncan's mobile but he'd switched it off. I didn't leave a message. What the hell would I say?

I wanted, more than anything, to call my dad. To tell him what had happened, to hear him tell me it was going to be OK. Four times, I think, I dialled my parents' number but couldn't bring myself to press the last digit. What on earth could he do, my poor dad? He was hundreds of miles away.

Eventually I heard the cars pulling into the yard and made myself get up to answer the door. Andy Dunn took one look at me and ordered me into the sitting room with a WPC. A blanket materialized and I sat, shivering, trying to answer the questions that she and a detective constable put to me. From the kitchen I heard Dunn's sharp intake of breath, the blasphemous exclamation of the sergeant accompanying him. There was no sign of Dana. Then I heard Dunn on the radio:

'Yeah, we've got a break-in. Some sort of organ left on the kitchen table. Looks like a heart . . . yeah, looks human . . .'

I pushed myself up, ignored the protests of the two officers and walked into the kitchen. The heart hadn't been touched. It lay, glistening, in a pool of blood. The smell, strong, metallic, sickening, was flooding the kitchen now. I tried not to breathe too deeply.

'I don't think it's human,' I said.

Dunn stopped talking into the radio, muttered something about getting back and switched it off.

'You don't?' he said. I thought he looked paler than normal, but it could just have been the result of being dragged out of bed in the small hours.

I shook my head. 'I thought it was, at first. But I've had time to think about it . . .' The truth was, I still wasn't sure. Looking at it again, I couldn't have placed a bet either way.

Another officer entered the room. 'There's no sign of a break-in, Andy. Nothing forced or broken.'

Dunn looked at him and nodded. Then turned back to me. 'So what is it?' he said. 'What is it from? Some sort of animal?'

I swallowed hard. 'Can I weigh it?' I asked.

Dunn shot a glance at his sergeant. 'I'm not sure . . .' he began.

'You'll need a doctor to confirm it one way or another. Might as well be me.'

Dunn said nothing. I crossed the room to where I'd left my work bag and fumbled inside until I found a packet of surgical gloves. Then I carried my kitchen scales over to the table.

'Mammalian hearts are all very similar in structure,' I said, trying to sound professional, knowing I was failing miserably. 'They have five major pipes, called the great vessels, coming out of them: the superior and the inferior vena cava, two pulmonary trunks and the aorta.' I touched the heart, turned it round. Blood, already starting to clot, poured from it and splattered the table. The WPC gave a faint gasp. I clenched my teeth together and took a deep breath. 'They also have two chambers, the left and right ventricle, both with thick, muscular walls, the left substantially bigger than the right. Also a right and left atrium. They're all here.'

'You don't have to . . .' began Dunn, but I did. I had to prove to them all, and to myself most of all, that I was not going to be freaked out – not for more than a few minutes anyway – by something I'd seen and handled countless times before. I picked the heart up and put it on the scales.

'Human hearts typically weigh 250–350 grams,' I said. The electronic reading on the scales said 345 grams.

'Within the range,' said Dunn.

'It is,' I agreed. 'And there's an outside chance this is the heart of a big adult male. Over six foot and powerfully built. But if I was putting money on it, I'd say it came from a large pig.'

The relief in the room was almost strong enough to reach out and touch. I was ordered back into the other room and questioned again. More police arrived. They dusted for fingerprints, walked the perimeter of the property with dogs and removed both the heart and the strawberries. Still no sign of Dana.

Eventually, Dunn came to join me on the sofa.

'You need to get some rest now,' he said, almost gently. 'I'm leaving a couple of constables in the house for the rest of the night. You'll be perfectly safe.'

'Thank you,' I managed.

'Duncan's back on Saturday, right?'

I nodded.

'You might want to find somewhere else to stay tomorrow. This is almost certainly some sort of sick practical joke but I don't like the fact that whoever got in here did so without breaking in. We'll be checking who might have keys to the house. A change of locks probably isn't a bad idea.'

I nodded again.

He reached out, touched my arm, seemed unsure what to do next and ended up giving it a feeble pat. Then he got up. 'Try to get some rest, Miss Hamilton,' he said again. Then he left.

I went upstairs thinking that, as practical jokes go, it was the least funny I'd ever heard of. And besides, it didn't feel like a joke to me. It felt as though someone was trying to scare the shit out of me.

13

'TOR, I FOUND THE RING.'

'What? You did what?'

It was seven forty-five the next morning; I was running late and driving too fast. Duncan had called to say he had an extra meeting scheduled – a really important one – and wouldn't be home till Saturday evening, if that was OK. He'd sounded so excited about the potential deal, so fired up, that I couldn't bring myself to tell him about what had happened the night before. I couldn't ruin a really big opportunity for him. I'd be OK for another night, I told myself. I could always sleep at the hospital.

So instead, I'd told him about all the stuff that had happened the previous day, things that had seemed so important at the time: finding the ring on my boot, checking the various registers and visiting both the Hawick family home and the graveyard. Speaking far too fast, praying he wouldn't notice how shaken I still was, I'd even told him about my plans to carry out an illicit search of dental records. He'd listened patiently until I'd just about done, then dropped his bombshell.

'I found it,' he was saying, 'months ago.'

I couldn't take it in. The ring had been stuck to the bottom of my wellington. It had been buried beneath six feet of peat with the dead body of its owner.

'Where? How?' I managed.

'In the bottom field. Last November, I think, before you came out. I was laying concrete to put the fence posts in. I just saw it, lying on a pile of earth. I must have dug it up.'

'But, what . . . you never said!'

'I didn't give it much thought. I wasn't even sure what it was. It was filthy and I wanted to get the job finished. I threw it into my tool box and forgot about it.'

And suddenly, it all made complete sense: the ring had been in Duncan's toolbox. I'd dislodged it when I'd been looking for something to cut the wire around Charles's leg and it had landed, to be found shortly afterwards, on the stair. It had been nowhere near my wellington and – more importantly – nowhere near the grave. The fence that Duncan had built around our bottom field was a good hundred yards downhill from where I'd tried to bury Jamie. The ring was a total red herring after all.

'But how did it get there?' Red herring or not, it still didn't add up.

'Good question. Assuming it really is the wedding ring of the woman who died – Kirsten, was that her name? Is it possible it wasn't? How clear was the inscription?'

'Not very.' I hadn't even been completely sure about the letters. Only the date was clear and, as I'd discovered, several weddings had taken place that day.

'Tor, you're not really going to check dental records, are you? At best it's a waste of time and at worst highly unprofessional, probably even illegal. Don't get involved any more.'

It's not often Duncan asks me to do something. When he does, I nearly always agree.

'No, of course not. You're right.' I meant it, too. It had all gone far enough.

'Good girl. I'll see you tomorrow. Love you.'

He hadn't said that in a long time. By the time I was ready to respond, he'd hung up.

I was on the edge of Lerwick now and drove quickly to the hospital. I glanced at the car clock. I was going to be ten minutes late. I parked the car and jumped out, wincing. It occurred to me that I might be coming down with some sort of summer flu bug: every limb was aching, I had what seemed like a raging hangover even though I'd drunk nothing the night before, and felt like I hadn't slept in a week. And now I was ten minutes late for a bollocking from Kenn Gifford.

He was waiting for me in my office, looking out of the window, already dressed in blue surgical scrubs, his long hair scraped back in a ponytail.

'How are you feeling?' he asked, turning round.

'Been better,' I replied.

I might feel like shit but Gifford wasn't looking his best either. His narrow eyes were little more than slits in his face and the shadows under them had deepened.

'Sorry I'm late,' I said. 'Duncan phoned on my way in. Slowed me up a bit.' I told Gifford about Duncan finding the ring. When I'd finished, he nodded.

'I'll call Joss Hawick. It's almost certainly not his wife's ring, but if he wants to pursue the matter he can call into the police station to identify it. If it is hers, it looks like we have a pilfering problem; a particularly distasteful one, at that, if someone is robbing the morgue. I'm sorry all this is happening, Tora, it can't be easy settling in with all these distractions. Can I get you a coffee?'

'Thanks,' I said, and he walked over to the coffee-maker in the corner and poured two cups.

'Do you have some sort of master key?' I asked.

He turned round, a steaming mug in each hand, and raised his eyebrows.

'I lock my office in the evening but you managed to find your way in and organize breakfast. Do you have croissants baking as well?'

'I'll happily nip out to the bakery. Mr Stephenson's been waiting three months for his bypass and I'm sure another half-hour won't hurt. But, no. Having a master key – and using it – would be pretty unprofessional, don't you think? Unless, of course, you're a cleaner. Like the one who was in here when I arrived and who let me stay and make coffee. Just thought you might need it.' He handed me a mug. The warmth in my hands was comforting, like a hug from an old friend. He was standing very close to me and I didn't move away.

'DI Dunn came by earlier,' he said. 'He wanted Stephen Renney to confirm the heart wasn't human.'

'And . . .' I prompted, although I was pretty certain I'd been right the night before.

Gifford led me to two easy chairs in the corner of the room. He motioned for me to sit and I did. So did he.

'From a pig,' he said. 'Andy's got people checking all the butchers on the islands. If anyone bought a heart in the last few days he'll soon know about it.'

'Is he still going with his practical-joke theory?'

Kenn nodded. 'I think he's right, don't you? Why would the killer, assuming he's still around, take such a huge risk? Supposing you'd seen him last night.'

Then I'd be dead right now.

'Andy's done his best to keep details under wraps,' continued Gifford, 'but this is a small place. Things get out. Any number of people might know that you found the body, about the missing heart, about her stomach contents. As jokes go it's not particularly tasteful but there are some very odd people around.'

'And I'm not exactly Miss Popular.'

'Oh, I don't know.' He stood up. 'You need somewhere to sleep tonight,' he said. 'I'd offer my spare room, but I'm not sure how that would go down with Duncan.'

Suddenly I couldn't look at him.

'Is Inspector Dunn making much progress with the murder investigation?' I asked, partly because I was sure the island police would have been more forthcoming with one of their own than they had been with me, and partly because a change of subject seemed to be called for.

'They've pretty much ruled out the victim being a local woman,' he said. 'She matches no one on the missing-persons list. Andy has his team combing similar lists for the rest of the UK. When they find a possible match they'll use dental records to confirm identity.'

Dental records that were, at that moment, in my briefcase. I must have looked guilty as hell, but if he noticed he gave no sign.

'It's not exciting, it's not glamorous, but it's good solid police work and sooner or later it should get results.'

'You'd think so, but . . .' I stopped. Kenn had known Dunn since school, he'd known me for a matter of days. Where did I really think his loyalty was going to lie?

'But what?' he prompted.

'It just seems . . . sometimes I think . . .' I stopped. Kenn was looking at me, waiting for me to go on. I was in for it now. 'He just doesn't seem to be taking it terribly seriously. First the body was an archeological find, then the victim couldn't possibly be local, and then last night was a practical joke. It's like he's trying to play it down all the time, make out it's less serious than it is.'

Kenn was frowning at me, but whether he didn't believe me and was annoyed, or whether he did and was alarmed, I really couldn't tell.

'Dana Tulloch thinks so too,' I went on. 'She hasn't said anything, she's far too professional for that, but I can tell the way she's thinking sometimes.'

He sighed. 'Tora, there's something you need to know about Sergeant Tulloch.'

'What?'

'I'm probably breaking all sorts of professional confidences now but, well, Andy Dunn and I go back a long way.'

'I know. You all do up here.'

He smiled. 'This is not Dana's first sergeant's job. She was a sergeant in Dundee. She also did a spell in Manchester. Neither job worked out and she agreed to two transfers. I get the impression this is her last chance in the force.'

I was amazed. 'But she's just so . . . competent.'

'Oh, she's bright enough. IQ off the stratosphere. One of the reasons she's lasted so long. But there are other problems.'

'Such as?' I didn't like this. The previous day I'd found myself warming to Dana, even starting to like her. It didn't feel right to be talking behind her back.

'I don't remember much of my psychology but I'd say she shows signs of obsessive compulsive disorder. I think there've been eating problems in the past, maybe there are still, she's very slim. And she has a compulsive interest in order and organization and external appearances. She's been known to throw a complete tantrum when someone moves a stapler on her desk.'

'So she's tidy.' I glanced round my office: utter tip, as usual. 'Christ, we could all do with having that problem.'

'Look at the way she dresses. Have you ever seen her less than immaculate? How does she afford that on a police sergeant's salary? And what about the car she drives? Not only is it a Mercedes but it looks like she just drove it out of the showroom. Every police officer I've ever met has a car like a municipal dump. You can't see the carpet for fag ends, the remains of takeaway dinners and Mars bar wrappers. That's if you get one of the more refined ones. Her car gets vacuumed every day.'

'What are you saying?'

He walked over to my window. 'She's believed to be seriously in debt,' he said to the seagulls outside. Then he turned round to me again. 'She can't stop spending money. Money she doesn't have. And she can't work as part of a team. She's secretive. Drives Dunn up the wall and makes her very unpopular with her colleagues. If people question her methods, she always assumes the problem lies with them; that there's some sort of conspiracy to get at her.'

I remembered her actions the previous evening, working with me rather than any of her colleagues, not letting them know where she was or what she was up to. It had seemed odd at the time; now it made more sense. And that was before her accusations against Gifford and Dunn, or her persuading me to carry out an illegal search of confidential records. Oh great, my new best friend was a fruit-cake!

'Dana Tulloch needs professional help, in my view,' said Gifford. 'You, on the other hand, need to come to terms with what's happened and move on.'

'You mentioned that before.'

'And it bears repeating. This case may never be solved.'

I looked at him and shook my head.

'Ask any police officer,' he continued. 'The chances of solving a murder are always greatest in the first twenty-four hours. Just one day goes by and the trail starts to go cold. This trail is two years cold and our friend down in the morgue matches no one on the missing-persons list and no one who had a baby on the islands that year. She almost certainly wasn't local.'

He was right, of course. The grown-ups are always right in the end. He looked at his watch. 'It's nearly nine. You have a clinic this morning?'

I nodded. A busy one. Ten appointments, followed by two planned Caesars this afternoon and discharging Janet and Tamary Kennedy.

'I'd better go too. Mr Stephenson will be wondering where I am.'

He was in the doorway when I called him back. 'Kenn, what does KT mean?'

He turned. 'Excuse me?'

'KT. I found it on the system, recorded against births in summer 2005.'

Light seemed to dawn. 'Oh yes, I asked that too. It means Keloid Trauma.'

'What?'

'Oh, it's a term we coined up here. You won't have come across it before. Hold on, let me think for a minute . . .'

He leaned against the doorframe, staring up at the ceiling. I watched him. The word 'keloid' refers to an over-reaction of fibrous skin tissue that sometimes occurs after surgery or injury. It can lead to a thickened or pronounced scar.

'There was a study here a while ago,' Gifford said, after a second or two. 'One of our graduate students led it. I was away at the time and can't say I've actually read the paper, so I'm going to sound a bit vague. Oh, I've got it. There's a genetic condition up here that results in severe scarring after perineum tearing in childbirth. When the next child comes along it can cause problems. Hence, Keloid Trauma.'

'Sounds like something I should watch out for,' I said, relieved that KT, at least, was a mystery I could cross off the list.

'I'll try and dig the paperwork out for you.' He turned to the door, stopped and then looked back over his shoulder.

'Duncan doesn't like me because I stole his girlfriend.' He grinned at me: a thin, mirthless elongation of his lips. 'More than once.'

14

I THANKED MY LUCKY STARS FOR A BUSY CLINIC THAT morning and for the fact that this really isn't a job you can do with your mind elsewhere. For four hours I monitored foetal heartbeats, measured blood pressure, checked for excess sugar in urine and examined abdomens in various stages of distension. I discussed, with a straight face, whether damp panties were likely to be the result of waters breaking early or late-pregnancy incontinence and I resisted throwing up my hands in despair at the woman in the thirty-eighth week of her fourth pregnancy who wanted me to describe the exact sensations felt during a Braxton Hicks contraction. *Well, you tell me, love.*

During my half-hour lunch break I grabbed a sandwich from the hospital canteen. Not feeling up to small talk, I took it back to my office and, with nothing to immediately occupy me, started getting flashbacks of the night before. My sandwich – rare roast beef – no longer seemed a particularly wise choice. Searching for something to take my mind off blood-covered organs, I found myself thinking of Kirsten Hawick, who'd been killed riding a horse not far away. I've been riding since I was seven and consider myself, modesty aside, pretty good. But hearing about Kirsten's accident had bothered me. The best of riders can be caught unawares and horses are notoriously unpredictable, especially on the roads. I wanted to know more. Had she been at fault? What had happened to the driver of the lorry? I switched on my computer and accessed the Internet.

The *Shetland Times* is not the only newspaper on the islands, but it's the one claiming the highest circulation. I found its website easily enough. I put 'Kirsten Hawick' and 'Riding Accidents' into the search facility and pressed Go. A few seconds later I was reading the account, from August 2004, of how a supermarket delivery lorry took a blind corner on the B9074 just a little too fast and of how the driver had been unable to stop when he found himself almost on top of the woman on the large grey horse. Kirsten had been pronounced dead at the hospital and there was a quote – bland and sympathetic – from the senior registrar. The police were considering a charge of causing death by dangerous driving.

There would be follow-up stories in later issues of the paper but I wasn't interested. I was staring at the photograph of Kirsten that accompanied the story. The caption described it as having been taken by her husband on a recent walking holiday. There were mountains in the background and an inland loch just behind her. She wore walking boots and waterproofs and looked very happy. Her hair was cut into a chin-length bob and was as straight as my own. The night before, looking at the photograph at the Hawicks' home, Dana and I had been deceived by a glamorous wedding hair-do and had compared it to the woman on the autopsy table with her long, corkscrew curls. When Kirsten Hawick died, her hair was short and straight. And that finally convinced me. I sighed, checked my messages – nothing from Dana – and logged off before heading down to theatre.

By six o'clock I was so tired I could have starred in *Night of the Living Dead*, but the thought of going home didn't hold enormous appeal. I found I was really missing Duncan. We had to try and use this coming weekend as a chance to reconnect, somehow. Perhaps we could catch the ferry up to Unst and stay with his parents for a couple of nights. Our Laser 2 was up there for the summer and we could do some sailing; maybe even a race or two if the local club was active this weekend.

Dana hadn't phoned and I was hugely relieved. I hadn't worked out what I was going to say to her, but I'd decided I wasn't going to do what she'd asked. I no longer believed the woman buried in my field was Kirsten Hawick. Any more digging on my part could get me into serious trouble and – more importantly – I'd promised Duncan. Somehow, I was going to have to get the dental X-rays back to her without anyone knowing she'd given them to me. I picked up a pile of midwives' timesheets that needed checking and signing, read through the first and scribbled my signature at the bottom.

If you're not getting close, why is someone trying to scare you?

I stopped, pen in mid-air. Then looked down. My briefcase was by my desk. I reached into it and pulled out the file.

I'd promised Duncan.

I shoved the file back down and closed the case. Last night had been a joke, a sick prank, nothing more. Gifford was right: news spreads like forest-fire in small communities. In the restaurant at lunchtime someone behind me had muttered, 'Have a heart, Nigel.' There'd been sniggers and a scuffle, the sound of someone being elbowed sharply in the ribs. I'd given no sign that I'd heard, but knew that my adventures were common knowledge and that more than one person on the islands was getting some fun out of them. I bent down to the timesheets again.

Someone stood in your bedroom. Watched you while you were asleep. Some kind of joke!

I scribbled my name on a third and a fourth timesheet. I can't say for certain that I read them.

They entered your house without breaking any windows, forcing any doors. Sound like an ordinary prankster to you?

I put down my pen and looked at my case again.

Can't hurt, can it, to rule Kirsten out once and for all?

I pulled the black and white films from the cardboard file and placed them on top of white paper on my desk. There was a noise outside, someone walking past in the corridor. I got up, meaning to lock the door, and found my office keys weren't in my handbag. Leaving keys at home is hardly a first for me so, thinking nothing of it, I took a spare set from the desk drawer and used them. Sitting back down again, I looked at the X-ray. It was what is known as a panoramic radiograph, showing every tooth present in the mouth.

Permanent dentition consists normally of thirty-two teeth and one of the first rules in studying dental radiographs is to count. There were thirty-one: fifteen uppers, sixteen lowers, only two molars in the upper right quadrant rather than the more usual three. There was what looked like a crown in the upper left quadrant; also a malformed root above one of the pre-molars in the upper right quadrant. Unlike all the other roots, this one had a distinctive distal curvature. Most of the teeth were regular, but there seemed to be a significant space in the bottom right-hand side, between the first and second pre-molar. Not big enough to suggest a missing tooth, just a gap that would be barely noticeable when she smiled. Several of the back teeth had been filled. I was no dentist, but I was pretty certain I'd be able to make an intelligent comparison of these films with any others that might be relevant.

The phone rang. It was the secretary whom several of the doctors share, with a call waiting from Dana

Tulloch. I asked her to tell Dana I was still in theatre and would get back to her later.

Glancing once more at my door even though I knew it was locked, I found the hospital's intranet site and tried to access the dental department. And found myself tripped at the first hurdle. As a consultant I have access to pretty much the entire site, but the dental unit politely requested a password. I thought about ringing the hospital's IT department but I was willing to bet all requests for new information had to be cleared by Gifford first. I got up and crossed to the window. His BMW was still in the car park. I took a puce-coloured folder from my cupboard and tucked the X-ray inside it. Then I left the room.

The recently opened NHS dental unit is in a separate building within the hospital complex, just a short walk away. I was still wearing my scrubs and I made sure my consultant's badge was visible just above my right-hand jacket pocket. What I wanted was a not-terribly-bright-or-interested dental nurse.

I pushed through the double doors and forced my best smile on to my face. The nurse/receptionist looked up. The name on her badge said Shirley. She didn't smile back or look at all pleased to have a visitor.

'Hi! We haven't met. I'm Tora Hamilton.' I held up my badge and waited until I'd felt sure she'd read it. 'Obstetrics,' I added, somewhat unnecessarily. Then I looked at her with what I hoped came across as polite interest. 'Are you new too?'

She nodded. 'Just three months,' she responded in a Shetland accent. So far, so good.

I leaned forward, trying for a friendly, confidential manner. 'The thing is, I've got a bit of an embarrassing problem.'

Suddenly, she looked interested.

'My predecessor left my office in a bit of a shambles and I'm trying to sort it out. I've just come across what appear to be dental records, but no indication of whom they might belong to. Now, I don't want to get Dr McLean into trouble, what with him just retired and everything, but these things shouldn't just be left around, should they? They're confidential?'

She nodded. 'Aye, they are.'

'The thing is, I have an idea whose they might be. If we could just check, I can leave them with you, you can file them where they belong and the problem's over with.'

'Isn't there a name on the X-rays?'

I tried to look as though I hadn't thought of that and pulled the film out. There was a code on the bottom that I recognized as belonging to the morgue but I felt pretty sure that Shirley wouldn't spot it.

'Whose did you think they might be?' she asked.

'Kirsten Hawick's. She's a patient of yours.'

'Thing is, we're about to close for the evening. Can you come back in the morning and see Dr McDouglas?'

I shook my head, looking sorrowful. 'I'm going to be in surgery all day,' I said, which was a big lie. The only place I planned to be the next day was in bed; exactly where I hadn't quite figured out. 'I guess we're just going to have to do this officially. God, the paperwork. For you as well, I'm afraid. Ah well, have a good time tonight. I guess you have plans?'

I started to turn away.

'You can call up the records yourself, you know. If you have a computer, that is.'

I turned back. 'I know, but I haven't got all my passwords sorted out yet. Too busy learning the ropes. I called the IT department before I came here but I think they'd all gone home for the evening.'

'Wouldn't surprise me,' she said, looking sympathetic. Then she appeared to have a brainwave. 'Is all you need the password then?'

I tried to look puzzled. 'I guess,' I said. 'Do you know it?'

'Sure,' she said and scribbled something down. Willing myself not to snatch, I reached out and took the Post-it note. I read what she'd written and then looked at her for confirmation. She smiled.

'Dr McDouglas's favourite film.'

'Mine too,' I replied, not entirely untruthfully. I thanked her and left.

Back in my office, I wasn't sure whether I was terrified at what I'd done or delighted by my own cleverness. Shirley would almost certainly tell her boss what had happened. Even if it didn't get back to Gifford, I could face some pertinent and difficult-to-answer questions from Dr McDouglas.

Did I really want to go on with this? So far, I

hadn't done anything wrong. Granted, I'd tricked a junior colleague into giving me information I shouldn't have, but I hadn't used it. I could always claim I'd had second and better thoughts and would probably get away with it.

My screen still showed the homepage of the dental department. I typed in *Terminator* and waited. Then I was in. I found patient records and typed in Kirsten Hawick.

There was nothing there.

Huge relief. And a tiny but rapidly growing seedling of frustration.

I thought for a bit. Kirsten hadn't been married that long when she died. Maybe she hadn't got round to changing her name on all her records. I typed in Kirsten Georgeson and there she was: details of her age, address, brief medical history, records of her visits, invoices for non-NHS treatment. And her X-rays.

The comparison wasn't as easy as I'd expected, as the format was different. The X-ray taken during the post mortem was just one film scanning from one side of the mouth to the other. Those produced during dental appointments tend to be taken in sections from inside the mouth. I had six small X-rays to compare to one large one. I started off in the top left corner, the section that I guessed would be easiest to distinguish. I was looking for a crown. Nothing.

Then I tried the bottom right corner for a small gap. Next, I tried to count the teeth. That was tricky due to the overlapping of teeth on more than one shot. It didn't really matter, though. I was as sure as I could be, without having a dentist sitting next to me, that the X-ray taken of the corpse didn't match the dental records of Kirsten Hawick. I'd known already, of course, but now even Dana would have to accept defeat. It wasn't her.

I got ready to close up the site and started thinking. Dana had told me that most dentists on Shetland are NHS. If that were true, then whilst patients might visit a number of different surgeries scattered over the islands, their records would be on this one central database and accessible by yours truly, courtesy of a rather weird password, which would probably be changed the minute the hierarchy found out I'd been meddling. This was my one chance.

Which you are not going to take. You've done what you set out to do, proved the body in the peat wasn't Kirsten; it's up to the police now.

But dental records, like all medical records, are confidential. Even police working on a murder investigation couldn't gain automatic access to them. A court order, at least, would be needed and from what I'd heard, there were no plans to apply for one. This was a pretty unique opportunity. No one on the murder squad could do what I was doing right now. The big question, though, was whether the search was even remotely manageable. Just how many dental records would I have to look at?

No, that is not the big question, Tora! The big question is: why aren't you packing up and going to find a room somewhere to spend the night?

I switched to the Internet and called up the site of the Scottish Census. I knew the population of Shetland was in the region of 25,000, including the migrant workers on the oilfields, but I had no idea how many women there were in the twenty-five to thirty-five age group. Which, you could argue, was a bit unprofessional for the resident obstetrician, given they were what management consultants call my prime target group. The Scottish Census for 2004 was the most recent available and it told me that the number of women on the islands aged between twenty and thirty-four was 2,558: an impossible number to check.

Good, that's settled then, let's go and get some rest.

Could it be narrowed down at all? Not everyone is registered with a dentist. I remembered reading somewhere that a lot of people neglect their teeth, something like half the population. That would bring the number down to around 1,200. And my friend from the field had had dental work. If she was an island woman and an NHS patient, her records were here for me to find.

She isn't an island woman. DI Dunn's investigation has ruled out all the missing women from the islands. You and Dana were wrong.

Don't like being wrong. I went back to the dental database, wondering if I could sort the data. I pressed the button for data sort and put in my criteria: female patients, resident on the island, aged between sixteen and thirty-four. I'd have liked to specify a narrower age band but the system wouldn't let me. Then I was looking at a list of names. I scanned to the bottom of the page. 1,700 patients. Still an impossible search. I got up and crossed to the coffee machine.

OK, think, tired brain, think. 1,700 women, aged between sixteen and thirty-four years old. There was a real, good chance the lady from the peat was one of them, if only I could . . . Of course! I shot back to my desk and scanned the list of search criteria. Yes! There it was: date of last appointment. My friend had been dead since early summer 2005; I just had to get rid of all the women who'd attended the surgery since then. I typed in '1 September 2005', which I guessed would leave a big enough margin for error, and pressed search. It took a few seconds, then . . . sixty-three women left on the list.

It was a manageable – if lengthy – search. Five minutes per patient to be really sure; it was already seven thirty and I was shattered. On the other hand, this really was my only chance. By tomorrow morning my unauthorized hacking would have been discovered and terminated . . .

quite probably along with your employment

. . . and I had to make it worthwhile.

In my desk drawer, under Filing and Misc., was a copy of the print-out I'd given Dana at the start of the week: the list of women who'd given birth on the islands during the spring and summer of 2005. I began to compare the two lists, looking for a woman who had given birth that summer and, simultaneously, ceased to feel the need for regular dental check-ups. It took some time, as both lists were sorted by date rather than alphabetically, but thirty minutes and two cups of coffee later I was pretty certain there were no matches.

Exhaustion hit me at that point. There was really no getting round the birth issue. The woman had had a baby and any woman who had done so on the islands that summer had to be on my list. She must have visited a dentist privately. Unfortunately, I still had to work till two a.m. and go through the sixty-three records or I'd never know for sure.

The phone rang. This was it then: Gifford summoning me to his office. I considered ignoring it but knew he'd just come and find me.

'Hello.'

'It's Dana. Are you OK?'

'I'm fine, just tired.'

'I have just had the devil of a row with my inspector. I can't believe no one called me last night. You must have been out of your wits.'

'Something like that,' I confessed. 'I was a bit surprised not to see you.'

'I'm supposed to be in charge of this blessed investigation. Can you believe what the official line is? I wasn't called out because there was no direct link to the case. What happened last night was just somebody's idea of a joke.'

Logically, I probably should have been disturbed that Dana took the events of the previous night as seriously as I did. And yet I found myself reassured.

I guess, given the choice, most of us would opt for *in danger* before *delusional*.

'You don't go along with that theory then?' I said.

'Are you kidding me? What are you up to right now?'

I explained about conning the nurse into giving me the password and my examination of Kirsten Hawick's records. If she was disappointed, she gave no sign. Then I told her about my plans to go through the rest.

'How many more do you have to look at?' she asked.

'Sixty-three,' I told her.

'I'm coming in to help. I don't like the idea of you being there on your own.'

I stood up, peered out of the window. Gifford's car was still there.

'No, you'll be far too conspicuous. I'll be fine. There's loads of people around. I'll call when I'm done.'

'Thanks, Tora, I mean it. Look, let me give you my address and home phone number. Come round, it doesn't matter what time.'

I scribbled the details down and she was gone. I was on my own and, in spite of all my best intentions and the well-meaning advice of those wiser than myself, I called up the first set of X-rays.

15

TWO HOURS LATER, I'D RULED OUT TWENTY-TWO of the names on the list. It was all starting to look like a complete waste of time, but I'm one of those people who can never leave a job unfinished. I knew I'd be here for the duration.

First, though: sustenance. I locked my office and went down to the canteen. I piled my tray high with fatty carbohydrates and added a Diet Coke. I ate like a robot, hardly lifting my eyes from the tray, and then went back to my office.

Another hour and a half, another two cups of coffee and either something was going wrong with the hospital electrics or I was seriously in need of sleep, because the room around me had grown decidedly dimmer. I looked up at the neon strips above me. I hadn't noticed any flickering but the light just wasn't what it had been a couple of hours ago. The sky outside seemed unnaturally dark too, even allowing for it not being far off midnight. There must be a storm coming.

I looked back at the screen, but could barely make it out. The sharpness of the X-ray image had blurred into a confused mass of shapes and shading. Words were indistinguishable. I knew I had eighteen more records to check, but it just wasn't possible. I'd print them off, go find a bed and read through them in the morning. I closed my eyes, shook my head and then opened them again. It was no better; if anything, worse: I was staring at a black screen with words that had been bright green. Now, they were no colour at all, just dullish marks of light that seemed to be growing in size.

I selected the print field and pressed the print command. There was definitely a problem with the electricity. Without my noticing, the lights had gone out completely and my room was a mass of shadows. From the printer at the other side of the room came a shrill, persistent beeping sound. Great: as invariably happens when it's important, it was out of paper. I started to get up and couldn't. I just about managed to push the keyboard out of the way before my head hit the desk.

The next thing I remember was my mobile ringing, somewhere in the distance. I raised my head and gasped out loud: there were demons in my skull, beating a tattoo on my brain. And someone had broken my spine; nothing less could cause this amount of pain. As nausea reared up I closed my eyes and counted to ten. Then risked opening them again. I was still at my desk; the room was in almost total darkness. My computer screen was blank but its low-pitched buzzing told me it was still switched on.

Without moving I managed to locate the ringing. My mobile was in the pocket of my jacket, which was hanging behind the door. I got up – oh my, it hurt – and crossed the room. I found the phone and looked at the screen. It was Dana. I switched the phone off. Heading back to my desk I found even walking was an effort, as though every limb had suddenly grown three times as heavy. What the hell was wrong with me?

By the time I reached my desk I felt slightly better. Just the simple act of moving had loosened me up a little. Then I remembered what I'd been doing. I pressed a key and the screen sprang to life. There was nothing there. I was looking at the screen saver. I grabbed the mouse and flicked round the screen, in case I'd accidentally minimized the dental records somewhere. They couldn't have just disappeared.

Except they had. I clicked again on the dental department's section of the site and once again it requested a password. I typed in *Terminator*.

Access denied.

I tried it again.

Access denied.

I looked round my office, as though the answer might lie on my walls, my desk. The room was tidy, nothing out of place. Except . . .

My desk was never that tidy. Papers were stacked up neatly. The cup I'd been drinking from was over by the sink. It had been rinsed out, as had the coffee pot. I hadn't done that. I crossed to the light switch and flicked. The lights flickered and flashed and then were fully on. Functioning normally. Which was a whole lot more than could be said for me.

I staggered to the sink and poured a cup of water. In my bag I found some of the painkillers Gifford had given me the other day and I swallowed two gratefully. I leaned against the sink, waiting for the pain in my head to subside, which it didn't, and for the aching in my limbs to fade, which, gradually, it did.

The hospital was silent. Downstairs, in and around the wards, there would be people and movement, noise and bustle; up here, just the faint electronic buzz of the lights and my computer. My watch said 04.26. I'd been asleep, or something, for over four hours.

I started to walk back to my desk and a flashing button on the printer caught my eye. *Paper tray empty* said the message on the small display. Without really thinking about it, I bent down, took a few sheets of paper from the cupboard beneath it and slid them into the paper tray.

The machine whirred into life and started sending out printed sheets. I picked the first one up. It was an X-ray of the upper left quadrant and the second molar had been crowned.

Stop it, Tora, enough is enough.

I picked up the next sheet. It showed the central and lateral incisors. The placement looked right. I picked up the next sheet. Then the next. I counted the teeth. Then, for the first time, I looked at the patient's name at the top of the page. I reached out and touched it, whispering it softly as I did so.

'Melissa Gair.'

I wanted to weep. I wanted to jump on my desk and scream my triumph to the rooftops. At the same time, I don't think I've ever felt calmer in my life.

I flicked through the print-outs that followed. I saw her birth date and calculated her age: thirty-two. I saw that she'd been married and that she'd lived in Lerwick, not two miles from where I was sitting. I saw that she'd attended the dentist regularly; appointments roughly every six months going back ten years or so, with hygienist's appointments in between. Her last appointment had been just before Christmas in the year 2003.

Which, of course, didn't quite fit. My head started to hurt more as I struggled to work out what was bothering me. The woman in my field was Melissa Gair. The records matched exactly. Yet why would a woman who attended her dentist religiously suddenly stop a good eighteen months before her death? Unless she'd left the islands temporarily, coming back only to meet an untimely end.

If that were the case, then her name might not be on my list of women who had given birth on the islands. I grabbed it and scanned as quickly as I could. No, Melissa Gair had not given birth here. She'd had her baby off the islands and then returned less than two weeks afterwards. Most women are not up for major upheaval in their lives two weeks after having a baby.

Something in her motives would surely give us a clue as to why she'd been killed.

I needed sleep very badly, but first I had to find Dana. I picked up the phone and dialled her mobile number but got an unobtainable tone. I almost stood up, but thought of one more thing I could check. It would help Dana, surely, to have as much information on Melissa Gair as possible.

I turned back to my computer and went into the main hospital records. I put Melissa's name into the search facility and waited for a few seconds, not really expecting to find anything. She'd been a healthy young woman and might never have been admitted.

Her name appeared. I opened the file, read it through once, then again, checking and double-checking the dates. My headache was back with a vengeance and I think only the certain knowledge that I was a split-second from throwing up kept me motionless in my seat. Had I moved, it would have been to ram my fist directly into the computer screen.

16

I SAW NO OTHER TRAFFIC ON THE WAY OVER TO DANA'S house, which was a good thing, because I'd probably have collided with it. I hit the kerb twice and scraped the paintwork leaving the hospital.

I parked, checked the address and climbed out of the car. There was no sign of Dana's car in the car park that I'd assumed would be closest to her house. I staggered like a drunk through the stone archway, down a flight of steps and a steep, cobbled slope. It was an hour or so before dawn and the sky in the east had lightened. The narrow streets of the Lanes, though, were still drenched in shadows.

The Lanes are one of the oldest and most interesting areas of Lerwick. They run downhill, in parallel lines, the quarter of a mile from Hillhead to Commercial Street, from where it's a two-minute walk to the harbour. The Lanes are flagged, steeply sloping alleys, interspersed with short flights of stone steps. It would be impossible to drive a vehicle down them; in places they are so narrow that two grown people would struggle to walk abreast. The buildings, a mixture of residential and commercial property, rise up to three and four storeys on either side. The Lanes are quaint, popular with tourists and much sought-after as trendy, town-centre homes. But when the light is poor and no one else is around, they are dark, decidedly eerie.

Three times, I'd tried Dana on her mobile but had got no response. At first, I'd assumed she'd gone to bed, but now that seemed unlikely. I'd found her door and had been banging on it for several minutes. No one was coming. She wasn't home and I was in no fit state to drive anywhere else. I climbed slowly back up to my car. On the back seat were my coat and an old horse blanket. I thought, briefly, about trying her mobile again but couldn't summon up the energy. She was almost certainly somewhere out of signal range. I wrapped coat and blanket around me and was asleep in seconds.

It was nearly dawn when the tapping on the window woke me. I was cold, stiff and acutely aware that the moment I moved I would regret it. The worst hangover I'd ever experienced – and I've had a few bad ones – was going to feel like a Shiatsu massage compared with what today had in store for me. But there was nothing else for it. Dana's incredulous face was staring down at me and I had to move. I sat up. Oh boy, so much worse than I'd expected. I reached for the lock and then Dana opened the door.

'Tora, I've been at your house half the night. I've been seriously—'

I waved her away, turned and vomited over the rear wheel of my car. I stayed there, bent double, for some time. I coughed and retched, trying to dislodge those sickening bits that stick in your nasal passages at such times and decided that sudden death had an awful lot to recommend it.

The next thing I remember is being half led, half carried, through Dana's front door and deposited on her sofa. She gave me, on my instructions, an unwise dose of ibuprofen and paracetemol and left to make hot, sweet tea and dry toast. While she was gone I tried to steady my nausea by focusing on her living room. It was exactly as I would have expected: immaculately tidy and undoubtedly expensive. The floorboards were polished oak, partly covered by a rug patterned in squares of rust, oatmeal and pale green. The sofas were the same shade of green, whilst the roman blinds on both windows picked out the rust and oatmeal colours. The fabrics looked the sort you might pay £50 a metre for. A flat-screen TV was fastened to one wall and there was a Bang and Olufsen stereo system under the window. Dana came back with the food and left the room again. I heard her running upstairs. She returned carrying a large duvet and wrapped it around me, like a mother with a sick toddler. I took a bite of toast and managed to keep it down. Dana sat down on a leather footstool in front of me.

'Ready to tell me what happened to you?'

'I worked half the night, spent the rest of it in the car,' I managed. The tea was scalding and totally wonderful.

She looked at me, then down at herself. Her linen trousers were creased but clean and still looked pretty good, as did the pink cotton shirt and matching cardigan. Her skin looked daisy-fresh and her hair as though it had been combed ten minutes ago.

'So did I,' she said. She had a point.

'First, I need to tell you what I found out,' I said. I'd been toying with how exactly I was going to do that since we'd entered the house. Duncan has a particularly irritating habit when he wants to tell me something and, for some reason, it seemed strangely appropriate for the circumstances.

'Tor,' he'd announce, 'I've got good news and bad news.' It really didn't matter how I'd respond, he'd have some half-witted wise-crack to hand which he'd invariably find hilarious and was guaranteed to irritate the hell out of me. 'I'll have the good news,' I'd say, with heavy reluctance. 'The good news is: there's not too much bad news!' he'd respond. We'd been doing it for seven years now and it really wasn't getting any funnier. Not from my point of view anyway. Still, I definitely wasn't myself that morning because I had an almost irresistible urge to use it right now.

Do you want the good news, or the bad news, Dana?

The good news? I know who our lady from the peat was.

The bad news? No, you are really not going to believe the bad news.

She was watching me closely. I realized she was very concerned and that I must look even worse than I felt. I took a deep breath.

'I found a match,' I said, watching the glint leap into her eyes and her face come alive. 'You'll need to get it checked, of course, but I am 98 per cent certain.'

She leaned forward and her hand brushed mine. 'My God, well done! Who was she?'

I took another gulp of tea. 'Melissa Gair,' I said. 'Aged thirty-two. An island woman; from Lerwick; married to a local man.'

Dana clenched her fist and made a little stabbing action with it. 'So why wasn't she reported missing? Why wasn't she on your list of summer 2005 deliveries? She wasn't, was she?'

'No, she wasn't . . .'

'Then how . . .'

'Because she was already dead.'

She stared at me. Three tiny furrows appeared between her eyebrows. 'Come again,' she said.

'I checked her hospital records. She was admitted on 29 September 2004, with a malignant breast tumour that was subsequently found to have spread to her lungs, back and kidneys. Her GP had spotted a lump just a couple of weeks earlier during a routine examination. She was transferred to Aberdeen for treatment but it didn't work. She died on the sixth of October, just three and a half weeks after being diagnosed.'

'Fuck!' I hadn't heard Dana swear before.

'You can say that again,' I said.

She did. And quite a lot more. She got up and walked across the room, stopping only when the wall made further progress impossible. She turned and walked back, again just stopping at the wall. Another turn and a few more steps. Then she stopped and looked at me.

'How sure are you about those dental records?'

At four in the morning I'd been pretty certain. Now . . .

'You need to have a proper dentist look at them but . . . I'm . . . I'm sure. They were the same.'

'Could she have been a different woman? Different woman, same name. Two Melissa Gairs living in Lerwick.'

I'd thought of that. I shook my head. 'Their birth dates were identical. So were their blood groups. It's the same woman.'

'Shit!' And she was off again, pacing the room and swearing. In a way, it was kind of nice to see the impeccable Dana losing control. In another, I wanted her to stop. She was making my head hurt more.

'It's déjà vu. It's déjà-fucking-vu. We went through this with Kirsten, convinced we'd found the right woman.'

'We have to forget about Kirsten. The dental records were totally different. It wasn't her.'

'I accept that. But it's still too much of a bloody coincidence. We find a body and a ring in your field. Both belong to young women who supposedly died in 2004. Except one of them didn't. One of them actually died – because our pathologists tell us so – almost a whole year later.'

'My head hurts!' I wailed.

'OK, OK.' She stopped pacing and came back to sit on her footstool. She lowered her voice. 'Now tell me what happened to you.'

I shook my head. 'It doesn't matter.'

She took hold of my hands, one of them still clutching an empty tea mug, and forced me to look at her.

'It matters. Now talk.'

I talked. I told her that, for the second time in two nights, someone had bypassed locked doors, not to mention considerable hospital security, to force their way into my presence. That for the second time, someone had watched me while I slept, that I had, once again, been completely at the mercy of someone who wished me harm.

'Nothing was left. No . . .'

'Little gifts? No. But he washed out my coffee mug and pot. Very thoroughly.'

'You think you were drugged?'

'It's possible. I haven't been feeling great the last few days, like I'm coming down with flu or something, but not this bad.'

'We need to get you to a doctor.' She saw the look on my face and allowed herself to smile. 'We need to do some tests,' she said. 'I don't know, blood tests or something.'

'Already done. I took some bloods before I left the

hospital. They're in my office fridge; I'll send them off on Monday. But until we know for certain, can we just keep quiet about this, please? It's only going to be a distraction.'

Dana nodded slowly but her eyes were dull and unfocused. I recognized the sign that she was thinking hard. I wondered how to breach the subject of my going home. I hated to leave her with such a bombshell but knew I couldn't carry on any longer. I stood up.

'Dana, I'm sorry, but I really need to get home.'

She looked up sharply. 'Will Duncan be there?'

'No,' I said, surprised. 'He's not back till this evening.' Which was probably just as well. I didn't want him to see me in this state.

'You can't go.'

'Umm?'

'You're safer here. Go upstairs. Have a shower if you like and then use the spare bedroom. When we know he's back I'll sign your release papers.'

I didn't move. I hardly knew this girl. I was far from sure I trusted her and I was letting her take control of me. She must have seen something in my face because her own expression sharpened. 'What?' she said.

I sat back down. I told her everything Gifford had said about her. She listened, her eyebrows flickered once or twice, but otherwise there was no reaction. When I finished, her mouth tightened. She was visibly angry but I didn't think it was with me.

'My father died three years ago,' she said. 'I lost

my mother when I was fifteen and have no siblings so I inherited the whole of his estate. He wasn't a rich man but he'd done OK. I got about four hundred thousand pounds. I bought the car, the house and the things you can see around you. It's nice to have some money but I'd much rather have my dad.'

She took a deep breath.

'I did not leave Manchester in disgrace. I left with an excellent record and first-rate references. I transferred to Dundee because I wanted to work in Scotland. I left Dundee because I began a relationship with another officer – a much more senior one – and we agreed it wasn't good for the force.'

She stood up, still annoyed, and crossed the room to her stereo system. She ran a finger along the glass case then inspected her fingertip for dust. I doubted she'd see any. Then she looked back at me.

'As for not fitting in here, well, they got that bit right. These islands are run by a small and very powerful clique of big, blond men who all went to the same schools, the same Scottish universities, and whose families have known each other since the Norwegian invasions. Just think about it, Tora, think about the doctors you know at the hospital, the head-teachers at the schools, the police force, the magistrate, the chamber of commerce, the local councils.'

I didn't need to think about it. I'd noticed more than once how many of the islanders fitted into the same distinctive physical type.

'Oh, the place is crawling with Vikings. One of its few redeeming features, I've always thought.'

'Try and name me more than half a dozen prominent islanders who are not local men,' said Dana, ignoring my feeble attempts at humour. 'They all know each other, they all socialize, they do business together, offer each other jobs and the best contracts. These islands are running the biggest jobs-for-the-blond-boys club I have ever come across and when, once in a blue moon, an outsider does manage to break in, he or she gets obstructed, delayed and frustrated every step of the way. Most outsiders, sooner or later, get driven out. It's happening to me and I suspect it's happening to you too. Sorry to go on a bit, but I happen to get pretty pissed off about it.'

'Clearly,' I said.

'I am not in debt, nor am I anorexic. I eat quite a lot but I work out most evenings. And yes, I shop a lot too. It's called displacement activity. I don't particularly like it here and I miss Helen.'

'Helen?' I said stupidly.

'DCI Helen Rowley. The officer in Dundee with whom I was – am still when we get the chance – having a relationship. Helen is my girlfriend.'

And no, I admit, I had definitely not seen that one coming.

'Now, you can stay down here and help me do some pretty arduous police work, you can go home and risk someone disturbing your rest for a third time in three days, or you can go upstairs and get some sleep.'

Not really too difficult a decision. I turned to leave the room.

When I awoke, it was to the sound of voices. Two voices, to be precise: Dana's and that of a man. I sat up. Dana's spare bedroom was small but as beautifully decorated and tidy as the rest of her home. A blind was drawn but behind it I thought I could see bright sunshine. There was no clock in the room. I walked to the window and raised the blind. Lerwick Harbour and the Bressay Sound. It was about midday, I guessed, which meant I'd slept for five hours.

I felt better. I was groggy from too little sleep and aching in all sorts of places but the horrible nausea had gone.

I sat down to slip on my shoes. Bookshelves lined one wall of the small room. The desk in the corner held computer equipment that looked state-of-the-art. Beside the monitor stood a framed photograph of Dana in Ph.D. graduation robes, standing next to a tall man with grey hair and fair skin. I was pretty certain it had been taken at one of the Cambridge colleges.

Dana and her guest were still talking quietly. I walked softly downstairs, but they must have heard me coming because the voices stopped when I reached the bottom step and silence heralded my arrival into the room below. They were sitting, but first the man, then Dana, stood as I walked in. He was in his early forties, maybe slightly above average height, with pale-blue eyes and thick hair of the colour known as salt and pepper. He was smartly dressed for a Saturday, possibly with lunch at the golf club in mind. He was attractive and – maybe more importantly – he looked nice. There were lots of lines around his eyes that suggested he laughed a lot.

'This is Stephen Gair,' said Dana.

I turned to Dana in astonishment.

'Melissa's husband,' she added, quite unnecessarily. I'd got it; I just couldn't believe it. She gestured towards me. 'Tora Hamilton.'

He held out his hand. 'I've been hearing a lot about you. How are you feeling?'

'Mr Gair knows you've been working all night,' said Dana. 'We've been waiting for you to wake up before . . .'

She looked at him, as if uncertain what to say next.

'Before we go and get my wife's X-rays checked,' answered Stephen Gair. Dana visibly relaxed.

'My, you have been busy,' was just about all I could manage. Was it really going to be that easy?

Somehow, without my noticing it, we'd all sat down again. The other two looked as though they were waiting for me to say something. I glanced from one to the other, then looked at Stephen Gair.

'Has Dana told you . . .?' Jesus, what had Dana told him? That I'd dug his wife up out of my field six days ago?

'Shall I summarize?' he offered.

I nodded, thinking, *Shall I summarize*? What kind

of talk was that for a man who'd just been given such devastating news?

'Last Sunday,' he began, 'a body was found on your land. My sympathies, by the way. The body was that of a young woman who was murdered – rather brutally, I understand, although I haven't been given the details – some time during the early summer of 2005. You've been using your position at the hospital to conduct a comparison of dental records. Your doing so was unethical and probably illegal but entirely understandable given your involvement in the case. Now, you believe you've found an exact match in the dental records of my late wife, Melissa. Am I right so far?'

'Absolutely,' I said, wondering what Stephen Gair did for a living.

'Except therein lies a problem. My wife died in hospital of breast cancer in October 2004. She'd been dead for months, possibly the better part of a year, by the time the murder took place. So the body on your land cannot be her. How am I doing?'

'You're cooking on gas,' I said, borrowing an expression of Duncan's. From the corner of my eye I caught Dana looking at me as if worried my head was still addled from the drugs I may or may not have been fed.

Gair smiled. Too bright a smile, or maybe I just couldn't cope with jollity this morning. 'Thanks,' he said.

'Trouble is, the X-rays match,' I said. 'Illegal

search or not, there's no getting round that. If she'd been my wife, I'd want to know why.'

The smile faded. 'I do want to know why,' he said. He no longer looked remotely nice.

Dana seemed to sense trouble. She stood up.

'Shall we go?' she said. 'Tora, are you OK to go straight away?'

'Of course,' I said. 'Where are we going?'

We were going to the hospital dental unit. Dana drove me, Stephen Gair followed behind. It took us ten minutes to get there and when we did, three cars were already parked in the car park. I was not in the least bit surprised to see Gifford's silver BMW and DI Dunn's black four-wheel-drive. A glance at Dana told me that she too had expected it. Stephen Gair got out of his car and looked over at Dana and me. He started to walk towards the entrance.

'He's dodgy,' I said.

'He's senior partner in the biggest firm of solicitors we have here in Lerwick.'

'Oh, well, there you go.' Neither of us moved. 'Do you think he tipped off the fuzz?'

'What do you watch on TV? And no, I think that was probably Dentist McDouglas. You might want to muffle that schoolgirl sense of humour of yours for the next hour.'

'Right you are, Sarge.'

Neither of us moved. 'What's with you and your inspector?' I asked.

Glancing across, I saw her face had clouded over

and wondered if I'd overstepped the mark. 'How do you mean?' she asked.

No going back now. 'You don't trust him, do you?'

Bracing myself for one of her put-downs, I was surprised to see her thinking about it.

'I used to,' she said eventually. 'We got on pretty well when I came here. But he hasn't been the same the last few days.' She stopped, as though worried she'd said too much.

'You give quite a lot away when you think no one's watching you,' I ventured. 'You weren't happy in the morgue that first day, you went out on a limb the evening we met Joss Hawick. And he left you off the guest list at my house the other night. You've disagreed all along about whether the victim was a local woman.'

She nodded. 'There's nothing he's doing I can specifically complain of, it just seems all the way along that my gut is steering me one way and he's sending me another.' We both watched as Stephen Gair pulled open the door to the dental unit and went inside. 'We should go,' said Dana.

We got out of the car. I was still wearing yesterday's scrubs and hadn't showered, cleaned my teeth or combed my hair in about twenty-four hours. Gifford was about to see me looking like death warmed up and there wasn't a damn thing I could do about it.

'The truth is in there, Agent Tulloch,' I said, as we headed for the swing doors.

She gave me a *will-you-pack-it-in* look, as the automatic doors opened for us and we walked through.

'I am deeply uncomfortable,' said Dr McDouglas, which struck me as just a little ironic coming from a dentist. 'Your actions are reprehensible, Miss Hamilton. You might do things differently where you come from, but I assure you, in Scot—'

'Let me apologize for—' Gifford interrupted.

'Oh no, you don't.' That time, it was me. I turned to Gifford. 'With respect, Mr Gifford, I can apologize for myself.' Fantastic phrase that – you can be as rude as you like to someone but as long as you put a *with respect* in front, you get away with it. I turned back to Dentist McDouglas, a tall, thin, arrogant shit whom I'd disliked on first sight. I was going to do it again. 'And with all due respect to you, Dr McDouglas, my actions are not our primary concern right now. If I'm wrong, you can instigate a formal complaint and Mr Gifford here will make sure it's dealt with according to the health authority's procedures.'

Gifford put a hand on my arm, but I wasn't having it. I was on a roll.

'On the other hand, if I'm right, then so much shit is going to hit the fan that any complaint against me will, frankly, get lost in the general hysteria.'

'Your use of profanities offends me deeply,' the sour, Presbyterian tooth-puller spat back at me.

'Yeah, well, digging up mutilated corpses offends me deeply. Can we get on with it, please?'

'We're not getting on with anything here. Not without the proper authority.'

'I agree,' said Andy Dunn.

I pointed at Stephen Gair. 'There's your proper authority. He is prepared to release his wife's X-rays for examination. Or at least, he said he was before we left. Have you changed your mind, Mr Gair?' As I said that, I knew, with a plummeting heart, that Gair wasn't going to back us up. He'd never intended to let us examine the records officially. He'd been playing us along, getting us to admit everything we'd been up to in front of the very people able to cut us off at the knees. Stephen Gair had sold Dana and me down the Swannee and we'd fallen for it.

'No, I haven't changed my mind,' he said.

OK, maybe I wasn't reading the situation too well. I decided to quieten down for a while.

'I think it would help to see exactly what we're dealing with here,' said Gifford. 'Who's got the X-rays?'

'Kenn,' said Andy Dunn, 'this is really not—'

'I have,' said Dana, ignoring her boss. From her bag she pulled the folder I'd given her that morning. She took out the large panoramic film taken in the hospital morgue and then the half-dozen smaller, overlapping shots – the ones that were definitely Melissa's – that I'd printed off the dental intranet site the night before.

'What do you think, Richard?' said Gifford.

Richard McDouglas looked at the films on his desk. So did the rest of us. From time to time, I looked up at his face but it was unreadable; a frown of concentration crinkling his brow, his lips curled in a scowl. Once, I risked looking at Dana but she was staring into space. I didn't want to look at anyone else.

After about five minutes, McDouglas shook his head.

'I can't see it,' he said. Sighs of relief all around the table.

Oh, for heaven's sake! 'Dr McDouglas,' I said quickly, before anyone else had a chance to open their mouths. 'Could you look at the second molar in the upper left quadrant?' He looked at Gifford, then at Dunn, but neither of them spoke. 'Look on the panoramic radiograph first, please.'

He did so.

'Would you say that molar has been crowned?'

He nodded. 'It would appear so.'

'Now look at the same tooth on your own X-rays.' I pushed the relevant film towards him. 'There, has that tooth been crowned?'

He nodded again, but didn't speak.

'Now, please look in the upper right quadrant. Do you agree there's a molar missing?'

'Difficult to say. Could be one of the pre-molars.'

'Whatever.' I pushed another film in front of him. The look of distaste on his face was a picture. I was being unreasonably aggressive, but enough was enough. 'This is the corresponding quadrant for Mrs Gair's X-rays. Is there a molar, or pre-molar missing?'

He counted the teeth.

'Yes, there is.'

Gifford leaned forward. He and Andy Dunn exchanged a glance. I was about to play my trump card.

'Dr McDouglas, could you please look at the root of this tooth.' I pointed to a tooth on the panoramic X-ray. 'I think this is the second pre-molar, am I right?'

He nodded.

'The root has a very distinctive curvature. Would you say it's mesial or distal?'

He pretended to study it but the answer was obvious.

'The curvature is distal.'

'And this one?' I indicated the same tooth on Melissa's X-ray.

He stared down. 'Miss Hamilton is correct,' he said eventually. 'There are sufficient similarities to merit a proper investigation.'

Stephen Gair pointed to the panoramic, then looked at Gifford. 'Are you saying this is my wife? That my wife is in your morgue? What the hell is going on here?'

'OK, that's it.' Andy Dunn had a loud voice and the proper air of authority when he needed it. 'We're going down to the station. Mr Gair, can you come with us, please? You too, Dr McDouglas.

At that moment, my beeper sounded. I excused myself and went out into the hallway to make a call. One of my patients was nearing the end of the second stage of labour and the baby was showing signs of distress. The midwife thought an emergency Caesar might be needed. I went back in and explained.

'I'll give you a hand,' said Gifford. 'Catch up with you later, Andy.'

Andy Dunn opened his mouth, but Gifford was too fast for him. He had the doors open and me out of there before anyone had time to object. I caught Dana's eye; she looked surprised and not entirely happy and I couldn't help feeling that we were being deliberately separated.

Once outside, Gifford strode ahead and I followed as best I could. It was difficult to keep up as we crossed the car park and walked up the flagged path that led to the main door of the hospital, so I walked faster than I really had the energy for and wondered when he was going to open his mouth and ball me out for the trouble I'd caused.

I had so many words bubbling inside me I didn't trust myself to get them out in the right order once I'd begun. I wanted to accuse him, to demand an explanation, to vindicate myself. At the same time, I was determined not to let myself down by incoherent babbling. It was up to him to speak first, to offer some sort of explanation and I was determined he was going to do it.

He still hadn't said a word as we entered the hospital, turned left past A&E and carried on towards the maternity unit. At the stairs he turned and started to climb.

'I thought you were coming to give me a hand?' I

said, realizing I sounded like a nagging wife but not caring. I had the moral high ground now and I wasn't budging.

He was on the fourth step up but he stopped and turned. The light from the staircase window shone brightly behind him and I couldn't see his expression.

'Do you *need* help?' he asked.

Instantly I felt stupid. Of course I didn't need help. But I wasn't about to be ignored either. Two nurses and a porter were coming along the corridor. Their conversation faded as they took in the obvious tension between us. 'You said you were coming with me,' I said, not bothering to lower my voice.

Kenn had noticed the others too. 'I needed to get away,' he said. 'There are things I have to do.' He turned and continued up the stairs. I stayed where I was, watching him. 'You're needed in maternity, Miss Hamilton,' he said firmly. 'Come and see me when you're done.'

The three staff members passed me and followed him up. One of them, a nurse I knew slightly, didn't even bother to hide the curious look and the half-smile she shot in my direction. She thought I was in trouble and wasn't in the least bit sorry.

I could hardly follow Gifford up the stairs, demanding an explanation in front of half the hospital. And he was right, I was needed in maternity. I turned, continued on down the corridor and, stopping only to scrub my hands and tie back my hair, strode into the delivery room.

There were two midwives in attendance; one a middle-aged, local woman who'd been doing the job for twenty years and had made no secret of the fact that she thought me superfluous. The other was a student, a young girl in her mid twenties. I couldn't remember her name.

The mother-to-be was Maura Lennon, thirty-five years old and about to produce her first child. She lay back on the bed, eyes huge, face pale and shiny with sweat. She was shivering violently, which I didn't like. Her husband sat by her side, nervously glancing towards the machine that was monitoring his baby's heartbeat. As I approached, Maura moaned and Jenny, the older of the two midwives, raised her up.

'Come on now, Maura, push as hard as you can.'

Maura's face screwed up and she pushed as I took Jenny's place at the foot of the bed. The baby's head was visible but didn't look as though it was coming out in the next few minutes. Which was what it needed to do. Maura was exhausted and the pain had become too much for her. She pushed, but it was a feeble attempt and as the contraction died away she fell back, whimpering. I glanced at the monitor. The baby's heartbeat slowed noticeably.

'How long has it been doing that?' I asked.

'About ten minutes,' replied Jenny. 'Maura's had no pain relief apart from gas and air, she won't let me cut her, she doesn't want forceps and she doesn't want a Caesarean.'

I glanced at the desk. Maura's birth plan, bound in red card, lay on it. I picked it up and flicked through.

About four pages, closely typed. I wondered if anyone but the mother-to-be had actually read it. I certainly wasn't about to.

I stood by the bed and then reached out and stroked away the damp hair that had fallen across Maura's forehead. It was the first time I had ever touched a patient in that way.

'How are you feeling, Maura?'

She moaned and looked away. Daft question. I took her hand.

'How long have you been in labour?'

'Fifteen hours,' replied Jenny, on Maura's behalf. 'She was induced last night. At forty-two weeks.' The last sounded slightly accusatory. No one wanted a pregnancy to last forty-two weeks, least of all me. By that stage the placenta is starting to deteriorate, sometimes seriously, and the percentage of stillbirths rises dramatically. I'd seen Maura a week ago and she'd been adamant she didn't want to be induced at all. I'd let her go the full forty-two weeks at her insistence but against my better instincts.

She jerked upwards for another contraction. Jenny and the student shouted encouragement and I watched the monitor. 'Who's the house officer?' I asked the student.

'Dave Renald,' she replied.

'Ask him to come in, please.'

She scurried out.

The contraction faded and one look at Jenny's face told me we were making no progress down at the sharp end.

I took hold of Maura's free hand. 'Maura, look at me,' I said, forcing her to make eye contact. Her eyes were glazed but they held my own. 'This has been an unusually painful labour,' I said, 'and you have done amazingly well to get this far.' She had, too. Inductions were always more intense and few managed without an epidural. 'But you have to let us help you now.'

I could see from the monitor that another contraction was building. I was running out of time.

'I'm going to give you a local anaesthetic and I'm going to try forceps. If that doesn't work, we have to go straight into theatre for an emergency Caesarean. Now are you OK with that?'

She looked back at me and her voice came out cracked. 'Can you give me a minute to think about it?'

I shook my head as the house officer and a nurse came into the room. In a bigger hospital, a paediatrician would usually be present at a forceps delivery, but here we had to make do with whoever was on duty. Jenny whispered something to the student and she scuttled out again to put theatre on alert.

'No, Maura,' I said. 'We don't have a minute. Your baby needs to be born now.' She didn't reply and I took her silence for acquiescence. I sat down. Jenny had the instruments all ready and began, without being asked, to lift Maura's legs into stirrups. I administered the anaesthetic into Maura's perineum and made a small cut to enlarge her vaginal outlet. I inserted the forceps and waited for the next contraction. As Maura pushed, I pulled, gently, gently. The head moved closer.

'Rest now, rest,' I instructed. 'Next one's the big one.'

She began to push again and I pulled. Almost there, almost . . . the head was out. I loosened the forceps, handed them to Jenny and reached . . . Shit! An inch of grey membrane appeared – the umbilical cord was wrapped around the baby's neck and I'd nearly missed it. I hooked one finger under it, pulling gently until I could loop it over the head and then, as I reached for the shoulders again, Maura gave one last push and they came out by themselves, followed by the rest of the baby. I handed the solid, slimy, unspeakably beautiful little body to Jenny, who took her up to meet her parents. There came the sound of sobbing and for a moment I thought it was me. I shook myself, wiped a sleeve across my eyes and delivered the placenta. The student – Grace, I remembered now, her name was Grace – helped me sew and clean our patient up. Her eyes were shining but she was quick and neat in everything she did. She'd make a good midwife.

Over at the paediatrician's table, the house officer had finished his checks.

'Everything's fine,' he said, handing the baby back to Maura.

17

I STAYED IN THE DELIVERY ROOM FOR ANOTHER FIFTEEN minutes, making sure mother and baby were OK. Then an orderly came to take Maura for a shower and I had a quick wander round the ward to check on the rest of my patients. We weren't expecting another birth before midweek so with a bit of luck it would be a quiet weekend. I decided I could be spared and headed for the exit.

Jenny, the midwife, was coming back into the unit as I left.

'Well done, Miss Hamilton,' she said, and instantly I suspected sarcasm.

'Is anything wrong?' I asked, hackles up.

She looked puzzled. 'Not now,' she said. 'But before you arrived, I really thought I was going to lose that one. And I haven't said that in a few years.'

She must have seen something give in my face because she stepped forward and lowered her voice.

'I spent fourteen sweaty hours with that lassie. I've been shouted at, kicked, sworn at and had my hand squeezed so tight it feels like the bones are broken. And it's your praises she and her man are singing right now, not mine.'

She reached out for my arm and gave it a squeeze. 'Well done, lass.'

I climbed the stairs to where the senior members of the medical team had their offices. Gifford's was the last along the corridor, the largest, on the corner. It was the first time I'd been in there and it came as something of a surprise, reminding me of private consulting rooms I'd visited during my student days: buttermilk-washed walls, heavy, striped curtains, brown studded leather armchairs and a dark wooden desk, whether antique or reproduction I couldn't tell. The desk was almost empty, with just a closed laptop computer and a solitary manila file. I was willing to lay bets it contained the records of Melissa Gair.

Gifford had his back to the door. He was leaning forward, elbows on the window ledge, staring out over the buildings towards the ocean. I didn't knock, just pushed the already open door; it made no sound on the thick, patterned carpet. He turned.

'How'd you get on?' he asked.

'It's a girl,' I answered, crossing the carpet to the middle of the room.

'Congratulations.' He stood there looking at me, the picture of self-possession. At any moment, he was going to tilt his head on one side, assume a polite but firm expression and ask, 'Will that be all, Miss Hamilton?'

Well, I was having none of it. 'I am this close—' I held up my left hand, making a pinch-of-salt type of gesture, 'just this close to throwing the biggest tantrum of my life. And you know what? I think I'd get away with it.'

'Please don't,' he said, crossing the room and leaning back against his desk. 'I have a splitting headache.'

'You deserve one. What the fuck are you lot playing at? Do you have any idea how serious this is?'

He sighed, looking suddenly tired. 'What do you want to know, Tora?'

'Everything. I want a goddamned explanation.'

His response was a weary smile, a small shake of the head and an exhalation of air from his nose – it was a laugh, as economical in mirth as it was in duration. 'Don't we all,' he said. He ran both hands over his face, sweeping his hair back and up. There were sweat stains under his arms. 'I can tell you what's happened while you've been in delivery. Will that do?'

'It's a start.'

'Do you want to sit down?' He nodded towards a chair. I did. In fact, I needed to, as though his despondency was infectious. The chair was absurdly comfortable and the room hot. I made myself sit upright.

'Detective Superintendent Harris is on his way over from Inverness. He is taking personal control of the situation. Andy Dunn came here twenty minutes ago to collect details of the two doctors and three nurses who treated Mrs Gair. Three of the five are currently at the station being interviewed. One is on holiday, the other left the hospital and is being tracked down. Mrs Gair's GP is also at the station.'

'What about you?'

He smiled again, reading my mind.

'I often take extended leave in the late summer or autumn. When Mrs Gair was admitted, I was in New Zealand. She'd been dead five days by the time I got back.'

I thought about what he was telling me. Was it really possible that whatever sick shit was going on here, Kenn Gifford had no part in it?

'The pathologist who carried out her post mortem is on sick leave in Edinburgh—'

'Wait a sec,' I interrupted him. 'Stephen Renney didn't do it?'

Gifford shook his head. 'Stephen's only been with us about eight months. He started just before you did. He's covering for our regular guy – chap called Jonathan Wheeler. What was I saying? Oh yes, Sergeant Tulloch is at this moment flying down to interview Jonathan. The report is here, though.' He gestured to the manila file on his desk. 'It seems pretty thorough. Want to see it?'

He reached over and I took the file, more because I needed time to think than because I really wanted to look at it. I flicked through. Extensive spread of the cancer into both breasts, lymph nodes and lungs. Secondary tumours in . . . and so it went on.

I looked up. 'Her grave. I mean, her official one. Where is it? Are they exhuming?'

'Not an option, I'm afraid. Mrs Gair was – or so we believed until now – cremated.'

'How convenient.'

'Nothing remotely convenient about this mess.'

'So how, exactly, does a woman who died of cancer three years ago end up in my field?'

'You want my best guess?'

'You mean you have more than one? I'm impressed. I can't even begin to start guessing.'

'Well, as theories go it's a weak one; wishful thinking probably describes it better. But what I hope is that we're looking at some sort of Burke and Hare scenario.'

'Body-snatchers?'

He nodded. 'Someone, for reasons of their own – which I would really rather not enquire into but I suppose I'm going to have to – stole her body from the morgue. An empty coffin – or more likely a weighted one – got cremated.'

It was ridiculous. Kenn Gifford, one of the brightest men I'd ever met, thought that load of rubbish was going to fly?

'But she didn't die in October 2004. According to the pathologists she died nearly a year later.'

'Her body was put in the peat nearly a year later. What if she was kept in a deep freeze for several months?'

I thought about it. For a split second.

'She'd had a baby. A dead body in a deep freeze

can't gestate a baby to full term.'

'Well, there my theory hits an obstacle, I'll have to admit. I just have to hope – and pray – that you and Stephen Renney got it totally wrong.'

'We didn't,' I whispered, thinking about the forensic pathology team from Inverness who'd also examined the body. We couldn't all be wrong.

'Peat's a strange substance. We don't know very much about it. Maybe it confused the normal decaying procedure.'

'She'd had a baby,' I repeated.

'Melissa Gair *was* pregnant.'

'She was?'

'I spoke to her GP. About forty minutes ago. Before the police picked him up.'

'You mean you warned him.'

'Tora, get a grip. I've known Peter Jobbs since I was ten years old. He's as straight as an arrow, trust me.'

I decided to let that one pass. 'So, what did he tell you?'

'She went to see him in September 2004, concerned about a lump in her left breast. She also suspected she was in the very early stages of pregnancy. Peter arranged a consultation with a specialist in Aberdeen, but two weeks later – three days before her appointment – she was admitted to hospital in great pain.'

He got up and walked across the room. 'Do you want coffee?' he asked.

I nodded.

Gifford poured from a machine very similar to the one I kept in my office and brought two mugs back. He handed one to me and then sat down in the other chair. I had to twist sideways to look at him. He stared straight ahead, denying me eye contact.

'The initial X-rays showed extensive spread of the cancer. No one here is really qualified to deal with that so a transfer was requested. She was kept as comfortable as possible and flown, briefly, to Aberdeen. They did an open-and-shut and brought her back here. They upped her pain relief and she died a few days later.'

Open-and-shut refers to a surgical procedure cut short following the discovery of an inoperable condition. The surgeon at Aberdeen would have opened Melissa up, seen that the spread was too extensive to be able to remove the cancer surgically and then closed her again. The surgeon would have been standing beside Melissa's bedside when she woke up. *I'm very sorry, Mrs Gair, but I'm afraid we weren't able to operate.* He might as well have donned a black cloak and carried a scythe into the room.

'Poor Melissa.'

He nodded agreement. 'Thirty-two years old.'

With a new life just beginning inside her. How sad was that?

Except . . . 'No, fuck it.' I was on my feet again and shouting. I couldn't believe I'd nearly fallen for that shit. 'Melissa did not die of cancer. Melissa died when someone took a chisel, rammed it between her breast bone, forced open her ribcage and then systematically hacked through five principle arteries and several smaller ones and pulled her heart, probably still beating, from her body.'

'Tora.' Gifford was also on his feet, coming towards me. I was breathing too fast and starting to feel light-headed.

'She died because some sick fuck decided she was going to and a whole load of wankers are lying about it. Probably you, too.'

He put his hands on my shoulders and I felt an immense flood of warmth wash into me. We looked at each other. Slate, his eyes were the colour of slate. He was breathing heavily and slowly. I found my own slowing down to fall into sync with his. The fuzziness in my head faded. There was a knock on the door.

'Is everything OK, Mr Gifford?'

'Everything's fine,' Gifford called back. 'Can you give me a minute?'

Footsteps retreated outside.

'Feeling better?' asked Gifford.

I shook my head, but more out of stubbornness than honesty. I was, a little.

Gifford lifted a hand and stroked it down over my head. It came to rest on the bare skin of my neck.

'What am I going to do with you?' he said.

Well, a few things sprang to mind because, in spite of everything, it felt very nice to be standing there with Gifford, in that ridiculously furnished room, being held – almost – in his arms.

'I hate long hair on men,' I said.

Don't ask me where that came from; or why I thought that particular moment, of all possible opportunities, was the time to utter it.

He smiled. A proper smile this time, and I wondered how I could ever have thought him ugly.

'So, I'll get it cut,' he said.

I took a step closer, dropped my head and stared at the fabric of his shirt, knowing the situation had strayed way beyond the bounds of what was appropriate and that I really, really, needed to snap out of it.

'Now comes the bit you're not going to like,' he said.

I looked up again sharply, even took a step back. What was it, exactly, that I was supposed to have been enjoying so far?

'You're suspended on full pay for a fortnight.'

I backed away. 'You are fucking well kidding me.'

He said nothing. He wasn't kidding.

'You can't do that. I've done nothing wrong.'

He laughed and walked back over to the window. Turning his back on me made me want to kick him, but I didn't move.

'Technically,' he said to my reflection in the windowpane, 'I think you'll find you've done quite a lot wrong. You've interfered in police investigations, you've broken any number of hospital regulations and you've disregarded some direct instructions from me. You've broken patient confidentiality and you've upset some senior members of the community and the hospital.' He turned round again. He was smiling. 'But that isn't why you're suspended.'

'Why, then?'

He held up his index finger. 'One – if you stay, you'll carry on exactly as you have been and I can't protect you for ever.'

'I won't. I'll leave it to the police now.'

He shook his head. 'Don't believe you. Two – as you so eloquently put it over in the dental unit, the shit is really going to hit the fan here in the next few days and a lot of people will be very unhappy. I don't want you being seen as the focus – or even the cause – of all that.'

'I don't care what people think of me.'

'Then you should. When this is all over, you'll still have to work here. You won't be able to do that if everyone dislikes you.'

'They won't like me more for running away. They'll think I daren't face them. Hell, if you tell them I'm suspended, they might even think I'm involved.'

'I'll tell them you're exhausted and deeply upset by what's been going on. You'll be the object of sympathy, not resentment. Three – I'm going to have a whole lot to do in the next few days to minimize damage to the hospital, not to mention my own reputation – I don't want to hear it, Tora,' he said, as I started to interrupt him. 'I'm not a policeman. The well-being of the hospital is my priority and I don't want you around distracting me.'

I didn't have an immediate answer to that one. Something that, had it not felt so completely out of place, I would have said was happiness was twisting around in the pit of my stomach.

'Four,' he said, startling me. There was a four? 'I want you where you're safe.' Happy feeling gone! I had completely forgotten, amidst the heady rush of discovery and vindication, that – to use a cop-show cliché – there was a killer about; and I had been poking my nose in where someone – maybe even someone at this hospital – didn't want it.

He stepped forward and he was holding me again, upper arms this time. 'You need some serious time off,' he said. 'You're obviously exhausted, you're white as a sheet, your hands won't stop shaking and your pupils look like you've taken drugs. Exposure to anything infectious right now would knock you flat. I can't have you working in a hospital.'

I had taken drugs, albeit unwittingly. Was it really so obvious? Or did Kenn know more than he was letting on? I wondered again how anyone could bypass my locked office door. Kenn had done it the previous morning. He'd claimed a cleaner had let him in, but . . .

There was a rush of cold air through the room as the door was pushed open. Kenn was no longer looking at me but at whoever was standing in the doorway. I spun round and my day was complete. It was Duncan.

'Hands off my wife, Gifford,' he said calmly. His face looked anything but calm.

For a moment, Kenn's hands remained on my shoulders and then the warmth was gone. I moved forward, away from him and towards my husband, who was not, it had to be said, looking particularly pleased to see me.

'What kept you?' said Gifford.

'Delayed flight,' replied Duncan, glaring back at him. Then he took a step into the room and looked round. He gave a short, unpleasant laugh. 'What are you – a Harley Street gynaecologist?'

'Glad you like it,' said Gifford. 'But my predecessor designed this room.'

Beside me, I sensed Duncan stiffen.

'I just can't justify the funds to change it,' said Kenn. 'What? Did he never invite you in?'

I looked from one man to the other. Duncan was furious and I could only imagine it was with me. But, Christ, wasn't he over-reacting a bit? Gifford and I may have looked more intimate than the average husband would like but we'd hardly been caught bonking on the sofa.

'What's going on?' I said, thinking I was using that phrase far too often these days.

Gifford turned to me. 'My predecessor. Medical director here for fifteen years before his retirement. Something of a mentor for me. Give him my regards, won't you?'

I looked at Duncan.

'Wake up, Tor,' he said irritably. 'He's talking about Dad.'

OK, really not keeping up here. 'Your father worked in Edinburgh. You told me.'

Shortly after we'd met, Duncan had told me his

father was a doctor, an anaesthetist, and naturally I'd been interested. He'd also told me that he'd worked away from home for most of his childhood, coming back only at weekends. I'd always assumed it went some way towards explaining why Duncan's family are the way they are.

'He came back,' said Duncan, 'round about the time I went to university. Where's your car?'

'Haven't a clue,' I responded. Things had been moving pretty fast lately and I'd lost track.

'Parked outside Sergeant Tulloch's house,' said Gifford. 'Safe enough – one would hope.'

I fell asleep minutes after Duncan started driving. My dreams were strange, disjointed ones about being in theatre with no notes and no proper instruments. The patient was Duncan's father and the face of the scrub nurse peering at me over her mask was that of Duncan's mother, Elspeth. We were in one of the original anatomy theatres, with a central operating table and circles of seats rising ever higher around it. Every seat was filled by someone I knew: Dana, Andy Dunn, Stephen Renney, my parents, my three brothers, friends from university, my old Girl Guide leader. I didn't have to be Sigmund Freud to recognize a classic anxiety dream. I jerked awake at one point when Duncan braked hard to avoid a stray sheep. We were not on the road home.

'Where are we going?' I asked.

'Westing,' he replied. Westing was his parents'

home on Unst, the place where he'd been born and brought up.

I thought for a moment. 'Who's looking after the horses?'

'Mary said she'd come over.'

I nodded. Mary was a local girl who helped me with feeding and exercising on my busy days. She knew the horses well and they knew her. They'd be fine. My eyelids were sinking again when I wondered if I should tell Duncan what had happened the night before. I also wanted to ask him what he knew about Tronal.

I glanced over. He was staring straight ahead, face muscles tight as though he was concentrating hard, even though he knew this road well and it wasn't nearly dark. Mind you, he was driving far too fast. Didn't seem like a good moment to talk. Maybe later. I closed my eyes again and drifted off. I woke briefly during the ferry crossing to Yell.

'Gifford phoned you, didn't he?' I asked. 'He told you about the break-in at the house.'

Without looking at me, Duncan nodded. It gave me an uncomfortable feeling. Duncan and Gifford might dislike each other but they were working together to manage me. Or were they? Maybe the intimate little encounter Gifford and I had shared had been staged for Duncan's benefit. Was Gifford playing both of us?

It doesn't take long to drive up Yell and by nine o'clock we were on the last leg of the journey.

Having known Duncan for seven years and

been married for five of them, I could still say with complete honesty that I did not know his parents. For a long time I found it strange, even a little distressing, coming, as I do, from a large and noisy, frank and nosy family, amongst whom talk is plentiful and secrets in short supply. That was until I realized that Duncan doesn't know his parents all that well either and that it wasn't something I should take personally.

Duncan is an only child. One who arrived relatively late into the marriage when, presumably, the certainty of children had long since given way to a half-resigned, half-resentful acceptance of something that may never be. One might have thought he would be all the more precious, all the more loved because of that, but that didn't seem to be the case.

They had never been a close family. Whilst his mother was as doting as one would expect an older mother of an only son to be, there was no comfortable familiarity in their relationship. I'd rarely heard them joke together or share memories of childhood. Still less frequently had I heard her scold him. Polite seemed to best summarize the relationship between Duncan and his mother, although occasionally one could have called it uneasy.

The relationship between Duncan and his father was easier to describe, although not to understand. It was formal, courteous and – to my mind, at least – distinctly cold. It wasn't that they didn't talk. They talked quite a lot – about Duncan's work, the economy, current affairs, life on the islands – but they never touched on the personal. They never went sailing together, or for walks over the cliffs. They never sneaked off to the pub while his mother and I were preparing dinner, they didn't fall asleep together in front of the TV afterwards and they never, ever quarrelled.

On the fifteen-minute ferry journey from Yell to Unst I asked, 'Did he retire early?' I had no idea how old Richard was but he barely looked seventy. Yet he hadn't worked in all the time I'd known him. I hadn't mentioned Richard the whole journey but Duncan knew immediately whom I meant.

'Ten years ago,' he replied, looking straight ahead.

'Why?' I asked. If Richard had left his post under some sort of cloud, that at least could explain why he was so reluctant to talk about his former profession.

Duncan shrugged without looking at me. 'He had other things to do. And he'd groomed his successor.'

'Gifford.'

Duncan was silent.

'What is it between you two?' I said.

Then he looked at me. 'Do I need to ask you that?'

'He said he stole your girlfriend.'

The light disappeared from Duncan's eyes and for a moment the face looking back at me was not one I recognized. Then he gave a sharp, angry laugh.

'In his dreams.'

The ferry was docking and the three other cars

making the late crossing had started their engines. Duncan turned on the ignition. As the ferry engines roared up and the heavy harbour ramp slammed down, he muttered something under his breath, but I didn't dare ask him to repeat himself.

18

UNST, LYING ON THE SAME LATITUDE AS southern Greenland, is home to around seven hundred people and fifty thousand puffins. The most northerly of all the inhabited British islands, it measures roughly twelve miles long and five miles wide, with one main road, the A968, running from the south-eastern ferry port at Belmont up to Norwich in the north-east.

Two miles after leaving the ferry we turned left along a single-track road and started to drive up and down the shore-edged hills. At the end of the road, just about literally, you find the handful of buildings that is Westing; and the cold, grand, granite house that is Duncan's family home.

Elspeth hugged Duncan and pressed her cold cheek against mine. Richard shook hands with his son and nodded to me. They led us into their large, west-facing sitting room. Drawn by the colours I could see outside, I walked over to the window. Behind me, a short silence fell; I bristled at a sense of being stared at, and then I heard the sound of a cork being pulled.

The sun was almost gone and the sky had turned violet. Close to the shore at Westing stand several massive lava rocks, all that remain of ancient cliffs that in past days withstood the might of the Atlantic. These rocks were black as pitch where the light couldn't catch them, but their beaten and jagged edges glowed like molten gold. The clouds that had been thick and threatening all day had become soft, dusky pink shadows and the surf bounced at the water's edge like sparks of silver.

There was movement beside me and I turned. It was Richard, holding out a glass of red wine. He stood beside me and we both looked out. The sun had disappeared behind the cliffs of Yell but, in doing so, had draped them in light. They looked as if they had been carved from bronze.

'The loveliest and loneliest place on earth,' said Richard, and he seemed to be voicing my thoughts.

I took a large gulp of wine. It was excellent. Elspeth and Richard's home had a huge cellar beneath it, but, unlike ours, it was kept well stocked. Richard took my arm and led me to an armchair near the fire and Elspeth scurried forward with a loaded plate. I surrendered myself to their hospitality and ate and drank gratefully, doing my best to respond to Elspeth's attempts at polite conversation.

Half an hour later, while Duncan and his father were discussing the state of the roads on the island

and plans to develop some of its peat resources, I excused myself and went upstairs to our room. When we stayed with Duncan's parents, we slept in the best guest room – not, as I had first expected, in Duncan's old room. That, he'd told me once, had been in the attic but had since been converted into storage. I hadn't asked what had happened to all his old stuff, all the dusty souvenirs of childhood.

I pulled my mobile out of my bag and checked messages. There were three from Dana and I felt a glimmer of affection for her. She, at least, was not part of the general conspiracy to get me out of the loop. I knew my mobile wouldn't work too well this far north so I risked using the landline in the bedroom. She answered on the second ring.

'Thank God, Tora, where are you?'

'Serving exile in the Siberian wastelands.' The bedroom phone was by the window. Our room faced east. I could see more hills, bathed in a rich rosy light, and the strawberry-pink waters of the inland lake behind the house.

'Come again?'

I explained.

'Well, that's probably good. At least you'll be safe up there.'

Why did everyone keep going on about my safety? It was unnerving, to say the least.

'Can you tell me what's been happening?' A puffin landed on the window ledge and looked directly at me.

'Of course. I just got back from Edinburgh. I went

to interview a Jonathan Wheeler. He's the regular pathologist at your place. Been on sick leave for a few months.'

'Yes, I've heard of him. What did you find out?' The puffin, bored with me, started wiping his multi-coloured beak against the stone of the ledge.

'Well, it didn't help that he'd obviously been warned I was coming. Your friend Gifford needs banging up for obstructing justice, if you ask me, but that's hardly likely to happen, is it, given that he and my inspector are old rugger-bugger shower buddies, sharing a soap on a rope and any number—'

'Dana!' Not that I wasn't enjoying her invective against Gifford but I knew my time was limited. I could hear movement downstairs.

'Sorry. Anyway, that notwithstanding, he seemed pretty straight. I took him down to Edinburgh nick, kept him sweating in the interview room for half an hour, gave him the full treatment. He remembered the case – well, he would, wouldn't he, having had his memory jogged by your boss – and was pretty forthcoming with the details. Haven't got my notes in front of me but it all seemed to square with what we'd been told. Young woman, malignant lumps in both breasts and extensive spread of the cancer through most of her major organs. I tell you what didn't fit, though.'

'What?'

'Well, apparently Melissa Gair was pregnant when she first went to her GP. Very early stages. Even Stephen Gair didn't know.'

'Gifford told me.'

There was a sharp intake of breath. 'Bloody man's a menace. Anyway, Melissa and her GP did a urine test that proved she was pregnant, but by the time of the post-mortem, three weeks later, she wasn't.'

I was sorry to dampen Dana's enthusiasm but I didn't want her chasing stray hares.

'That's very easily explained.'

'How?'

'Lots of early pregnancies fail to develop. Eggs get fertilized and the pregnancy hormone appears in the woman's blood, giving a positive pregnancy test, but then the egg dies. Melissa could have had a period between her visit to the GP and being admitted to hospital that was actually a very early miscarriage. Given the invasive nature of the cancer, I'd say that was pretty likely.'

There was silence, while Dana processed the information I'd just given her.

'Dana,' I continued, when she still hadn't spoken. 'I've been thinking about something. Maybe the woman who was admitted to hospital with cancer, who died there, the one you've been researching all day, wasn't Melissa Gair. Maybe records got mixed up.'

'We thought of that.'

'And . . .'

'It was her. Her GP is adamant that Melissa came to see him. He'd known her for years. We also spoke to the receptionist at the practice. She knew Melissa, too. The hospital staff didn't know her personally but I've shown them photographs and they're pretty sure it was her. Of course, she'd changed quite a bit by the time she was admitted. Pain does that to people, apparently. But they all, distinctly and separately, remembered her hair and her skin. She was a striking-looking woman.'

'They could be lying.'

She was quiet for a moment.

'Well, possibly. But their stories all match perfectly. We've been over it with them time after time and nothing budges.'

I thought for a moment. 'Did she have a twin?'

'No. An older brother, lives in the States.'

'So were Stephen Renney and I wrong? Was I wrong about the dental records?' I couldn't believe it, but it seemed the only possible explanation.

'No, you weren't wrong. We've had another dentist look at the records. The body in the morgue is definitely Melissa. And another post-mortem has been carried out. She most certainly had a baby. They also found a small lump in her left breast. It's being tested but they think it probably wasn't malignant.'

I was quiet for a moment. My brain simply could not compute the facts I was feeding into it.

'We're going round in circles,' I said eventually.

'Tell me about it.'

'So what happens next?'

'No one seems to know. The hospital staff and the GP have all gone home. So has Stephen Gair.'

'You let them go?'

Even over the phone line I could feel Dana's

frustration. 'Tora, who is our suspect? What do we charge them with? We have six – no, seven – respectable members of the medical profession all saying the same thing: a woman called Melissa Gair was admitted with acute breast cancer in September 2004. Given the advanced stage of the disease, she wasn't expected to live beyond a few weeks and she died in hospital. Everything was done by the book. There's no reason to doubt their stories.'

'Other than the obvious,' I snapped. The puffin whipped its head in my direction and took off. Within seconds it had disappeared over the cliffs.

'We'd have to prove that seven of them colluded, together with Stephen Gair himself, to fake a death. We haven't a clue how that could have happened, or what their motive was. We can't even begin to start constructing a case against them.'

I couldn't think of anything to say. Then I could. 'Life insurance. How much was she insured for?'

'I'm checking Gair's finances but probably not enough to pay off seven other people as well. The other thing is that Stephen Gair has identified the body in the morgue. He says it's definitely his wife.'

'The one he watched die three years ago.' My voice was rising.

'Hold your fire, Doc, I'm just the messenger. My point is, would he make a positive identification if he was involved in foul play three years ago?'

'Tor, are you OK?' Duncan was standing at the bottom of the stairs, shouting up at me.

'I have to go,' I said to Dana. 'I'll call you.'

* * *

Duncan had his back to the peat fire. His parents sat close by. Even in May the air on Unst had a distinct chill to it. Duncan, I noticed, had finished the wine and moved on to Lagavulin, a single Highland malt that makes me think of rancid bacon.

'Who were you calling?' he asked.

'Dana,' I said, wondering if now was a good time to start acquiring a taste for single malt. One Melissa Gair: two very different deaths. How could one person die twice?

Duncan closed his eyes briefly. He looked sad, rather than angry, which made me feel guilty – which made me feel angry again. Given everything that was going on up here, why should I, of all people, be made to feel guilty?

'I do wish you'd leave it,' he said softly, in a tone that suggested he knew I wouldn't. From the corner of my eye, I saw Elspeth glance at Richard, but neither asked what it was, exactly, I was supposed to leave. I guessed they already knew.

Over Duncan's shoulder I spotted something that I suppose I must have seen several times, but had never really thought about before. I walked over and with one index finger began to trace the outline.

The fireplace in the sitting room of Richard and Elspeth's house is huge. It must measure six feet in length and be about four feet deep. The central grate is about two feet square and the base of the chimney a similar dimension. It has a terrific draught and the fires it creates on high days and holidays are small bonfires. I wasn't looking at the fire, though – a relatively modest one for a spring evening – but at the stone lintel that ran across the top of the hearth. About eight feet long, seven inches high, supported on either side by strong stone pillars. Carved into the granite of the lintel were shapes I recognized: an upright arrow, a crooked letter F, a zigzag like a flash of lightning. They were repeated several times, sometimes appearing upside-down, sometimes inverted, like a mirror image, and an angular pattern had been carved around the edge of the lintel. The whole effect was more elaborate but still bore a striking resemblance to the carvings in our cellar at home. And the five Viking runes from our own fireplace that Dana and I had puzzled over were all here.

'You've spoken to Sergeant Tulloch yourself, Richard,' I said, tracing the shape of the rune I was pretty certain meant Initiation. 'She needed your advice on some runes carved on the body I found.'

Out of the corner of my eye I saw Elspeth wince.

'Yes, I remember,' said Richard, speaking slowly as he usually did. 'She'd already found a book on the subject. I told her I had nothing to add to the interpretation offered by the author. I referred her to the British Library.'

And a whole heap of good that would have done poor Dana, stuck up here on Shetland. I simply couldn't believe my father-in-law had nothing useful to say on a subject so integral to the islands' history. Was he joining the general conspiracy to keep

Tora's little nastiness under wraps? I realized that if Melissa's murder was connected to the hospital, as seemed highly likely, then as a former medical director Richard Guthrie might have a strong interest in muffling the facts. I started to wonder if the instinct that had sent me to Unst for my personal safety had been entirely sound.

'These are the same as the carvings in our cellar,' I said, wondering how Richard would deal with a straight question. 'What do they mean?'

'I'll gladly lend you a book in the morning.'

'Initiation,' I said, my finger still tracing the outline of the rune.

Richard joined me at the hearth. 'Maybe you don't need a book.'

'Why would someone carve the rune for Initiation into the hearth of a house?' I asked. 'It makes no sense.'

He looked down at me and I had to steel myself not to step backwards. He was a tall man, built on a very large frame. His physical presence, along with a formidable intellect and quick wit, had always made him immensely intimidating. I'd never crossed swords with him before and I could feel my heart rate starting to speed up.

'Nobody really knows what these runes mean,' he said. 'They date back thousands of years and the original meanings and usage have almost certainly been lost. The book Sergeant Tulloch had offered one set of interpretations. Others exist too. You simply take your pick.' As though bored with the subject he sighed and moved towards the door. 'Now, if you'll all excuse me, I'm going to bed.'

'Good idea,' said Elspeth, getting to her feet. 'Do you two need anything before you go up?'

'You don't look much like your dad,' I said, as Duncan started to undress.

'You've said that before,' he replied, his voice muffled by the sweater he was pulling over his head.

'He's much bigger, for a start,' I said. 'And wasn't he blond when he was young?'

'Maybe I take after my mother,' said Duncan, unbuttoning his jeans. He was still annoyed with me.

I thought about it. Elspeth was short and, not to put too fine a point on it, dumpy. There was no immediate resemblance to Duncan that I could think of, but the flow of genes is notoriously unpredictable and you never know quite what human cocktail each act of reproduction is going to kick up.

'Are you going to shower before you come to bed?' asked Duncan, and at last I'd found someone honest enough to admit I smelled like a skunk in mating season. I showered for a long time and when I got back to the bedroom Duncan was asleep. Five minutes later, mere seconds before I too drifted off, it occurred to me that whilst Richard Guthrie might bear little resemblance to his son, he bore quite a lot to Kenn Gifford.

19

I WAS AWOKEN BY LIGHT, LOTS OF IT, FLOODING THE room and coaxing me out of sleep. The curtains of our east-facing window were open and Duncan stood by the bed with a steaming mug of tea.

'You awake?'

I looked at the tea. 'Is that for me?'

'Yup.' He put it down on the bedside table.

'I'm awake.' I was amazed at how much better I felt. There really is nothing like a decent night's sleep.

Duncan sat down on the bed and I smiled at him. I'm a sucker for tea in bed.

'Wanna come sailing?' he asked. He was already dressed.

'Now?'

'Bacon sandwiches in the clubhouse,' he tempted.

I thought about it. Spend the morning hanging around the house, searching for polite things to say to Elspeth, trying to avoid a row with Richard, or . . .

'You feel the need . . .' I said to Duncan.

He jumped up from the bed. 'I feel the need for speed!' he finished. We slapped a high five.

Twenty-five minutes later we were at the Uyea clubhouse, tucking into bacon sandwiches washed down with strong, milky Nescafé and looking out over Uyea Sound to—

'My God, that's it!' I said, between mouthfuls.

'What?' mumbled Duncan. He was already on his second sandwich, fully kitted up and fastening his lifejacket.

'Tronal island,' I said. 'There's a maternity clinic there. And an adoption centre.'

'Come on,' said Duncan, getting to his feet. 'We have an hour and a half before it pours down.'

Directly above us the sky was as blue as a robin's egg but out over the ocean, several miles beyond Yell, low clouds hung ominously. The wind was strong, about a force five, and coming in an easterly direction. Duncan was right: the storm was on its way.

'It can't be much more than quarter of a mile away,' I said, my eyes still fixed on Tronal as we pushed the dinghy down the slipway.

No reply.

'Can we go?' I said as we reached the water's edge and Duncan began to lift the boat off its trailer.

'No, we bloody well can't,' he replied. 'For a start, it's private land and the navigation's a bugger. There are rocks that'll rip the hull off before we get near.'

Duncan couldn't stop me looking, though, as we

sped away from the jetty, he at the helm and I controlling the jib. I realized I must have seen Tronal a dozen times or more but had never really registered it. I don't think I'd even realized it was an island. The coastline of Shetland undulates and twists so much that it's often difficult to tell what's attached to the land you are on and what isn't.

Tronal sat low in the water, without the mountainous cliffs that characterize so much of Shetland. In the early-morning light, against the blue backdrop of the sky behind, I could see tracks and, behind one ridge, the tops of buildings. No other obvious signs of life.

The wind was perfect and the dinghy was tearing along, but starting to keel over. Duncan signalled to me to put the trapeze out and a few minutes later I was skimming just inches above the water, at a speed that felt like flight. We bounced high on a few rogue waves and the spray stung my eyes. Beneath me, the sea looked like a shimmering mass of diamonds.

'Ready about,' called Duncan, and as I prepared to tack I saw that we were now only yards from Tronal. A crumbling stone wall rimmed the lower reaches of the land and, just a foot or so outside it, a barbed-wire fence. The land the double barrier enclosed had been tilled and green shoots of some early crop were forcing through. I saw a man on his knees, digging. He wore dull brown overalls and was almost invisible against the earth. He stopped working and turned round. I followed his gaze and saw a woman some twenty yards further up the hill.

'Lee-ho!' called Duncan and the dinghy turned, disorientating me, as it always does. When I got my bearings and glanced back we were already too far away to make anyone out against the dull backdrop of the island.

We were now heading south-west. Given the strong winds and the approaching storm, Duncan had chosen to steer us not out towards the North Sea but into the much more sheltered waters that lay between Unst to the north, Yell to the west and Fetlar in the south. We tacked again and Duncan had to shout at me to pay attention. But my mind was full of the woman I'd just seen. I couldn't be sure, I had seen her so briefly, but she'd looked in the later stages of pregnancy. I wondered if she were one of the unhappy souls about to give up her baby.

The boat was keeling hard, even though I was fully out on the trapeze, and Duncan wasn't looking particularly relaxed. Although these waters are more sheltered than the open seas to the east and west of Unst, the winds are notoriously flukey. Whatever the prevailing conditions, there are so many headlands and islands for the gusts to bounce off that you never really know what's going to hit you and when. We'd also strayed into the triangle of sea that the ferries use and had to keep a sharp lookout; those beasties move fast and they won't shift their course to avoid a careless dinghy. We sped up past the small island of Linga and I breathed a sigh of relief as we passed Belmont and were out of reach of the big boats. The thing about sailing that non-sailors never quite understand is that your mood can shift so quickly from exhilaration to anxiety to mind-numbing terror. Right now I was into anxiety and climbing. The wind seemed to have picked up, the trapeze was not stabilizing the boat and the rigging was starting to creak.

'Get back in,' Duncan yelled at me, none too soon, and I started to pull myself back towards the marginally greater comfort of the boat.

At that moment, there was a deafening crack. *Thunder*, I thought, *the storm's an hour ahead of schedule.* Then I heard a loud tearing noise and a cry of warning from Duncan. I was thrown up in the air and came down in the cold waters of Bluemull Sound.

Instinct had turned me the right way up and several feet above me I could see sunlight and clear, sparkling water. I kicked hard and broke through the surface. I coughed over and over, with no time in between to take in more air. I started to go down again.

Back under the surface, I remembered that although I was wearing a life jacket, it wasn't inflated. Forcing myself not to panic, kicking hard to keep myself from sinking too deep, I fumbled under the canvas flaps of my jacket for the red pull toggle. I had only to tug on it and the jacket would automatically fill with air, propelling me to the surface. Except I couldn't find the damn thing!

I knew I had to stay calm, so I gave up and went for the surface again. This time I managed to control the coughing just long enough to breathe in. The water was choppier than I'd thought and all I could see were the short, aggressive waves that bounced around me. No sign of the boat. Nor of Duncan.

I gave up on the toggle and fumbled for the air inlet that allows you to inflate a life jacket manually. I found it easily enough, ripped off the stopper and started to blow. After eight blows I was exhausted. I replaced the stopper and lay back in the water. My natural buoyancy kept me on the surface but the waves splashed so aggressively into my face that I felt myself panicking again. I pulled upright. Sixteen puffs later and I had to admit defeat. The life jacket was not inflating and I was exhausting myself for nothing.

I think I almost gave up at that point. I sobbed aloud and tried to yell but I could barely hear my own voice above the wind. I tried to raise myself higher in the water, to get some sort of bearing. The Bluemull Sound was no more than half a mile wide at this point and I appeared to be directly in the middle. I turned round in the water and caught sight of the boat, little more than a white speck, a quarter mile, maybe more, further up the Sound. Its sails were dragging in the water and it looked as though the mast was gone. There was no sign of Duncan.

I thought quickly. Unst or Yell? Unst looked closer and, instinctively, it felt right to head for home, but the cliffs are steeper and far less forgiving than those on the neighbouring island. There'd be little point in reaching land only to die of exposure at the foot of a thirty-metre cliff. I turned for Yell and started swimming.

Several minutes later, I'd made no progress through the water. I couldn't remember what the currents were like here in the Sound but I guessed I was swimming against one. I looked around again, hoping in the face of no real probability that someone would see me: a passing fishing boat, a cliff walker, another dinghy, anyone. That's when I saw the thing that was to save my life: not ten yards away and barely visible against water that was getting darker and greyer by the minute was a broken-off chunk of wooden pallet. I swam for it. Several times I touched it only to have it swept away, but finally I had it. I gripped it tight and started to kick.

The wind got up; the waves became choppier and the rain heavier. From time to time, sea-birds dived close, cawing at me. At first, I thought they were merely curious, then I got to wondering if they were trying to tell me something: *not that way – you're heading straight for a rip-tide, swim south now – the current will take you in.* After a while, I wondered if the prospect of carrion was the real attraction.

I know exactly how long I spent in the water that day because I always wear a waterproof wristwatch when I'm sailing. Having the watch helped almost as much as having the pallet. It kept at bay the bewildering disorientation of not knowing how much time was passing and it enabled me to set little targets for myself, even play games. I would swim for ten minutes and then rest for two, timing it to the second. Then I would lay bets with myself. How many more minutes before I could recognize sea birds on the cliffs? How many more before I could make out wild flowers on the rocks?

The pallet kept me afloat; the watch kept me sane; and my legs, strong from years of daily horse-riding, kicked me back to land.

It took three hours and twenty minutes to swim the quarter-mile from where the dinghy capsized to the island of Yell. That's the equivalent of about thirty lengths of a twenty-five-metre municipal swimming pool, and if it seems wimpishly slow, then you have to remember that swimming pools do not, as a rule, have tides, nor currents, nor freezing temperatures, nor heavy rain pelting down on you. But eventually it was over and by ten minutes to twelve I knew that if death by drowning was to be my fate, it wasn't going to happen that day. Thirty seconds later I staggered on to the beach.

Death from exposure was still on the cards, though, and I had to get moving. I pulled myself to my feet and looked around. Ahead of me was a cliff: not massively high but a cliff nonetheless. The beach was very narrow, hardly more than a strip of sand, and behind a very thin causeway there was a small lake. Two streams fed it, running down from the cliff-top above, and I realized they offered my best route up.

I started upwards. The stream I was following had cut out numerous little ledges and gullies over the years, and climbing wasn't difficult. The biggest danger was that I would get careless and slip. Before I reached the top I saw a car drive past, not thirty yards away from me, but the driver was staring straight ahead. I kept on going and collapsed at the roadside.

The rain was striking my face like a whip with a thousand tiny lashes and if a patient had arrived in A&E shivering as violently as I was doing, I'd have been seriously concerned. Yet I found I had enough strength left to start worrying about Duncan. Would it really be worth surviving only to find that he hadn't? He was a better swimmer than I, but what if he'd been hit by the mast? I found I had enough energy left to cry.

By twelve-fifteen I hadn't seen another car and had no choice but to start walking. I was barefoot. Shortly after the accident my sailing boots had filled with water. I'd kicked them off but I'd have been glad of them – of anything – now. The roadside verges were made of coarse grass, mud, shingle and more stones. After ten minutes my feet were bleeding.

I walked along the road until I came to Gutcher, from where the Yell–Unst ferry leaves, and stumbled into the green-painted, wooden-built café just by the pier.

'Dat in traath!' said the woman behind the counter at the sight of me. There were two other people in the café, a boy of about ten and a woman whom I took for his mother. They said nothing, just stared.

'Do you have a phone I could use?' I managed.

'I've been in a sailing accident,' I added, although I'm sure it was hardly necessary.

'Yan!' yelled the woman, her head half turned towards a door at the back of the café, her eyes fixed on me. 'Da lassie is haff drunned.'

They brought me a phone but I couldn't dial the number. I couldn't even remember it, but I managed to tell them who I was and they put the call through. It seemed to take a long time and all the while I was bracing myself for the news that Duncan hadn't made it back. I think I retreated to somewhere inside my head, only vaguely aware of movement and sound around me. I was given hot tea that I couldn't even hold and someone put a car blanket around me. I became the object of the gentle curiosity and unconditional kindness that you only find in small communities. And I waited to be told the news of my husband's death.

20

DUNCAN WAS NOT DEAD. DUNCAN CAME RACING into the café an hour later, a little whiter in the face than normal but otherwise perfectly OK. Later, I learned the dinghy hadn't capsized, just broached violently and then righted itself. Duncan had managed to cling to the tiller and remain on board, but with the mast gone and the sails ripped, it was pretty much uncontrollable, and heading for the cliffs. He'd inflated his life jacket – working perfectly, thank you – and prepared to bail. Then he'd had the good fortune to be spotted by a passing boat. Rob Craigie, owner of one of the largest salmon farms on Unst, had been returning from an early-morning check of his offshore cages. He'd rescued Duncan and the two of them had spent the next hour looking for me. In the face of a steadily worsening storm, Duncan had eventually been persuaded to return to Unst and call out the coastguard. By the time the phone call from the Yell café reached the Guthrie home, I had been missing for nearly four hours.

I don't remember much about the journey back to Westing. Just that Richard drove and I sat in the back, huddled close to Duncan. No one spoke much. It took longer than it should have because the bad weather was delaying the ferries, but eventually, around mid afternoon, we arrived back. Elspeth had built a huge fire in our room and put extra quilts on the bed. Duncan helped me take a hot bath and then dressed me in a pair of Richard's flannel pyjamas. Richard checked me for concussion, gave me painkillers for my headache and Temazepam to help me sleep. I didn't argue, although I doubted I really needed it. Sleep was the only thing I felt I could handle just then.

Voices woke me. I was still drowsy. I wanted to go back to sleep. I closed my eyes and snuggled down.

Duncan was shouting. I'd never heard raised voices in that house before. I opened my eyes again. The curtains were drawn and a soft lamp glowed in the corner of the room. I turned to look at the clock. It was a little past seven in the evening. I sat up and felt OK, so I climbed out of bed.

The door was slightly ajar. I could hear Richard now. He wasn't shouting – I doubted him capable of doing so – but he was arguing. I moved out into the corridor and hovered uncertainly at the top of the stairs.

The door to Richard's study was open and Duncan appeared in the doorway. He stopped and turned, looking back into the room.

'I've had enough,' he said firmly. 'I want out. I'm getting out!'

Then he was gone: along the corridor, through the kitchen and out of the back door. I had the weirdest feeling that he was gone for good; that I was never going to see Duncan again.

I moved down the steps. Four steps down, I realized that Richard wasn't alone in his study. Elspeth was with him. They were arguing too, but very quietly. Another step down and I realized she was pleading with him.

'It's unthinkable,' said Richard.

'He's in love,' said Elspeth.

'He can't do it. He can't just walk away from everything he has here.'

I froze, one hand gripping the banister; then, forcing myself to move, I backed up on legs that were suddenly shaky again, one step . . . two . . . three. At the top I ran along the corridor, back into the guest room and climbed back into bed. The sheets had cooled in my absence and I started to shiver. I pulled the quilts up over my head and waited for the trembling to slow down.

Duncan was going to leave me? Of course, I knew things hadn't exactly been great between us for some time; even before we moved to Shetland he'd changed: laughing less, talking less, being away more. I'd put it down to the stress of an impending move and our difficulties in starting a family. Now, it seemed it was so much more. What I'd seen as a bad patch, he'd recognized as the end.

He'd found a lifeline and was bailing.

Was there any other explanation for what I'd just heard? Try as I might, I couldn't find one. Duncan was going to leave me. Duncan was in love with someone else. Someone he'd met on one of his trips away? Someone on the islands?

What the hell was I going to do? I had a job here. I couldn't just up and leave after six months. I could wave goodbye to any future consultant's post if I did that, even supposing I'd be allowed to leave the islands given everything that was going on. I'd only come to this godforsaken place to be with Duncan. How was I ever going to have a baby now?

My tears, when they came, were hot and stinging and I had to bite hard on my arm to keep from howling out loud. My headache was back with a vengeance. I couldn't face going downstairs to find Richard so I got up to see what I could find in the bathroom. There was nothing in the cabinet, nor in the toilet bag that Duncan had packed for me. Duncan's bag lay next to mine on the window ledge.

I started sobbing again at that point, but my headache was getting worse. I pulled down his bag and looked inside. A soggy blue flannel, razor, toothbrush, ibuprofen – thank God – and another packet of pills. I picked them up without really thinking about it and read the label: Desogestrel. Inside were three rows of small white pills, pressed into foil. Desogestrel. The name meant something but I couldn't place it. I hadn't been aware of Duncan having any condition that required a daily pill, but then again, I was learning quite a lot about Duncan that evening.

I took two ibuprofen, replaced Duncan's bag on the shelf and went back to bed, steeling myself for a restless night. I think I fell asleep in minutes.

Duncan didn't come to bed. I'm not sure what I would have said to him if he had. Some time in the night I woke to find him standing over the bed, looking down at me. I didn't move. He bent down, stroked the hair lying over my temple and went out again.

Shortly before dawn, when the dull grey light outside the window was starting to gather colour, I woke and the first thought in my head was that I knew what Desogestrel was. Had I been myself, I think I'd have recognized it immediately. Desogestrel is a synthetic hormone, known to reduce levels of testosterone in the male body and thus prohibit the production of sperm. For several years it's been used in clinical trials aimed at perfecting a male contraceptive pill. Combined with regular injections of testosterone to maintain balance in the male body, it's proven reasonably effective. Although not yet available as a prescriptive medicine, it was only a matter of time.

Duncan, it seemed, was ahead of the game. And I'd discovered the reason why, after two years of trying, I'd been unable to get pregnant.

21

'I'LL BE BACK BY WEDNESDAY, THURSDAY AT THE latest,' said Duncan.

'OK,' I replied, without turning round. I'd pulled an armchair over to the window and was looking out across the moor behind the house. The first heather was just beginning to bloom, casting a rich, claret-coloured haze over the hilltops. The rain had stopped but there were heavy clouds overhead, and their long shadows clutched the moor like the claws of a miser grasping something precious.

'We'll be home for next weekend,' he continued. 'Maybe try and get the garden sorted out.'

'Whatever,' I said, watching an arrowhead of snow-white birds with grey wings fly past the window.

Duncan knelt down beside me. I felt a tear roll down my cheek but if I carried on staring straight ahead, he wouldn't be able to see it.

'Tor, I can't take you with me. Dad says you're not fit to travel and I've back-to-back meetings for the next few days. I wouldn't be able to look—'

'I don't want to come,' I said.

He took hold of my hand. I let him but didn't return the pressure.

'I'm sorry, honey,' he said. 'I'm really sorry about everything you're going through.'

I'll bet you are, I thought, but I couldn't bring myself to say it. I couldn't say the few bitter words that would bring everything out into the open. I wasn't in denial, exactly; I just didn't need to hear him say it.

He hung around for another few minutes and then, kissing me on top of the head, he left. I heard the car engine start up and then fade away as he drove down the cliff road towards the ferry.

I forced myself to get up, knowing I couldn't stay in the house all day, obsessing about Duncan and my now very uncertain future. Official invalid or not, I was going out for a walk. I dressed and went downstairs. Luckily, only Elspeth was in the kitchen. Richard might have tried to stop me going out.

For the first half-mile I followed the coast road south. When the road veered inland towards Uyeasound, I took a detour, round the hill of Burragarth towards St Olaf's Kirk at Lundawick. Dating back to the twelfth century, this is one of the few remaining Norse churches on the island. It's a popular spot with tourists, mainly for the views it offers over the Bluemull Sound towards Yell. That day, though, I was alone as I walked round the ruin and looked out across Lunda Wick. Although the winds had died down, the waves they'd left in their wake were still jumping angrily up and down. It would have made uncomfortable sailing conditions; not that I had any desire to get back in a boat.

All around me, perched on stones, launching themselves from rocks, sliding and bouncing on the wind, were hundreds of the seabirds for which these islands are famous: kittiwakes, gannets, fulmars, terns and skuas raced round my head, screaming at each other and at me. As I watched, my head twisting this way and that, a frenetic excitement seemed to grow in their midst. Then, almost as one, they dived over my head and down, straight into the wick, and hurled themselves amongst a shoal of sand eels. There was a frantic whirl of feathers, a blizzard of sleek bodies as they fought and feasted, binged and bickered.

I was wondering if I had the energy to walk into Uyeasound for a coffee when I noticed the standing stone, not ten yards from the road. It stands about twelve feet high, just askew of the perpendicular, covered by pale-grey lichen. I wandered over to it, more for the purpose of filling time than anything else. The stone was smooth – except for the shapes that had been carved into it. Not the same markings exactly, but similar enough for me to be pretty sure I'd find them amongst the runic alphabet in Dana's library book. More runes. I wasn't sure I really cared any more, but it was still much easier to think about runes than about Duncan.

I set off down the road again. Ten minutes later, my mobile rang. It was Dana.

'I heard about the accident. Are you OK?'

'I'm fine,' I said, because that's what you always say, isn't it? 'How could you possibly have heard . . .?' The line started to crackle and I stood still. It cleared again.

'. . . at the station saw the coastguard report and recognized the name. Look, can I do anything? Do you want me to come up?'

I was touched. And for a second, I would have given anything to have her company, but knew it would have been ridiculously selfish. Dana had far too much to do to come and babysit me. I started walking again.

'Thanks, but the outlaws are looking after me. Anything new?'

'Sort of. I was planning to call you anyway. Can you talk right now?'

I looked round, saw a rock, plonked myself down on it. 'Sure, go ahead. Although I'm not sure how long the signal will last.'

'I've been talking to Melissa Gair's GP again. I wanted to check something he told me.'

'Go on.'

'He said that, whilst the lump in Melissa's breast was definitely worthy of checking out, it hadn't unduly worried him at the time. At the worst, he'd thought it would be a malignant tumour in the very early stages. He'd been amazed, he said, to hear about her death so soon afterwards. He didn't say it was impossible, but I couldn't help feeling that's what he was driving at.'

The wind was getting up; I pulled my jacket up

higher around my neck. 'And you want to know what I think?'

'Yes,' she said, none too patiently. 'What do you think?'

'Well, it would certainly be very unusual,' I replied. 'But sometimes it happens that way. Maybe Melissa didn't spot the lump straight away, so it could have been growing for quite some time before she even went to the GP. Maybe he didn't realize quite how extensive it was.'

'Not impossible, then?'

I was getting cold so I moved on again. 'No, not impossible.'

She made me repeat myself. I lost her for a few seconds and then she was back again.

'Did you find anything on Stephen Gair?' I asked.

'I went to see him at home yesterday. Nice place. Met his new wife and a child they say is hers from a previous relationship.'

'Right,' I encouraged, not really sure where she was going.

'It's a little boy. Not quite two years old. Name's Connor Gair. Stephen's officially adopted him.'

'Nice. And . . .'

'Looks a lot like his new stepdad. And they seem very close.'

I couldn't see how that was remotely relevant. I had no interest in Stephen Gair's family life. I was a bit preoccupied thinking about my own – or lack of it.

'He has carrot-coloured hair, gorgeous fair skin

and very fine features. His mother, on the other hand, is quite dark.'

I thought for a moment. Light dawned. 'Blimey!' I said.

'Quite.'

She started crackling again so I told her, without being sure she could hear me, that I would phone her that evening. I carried on into Uyeasound, a scattering of buildings around a small, natural harbour.

I found the coffee shop easily enough. A couple of hikers sat at one of the tables; a man in a business suit at another. That left three tables free. I chose one and sat down. An elderly woman poked her head out of a door at the back of the room, glanced round, didn't appear to notice me and disappeared again. I pulled a biro out of my coat pocket and picked up one of the paper napkins on the table. I started to doodle. And think.

Connor Gair; a fair-skinned, two-year-old boy. Given my own preoccupation with babies, it's hardly surprising that since finding out that the murdered woman had given birth, I'd been wondering what had happened to her baby. Had the baby died too, I'd asked myself many times, or was it alive somewhere, oblivious to what had happened to its mother? Had Dana now found that baby?

Well, if Stephen Gair was bringing up his own son by Melissa but passing him off as the child of his new wife, he had to have been involved in Melissa's death. There was no getting round that one.

'Ye writin to da Trowie folk?'

I jumped. The waitress had returned and was looking down at the napkin. I'd drawn several of the runes I remembered from the standing stone.

'Oh,' I said, 'they're runes. From the standing stone up at Lunda Wick.'

She nodded. 'Aye, da Trowie marks.'

The Shetland dialect can be pretty strong and the locals aren't above exaggerating it a bit to perplex their visitors.

'Sorry, but what's Trowie?'

She grinned at me, showing bad teeth. Her once-fair skin had been burned red by the wind and her hair was like dead straw. She looked about sixty; she could have been anything from forty-five upwards. 'Da Trows,' she said. 'Da grey folk.'

It was a new one on me. 'I thought they were runes. Viking runes.'

She nodded and seemed to lose interest. 'Aye. Dey say dey came fra the Norse lands. What'll I get ye?'

I ordered a sandwich and coffee and she disappeared back into her kitchen. Trow, Trowie? I wrote it down, guessing at the spelling. I'd never heard the word before but it might well be significant. What I'd assumed were Viking runes, she'd called Trowie marks. Who were the Trows? And why would they carve their marks on Melissa's body?

I waited for her to come back but the café was filling up. When she brought my order, she plonked it down and turned to another table. I could come back later, when the café was quieter, or I could find a library. Now, that was a thought. I had access to the best library on Unst, one that specialized in island folklore and legend. Always assuming I could successfully navigate the librarian. I ate quickly, got up and paid my bill.

I was lucky; Richard was still out and Elspeth only too happy to be left alone all afternoon. By five o'clock, I knew more about the history of Shetland than I'd ever wanted to. I'd learned that Viking warriors had invaded in the eighth century, bringing with them the old pagan religions of Scandinavia. Christianity had arrived two hundred years later, but by that time the Norse pagan beliefs were deep rooted and had clung hard. As had the Nordic culture.

Though geographically closer to the coast of Scotland, the Shetland Isles had been part of a Norse earldom until the late fifteenth century. Even after the islands passed under Scottish rule, the sea continued to insulate them, preserving a whole store of tradition. The dialect was still heavily interspersed with old Norse words, many of which had been adapted and localized. The word Trow being a case in point.

Trow, I discovered, was an island corruption of the Scandinavian word *troll*. According to legend, when the Vikings had arrived for a spot of rape and pillage, they hadn't come alone – they'd brought the Trows. Most of the early references I found described the Trows as quite endearing creatures, albeit stomach-churningly ugly: cheerful, happy people, who lived in splendid caverns in the ground, were fond of good food, drink and music, but hated churches and anything connected to religion. Humans took care not to offend them on account of their supernatural abilities.

They had powers to charm and hypnotize, and liked to lure away humans, particularly children and pretty young women. They also had the gift of making themselves invisible, especially at night-time and at twilight. Strong sunlight, depending on which version of the stories you read, was either uncomfortable or fatal.

I found stories of Trows stealing into homes at night-time, to sit around the fireside and help themselves to household produce, tools or – their favourite – items fashioned from silver; and of islanders leaving gifts of fresh water and bread out for their Trowie visitors, like children leaving mince pies out for Santa Claus. I learned that Trows were powerless when confronted with iron.

It was all quite harmless, entertaining stuff. Until I got to the Unst versions of the stories. Then things took a decidedly darker turn.

Gletna Kirk, for example, not far from Uyeasound, had never been completed, thanks to the Trows. Any building work done on one day would be found strewn down the next. One night, irritated by the lack of progress, the officiating priest had stayed at the site to watch. He'd been found dead the next morning. His murderer was never found, the building work was abandoned and Trows had copped the blame.

I read that the numerous tiny hillocks around the islands were believed to be Trow graves, the creatures, it seemed, being particular about how they were buried. Trows believed that if their bodies didn't lie in 'sweet, dark earth', their souls would wander and turn malicious. Many Trows were buried together, preferring company, even in death. Even today, it was claimed, an islander, discovering disturbed ground on his land, wouldn't investigate, in case he uncovered a Trowie grave and set loose an evil spirit.

I am not remotely a superstitious person, but as I read that something cold pressed itself against my spine.

Other stories told of women seen out walking in the twilight, at the same time that they died peacefully in their beds at home. I read that whenever the Trows stole an object, they left in its place a perfect replica, known as a stock. When they stole a person, they left a semblance. I looked *semblance* up in a dictionary of folklore: 'A wraith-like creature,' it said, 'little more than a ghost, but bearing a strong physical resemblance to a human.' Richard's study lay on the eastern side of the house and, this late in the day, no sunlight found its way through the large bay windows. I realized that I was shivering.

In relation to Unst, I found no stories of mischievous, hobbit-like creatures. Instead, there were several brief references to the Kunal Trow, or King Trow: human in appearance but with great strength, unnatural long life and considerable supernatural powers, including that of hypnosis and the ability to make himself invisible.

In one book I looked at the Kunal Trows were described as a race of males, unable to beget female children. To reproduce, the Kunal Trows stole human women, leaving behind semblances in their place. Babies born of these unions were always strong, healthy sons. And yet nine days after giving birth, the mothers died.

I found several references to a book by a Scottish woman, who was generally considered to be the expert on the Unst Kunal Trow. I was sure Richard would have a copy of it but it wasn't anywhere obvious.

Well, it was all very interesting, but it wasn't getting me any closer to interpreting my runes or Trowie marks.

Earlier, I'd found a copy of the same book on runes that Dana had borrowed from Lerwick public library. I picked it up again and opened it at the preface.

Runes are the language of life: they heal, they bless, they bring wisdom; they do no harm.

I wondered what Melissa Gair might have said about that.

Richard had told me that one could find different interpretations of the runes. Dana and I had made no sense of the meanings offered in this book, but maybe Richard had others. I stood up and scanned the room. I'd seen district public libraries in London with fewer books. It was the largest room in the house and each of its walls was lined, floor to ceiling, with shelves fashioned of dark oak. The west wall contained his Shetland collection, including the works on myth and legend that I'd been skimming. The lower shelves were piled high with leather-covered box files, each one neatly labelled in Richard's tiny handwriting. The first one I looked inside contained several thin paperbacks on the Shetland dialect. I was nervous about rummaging through many more. It was one thing to be found in here looking at books. To be found going through boxes of papers was another matter. Then I saw it: a box at the bottom of a pile labelled *Runic Scripts and Alphabet*. At that moment the door opened.

I made myself turn round slowly and smile. Richard stood in the doorway. He only just made it into the room without ducking his head.

'Can I help you find something?' He'd been out walking and brought the smell of the moors with him. I noticed he was still wearing his outdoor boots and coat.

'Maybe something light,' I replied. 'In case I have trouble sleeping.'

'Mrs Gaskell is probably the closest thing to Mills and Boon I have,' he said. 'Or maybe Wilkie Collins; he's usually good for a cheap thrill.'

I stood up. 'Why did you never mention you worked at the Franklin Stone?'

He didn't flinch. 'Would you have been interested?'

I stared at him, more than ready for a fight. 'Did you get me my job? Did you put in a good word for me with your protégé?'

I watched him closely. 'No,' he said simply. I was sure he was lying.

'Why do Kenn Gifford and Duncan hate each other? What happened?'

His eyes narrowed. 'Kenn doesn't hate Duncan. I doubt he gives him much thought at all.' He shrugged, as if the matter was too trivial to be of interest. 'Duncan can be childish sometimes.'

His eyes left me and fixed on the pile of books I'd left on the carpet.

'My books are very carefully arranged. I find it difficult if someone displaces them. I'll be happy to find you anything you need.'

I bent down and picked up the scattered books.

'Leave them, please. Elspeth has made tea.' I knew he wasn't going to budge until I left, so I walked out.

22

THE NEXT MORNING, RICHARD LEFT EARLY. FOR a retired man, he spent a lot of time out of the house and I realized I had no idea where he went or what he did. Since the previous evening, though, we'd been distinctly frosty with each other and it didn't seem like a good time to ask. Shortly after breakfast, Elspeth left too on a shopping trip. She asked if I'd like to go with her but I truthfully pleaded a headache and tiredness and, after fussing a bit, she went. I waited for the sound of her car engine to fade and made straight for Richard's study, only to find the door locked.

I stood behind it for a moment, steaming. Then I ran upstairs. In my handbag I knew I'd find a few hairgrips. I grabbed four from the debris at the bottom and started bending them into shape.

I grew up with three brothers, all older than I, in a Wiltshire farmhouse three miles from the nearest village. After school they were my only companions. Consequently, I understand rugby, can keep score in cricket and explain the offside rule in soccer. I can name every bug and insect that crawls on British soil and can perform some pretty impressive stunts on a skateboard. I gleaned my early knowledge of sex from *Playboy* magazines and, coming to the point now, was pretty certain I could still pick a lock.

The lock was old, which helped. It was also a little loose in its casing, which didn't. It took me fifteen minutes. Inside the study, I went straight for the box file I'd noticed the evening before. It contained six copies of a magazine I'd never heard of: *Ancient Scripts and Symbols*, some photocopied pages from books and several dozen sheets of coarse paper, on which the runic symbols had been hand-drawn with explanatory paragraphs by each.

Three runic symbols had been carved into Melissa Gair. One was a streak of lightning, wasn't it? No – that was around the hearths. A kite – that was it – like a child's drawing of the bow on a kite string. I flicked through the sheets. There it was: Dagaz. The translation offered for its name was Harvest and its primary meanings were listed as Fruitfulness, Abundance, New Life. Harvest. Now why would someone carve that on a woman's body? Harvest is a medical term, used when an organ is removed for donation. Melissa's heart had been removed. Did Harvest refer to her heart – or to something else? I scanned through the pages, looking for other familiar symbols. I couldn't picture the second rune but the word *fish* kept springing to mind and after a moment or so I found an angular fish shape, called

Othila or Fertility. It was described as the symbol for Womanhood and Childbirth. Not too difficult to see the connection there.

The third rune had been simple, just two crossed lines. I found it: Nauthiz, or in English, Sacrifice. Its meanings were listed as Pain, Deprivation, Starvation.

I think I stared at the words for a very long time, long after they blurred over and I ceased to see them clearly. But if I closed my eyes they were still there. Pain. Deprivation. Starvation. What on earth was I dealing with here? And Sacrifice? What kind of monster carves words like those on a woman's body?

And what a difference. With Dana's library book, we'd interpreted the three runes as meaning Separation, Breakthrough and Constraint, and had seen little significance at all. According to Richard's script, though, the runes seemed decidedly more apt: Fertility – a woman able to bear children; Harvest – the new life emerging from her body; Sacrifice – the price she has to pay. I'd learned that the runic carvings on Melissa did have meaning and – very disturbingly – that my father-in-law knew about them and had chosen to keep quiet. I also realized Dana's library book hadn't been so far off. Constraint seemed to fit quite naturally in a group containing words like Sacrifice, Pain and Deprivation; likewise Breakthrough had connections to words like Harvest and New Life. It was just a question of where the focus and emphasis lay.

Something started niggling at me. There was more there if only I could see it; something new; something in the meaning of the words, something I was missing.

On a desk in a far corner stood a fax machine. I took the sheets of paper over to it, copied them and tucked them into the pocket of my jeans. Then I left the room, taking a few minutes to re-lock the door behind me.

I had to call Dana. She didn't answer her mobile or her home phone. Through directory enquiries I found the number of the Lerwick police station, but got her voicemail. While I was wondering what to do next, the phone rang. I answered and a male voice asked for Richard.

'It's McGill. Tell him his son's boat has been retrieved. It's down at my yard. I need to know what he wants me to do now.'

I promised to pass on the message and got the address of the boatyard. I'd put the receiver down before I realized it was really up to me to deal with it. The boat belonged to Duncan and me. *Duncan and me.* How much longer would I be able to say *Duncan and me*? I felt tears rushing up. No. Not now. I couldn't deal with it yet.

The boatyard man hadn't said whether it was a question of repair or scrap and I hadn't asked. I could go and look. Anything was better than hanging around with nothing to do and too much time to think.

I phoned Dana's voicemail again and explained

about the new runic meanings I'd found and about the local woman calling them the Trowie marks. Anxious not to run out of time on her answering system and speaking far too quickly, I ran through the various stories about trows and Kunal Trows and suggested she investigate any island cults with links to old legends. I left it at that, not mentioning Richard. It might be nothing more than bloody-mindedness on his part and, when it came to it, I was a bit reluctant to shop my husband's father.

Borrowing Elspeth's bicycle, I rode to Uyeasound and found the boatyard. A red-faced, red-haired islander in his late teens told me McGill had gone out for half an hour and led me inside the hangar where several boats, in various stages of repair or construction, were balanced on wooden piles. Our Laser lay against the wall in a far corner. A chunk of the bow was missing, the port side badly dented and scraped.

'You own this boat?' asked the lad.

I nodded.

He shifted from one foot to the other, looked at the boat, then at me. 'Insurance job, is it?'

I raised my head and looked at him. 'Sorry?'

He looked round at the wide double door, as if hoping help would come. It didn't; the two of us were alone.

'Are ye plannin' an insurance claim?' he muttered again.

'I suppose so,' I said. 'Why?'

‘Ye’d better see Mr McGill,’ he said, moving away from me.

‘Wait a minute,’ I called after him. ‘What’s the problem with an insurance claim?’

He paused, seemed to make up his mind, then walked back.

‘Thing is,’ he said, still without looking at me. ‘Thing is, I wouldn’t. We’ve had a lot just lately. Boat accidents. They always send someone. They investigate, you see, the insurance company. Find out what really happened.’

‘What do you mean?’ I said. ‘The mast broke.’

Then he gave me that half-pitying, half-amused look we all use when we know someone is lying to us. And they know that we know. And we know that they know that we know.

Except I didn’t.

I walked over to the boat. It was upturned but there was room to lift it and I did.

‘Hey!’ he shouted.

I shoved hard and it turned over. Now I was looking at the cockpit. Just an eight-inch stump remained where the mast had been. Most of the rigging was gone too but part of the main sail was still attached.

The boy was beside me now. He pointed to the mast stump. ‘You make an insurance claim and you’re going to end up in court,’ he said. ‘No one will believe that snapped. It was sawn through, to nearly halfway.’

23

I MADE IT BACK INTO TOWN AND HEADED OUT along the B9084, sick to the stomach at what I'd just learned. Our sailing accident had been nothing of the kind. The dinghy had been sabotaged. I remembered that my life jacket hadn't inflated and felt worse still. At the Belmont pier I had to wait the ten agonizing minutes it took for the ferry to arrive. All the while I was thinking, had I done the right thing? I had to get off Unst and this was the only way I knew. But they'd guess where I'd gone. They'd be waiting for me at the other dock.

The ferry arrived. The four waiting cars drove on and I followed. Two more cars arrived and I looked carefully at the occupants. No one I recognized. As the air filled with a pungent smell of diesel and the growl of the engines drowned out most other sounds, soft rain started to fall. I pulled my coat collar up and hunched forward, fixing my eyes on Yell, willing it to get closer and, at the same time, dreading the moment we arrived.

* * *

I had too much time to think, on that long and piecemeal journey back to the main island. Someone wanted me dead. I didn't need to ask why. I'd unearthed what was meant to stay hidden for all time. Had I left it at that, had I allowed the police to go through the motions of their investigation, I'd probably still be safe. But frustrated by their lack of progress, feeling an interest that was nothing short of personal, I'd interfered again and again. Without my search through the dental records, who would have dreamed of linking a mutilated corpse with a death from cancer? Without an identity the crime would never have been solved, but thanks to yours truly, someone had cause to fear. And now so did I.

From leaving the boatyard to arriving back on the main island, my thoughts remained resolutely self-centered. Then I remembered Dana. I stopped cycling and fumbled in pockets for my mobile. My brain was still functioning well enough to work out that I couldn't be the only one in danger, and that it wasn't just one potential assassin Dana and I had to worry about. In fact, the more I thought about it, the more it seemed a question not of who *was* involved but of who *wasn't*.

Something very dodgy had occurred when Melissa was admitted to hospital. Whatever Kenn Gifford claimed about being in New Zealand at the time, he still ran the place. He had to have been involved, but he couldn't have acted alone. The local police had gone through the motions of an investigation: from the start, Andy Dunn had gone out of his way to play down the murder, keep it out of the media, send Dana in the wrong direction. Stephen Gair had watched his wife die, had arranged her cremation, only to identify her body on a mortuary slab three years later. And, as I'd just discovered, someone on Unst had sawed through the dinghy's mast and sabotaged my life jacket. Just how many of them were there?

Not Dana, though. Dana had been as persistent and determined as I. If someone wanted me out of the way, she was a target too and I had to warn her. Trouble was, I didn't have my mobile. I'd left it at Richard and Elspeth's house.

I realized that I hadn't spoken to her since late yesterday morning. I'd tried and failed the previous evening to find her and again this morning. It hadn't worried me at the time but it was worrying me now.

Back on the main island I rode to Mossbank, a small town on the east coast where I had fifteen minutes to spare before the last bus of the day left. As I was folding up Elspeth's bicycle and tucking it into the luggage rack I caught a glimpse of a police car through the back window of the bus. The car was parked not twenty yards away and the driver, from what I could see, was closely watching the last passengers get on board.

The bus set off. For the first mile or so I couldn't help glancing behind every few minutes but there was no sign of the police car. After a while I started to relax and to feel, temporarily at least, safe. I didn't imagine even the most determined assassin would attack a dozen islanders on a public bus just to get at me. I was able to rest for an hour and eat a sandwich. By the time we arrived back in Lerwick I had the outline of a plan.

First, find Dana. I had to fill her in with what I'd learned since being on Unst and I had to warn her. Second, get off the islands. Go home briefly, collect clothes and important personal papers and get to the airport. Spend the night there if necessary but catch the first plane to London and then a train to Mum and Dad's house. Third, get some career-focused advice on what my options were. If I left the Franklin Stone now – claiming undue stress – what were my chances of getting a decent job? Four . . . I didn't really have a Four. Find a good divorce lawyer, maybe.

We pulled into Lerwick bus station just after four o'clock. I got off and unfolded the bicycle. And there was the police car again, tucked away behind another bus. Nothing I could do. I jumped on the bike and set off for Dana's house. I didn't have much hope of finding her there but, with any luck, my car would still be parked near by.

By the time I turned into the car park above Dana's house my neck was sore from the number of times I'd turned to check the road behind me, my chest was starting to feel tight and my head woozy. But I was cheered by the realization that Dana was home. Or at least, her car was. My own car was where I'd left it, and – I quickly checked – the keys were still in my coat pocket.

I left the bike leaning against my car and ran out of the car park, down a flight of steps and along a few steps of the lane. I banged on the door. The noise seemed to echo inside, as though the house was empty. I started to think that maybe I wasn't about to see Dana again after all. I banged again.

'Do you have keys?'

I spun round. I hadn't heard anyone approach but Andy Dunn was right behind me. Too close.

'I've been knocking for ten minutes,' he said. 'If she's in, she can't hear us. When did you last talk to her?'

I couldn't reply.

He took a step closer and put his hands on my shoulders. I wanted to shrug him off and run back up the path, leap into the car, on to the bicycle, anything, but I couldn't move.

'Miss Hamilton, are you OK? Do you need to sit down?'

I felt myself relax a little. 'I'm fine, thank you. I need to see Dana.'

He didn't ask why. He dropped his hands and turned to look at Dana's grey front door. Then he bent down, raised the cover of the letter box and peered inside.

'So do I,' he said. 'When did you last talk to her?'

I took a moment to remember. He rose and turned to me. He had very deep-set eyes, a dull blue in colour. The skin around them was coarse and deeply lined, heavily freckled. He looked as though he'd never been indoors in his life.

'Tora!' he said sharply.

'Yesterday morning,' I replied. 'I've left several messages.'

'Stand back,' he ordered. I did and then watched as he backed away for several paces then charged the door at a run. His shoulder connected and the door, which had seemed sturdy enough just seconds ago, buckled under the force and crashed inwards.

'Wait here.' He disappeared inside the house. I could feel reality slipping away from me again. I stood there for five, maybe six minutes. I was aware of sounds around me: children playing in a garden a little way further up the lane, a large ferry coming into harbour, DI Dunn moving swiftly through the downstairs rooms of Dana's house; also a rhythmic thumping noise, loud in my ears, that I couldn't place at the time but I think now must have been the sound of my own heartbeat.

Dunn ran upstairs. I heard doors slamming. Silence. I started to pray.

Then his footsteps, thudding down the stairs. He jumped the last three, strode across the small hallway and looked directly into my eyes. Much of the colour seemed to have drained from his face and there was sweat on his temples. For a second, maybe longer, he just stared at me. I don't remember seeing his lips move but I was sure I heard his voice anyway.

You can go upstairs now. Look in the bathroom.

I stepped into the house. I heard the click and crackle of a radio and Dunn's voice, urgent and unsteady, behind me. I started to climb the stairs, knowing where I had to go, what I'd find when I got there. There was a hiss of static and Dunn's voice again. I carried on climbing.

'Hey!' he yelled and then there were footsteps running back into the house. I'd reached the top of the stairs and had pushed open the bathroom door.

Footsteps, running up the stairs. Heavy breathing. Dunn was behind me, his hands on my shoulders again. 'What are you doing?' he said gently. 'Come on down.'

I tried to move forward but he held me back.

'You need to come downstairs.'

'I need to check for vitals.'

He must have seen some sense in that because he let me go. I took a step forward and leaned over the bathtub. I picked up Dana's left arm. It was pale and slender, like that of a child, and blood was no longer pumping from the three-inch gash that stretched diagonally across her wrist. Her skin felt cold but soft, so soft, like the smooth depression at the base of a baby's spine. I knew I would feel no pulse. I gently put her arm back down at her side and felt her neck. There was nothing there to find. Nothing to offer even the faintest glimmer of hope. One glance at her face had told me that, but I hadn't even needed to look at her face. I'd known. From the moment I'd hammered on the door of her house and heard emptiness inside, I'd known.

DI Dunn was holding me again and my field of

vision was blurring. I could no longer make out the tiled walls of Dana's bathroom, or the window ledge with its colourful glass sea-creatures, or the door. Just the white tub, Dana herself, like a beautiful statue, and the blood.

24

When I came round, my first thought was that I was still in the house and DI Dunn was leaning over me. Then I realized the eyes were more slate-grey than blue-grey and that the hair was dull blond with no hint of ginger.

'What time is it?' I managed.

Gifford looked at his watch. 'Eight twenty,' he replied.

'What did you give me?' I asked.

'Diazepam,' he said. 'You were pretty wired up when they brought you in. Had me worried for a while.' Diazepam is a mild sedative. If he was telling the truth I'd be woozy for a couple of hours but otherwise OK. I decided to put it to the test by sitting up. Harder than expected.

'Easy.' He wound the handle that lifts a hospital bed into a sitting position. Then he took hold of my wrist. I looked down in alarm but it was whole and unmarked. Gifford held it for half a minute while he checked my pulse. Then he took my blood pressure, shone a light into my eyes and held up several fingers for me to count. I waited until he'd finished and pronounced me OK; somewhere near the end of my tether, but basically sound.

'Where is she?' I asked.

He looked confused. 'Well, I imagine she's downstairs. Tora, promise me you won't—'

'I promise,' I said, meaning it. I had no intention of seeking out Dana. Dana had gone; somewhere I wasn't ready to follow.

'I'm so sorry,' said Gifford.

I didn't speak.

'I guess we never really know what's going on in someone else's head.'

'I guess not.'

'She was under a lot of stress. Had been unhappy for a long time.'

'I know. I just wish . . .'

'There was nothing you could have done. When suicides are determined, nothing will stop them. You know that.'

I nodded. I knew that.

'I spoke to Duncan. He's coming back but he can't get a plane before tomorrow morning.'

I looked at him. 'I might . . . I think I'll go to my parents for a few days. Will that be OK, do you think?'

Gifford took hold of my hand again. 'I'm sure it will,' he said. 'DI Dunn needs to speak to you. I told him to wait till morning. I'm keeping you here overnight.'

I nodded again. 'Thank you.'

Gifford wound my bed back down and I closed my eyes.

People tend not to warm to me. I don't know why, although heaven knows I've asked myself the question often enough over the years. What is it about me, exactly, that they find so unappealing? I can't work it out and no one's ever told me. All I know is that I've never found it particularly easy to make or keep friends.

I remember one incident from primary school: my class of eight-year-olds were exuberant that day and the teacher, Mrs Williams, was threatening that the worst offender would be moved to an empty single desk, right down at the front of the classroom. I was out of sorts, fed up with the yattering and fidgeting of the five other children on my table, so I stuck my hand in the air and asked to move. I'd meant that I wanted to go to the quiet desk but Mrs Williams misunderstood and thought I was asking to move elsewhere in the room. She asked me where I wanted to go; struck by the new possibilities, I looked around.

Across the classroom, a boy shouted that I should come and join his table. Then, one by one, most of the class took up the same cry. Everywhere I looked children were begging me to come and sit at their table. I guess they all got caught up by a sense of competition; I doubt if it was any genuine liking for me that was spurring them on, but I couldn't know that at the time. For several minutes I basked in the clamour before choosing a new spot and being enthusiastically welcomed by my new table-mates.

The incident sticks in my mind because it is the only occasion I can remember feeling valued by those around me. The only time I ever felt popular.

In secondary school I always seemed to find myself one of a threesome. I'd start out with a best friend and then, somewhere along the way, someone else would appear and our two would become three. Slowly but relentlessly, the interloper would spend more and more time with us until I couldn't ignore the fact that she was seeing more of my best friend than I was. Time and time again this happened, until I didn't know what it was like to have a best friend all of my own.

So I learned not to expect too much from other women. I went through medical school without getting particularly close to anyone. I wasn't a dork, spending every night in studying, and no one would have called me Norma No-Mates. But never that special someone, the one whom you absolutely have to speak to every couple of days, who will feed you chocolate and sympathy when your heart is breaking, whom you know will be maid of honour at your wedding and godmother to your first-born child.

I was startled by voices outside the door and I braced myself to feign sleep.

'At least she's on hand if she's needed,' said a voice, one I recognized as belonging to one of the student midwives.

'Can't see it happening,' said an older woman, whom I thought might be Jenny. 'I've never seen a healthier batch of babies. Must be something in the water this spring.'

The midwives moved on and I sank back into my pit of self-pity.

I'll say one thing for myself: I'm never pushy. I rarely take the initiative with girlfriends, always waiting to be phoned, for the other person to suggest getting together. I never complain when friendships start to cool, never grumble when the message pad is continually empty, when I see girls I know on jaunts to which I haven't been invited. I accept it as the norm, bottle up my loneliness and stick it on the shelf with the rest.

The point behind this self-indulgent rant is that with Dana, the whole process had begun again. Dana had gone from being someone I didn't much like to someone I trusted without question. More than that, I was starting to enjoy being with her. Gradually, over the past ten days, Dana had got a little closer to becoming a friend. Until, some time during the course of the day, while I'd been scurrying down the islands like a panic-stricken rabbit, she had lain down in a bath of her own blood.

I opened my eyes. Thank the Lord for chattering midwives. I knew what had been bothering me since that moment in Richard's study when I'd learned that one of the symbols on Melissa's body meant Harvest. I knew what I had to look for next.

I was in an ancillary private room attached to one

of my wards. I found my clothes and dressed quickly. It was a quarter to nine and the hospital would be quietening down for the night. I took a glance at the chart fixed to my bed. No medication had been prescribed for me during the night; with luck, I wouldn't be missed until morning. I opened the door. Three of the beds in the outer ward were occupied. One woman was sitting up, feeding. The other two appeared to be sleeping, their tiny appendages panting softly in transparent cots. Unnoticed, I walked slowly towards the door and out into the corridor.

I needed a computer but couldn't risk going to my office. In a room two doors down from my own I turned on the desk lamp and switched on the desktop. My password was still valid and after a couple of minutes I was in the system.

Batch was the word Jenny had used that had struck a chord with me while I lay in my room musing about friendship. I was looking for a batch.

25

IN RICHARD'S STUDY, I'D FOUND AN INTERPRETATION of Melissa's runes that had finally started to have some meaning. But one of them still hadn't made much sense. I could see where the . . . artist (shall we call him?) was coming from with Fertility and Sacrifice, but Harvest? In medical circles we use the word Harvest when we talk about an organ being removed for transplant and I'd toyed with the idea that it might refer to the missing heart. But really, what's the likelihood of an ancient cult using a modern medical term? The more I thought about it, the more likely it seemed that Harvest was a reference not to the heart, but to the baby.

Which brought me neatly to the next key question. Generally speaking, how often do you come across a harvest of one? Use the word *harvest* as a noun and it's decidedly plural in its implications, conjuring images of fruitfulness and plenty. And I already knew that at least one other young woman had met an untimely death in 2004, the year Melissa had supposedly died. Kirsten Hawick, who'd been hit by a lorry while out riding her horse, had been a similar age to Melissa and had been pretty similar in appearance. Plus, a wedding ring that was probably hers had been found in my field. I'd never truly accepted that as coincidence.

Melissa hadn't died and been cremated in 2004; her body, still in the morgue, offered irrefutable evidence of that. Whilst I couldn't begin to imagine how it had been achieved, her earlier death had to have been faked; so had the same thing happened to Kirsten and maybe other women as well?

Were there more bodies to be found?

The first thing I had to find out was how many female deaths were recorded in 2004 and I accessed the General Register Office for Shetland on the Internet. It wasn't the most user-friendly of sites but after a bit of poking around, I had it: a simple table, covering deaths that had occurred on Shetland, grouped in five-year age brackets, between 1983 and 2007.

In 2004, the year Melissa's and Kirsten's deaths had been recorded, there had been 106 female deaths on the islands. Scanning across the row I found that, as you would expect, the majority of them fell into the older age groups, from age 65 upwards. Down at the lower end of the scale, of course, deaths were far less common. In this particular year, no females had died aged between 0 and 19. In the 20–24 bracket though, five had. In the 25–30 bracket, three women had died and in the next one up, 30–34, four women had died. A total of twelve young women dead in one year.

Seemed like quite a lot to me.

I looked next at 2005. Only six women in the corresponding three age brackets had died. In 2006, there had been only four such deaths.

2006 was the latest year for which stats had been collected so I went back in time. In 2003, two women in the age range had died. 2002 had been a particularly good year for young women with no deaths recorded. 2001, on the other hand, recorded eleven deaths.

I went further back. 2000 had seen six mortalities, there were just two in 1999, but an impressive ten in 1998. 1997 saw a modest two, as did 1996, but – would you believe it – in 1995 eight women had met a premature end.

I went back as far as the table did, to 1983. I'm no statistician but even I could see a pattern emerging. Every three years a modest but significant blip appeared in the female death rates. Now, what the hell did that mean and, more importantly, why had no one spotted it before?

I looked again at the total column, to see if the pattern was reflected there. The number of total female deaths on Shetland ranged quite considerably from just 86 in 2003 to 154 in 1997. I looked for quite some time but there was no discernible three-year pattern that I could see; the spread of deaths, the difference in the numbers, appeared totally random. Whatever was going on in the three age groups representing young adult women was being hidden by the larger numbers involved in the female population as a whole. When you added male deaths into the equation, the chances of someone spotting what I'd just seen were non-existent.

Which might explain why no keen-eyed statistician at the General Register Office had spotted the anomaly. Taking the Shetland population as a whole, nothing was happening; and, when you considered that the death rate on Shetland is actually lower than the rest of Scotland, there'd be no reason for anyone to look more closely at the figures. The numbers were simply too small to show up on anything other than a very focused search.

I sat back to think about it.

I'd gone looking for one batch; I'd found seven. At least seven years in which the female death rate leaped way beyond the norm. If these figures were shown to someone in authority, surely they'd be enough to convince them that something odd was going on. Unfortunately, I had no idea whom to approach. Whilst I couldn't believe the entire Northern Constabulary was corrupt, without Dana how would I know whom to trust and whom not? More significantly, if some of these deaths were suspicious (or – not to put too fine a point on it – if they hadn't actually occurred), then how could some very senior people at this hospital not be involved? Could I rely on anyone to back me up? I decided I needed more details. Who were these dead women? How had they died? I'd start with

2004, the year Melissa had supposedly died.

I left the Internet, went into the hospital's own records and called up details of mortalities for 2004. There were 106 female deaths in total that year, out of which I was looking for just twelve. This was going to take some time and I was still woozy from the sedative Gifford had given me.

Fortunately, the list of mortalities included a name and a date of birth. It took about thirty minutes – of jumping out of my skin every time I heard a noise in the corridor – but eventually I had my list of twelve women, aged between 20 and 34, who died that year. I scribbled their names, ages and an abbreviated cause of death on a notepad I found on the desk.

Melissa Gair	32	breast cancer
Kirsten Hawick	29	riding accident
Heather Paterson	28	suicide
Kate Innes	23	breast cancer
Jacqueline Ross	33	eclampsia
Rachel Gibb	21	car accident
Joanna Buchan	24	drowning
Vivian Elrick	27	suicide
Olivia Birnie	33	heart disease
Laura Pendry	27	cervical cancer
Caitlin Corrigan	22	drowning
Phoebe Jones	20	suicide

I stared at the list for five, ten minutes, looking for anything out of the ordinary. There was nothing, really, except that there seemed too many of them.

Otherwise, the causes of death were exactly what you might expect. When young women die, it's usually as a result of an accident or deliberate self-harm. Other than that, you might expect a few cases of heart disease and cancer and, occasionally, problems associated with childbirth.

I looked back to my first list, the one I'd printed off the General Register site. A very crude calculation told me that when you removed the blip years from the equation, the average number of young women to die on Shetland each year was 3.1. Using just the blip years, the average leaped to ten. Every three years, six or seven more women than usual were dying.

Was it remotely possible to fake that number of deaths; to spirit these women away, keep them alive for a further year, before murdering them as brutally as Melissa had been murdered? And – big question coming up – had they, like Melissa, given birth shortly before death?

I turned back to the list of twelve women who'd died in 2004. Melissa and Kirsten hadn't died natural deaths, I was sure of that now. But which of the others had shared their fate? Vivian? Phoebe? Kate? Which of these women had been abducted, kept prisoner for the better part of a year, given birth alone and terrified? What had been their biggest fear at the end – fear for themselves or for what was going to happen to their babies?

A harvest of babies. At last I'd said it. It must have been bouncing around in the back of my mind ever since the post-mortem, when we'd learned that my lady from the peat had had a baby. What had happened to that baby, I'd asked myself immediately. In Richard's study, discovering that one of the runes meant Harvest had almost got me there but it had taken Jenny's passing comment about batches to give me the shove I needed.

OK, think, Tora, think. If these women were being abducted, they had to be kept somewhere; somewhere secure and out-of-the-way, but local all the same. They were buried here – in my backyard, for God's sake – so they couldn't have left the islands. It needed to be somewhere with medical facilities, where babies could be safely delivered. Jesus! It was obvious.

I started typing again and brought up the obs and gynae pages. I'd produced this list once before, the day after I'd found Melissa: the details of all births on the islands between March and August 2005 – the time Melissa's baby would have been born. I printed it off and sat looking at it, refreshing my memory. One hundred and forty births. According to Dana, most of the women named had been accounted for, found alive and well, but I already knew I was dealing with clever, impressively resourced people. If you could fake a death in a modern hospital, you could falsify pretty much anything.

I went down the list, marking entries as I went. Soon, every birth that had taken place on Tronal was highlighted in yellow. I was looking for six or seven; I found four. It was too few to suggest an easy answer; and yet Tronal was the ideal place: remote enough to offer privacy but accessible for those with their own boats and able to cope with the difficult navigation. It had a modern maternity facility and its own resident obstetrician. I realized, with a sinking heart, that it also had a qualified anaesthetist well within commuting distance.

Oh, Christ!

My father-in-law was involved in the facility on Tronal. He had to be; that was where he went when he left the house most days. I remembered what Stephen Renney had said about Melissa being heavily anaesthetized before she was killed and nausea reared. Richard had been Medical Director at the Franklin Stone before passing on the reins to his protégé, Kenn Gifford. If deaths were being faked at this hospital then the medical directors were ideally placed to oversee it happening.

Suddenly I was sure Richard was involved. Probably Kenn, too. And Dana and I had both had our doubts about Andy Dunn. One of them had watched Duncan and me set off in our dinghy, believing that I wouldn't survive the trip. They'd conspired to murder me. And they would try again.

I'd been staring down at the papers on the desk but a flickering of the screen made me look up. A message had flashed up.

AN ILLEGAL OPERATION HAS BEEN PERFORMED AND THE SYSTEM WILL BE CLOSED DOWN.

Then the screen went blank. I'd seen the message before. It might mean nothing. In any case, my time was up. I switched off the computer, gathered up the papers and grabbed my jacket from the back of the chair. The papers went into my pocket. I switched off the desk lamp and walked to the door.

Standing in darkness, listening hard, I could hear the usual hospital sounds, but all at a distance. The corridor outside was uncarpeted and I was sure I would have heard someone approaching. Risking it, I opened the door and glanced left and right. Voices. The door to my own office was open and I had to walk past it to get out. No use hanging around. Thanking my lucky stars I was wearing trainers and could move reasonably quietly, I walked quickly past my door, out through the swing doors at the end of the corridor and down the stairs. Praying I wouldn't bump into anyone I knew, I went out through A & E; not the route I'd have preferred as it was always the busiest part of the hospital, but it was the fastest way out. In the car park, I paused to think. It was nine fifty-five in the evening and I needed transport. Somehow, I had to get back to Dana's house to collect my car. I started to walk through the car park and then stopped. And almost laughed.

My car was parked in the area reserved for hospital staff. My keys were still in my pocket. Someone had even put Elspeth's bicycle in the back.

It was too late to leave the islands that night, but that part of the plan had changed anyway. I was going nowhere. I had more to find out and – priority for the morning – I was going to tell people I could trust. The one person I was going to find, somehow, was Helen. Dana's Helen. She was a high-ranking detective in Dundee. If Dana trusted her that was good enough for me.

First I needed some clothes and a sleeping bag, in case I ended up spending the night in my car. I parked a quarter of a mile down from the house, tucking the car away behind some garages. Then I pulled Elspeth's bicycle out of the back and cycled, in the late twilight, up the hill. I walked round the house once, peering into all the downstairs windows, but it seemed empty. As softly as I could, I turned the key and slipped inside. The mail lying behind the door scraped against the tiled floor. I closed the door and listened. Nothing. I was pretty sure the house was empty but I was jumpy all the same. I ran upstairs, found a holdall and threw some clothes into it. My sleeping bag was on top of the wardrobe and I grabbed a pillow from our bed for good measure. My jewellery, what little I possessed, went in the bag too. Last, I found Granddad's old horse gun and tucked it away under some clothes.

I stood in the doorway of our bedroom and it occurred to me that I might never see this room, this house again. It was only polite to leave a note.

On our dresser was a photograph of Duncan and me on our wedding day. He, tall and elegant in full morning dress, was kissing my hand at the door of the church. I was draped in cream lace and, for the only time in my life, looked feminine. I'd always loved that photograph. I picked it up, dropped it and stamped down hard with my right foot. The glass shattered and the wooden frame cracked at one corner. Should get the message across.

I struggled downstairs, not entirely sure how I would balance everything on the bike. The answer machine was flickering. Five messages. They could be important. I pressed play:

'Tora, this is Richard. It's just gone noon on Tuesday. Elspeth and I are concerned about you. Please call.'

Yeah, I'll bet you're concerned. I pressed erase.

'Tor, it's me. What's going on? I've been trying your mobile all day. Will you phone me, please?'

Erase.

'Tora, look – this really isn't funny. Everybody's worried about you. Just let us know you're OK . . . It's really difficult for me to get away at the moment. Jeez, Tora, just phone, will you?'

Erase.

'It's me again. I just heard about Dana. I'm so sorry, sweetheart. I'll be back tomorrow morning. Can you phone, please, just to let me know you're OK? . . . I love you.'

Well, call me a sucker if you like, but I couldn't erase that one. I pressed the button for the last message. New voice.

'Tora, this is a bad idea. You need to come back in now. I hope to God you're not driving. Let me know where you are and I'll come and pick you up.'

Like that was really going to happen. I pressed erase. It worried me though. If Kenn had told the local police I was driving around under the influence of sedative drugs I could expect to be picked up within minutes of leaving home.

I carried my stuff to the door and bent to pick up the mail. I was planning to dump it on the coffee table in the living room but one item caught my attention. It was a lilac envelope, with *Tora* handwritten on the front. There was no stamp and I could feel something heavy and hard inside. I opened it, took out a gold key and read the short note; the first I'd ever received from beyond the grave.

26

SOMEHOW I MANAGED TO FREEWHEEL ELSPETH'S bike back down the road to where my car was parked. I struggled to get my bags and the bike into the back and start the engine. I think it would have been tricky even if I hadn't been sobbing.

It started to rain as I set off back towards Lerwick. I couldn't stop crying. I thanked God it wasn't quite dark because I had to drive fast. They'd look for me on this road. Once I hit the edge of Lerwick it would be easier to hide. They'd never guess where I was going.

> *Tora* [Dana's note had said]
>
> *Just spoke to your mum-in-law. Is she always like that?*
>
> *Your message very helpful. Things are starting to come together.*
>
> *Assume you're heading back here. Don't stay home by yourself. Come to my house. Let yourself in and wait.*

Worried about you! Get in touch soon, please.
Dana

She'd put both the date and time of writing in the top corner. Twelve noon that day. I realized it would be crucial in establishing time of death and that I ought to hand it over to the police immediately. Knowing my luck, I'd have the opportunity some time in the next five minutes.

But no patrol cars pulled me over on the short drive back to Lerwick. Once I was off the highway I felt a bit safer. It took me a few more minutes to get to the Lanes and, driving past Dana's usual car park, I headed for the next one along.

The front door had been repaired – quick work, guys – but the key still worked. Dana's hallway seemed still, silent. I stood for a long moment, listening, and realized the house wasn't silent at all. Houses never are. I could hear faint gurgles of water heating up; a soft buzz of electronic equipment; even the ticking of a clock. Nothing to send my already racing pulse-rate into orbit. I'd brought a flashlight and, switching it on, I walked through the hall to the kitchen. The room was spotless. The floor looked freshly scrubbed, the stainless steel around the sink area was gleaming. Without really thinking what I was doing – maybe I was hungry and acting subconsciously – I crossed to the fridge and opened it.

Dana had been shopping. The salad tray was

full. A giant tub of apricots sat on one shelf, several wrapped Continental cheeses on another. Natural yoghurt by the bucketful. Two litres of skimmed milk, a litre of cranberry juice and a bottle of good white wine sat in the fridge door. Above them nestled a row of organic eggs. No meat or fish. Dana had been vegetarian.

I thought about eating but knew I couldn't. I closed the fridge door and left the kitchen. I had to go upstairs.

One step at a time, I retraced the last journey I'd made in this house, thinking, as we all do at such times, if only . . . If only I hadn't panicked on Unst; if only I'd gone back to Richard and Elspeth's house and stolen Elspeth's car instead of her bicycle, I'd have been back on the main island in a couple of hours, I could have been here before Dana . . .

The bathroom door was closed. I pulled my jacket up over my hand and pushed at it. Then I shone the flashlight all around.

Spotless.

The bath had been scrubbed. I remembered small pink splashes on the tiles from earlier in the day. They had gone. The ceramic tiles on the floor were clean but, as far as I could remember, they had been earlier. Dana had been as neat and clean in death as she had been in life. I backed out and pulled the door shut. There was nothing for me in here.

I walked past Dana's bedroom. I was heading for her spare room, where I'd slept briefly a few days earlier and which I knew doubled as a study.

Her desk was practically empty. I knew she kept her case notes in a pale-blue folder but there was no sign of it in the room. I pulled open the desk drawer and counted twenty folders in hanging files. Each was labelled in lilac ink on a buff-coloured card: House, Car, Investments, Pension, Travel, Insurance . . . and so on. I thought of the three battered box files at home that served as my own filing system. Maybe if she'd stayed around longer, Dana could have taught me to be tidy, to be organized. Maybe just a few hints.

I closed the drawer. I was probably wasting my time. Anything pertaining to the case would have been removed already by the police. I was sure I remembered a desk-top computer from my previous visit but it was gone now. Only a printer remained and a few trailing leads. And a pile of books stacked neatly to one side.

The top one caught my eye because I recognized the author. Wilkie Collins, I read, remembering Richard's taunt about Wilkie Collins being suitable for a retarded reader like myself. *The Woman in White.* I'd have dismissed it as Dana's bedtime reading, except it wasn't by her bed, and she'd marked several pages with little yellow Post-it notes. I picked it up.

Next in the pile was *Shetland Folklore* by James R. Nicholson. Again, some pages had been marked with Post-it notes. Then I found *British Folklore, Myths and Legends* by Marc Alexander. The title on thc bottom of the pile was familiar, although I hadn't seen a copy before. I flicked open the hardback cover and saw that it was a library book; very recently taken out judging by the return date stamped inside. It was the book that I'd found several references to in Richard's study, the one that might tell me more about the Kunal Trows. Dana had taken my comments about local cults seriously. The book held a lot of Post-it notes. I sat on the bed and started to read.

The first story to have caught Dana's attention was that of a macabre discovery of a large number of human bones during building work on Balta. Locals had muttered about an ancient burial ground but the bones (all from full-grown adults) had been discovered in no order, just flung together, and there had been no signs of memorial stones. On the accompanying Post-it, Dana had written: *Were bones female? Is story true? Can date be ascertained?*

On a later page I read about a rock that rises out of the sea near Papa Stour, known locally as the Frow Stack or the Maidens' Skerry. At the time the author was writing, the remains of a building could be seen on the rock. Local rumour held that the Frow Stack was used as a prison for women who 'misbehaved themselves'. Another rock, the Maiden Stack, with a very similar story attached to it, could be found on the east side of Shetland. Dana's commentary read: *Island stories of women being imprisoned. Any human remains found on either rock?*

A few pages further on and she'd found another story of unorthodox graves: a great number of small mounds on the island of Yell. The whole hillside, according to local tradition, was covered in graves and people avoided the spot. Dana's notes suggested increasing frustration. *When?* she had written. Dana had wanted facts and evidence, real leads she could follow up with meticulous police work. The book was only offering stories. Interesting stories, though. If the author was right, several times on these islands, hidden and unconsecrated mass graves had been discovered. I wondered how many more there might be. And I was growing more certain by the minute that Melissa had not lain alone on my land.

I lost all track of time as I read on through the books Dana had marked with Post-it notes, learning more and more about the strange and sometimes ghastly history of the islands. I found numerous other stories: of young women, children, even animals being stolen by Trows, their semblances left behind only to die shortly afterwards. The cynical amongst us would claim, of course, that the semblances were nothing of the kind, that the deaths had been of natural (or, more likely, human) causes and that the Trows had had nothing to do with it. One could argue, and half of me was tempted to, that the Trows had taken the blame for an awful lot of human mischief on these islands over the years. But still, the sheer number of stories impressed me. Over and over again, the same theme appeared: someone was taken, a semblance was left behind, the semblance died.

Of course, I didn't believe in semblances. If deaths had been faked in order to conceal kidnappings

– which was basically what all these stories boiled down to – then it had been achieved by natural means. I wasn't going down any supernatural route.

Trouble was, I wasn't going down any route. The words were starting to jump around on the page and I was done with thinking for one day. I put the book I was struggling to read down on the floor beside me and allowed my eyes to close.

In my dream, I closed the back door on Duncan and the sound of wood slamming into the door frame rang out around the house. I woke up. It hadn't been a dream. Someone had entered the house. Someone was moving around, softly but quite audibly, downstairs.

For a second I was back in the nightmare world of five nights ago. He'd come back. He'd found me. What the hell was I going to do? *Lie still, don't move, don't even breathe. He won't find you.*

Ridiculous. Whoever was here, he'd probably had the same idea I had. He was looking for something and soon his search would bring him to the place where Dana worked.

Hide.

I felt beneath me. The bed was a divan. There was no wardrobe in the room. Nowhere someone of my size could hope to go unnoticed. Especially if it was me he was looking for.

Escape.

Only sensible option, really. I sat up. My car keys

were on the desk. As I picked them up they chinked together.

I reached for the window. The handle wouldn't move. Of course Dana would lock her windows. She was a police officer. I looked closer. It was double-glazed. Breaking it might be possible but would make too much noise. I had to go down. Get past him somehow.

I reached into my holdall and rummaged around until I found the extra bit of protection I'd brought from home. Grasping it tightly in my right hand I walked to the door, pressed the handle softly and opened it. From downstairs came a faint bump. I crossed the hall, mentally blessing Dana for putting carpets on her stairs and landing. Downstairs were hardwood floors and ceramic tiles. But I still had to get downstairs.

At the top of the stairs I paused and listened. Faint sounds were coming from behind the closed kitchen door. I peered over the banister. There were two doors leading from Dana's kitchen, not counting the external back door: the first, the one I was looking at, led into the hall; the second into the living room. I was planning to go that way, throw something back into the hall to distract whoever it was and then, when he went to investigate, slip quietly through the kitchen and out the back door. Once outside I could climb the garden wall and run like hell back to the car.

Five more steps, six. My right hand was sticky with sweat. I checked the trigger. Loosened the safety catch.

The bottom step creaked.

I crossed the hall and into Dana's living room. It was darker than it should have been. Someone had pulled the curtains. I stopped. Listened. My right hand was up now, in front of me, but it was shaking.

Then something hit me square in the back and I went down hard.

27

I LAY ON THE FLOOR, THE SIDE OF MY HEAD PRESSED against Dana's oak floorboards, my right hand empty.

The weight pressing me down moved. I jabbed my elbow back hard and heard someone grunt. Then that solid weight was on me again. My right arm had been captured and was being twisted behind me. I squirmed and bucked and kicked backwards with both feet. My first three blows made contact and then the weight shifted forward.

'Police! Keep still!'

Yeah, right! One of the hands holding my right arm was released, presumably to grab a hold of my left hand and get cuffs on me. But he wasn't strong enough to hold me with one arm.

I took a large breath – tricky because with that weight on my chest my lungs could barely function – and twisted round. The figure on top of me slipped sideways. I was on my feet. So was my opponent. We stared at each other. In the darkness I could make out a tall figure; short, blond hair; neat, regular features. I resisted the temptation to say 'Dr Livingstone, I presume,' because I now knew who I'd been scrapping with.

'Who the hell are you?' she said.

'Tora Hamilton,' I answered. 'A friend of Dana's. She gave me a key.'

It occurred to me that that might not have been the wisest response, but the woman seemed to relax.

'I work at the hospital,' I added. 'I've been helping Dana with one of her cases. The murder. The body was found in my field. I found her.'

I stopped gabbling.

The woman nodded her head. 'She told me.'

I was breathing normally again. My head was sore but had stopped spinning.

'I'm truly, truly sorry,' I said, hearing my voice crack.

Detective Chief Inspector Helen Rowley stared at me for a long time. I could hear the central-heating system creaking as it cooled down for the night. Outside a dog barked.

'Can you believe she killed herself?' she asked me, so softly I could barely make out the words. She wasn't really expecting an answer, but I'd spent the better part of eight hours waiting, longing, to be given the chance to say what I said next.

'Not for a fraction of a second have I believed she did that.'

Helen's eyes glinted in surprise, then narrowed

as she caught up with me. 'What are you talking about?' she whispered.

'Have you seen the fridge?' I asked, the first thing that came into my head. 'You think Dana would stock a fridge hours before taking her own life?'

If anything, the stare intensified. She didn't believe me. And she was quickly becoming angry. But I was already there. Helen was supposed to know Dana better than anyone. Why was it up to me to convince her of the blindingly obvious?

'If Dana – the Dana I knew – had planned to kill herself she'd have emptied her fridge, put the contents in the bin, wheeled it down to the bottom of the drive and then cleaned the fridge with Dettol,' I said, with a bitterness I knew was unfair but couldn't help. 'Oh, and she'd have taken back her library books as well.'

Helen took a step back and fumbled against the wall. The room filled with light and I could see her properly. She wore a padded green jacket and baggy combat-style trousers. She was tall, almost my height, and her hair wasn't short, it was pulled back in a plait. She was attractive. Not pretty, exactly, but with a clean jaw-line and brown eyes. I realized with a jolt of surprise that she looked quite a lot like me. She looked round and then sank on to one of Dana's sofas.

I made myself keep quiet for a few seconds. I had so much to say, I didn't trust myself to get it all out coherently. When I thought I could speak without blithering, I continued:

'About four years ago, I spent some time working with suicides. Failed suicides, of course, tricky to talk to the ones who . . . well, they have various reasons, come from various circumstances, but they have one thing in common.'

Helen had curled herself forward, arms crossed in front of her body, hands gripping her upper arms. She spoke to the rug at her feet. 'What's that? Despair?'

'I guess. But the word I was going to use was emptiness. These people look into their future and they see nothing. They believe they have nothing to live for and so they don't.'

She looked at me. 'And that wasn't Dana?'

Forcing myself to speak slowly, I leaned closer. 'No way was it Dana. There was just too much going on in her life. She was determined to get to the bottom of this case . . . furious at the lack of cooperation she was getting. I've spoken to her several times over the last few days. She was fine – worried, angry, edgy – but definitely not empty. She wrote a note to me this morning. I'll show it to you; it's upstairs somewhere. It's not the note of a suicide. Dana was not a suicide.'

'They told me she'd been struggling to fit in, not relating to her colleagues, missing her old force . . . missing me.' Her voice was unsteady.

'Probably all true. But not nearly enough.'

'She phoned me yesterday evening. She was worried, she wanted my help, but you're right, she didn't sound . . .'

We were still, for a while, and silent. I was

wondering whether I should offer to make tea when she spoke again.

'This house is so like her. She could make homes beautiful. Her flat in Dundee was the same. You should see my place. Total mess.'

'Mine too,' I agreed, but inside I was getting edgy again. My relief at finding Helen was giving way to anxiety. Sooner or later I was going to be found. I would be taken down to the station – ostensibly to make a statement – and find myself stuck there for as long as they chose to keep me. I'd thought I needed Helen but I didn't need her grieving and helpless. I wanted her functioning.

'What the hell is that?' she said.

I followed her gaze along the floor. 'A humane killer,' I said. 'For putting horses down.'

For a second I thought she was going to laugh.

'Jesus,' she said. 'Is it legal?'

I shrugged. 'Used to be. Back in the 1950s.'

'Mind if I put it somewhere safe?'

'Be my guest.'

She stood up, retrieved the gun and put it on the top of a dresser. When she faced me again, the skin around her eyes was blotched pink but I could see she was a long way from breaking down.

'Did you kill her?' she asked.

I felt my mouth drop open but I was totally incapable of replying. Whatever she saw made her relax, even half smile.

'Sorry. Had to ask. So who did?'

'I'm not sure. But probably not one person acting

alone. And it was almost certainly connected to the case she was investigating. I think Dana was close to finding something out. Me too. I think someone tried to kill me, a couple of days ago.'

I told her about the sailing accident, about my discovering the sawn-off mast. When I'd finished she was silent. Then she stood up and walked across the room. She stood in front of a picture I hadn't noticed before, a small pencil-drawing of a terrier surrounded by high-heeled, female legs. I had no idea whether she believed me or thought me a total fruitcake.

'I was going to contact you in the morning. To ask you to help me,' I said.

She turned round again and her face had hardened, just fractionally.

'Help you how?'

'Well, stay safe for one thing. But also to find out what's going on up here and who killed Dana.'

She shook her head. 'You need to let the police handle that.'

I jumped to my feet. 'No! That's just it. The police will not handle it. Dana knew that. That's why she didn't trust her colleagues, found it hard to work with them. There is something very, very wrong up here and somehow the police are involved.'

She lowered herself back on to the sofa. 'I'm listening,' she said.

I sat down too. 'This is going to sound a bit weird,' I began.

* * *

Twenty minutes later I finished. A glance at the clock told me it was a quarter past midnight. Helen got up and left the room. I could hear her rustling about in the kitchen. After a minute or two she came back with two glasses of white wine.

'You were right,' she said. 'That did sound weird.'

I gave her a shrug and a goofy half-smile. Well, I had warned her.

'Trolls?' she said, giving me an *are you serious?* look.

I sipped my wine. It was good; crisp and clean, very cold. 'Well, no. Not real trolls. Obviously not real trolls. But some sort of cult that's based on an old island legend.'

'People who think they're trolls?'

She was wasting my time. I stood up.

'Sit down,' she barked. 'Dana didn't think you were an idiot and I'm going to give you the benefit of the doubt.' She glanced up towards the dresser. 'In spite of some evidence to the contrary.'

I scowled, like a teenager who'd just been ticked off. Helen was looking through notes she'd made while I'd been talking and didn't see my expression. I sat back down again.

'OK, I need to put Shetland folklore on one side for a moment and concentrate on what we know,' she went on. 'You dug up a body in your field that has since been positively identified as that of Melissa Gair. She'd been dead about two years, and shortly before her death she'd had a baby.'

I nodded.

'Reasonably straightforward so far, if a bit gruesome. The complication comes because Melissa Gair is supposed to have died almost a year earlier. We have a woman who died twice. The earlier death was well documented and witnessed and, on paper at least, is hard to disprove. The second death has the edge, of course, because it has a body to back it up.' She stopped to take a sip of her wine.

'Bit of a tricky one,' I agreed.

'You're telling me. Now, because of certain markings on the body, and because of a ring found in your field, you started to think that more than one woman might have been murdered.'

I nodded again.

'So, you looked up mortality statistics on the islands.' She bent down and picked up the notes I'd made at the hospital. 'If your figures are correct . . .'

'They are,' I interrupted. She frowned at me.

'If they're right, they indicate – I admit – a definite pattern. Every three years, the death rate among young females does seem to increase. OK, now we move from fact on to theory. You theorize that a number of these women . . .'

'Around six every three years.'

'Right. A number of these women were abducted. Their deaths were faked – in a busy, modern hospital – and they were held somewhere against their will for a whole year.' She looked down again. 'Your best guess is this island called Tronal. During that time they were . . . impregnated?' She grimaced. So did I.

'Or they could have been in the early stages of

pregnancy when they were taken,' I said. 'Like Melissa was. There are just so many stories on these islands about young women, pregnant women and children being abducted, about human bones being discovered. God, this place has more mass graves than Bosnia.'

'Umm. And these crimes are being committed by grey-clad men who live in underground caverns, love music and silver and fear anything made of iron?'

I said nothing, just glared.

'OK,' she said at last, 'back to the missing women. You think while they were being held prisoner they had babies. Then they were killed. Their bodies were brought back to the mainland and buried in your field.'

Helen stopped.

'Yes,' I said. 'That's what I think happened.'

She said nothing.

'It's exactly like the legend,' I rushed on. 'The Kunal Trows steal human wives. Nine days after their sons are born – it's always a son because they're a race of males – the mothers die.'

'Tora . . .'

'Melissa Gair was killed between a week to ten days after giving birth.'

'Whoa, whoa . . . Is it remotely possible to fake death in a hospital? Really?'

'Not so long ago, I'd have said definitely not. Now, I think it could be.'

'How?'

'Quite a lot of people would have to be involved:

several of the medical staff, maybe an administrator, definitely the pathologist. I'm not sure you could fool a trained medic, but a layman, especially a distressed relative . . . if there was a lot of fuss, plenty of distractions . . . and if the patient was very still, maybe heavily drugged into a coma-like state.'

Helen was whirling the wine round in her glass, staring at the patterns it made. She was giving nothing away but I sensed she was listening.

'And I think they use hypnosis,' I went on, thinking what the hell, in for a penny . . .

She stopped twirling. 'Hypnosis?' she said. Seeing the look on her face, only the fact that she hadn't already clapped me in handcuffs and phoned her colleagues gave me the courage to go on.

'Hypnosis isn't hokum,' I said quickly. 'It's been scientifically proven. Plenty of psychiatrists practise it. You can alter someone's perception by planting ideas in their head. I think it just possible that a grieving relative could be shown an apparently lifeless body and be led to believe that person was dead.'

Helen was silent. Then her head started to shake. She wasn't buying it.

'All the stories I've read emphasize the Trows' ability to hypnotize people.'

'They're just stories.' She looked incredulous. As well she might. But she hadn't been in my shoes for the last ten days.

'I don't think so any more. I'm sure my boss at the hospital can do it. There was an incident a short while ago with my horse. He put me in some sort of trance; made me do exactly what he told me. And I think he's done it a couple of times at work too. He puts his hands on my shoulders, looks me in the eye and talks to me. And my mood just changes. I feel calm and happy to do whatever he says.'

Helen's head was still now, but I couldn't tell whether she was convinced or not. 'And there are drugs that can do what you said – make someone look dead?'

'Absolutely. Just about any sedative, if you take enough of it, will drop the blood pressure so low that finding a peripheral pulse would be all but impossible. It's risky, of course; you could easily give the patient too much and end up killing them. But a skilled anaesthetist would probably manage it.'

I gave her time to think about it. And I thought about the skilled anaesthetist I knew.

'How much of this did you discuss with Dana?' she asked.

'I didn't get chance. But I left messages. I told her about the Trow legends. And I know she took me seriously because she has all the books upstairs. She didn't say anything to you when she called?'

Helen sighed and took another gulp of wine. It was arguable which of us was drinking fastest. We needed to slow down. I, especially, needed to slow down.

'No,' she said. 'She wanted to see me. I could tell she was worried. She didn't want to talk on the phone.'

'She learned too much,' I said, wondering if I'd

ever be able to deal with that knowledge. Because of me, because of the messages I'd left her, Dana got too close to whatever was going on up here. She'd paid the ultimate price for my meddling.

As if sensing my thoughts, Helen put a hand on my shoulder. 'I'm not dismissing the stats you found, but I'm struggling with this Trow business. We still only have one body. Let's work with that, shall we?' She stood up. 'Come on, let's see what Dana has to say about all this.'

I looked up at her stupidly. What was she planning, a séance?

'Let's go and check her computer. I know her passwords.'

I shook my head. 'Her desk is empty. The police took it.'

'Oh, you think?' she said, and turned to go up-stairs.

28

IN THE MAIN BEDROOM HELEN HOPPED UP ON TO A chair in front of the large oak wardrobes and opened the middle of three cupboards that ran along the top. Then she handed down a small canvas suitcase trimmed with red leather. Something large slid around inside. She pulled open the zip and took out a small laptop computer that I recognized immediately.

Helen grinned at me but there was no light in her eyes.

'The desktop belonged to the Force. This was her own. Dana always copied everything important. Really sensitive stuff she only ever put on here.'

She carried it through to the spare room and fiddled around with leads for a few seconds before opening the laptop. The screen sprang to life. I glanced towards the window. The blind was drawn but I was sure traces of light would be seen outside.

Helen was already busying her way through

Dana's filing system but I was too edgy to sit down and join her.

'Helen.'

She looked up.

'You should know the police are almost certainly looking for me.'

She leaned back in her chair and raised her eyebrows. It was such a Dana-like gesture that I didn't know whether to smile or sob.

'They want to question me about what happened here today – I mean yesterday. I sort of checked myself out of hospital earlier. Unofficially.'

'Do they know you have a key to this house?'

I shook my head.

'They'll probably work it out. We need to get a move on.'

I joined her at the computer. We were looking at a list of files, each one numbered.

'Dana gave her cases different numbers from the official ones,' Helen explained. She was clicking on the bottom of the pile, where the more recent cases were likely to be.

'She was strong on security,' I said, remembering Kenn Gifford's comments about Dana's paranoia.

'She was right to be,' snapped Helen. 'The average nick would make a sieve look watertight. Here we go.'

Case number Xcr56381 opened up. It was a folder containing a number of files. As I scanned down the list something heavy and cold started to grow in my chest.

The first file was named *Missing Persons*. Sub-files covered *Shetland, Orkney, Scotland* and *UK*. The second file was named *Babies*. Sub-files were called *Franklin Stone Deliveries*, and *Tronal Deliveries*. Then came *Financial Records*. In that section was a series of names: some I didn't recognize, several I did. *Andrew Dunn, Kenn Gifford, Richard Guthrie, Duncan Guthrie, Tora Hamilton*. Not Stephen Gair, though; he had a file section all to himself, with a sub-file for his firm, *Gair, Carter, Gow*.

'Spouse is always the first suspect,' said Helen, opening up the files on Gair. 'Dana wouldn't neglect the basics.'

There were a few personal details; his education, early years practising; the dates of his two marriages, to Melissa in 1999 and then to an Alison Jenner in 2005. Most of it, though, was work related.

We looked first at a summary of information about Gair's firm of solicitors: Gair, Carter, Gow, based in Lerwick but with offices in Oban and Stirling. Most of their business seemed to come from handling commercial contracts for the larger local oil and shipping companies. I noticed, with a pang of alarm, that Gair acted for Duncan's company and, with no real surprise, that they were legal advisers to the hospital. They also had departments that dealt with family law, conveyancing and trust and probate.

A pulse behind my left temple was threatening to become painful as we slowly ploughed through page after page of statements from the First National Bank of Scotland. Gair, Carter, Gow had numerous accounts. Each of its three branches had both a commercial account and a deposit account; after a few minutes it was clear the firm held substantial reserves. There were also six client accounts, sorted according to type of client.

'How the hell did Dana get all this stuff?' I asked. 'I can't believe Stephen Gair just handed it over. Could she have got a warrant this quickly?'

'Unlikely,' said Helen, without looking up.

'So . . . how?'

'Best not to ask,' said Helen. She closed down one client account and opened up another. Then she paused and looked at me. 'Let's just say Dana wasn't as strong on procedure as she was on security. In fact it was her unorthodox approach that got her transferred from Manchester to Dundee a few years ago. I was told to keep an eye on her, make her see the error of her ways. Needless to say, I failed.'

'She got all this illegally?'

'Almost certainly. There's very little Dana didn't know about computers. She did her Ph.D. in software creation. She had a particular expertise when it came to hacking into financial institutions.'

'How? How did she do it?'

Helen sighed. 'Tora, I don't know. I really didn't like to ask too much. But my guess is that when she moved here, she would have opened accounts for herself in every bank and financial institution based on the island. She'd have visited them frequently, getting to know the staff, copying down account numbers and sort codes. She'd have tried to work out passwords by watching people type on their keyboards. When she was at your house, did you ever notice her looking at private papers?'

'Yes,' I said, remembering a time I'd seen her staring at our kitchen noticeboard where we pin our most recent bank and credit-card statements.

'She had an amazing memory for numbers. And given how much she knew about writing software, she'd have known how to bypass most security systems.'

Well, Dana the villain. Who would have thought it?

'But,' I was struggling with my knowledge of the law, 'if information is obtained illegally, doesn't it jeopardize an investigation?'

'Only if you try and use it. Which Dana would never have done. Once she knew what was going on, she'd have found proof using normal routes. OK, look, Dana has put several flags on this one client. Shiller Drilling. Heard of them?'

'Vaguely. I think it's one of the larger oil companies.'

Helen was looking at one of Gair, Carter, Gow's client accounts for the previous financial year. Dana had flagged numerous entries, all relating to Shiller Drilling.

'Law firms have to keep separate client accounts by law, you know that?' asked Helen. 'Any money the firm handles but which belongs to a client has to be kept separate from the firm's own money.'

I must have looked a bit stupid because she took a deep breath and tried again.

'If you buy a house, you hand over money to your solicitor. He keeps it in his client account until it's time to pay it to the vendor. It's supposed to ensure transparency and accountability.'

I nodded. 'This money we're looking at – it belongs to clients, to Shiller Drilling, for example, not to Gair, Carter, Gow.'

'Exactly. Looks to me like Shiller Drilling were realizing quite a lot of assets that year. Look . . .'

Helen pointed out the first three entries that Dana had highlighted.

11 April TRF
Shiller Drilling sale: Minnesot.ranchland $75,000.00

15 June TRF
Shiller Drilling sale: Boston.prop $150,000.00

23 June TRF
Shiller Drilling sale: Dubai.seafront $90,000.00

There were more; too many to count at a glance, all apparently relating to income from land and property sales. At the bottom of the sheet, Dana had written a footnote.

NB: Total year's incomings re Shiller Drilling – $9.075 million US dollars, £5.5 million sterling (current exchange rate). Cross Reference 3.

Helen called up the search facility and typed in 'Cross Reference 3'. It took a couple of seconds and then another page of figures filled the screen. Helen flicked to the bottom of the page. 'Manganate Minerals Inc. Annual Report and Accounts.' Dana had cross-referenced Gair, Carter, Gow's client account with the annual report of a . . . mineral company?

Helen drummed her fingers on the desk. Then she flicked the screen back up.

'Of course. Manganate whatsit is a group holding company. Shiller Drilling is part of the group.'

She was right. Shiller Drilling was there, tucked away in the left-hand column, headed 'Income from Property and Land Sales'. Helen traced her finger horizontally across the screen. According to the annual report, Shiller Drilling had sold $4.54 million of land and property that year. Helen immediately flicked to another icon and opened up a calculator. She pressed a few keys and grinned at me. I was having trouble following. The calculator was showing 2,751,515.

'And what would you expect that to be?' Helen asked.

I was catching up slowly. 'Five and a half million?' I ventured, remembering the note Dana had made at the bottom of Gair, Carter, Gow's bank statement. 'It should be five and a half million pounds sterling.'

'Clever girl,' said Helen. All traces of her weariness seemed to have vanished. 'So, Gair, Carter, Gow's client account shows some two and three-quarter million pounds of income from overseas land and property sales that does not appear on the client company's annual report. So where is that money really coming from?'

'Different accounting period?'

She looked at me sharply.

'Good point. So if it's just a discrepancy of accounting periods, you would expect to find the missing millions . . . where, exactly?'

I thought for a second. 'The previous accounting period? Or maybe the subsequent one?'

She nodded. 'I can't believe Dana didn't have those.' She started flicking again and in a few seconds we had bank statements for the same client account for the previous financial year. Another footnote from Dana:

NB: Total year's incomings re Shiller Drilling – $10.065 million US dollars, £6.1 million sterling (current exchange rate). Cross Reference 2.

Putting 'Cross Reference 2' into the search facility took us to another of Manganate's annual reports and Helen, with the aid of the calculator, converted US dollars to pounds sterling. Again, the annual report showed substantially less income from overseas land and property sales than did the solicitors' client account.

We did it once more. Dana had gone back just three years. The story was the same. Several million pounds a year were coming into the Gair, Carter, Gow's client account ascribed to overseas land and property sales on the part of Shiller Drilling, but a cross check with the holding company's annual reports left a good portion of the millions unaccounted for.

'Did she ever sleep?' I muttered, mainly to myself.

'Not much,' said Helen. 'She rarely went to bed before one or two in the morning. Couldn't switch her brain off.'

I was looking down the columns of numbers and text notes. The law firm's statement showed debit as well as credit entries; as sales of land and property were completed, the proceeds were transferred into client bank accounts, most of which were referenced by name.

'Any point adding up all the debits to Shiller Drilling?' I asked. 'See what they amount to?'

'Can't hurt,' said Helen. 'I need to pee.'

Helen got up and I scanned the debit column, noting all the entries relating to Shiller Drilling. And spotted something. Not all the debits to Shiller Drilling had the same bank account reference. The money was being directed to two different accounts. I made a note of the reference number of each.

The lavatory flushed and I heard Helen going downstairs. I really wanted to know what information Dana had on Duncan, Richard, Andy Dunn and Kenn, not to mention on me. I hovered the curser over Duncan's name for a second, then opened the file on Andy Dunn and went straight to his bank account. Helen returned carrying two glasses of water.

'He likes to live well,' she muttered, sitting down beside me. The same thing had occurred to me too.

Substantial payments went out each month: to a car leasing company, a wine merchant, overseas flights. The size of his monthly mortgage payments made me blink.

'What would an inspector earn up here?' I asked.

'Not that much,' said Helen, who suddenly looked deadly serious. 'And where's that coming from?' She was pointing to a credit entry for £5,000. We flicked back through the months. There were several entries for similarly substantial sums. Each carried a reference number, presumably of the bank account that the money had been transferred from. As my heart-rate speeded up a fraction, I scribbled it down. CK0012946170. I'd seen that number before, I was sure of it.

'Hang on a minute,' I said, grabbing the mouse from Helen. I went back to the Gair, Carter, Gow's client account, scrolled through until I found the right place and then pointed my finger at the screen.

'Look,' I said, 'I thought I recognized it. It's the same number.' There it was, CK0012946170. The first two letters had struck me. CK had made me think of Calvin Klein. We checked the column of figures. There were twelve transfers from the Gair, Carter, Gow client account to the CK reference number, spread throughout the course of the year, totalling some two and a half million pounds.

'This isn't good,' said Helen to herself.

'Am I following this?' I said. 'We have unaccounted-for millions coming in from overseas. Stephen Gair is directing a good proportion of them to this bank account and then Andy Dunn is getting a monthly payout from it.'

'Looks that way,' said Helen. 'Shit!' She looked at her watch. 'Shit,' she said again.

Helen was starting to take me seriously. Which should have made me feel better. But she was also looking worried. She'd obviously just realized what I'd known for some time. The last flights had left hours ago. No way off the islands until morning.

'You should check Gifford,' I said. 'If there's stuff going on at the hospital, he has to be involved.'

She nodded and took the mouse back.

'Spartan,' she said, opening up the file on Kenn Gifford. She was right. I'd rarely seen an account statement as short or as simple as the one I was looking at. The salary came in monthly – substantially more than mine, even allowing for the seniority of his position – and then two-thirds of it went out again to a savings account. He took out a largish sum in cash each month and that was it; no standing orders, direct debits or monthly payments of any kind – well, just the one: £1,000 came into his account regularly every month: reference number CK0012946170.

'How long ago did you leave the hospital?' Helen asked me.

'About four hours,' I said.

'Shit, we need to get out of here.' She made no move to get up though, but flicked open the file on Richard Guthrie and went straight to his current bank account. Dana had flagged two entries: the first a credit payment of £2,000 from the same numbered bank account that Gifford and Dunn were receiving money from; the second another incoming payment of £2,000, referenced *Tronal Med Salary*. I'd been right. Richard Guthrie was still practising: at the Tronal Maternity Clinic. A quick flick through the months showed the two entries were repeated on a monthly basis.

'I really need to check your husband out,' said Helen.

'I know.'

She opened up Duncan's file and I found myself crossing my fingers. Dana had produced a brief biography of his university and career and had found a few press cuttings about his new company. And she had his bank accounts, both business and personal.

It was as though the air had grown thinner in Dana's small study. I was suddenly finding it harder to breathe. I watched as Helen flicked through the pages, seeing the same entry repeated month after month: £1,000. Guess the reference number.

Helen looked at me, put her hand on my shoulder. 'Are you OK?' she asked. I nodded, although I was far from OK. I wasn't looking at the screen any more.

'There's something else,' she said. 'Late last year. Does this mean anything to you?'

She pointed to an entry in early December. A huge sum of money, hundreds of thousands of pounds, had come into Duncan's account from the CK bank account before going out again just days later – to

Gair, Carter, Gow's client account.

'We bought the house the first week in December,' I said. 'That's how much we paid.'

'Looks like Stephen Gair handled the sale,' said Helen.

'Duncan told me the money came from a trust fund,' I said.

'Your husband uses a telephone bank,' she said in a gentle voice, as though dealing with an invalid. 'Do you know his security details?'

I thought about it, started to shake my head, then thought some more. He'd never actually told me, but I'd heard him on the phone to the bank dozens of times. His memorable date was 12 September 1974, my birthday; and his memorable address was 10 Rillington Place, a sick joke that only he found funny. I knew his mother's maiden name, McClare; it was only his password I would struggle with. But, thinking hard, I knew several of the letters. It contained a P, a Y, an S and an O. I wrote them down. Passwords need to be memorable, so people choose names of things or people they like. I ran through the names of family members, best mates from university, even pets, but came up with nothing.

'What does he enjoy doing?' said Helen.

'Plays squash,' I managed.

'Famous squash players,' she said.

'There aren't any. It's pointless anyway, they'll never believe I'm Duncan Guthrie.'

'Lower your voice.'

I dropped it an octave. 'They'll never believe I'm

Duncan Guthrie,' I said in a ridiculous imitation of a man.

'Speed it up and hold your nose, like you have a cold.'

'Oh for God's sake, you do it. You're supposed to have the monopoly on butch around here!'

Helen exhaled through her nose, like a mother at the end of her patience with a particularly tiresome toddler.

'Osprey,' I said, realizing my little outburst had made me feel better. 'His first boat was an Osprey. That's it.'

'Ready to have a go?' she said, picking up the phone.

I shook my head. 'I don't know.'

'We really need to know exactly where that money is coming from.'

I took the phone from her and dialled the number of the bank. When I gave Duncan's name the girl queried me immediately and I thought the game was up. I turned away from the phone, faked a sneeze and then turned back.

'Sorry, 'scuse me. Yes, Duncan Guthrie.'

'From your password, Mr Guthrie, can I take letter number three?'

Fifteen seconds later I was through security. 'I've been going through my account; first time for months, to be honest, and there are things in there I can't remember setting up.' I broke off to fake a fit of coughing. 'I was wondering if you could just explain some of the entries for me?'

'Certainly, what are you unsure about?'

I quoted a number and an amount. There was a moment's silence while she checked.

'That one is a monthly direct debit to Body Max Gym and Personal Training, Mr Guthrie. Do you want to cancel it?'

'No, no, that's fine. Must start using that gym. But I've also got myself a bit confused about some of the monthly retainers I get from clients. There's one referenced CK0012946170. Can you confirm where that comes from . . . ?'

Another short pause. 'That payment is referenced from the Tronal Maternity Clinic.'

I said nothing. The seconds ticked by.

'Mr Guthrie? Is there anything else I can help you with?'

'What?' hissed Helen beside me. 'What is it?'

'No. Thank you, that's great. Thank you very much for your help.'

I put the phone down. 'Tronal,' I said. 'It's all about Tronal.'

Helen's eyes flickered over my shoulder to the window. She jumped up, crossed the room and stood looking out. Then she leaned over to the wall, switched out the light and went back to the window. I didn't like what I could see on her face. I got up too. Dana's study looked down towards the harbour. Three police cars had pulled up just below us on Commercial Street, lights flickering but sirens turned off. As we watched a fourth car joined them.

'Can't help thinking that's something to do with you,' said Helen.

'Arrest me.'

'What?'

'Arrest me. If I'm in your custody they can't do anything.'

She took her eyes from the window for a second. Almost seemed to be thinking about it, then gave a slight shake of her head.

'We're on their patch. It won't work.'

'If you leave me with them, they'll kill me. Like they killed Dana. It will look like an accident, maybe suicide, but it will be them. I hope you remember that.'

'Get a grip!' Helen pushed past me, back to the desk. She shut down the computer programme and folded up the laptop. Then looked over her shoulder.

'Do you have a car?'

I nodded and she led the way as we fled the house. We went out through the back door, just as we heard hammering on the front. She locked the door, glanced around the small walled garden and set off. I followed. When we reached the top, Helen climbed on to a large terracotta planter and peered over the wall into the next garden. Then she leaped up, scrambled for a few seconds and disappeared.

'Swing the bag over,' she ordered softly. I did so, then climbed over myself. I wasn't as stealthy as Helen but a couple of seconds later I was on the same side of the wall. We set off, heading uphill in the direction of the car park, but the only way out of the second garden was via the lane where the police would be waiting. The wall was lower in this garden, and at the top we were able to hide behind a lilac bush and look over. Three uniformed constables, a man in a brown leather jacket and another, much taller man whom I was pretty certain was Andy Dunn all waited outside Dana's front door. As we watched, one of the constables ran at the door and it buckled inwards for the second time that day. The police disappeared inside the house; Helen and I leaped over the wall, ran up the lane, climbed a short flight of steps then ducked left through a stone archway into the car park. We ran to my car and climbed inside.

I was pulling out of the car park when in my rear-view mirror I saw lights flick on upstairs in Dana's house.

29

'THEY'LL EXPECT US TO HEAD FOR THE AIRPORT,' said Helen. 'They'll be watching the road south.'

She was right, and even if we made it to Sumburgh, we could hardly just park and wait for the first plane. Well before daybreak, the people who were looking for me would have every airport, every ferry port covered.

My stomach churned. Helen was a good ally to have: she was gutsy, intelligent and not easily intimidated; but I didn't think even she could hold out against the entire Northern Constabulary for long once they found us. And finding us would be the easiest thing in the world. There are just so few roads on Shetland; disappearing into a complicated labyrinth of back streets was simply not an option. If we were to avoid being picked up in the next hour we had to get off the roads.

'I can't get a helicopter out here until morning,' she said. 'What time is dawn?'

'About five a.m.,' I replied. In summer I often rose that early to ride my horses before work. Now, there was a thought. Helen was drumming her fists against the dashboard, obviously thinking hard.

'Tora, listen,' she said after a second. 'I can't start flinging accusations around about a senior police officer without a lot more proof than we have already. We need more time.' She looked at her watch. 'It's almost two,' she said. 'Can you hide us for three hours?'

I thought of going home: not good, practically the first place they'd look. I thought of going back to the hospital: plenty of quiet areas this time of night but I'd almost certainly be recognized. I thought of cruising downtown Lerwick, looking for an all-night café or even a nightclub: potentially quite a good idea, except I was pretty sure there weren't any. Helen and I couldn't hide amongst people; there simply weren't enough of them on Shetland.

'Can you ride?' I asked.

Fifteen minutes later I was parking, for the second time that night, some way down the hill from our house. Charles and Henry heard us coming and trotted over to the fence. A few Polo mints each and they were perfectly amenable to being tacked up. I was a bit anxious about Charles's leg; dealing with a lame horse in the middle of nowhere wasn't a prospect I relished, but it seemed to be healing well and as long as we took it easy it should hold up.

Dana's laptop, the books from her desk, our

money and Helen's mobile went into two saddlebags; everything else we had to leave behind. I helped Helen on to Henry then climbed on to Charles. The horses were excited about the prospect of a moonlight outing and skittered about. Helen sat rigid, her knuckles white against the reins. As we set off I felt a pang of misgiving; riding at night isn't a British Horse Society recommended activity, especially over rough ground with a barely sound horse and an inexperienced rider.

Our property is on the hill above Tresta and I was able to guide us through a field and out of the village before we turned on to the main road; which was probably just as well, because I don't think I'd ever appreciated what a racket the hoofs of two large horses make on a tarmac surface. Fortunately, Charles was walking well forward, excited about his first real exercise in a week, but setting a good pace that Henry was happy to follow. I wanted to trot, to get off the road as quickly as I could, but I didn't dare risk it until Helen felt a bit more confident. I could hear her swearing softly to herself as Henry's hoofs slid on smooth tarmac or clattered against loose stones.

As we moved east from Tresta we lost much of our light. The moon disappeared behind a cloud and the hills seemed to close in around us. We reached the point where the road is cut through the rock of the hills. Neither Helen nor I had much night vision yet and even the horses were struggling. I've always hated the feeling when a hoof slides along the road and a quarter of the horse sinks beneath you, and I had a pretty good idea of what Helen must be going through.

We rounded a bend and to our left the hill became a cliff, towering above us. To our right, the land fell away, down towards Weisdale Voe, one of the biggest of the mainland water inlets. In the daylight, this was a well-known beauty spot; at night, without the richness of colour or the sharp contrast of light playing on land and water, the landscape looked empty and unfinished. The rocks were dark and alien; barren, as though incapable of supporting life. In spite of the twinkling lights down at the water's edge the land around us felt hostile.

As we walked on, I tried to make sense of what we'd discovered in the last couple of hours. Following Dana's lead, we'd found what appeared to be an illegal money trail: huge sums entering Stephen Gair's business accounts from unknown sources, much of it being forwarded to a Tronal account, only to be distributed again to prominent men on the islands; including my own husband. Where was all that money coming from? What sort of activity could generate such large amounts? And was there any possibility that we'd misinterpreted what we'd seen? That Duncan, Richard, even Kenn, weren't involved in Melissa's and Dana's deaths.

Half a mile on, I heard what I'd been dreading: the sound of a car. I pulled Charles tightly into the side of the road and behind me Henry, rather than Helen, did the same thing. I could see lights ahead. Charles started to fidget and I tightened the reins. 'Steady,' I muttered. 'Hold him steady,' I called over my shoulder. The car was almost level with us, we heard the sudden loss of acceleration as the driver saw us and moved his foot towards the brake. The car didn't stop but continued its way out west.

A quick word to reassure Helen and we were off again. Soon we reached the point where we could turn off on to a smaller road. Now we were heading almost due north along the B9075 to Weisdale. The chances of meeting a speeding car reduced, but not those of being heard and recognized. We had to get through the village quickly and I was going to risk a trot. Checking that Helen's stirrups were short enough, I reminded her to keep her heels down and tighten up contact on the reins. Then I encouraged Charles forward.

Henry drew level with us. I glanced over and gave Helen what I hoped would be an encouraging smile. She was rising to the trot, but rather overdoing it and missing a few beats. She'd ridden a bit, she'd said, but wasn't up to jumping or galloping. She was a hell of a trouper, though.

'Where are we going?' she asked, having to shout above the sound of the hoofs. It was a good sign that she felt relaxed enough to talk.

'We're heading north through the Kergord valley to Voe,' I answered. 'A friend of mine has a couple of horses there. She'll keep these two in her field until I can arrange to have them collected.'

'Is there road all the way?' she asked hopefully. We

were passing Weisdale Mill and I could see light in the house next to it.

'No. We've got about half a mile of this road and then a farm track for another three-quarters. Then we're in open country.'

There was silence while she considered the implications of riding across country in the dark.

'Have you ridden this way before?'

I nodded. There seemed little point adding that on the one occasion I'd done it previously, it had been in daylight, with perfectly sound horses and an experienced local guide.

'How long will it take?'

'Couple of hours.'

'We should have brought food.'

I too was starving. I didn't want to think about when I'd last eaten. Except once I started I couldn't help it. About twelve hours ago, I reckoned: a chicken and mayonnaise sandwich on the bus. I was regretting my squeamishness over Dana's fridge.

Ahead of us reared dark shapes, rare enough in this landscape to seem strange. They were trees: the Kergord plantations, covering about eight to nine acres in total and possibly the only woodlands on Shetland; certainly the only ones I'd ever seen.

The sound we were making changed from the clatter of hoofs on a track to the crunching of dead leaves. Last time I'd ridden this way, my guide had told me how in late spring the woodland carpet is covered with tiny yellow celandines. I tried to make them out but the cloud and the tree cover made it impossible. A flapping and cawing above us made both horses jump. Rooks whirled in the sky, scolding us for waking them.

We'd reached the farm track and I slowed the horses to a walk as we were forced to navigate around a cattle grid. The brief trot had settled them and their pace was steadier.

The horses walked on and the hills rose up around us, casting their shadows across the valley as the night grew darker. I felt panic rising again and told myself to calm down. Horses had been used for transport at night for hundreds of years. Charles and Henry could deal with this, and so could I.

After a few minutes I judged Helen was relaxed enough to talk again.

'Well, I guess millions of pounds don't usually appear from nowhere without something dodgy going on. Any idea what?'

Helen risked taking her eyes off the path ahead. 'I've been thinking about that,' she said. 'I wonder if they're selling babies. Maybe to wealthy couples from overseas, countries where private adoption is the norm and money changes hands. Most of the money we saw seemed to be coming from the United States.'

The same thought had occurred to me, but, knowing what I did about Tronal, it didn't seem possible. 'According to the records, only about eight babies are born there every year,' I said. 'They'd need more, wouldn't they, to generate that sort of income? And what about the babies who are supposed to be adopted locally? Where are they coming from?

'Eight babies, huh? A maternity clinic on a private island for eight babies a year? Seem likely to you?'

'No,' I said; that had never seemed even remotely likely.

We'd reached the end of the farm track. We had to go past a few farm buildings and we'd be in open country. At that moment the front door to the farmhouse was flung open and a man appeared. He was short and substantially overweight, close to seventy years old and dressed in a torn string vest and baggy grey jogging pants that hung low on his hips. His feet were bare and I guessed he'd risen from bed too quickly to find his spectacles; he was scowling and squinting, as though struggling to see us properly. A fact that caused me no small level of disquiet, given that he was staring at us down the barrel of a twelve-bore shotgun.

30

I WAS BROUGHT UP IN THE COUNTRY, MY FATHER AND brothers were members of the local shoot, I'm even quite handy with a shotgun myself and I know the damage one of those things can do at close range.

It was a tense moment.

Helen held her right hand out in front of her. For a second, I thought it was a gesture of surrender.

'Police. Put your weapon down immediately, sir.' She was holding out her ID. Slowly, I dug my hand into my jacket pocket, found my hospital ID and brought it out. I held it up, confident that Jogging Pants would never be able to make out the details.

Far from sure, he lowered his shotgun. 'What's going on?'

'Night patrol, sir,' said Helen. 'Now, I need you to put your weapon on the ground. Right now, sir. Aiming a weapon at a police officer is a very serious offence.'

I had to bite my lip. Night patrol! He seemed to be

buying it, though. His knees buckled under him and his shotgun slipped to the ground. With an effort, he straightened up.

'Will I just be phoning the local station?' he muttered.

'Certainly, sir,' said Helen. 'They'll need you to go in to sign a statement, so you may prefer to leave it till morning. And you should take in your shotgun licence. They'll need to check the serial number.'

I loved this woman. Although shotgun licences could be obtained reasonably easily, it was common knowledge that numerous farmers hadn't bothered.

'We'll be on our way now, sir. I'm sorry to have disturbed you. Please give my apologies to your family. Sergeant, will you get the gate?'

I rode forward, jumped down and pushed open the gate that led from the farmyard into the valley. Helen rode past without looking at me. I pushed the gate shut and jumped back into the saddle. I trotted forward to catch up and we walked in silence until I judged we were out of earshot. Looking back, I saw that Jogging Pants had gone inside and closed the door but the light still shone from an upstairs window. As I watched, it flicked off.

'You couldn't have made me an inspector?' I asked.

She glanced over and seemed to force a smile. 'Night patrol,' she said. 'Oh God, Dana would've loved that.'

And then she crumpled, from the top down. First her face collapsed, then her shoulders sagged forward, then she fell until she was leaning against Henry's mane. Her body jerked in great, racking sobs and she began making the sound you only ever hear from someone suffering the deepest grief: a primitive noise, halfway between a howl and a scream. Henry shuddered in protest. Charles, the more highly strung of the two, whinnied and started to jump sideways. I steadied him and, leaning over, took Helen's reins from her hands and pulled them forwards over Henry's head. We walked on, I leading Henry, as Helen's sobs gradually grew softer and less insistent. After a while she was quiet. I glanced back; she was wiping her face on her sleeve. She looked like she'd aged ten years.

'Sorry,' she muttered.

'No, I'm sorry. I shouldn't be putting you through this. You can't possibly be up to it.'

She straightened in the saddle. 'Was Dana murdered yesterday?'

I thought very carefully before I answered her. I wasn't playing at Nancy Drew any more. This was real and very, very serious. 'Yes,' I said, 'I think she was.'

'I'm up to it. Can I have my reins back?'

We walked on for a few minutes. On either side the hills loomed high above us, deep shadows against a charcoal sky. We were about as far from the sea as it is possible to get on Shetland – which isn't far, three or four miles at most – but it seemed the landscape had changed when we entered the valley: the scents became those of land rather than sea, the musty dampness of peat, the ripeness of fresh vegetation. The wind had lost some of its ferocity, just buffeting us gently every few minutes, lest we get complacent.

Every now and again the moon appeared from behind a cloud and in its light the ground sparkled as though showered with broken glass. We were walking over flints gripped tight by the land, and they shone around us in the moonlight.

We came to the first of several streams that we had to cross. As I urged Charles over, he tugged his head forward and bent to drink. Henry copied him.

'Is this water drinkable?' asked Helen.

I was pretty parched too. The wine I'd drunk earlier had had its usual dehydrating effect.

'Well, these two seem to think so,' I said, jumping down. Helen followed suit and the four of us drank the ice-cold, slightly peaty-flavoured water. Helen washed her face; I splashed copious amounts over my head and felt better immediately. Still starving hungry, though.

Out of the corner of my eye I saw something moving towards us; something too large to be a sheep. I cried out, every nerve-ending in my body prickling. Helen was beside me in a second. Then we both relaxed. The one shape had become several and they were all heading our way. They were a dozen or more native Shetland ponies. I'd forgotten this valley was home to a large herd.

Horses are immensely social creatures and the herd, spotting two strangers of their own kind, had come up to say hello. They seemed not remotely perturbed at finding two humans as well. Two of the bolder ones started nuzzling my legs; one even allowed Helen to bend down and pet her.

'You know it could catch on,' I said, watching Henry rub muzzles with a grey mare that could only have been nine hands high.

'What could?' said Helen.

'Mounted police on the Shetlands,' I said. 'There's a whole mass of terrain that's totally inaccessible by road and no shortage of native livestock.'

'Worth thinking about,' agreed Helen. 'Course the mounties would have to be midgets.'

'You'd need to rethink the height rule.'

'Maybe special dispensation for Shetland. How many of these ponies do you have up here?'

'Not sure anyone knows. They breed like rabbits, apparently. A lot are sold – to pet centres, model farms, that sort of place. And as children's mounts. They're incredibly popular. Exported all over the wor—' I stopped, realizing what I was saying.

'Like Shetland babies?' asked Helen.

'Possibly,' I said, 'except . . .'

'Where are they all coming from?' she prompted.

I nodded.

Helen frowned, appeared to think for a moment. 'Let's just say there are more babies being born there than appear on your register,' she said at last. 'Let's say that Stephen Gair, Andy Dunn, Kenn Gifford . . . all the men whose records we checked earlier . . .'

'It's OK,' I interrupted. 'You're allowed to mention Duncan and Richard.'

She gave me a half smile. 'Suppose they are involved, making a whole packet of money from it, and somehow Melissa Gair found out, threatened to go to the police. That would be motive enough, wouldn't it, to get her out of the way?'

'I guess.'

'But why not just kill her, stage an accident? Why fake her death and keep her alive for so long?'

'Because Stephen Gair knew she was pregnant. He wanted his child.' I explained Dana's theory about the boy Stephen Gair called his stepson being, in fact, his own son by Melissa. Helen seemed to shrink a little inside herself at the mention of Dana, but managed to hold it together.

'Hell of a risk,' she said. 'And why cut out her heart? Why those weird symbols on her back? Why bury her in your field, for God's sake? Why not just dump her out at sea?'

'Because they have to be buried in sweet, dark earth,' I whispered, not really intending that she should hear.

She gave me a look. 'Are we back to trolls again? I can't do trolls right now. We need to get moving.'

She gathered up her reins and lifted her foot to the stirrup. She was mounting from the wrong side but I didn't say anything. Henry would probably go with it. Then she stopped.

'Do you want me to hold him?' I offered.

'Shut up,' she hissed. 'Listen.'

I listened. Soft whinnying from the ponies, gentle slurping as several of them drank, whistling of the wind down from the hill tops. And something else. Something low, regular, mechanical. Not a sound of nature. Something insistent; something approaching.

'Shit!' Helen threw the reins forward over Henry's head and started pulling him towards a steep overhang of rock at the valley's edge.

'Come on,' she urged. The noise was getting louder. The ponies could hear it now and didn't like it. Several of them kept breaking away from the group, sprinting off and then back again. Helen had reached the outcrop. I made it a few seconds later. We backed close to the rock, pulling the horses up against us. We held their heads and tried to keep them still as we waited for the helicopter to approach.

'The farmer phoned the police after all,' I whispered, as though people in a helicopter still half a mile away could hear us.

'More likely they found your car,' said Helen. 'Does everyone know you have horses?'

I thought about it. Duncan, of course, would know immediately that the horses were missing, but he was off the islands. Gifford! Gifford knew. And Dunn, of course. In fact, pretty much the entire Shetland police force. Richard. Yes, just about everyone knew I had horses.

The helicopter was close now and we could see the searchlight, a huge beam of brightness lighting up the valley. I tightened my hold on Charles. The Shetlands, seeking security in numbers, had all followed us to the overhang. Unlike Charles and Henry, though, they were far from still: they pushed and bustled each other, jumping around and squabbling in their efforts to stay as close as possible to the bigger horses.

'Skit! Scram! Get out of here!' hissed Helen. 'Little buggers are going to draw attention to us.'

The chopper was directly above us now. The cascade of light was alien, terrifying in its intensity, illuminating the landscape in a ghostly parody of daylight. Outside the light, though, all appeared pitch black, unnaturally dark for Shetland, and for the moment the dark cloak covered us.

The helicopter passed overhead. I held my breath, hardly daring to hope. It travelled maybe half a mile to the north and then swung a 180-degree turn and headed back towards us.

'They've seen us,' I whispered again. I couldn't help it; it was instinctive to keep my voice low.

'They've seen something,' said Helen. 'Stay still.'

This time the chopper wasn't lighting up the centre of the valley but had shifted twenty metres or so to the west; a small but crucial adjustment, given that this time the searchlight could hardly miss us.

'I should have untacked the horses when we first heard it,' I said. 'No one would think twice about finding two untacked horses out here. Without them, we could have hidden behind rocks.'

Helen shook her head. 'They'll have surveillance equipment,' she said. 'They'll be able to spot body heat. Actually, these little tykes might just save the day.'

The Shetlands seemed to fear the light more

than the noise. As it grew closer they broke cover, scattering across the valley, seeking the safety of darkness. The chopper swerved and followed them just as the light touched on Henry's brown tail. The dominant stallion set off south at a gallop, most of the herd veering round to follow him, and, like a new recruit, the chopper went too, increasing the panic among the scared little animals. The herd turned, so did the chopper. It began to circle; the light edged closer. A mare and her foal that had stayed with us broke away at this point and the helicopter circled again. It rose higher in the sky and moved north. It turned back but this time kept clear of our rock overhang and headed north again.

Charles and Henry started to fidget but Helen and I hardly dared move as the noise of the helicopter's engines faded.

'I can't believe we got away with that,' I said, when it felt safe to breathe again.

'They saw movement and probably body heat but assumed it was the ponies. God bless them.'

The ponies had calmed down but were staying clear of us.

'Will they come back?' I asked.

Helen shook her head. 'Impossible to say. They've got a lot of terrain to cover. I think we need to get moving. We'll hear them if they head back.'

We mounted and set off again. The tension of the last few minutes seemed to have sapped me of energy. It was all I could do to point Charles in the right direction and urge him forward.

'How much further do we have to go?' asked Helen.

I looked at my watch. It was coming up for three a.m. The incident with the helicopter had slowed us down.

'Another forty-five minutes,' I guessed.

'Christ, my ass is sore.'

'Wait till tomorrow. You won't be able to walk.'

At that moment the world around us changed.

We'd been travelling through a landscape of black and grey shadows, of cliffs topped with scrubby remnants of vegetation, silhouetted against a deep indigo sky. Of subtle hues there was an endless variety, of real colour there was none.

And then a great draper in the sky unleashed a roll of finest green silk; it hung in the air, several miles high, stretching as far as we could see, shifting and gleaming, changing constantly, giving off and reflecting back a light that was all its own. The sky grew blacker around it. Trees and rock formations were thrown into harsh relief as the draper shook his cloth, the silken sky rippled, and shades of pale green I'd never dreamed of danced before us.

The horses stood, frozen to the spot.

'Oh my God,' whispered Helen. 'What is it?'

From the north-west came a soundless explosion of colour, as though heaven had thrown open a window, allowing awestruck mortals below a glimpse of the treasures beyond. Cascading down came beams of silvery green, of a rich deep violet, and of the warmest, softest, rosiest pink you could imagine; it was the colour of love, of girlish dreams, of a warm and happy future that I would probably never know. It was colour so incredibly rich, and yet so fine that through it we could still see the stars.

And so we joined the ranks of the few privileged souls who, thanks to a lucky coincidence of time, geography and atmospheric conditions, have been permitted to glimpse the Aurora Borealis.

'The Northern Lights,' I said.

Silence.

'Wow!' said Helen.

'Doesn't nearly come close,' I agreed.

Silence again.

'How?' she said. 'How does it happen?'

I took a deep breath, ready to reel off a lengthy and extremely tedious explanation of charged particles from the sun colliding with atoms of oxygen and nitrogen. Then I changed my mind.

'The Inuits called them gifts from the dead,' I said. Then, surprised at my own daring, let alone the sentimental depths to which my normally cynical nature could plummet, I added, 'I think Dana sent them.'

Helen and I watched the lights glimmer and ripple for a further ten minutes before fading. We lost more time but it didn't seem to matter. We had gained strength.

'Thank you,' whispered Helen, and I knew she wasn't talking to me.

* * *

Shortly before three thirty we arrived at my friend's livery yard in Voe. The stable-block was empty but I could see her two horses peering at us from a nearby field. I slid off Charles and ran my hands over his injured leg. It had held up but he was going to need a few days rest. I found buckets and gave both horses a long drink and an armful of hay. Then I untacked them, released them into the field and carried the saddles and bridles over to the tack room. The key was where I expected to find it, beneath an earthenware flower tub.

My friend's tack room doubles as an office and there was a phone line. I pointed it out to Helen, closed the door behind us and headed straight for a drawer in the desk. I was in luck. Half a packet of Jaffa cakes, a nearly full box of Maltesers and three tubes of Polo mints. I divided the bounty and we ate ravenously for five minutes. Feeling slightly better but still sore and weary, we plugged in Dana's laptop.

31

THERE WAS ONLY ROOM FOR ONE AT MY FRIEND'S cramped desk so Helen took the chair and I lowered myself on to a straw bale and leaned against the stone wall of the tack room. I didn't think I'd ever been on a less comfortable seat, but I knew I could be asleep in seconds if I allowed my eyes to close. From the saddlebag I retrieved Dana's copy of *The Woman in White*. As I did so, several folded sheets of A4 paper fell out of it.

At the desk Helen broke off typing to cough and then spit into her hand. She caught me looking at her.

'Bloody Maltesers are covered in hairs,' she grumbled before resuming typing.

'Dog hairs if you're lucky, horse hairs if you're not,' I muttered.

''Scuse me?' she said, her fingers still tapping away.

'Something my dad used to say at mealtimes,' I said. 'I grew up on a farm. With horses. Food hygiene wasn't something we worried too much about.'

'If I find another I'll pass it your way. What are you doing?'

'Staring vacantly at a sheet of paper, hoping the words might come into focus some time before dawn,' I answered.

'You should sleep,' she said. 'You should probably still be in hospital.' She leaned to one side and spat again, less delicately this time. 'Shit, what is this?'

'You eat a pound of muck before you die,' I said.

This time she let her hands fall on to her lap and turned round to me. 'What?'

'Dad again. He got it from his dad. It's called a Wiltshire Wisdom. When I was young, I took it literally – you know, imagined that when I'd eaten exactly my pound of muck, that would be it – curtains – even if I was only seven and healthy as a horse. It terrified me for a while. I used to scrub fruit till I bruised it. One time I even tried to use bleach on a biscuit I dropped on the floor.'

Helen was staring at me. I dropped my eyes to the floor, feeling ridiculous.

'Are you OK?' she asked tentatively, as though not too sure she could deal with an honest answer.

I nodded without looking up.

'You're allowed to have a good howl. I did.'

I bit my lip, took a deep breath. 'Not sure I'd be able to stop,' I managed after a second or two. Helen said nothing but I could feel her staring at me. 'Duncan's leaving me,' I said. 'He's met someone else. I suppose I should be thankful, really, given everything that's . . .'

Helen started to push herself up from the desk to come towards me.

'When can you phone for a helicopter?' I asked.

She said nothing for a second, then sat back down. 'An hour or so. Not too long.'

I forced myself to concentrate on the papers in front of me. After a minute or two, I was able to blink away the tears and read them.

Right at the start of Dana's investigation I'd given her a print-out of births on the islands. She'd transferred it all on to her laptop but had kept my original and I was looking at it now. She'd gone over several entries with a pink highlighter pen. The four highlighted entries were all births that had taken place on Tronal between March and August 2005. I'd done exactly the same thing some hours previously.

Again, I noticed the initials KT. Seven entries. What had Gifford said they abbreviated: Keloid Trauma? It had made a certain sort of sense the way he'd explained it but it wasn't a term I'd come across before. Wondering if the entries had anything else in common, I checked the timing and found nothing; they were spread fairly evenly over the six-month period. Next I checked locality; three had been born at the Franklin Stone, another elsewhere in Lerwick, one on Yell, one on Bressay and one on Papa Stour. The weights of the infants varied but all were within the normal range, if anything slightly on the heavy side. A couple had been Caesareans but the rest were normal vaginal deliveries. They were all boys. I checked again. Not a single girl among them. *Race of males.*

I'd had it. I settled myself down on the straw and drew my jacket up around me. My consciousness closed down just about the same moment my eyes did.

'Tora.'

Didn't want to wake up. Knew I had to.

'Tora!' Firmer this time. Like Mum on a school day. Had to be done. I pushed myself up.

Helen was standing over me. The door to the tack room was open and it was light outside. Helen had packed both bags and had one slung over each shoulder.

'We have to leave,' she said. 'Can you walk a mile?'

I stood up. Speaking seemed like too much effort so I didn't try. I drank some water, scribbled a note to my friend and then walked out into the sunlight. Helen locked up behind me and replaced the key. I glanced over to where Charles and Henry were grazing and felt as though I was leaving my children behind. Helen set off towards the yard gate and I followed. She held it open for me.

We started to walk down the road towards the tiny town of Voe. My shoulder blades felt as though someone had put a knife in between them and my legs were shaking. I was light-headed again, but this time with exhaustion and lack of food rather than panic. I hadn't the energy left to panic.

'Where are we going?' I asked. I looked at my watch. Five-thirty a.m.

'Pub at the bottom,' Helen replied. 'There's a car park. Chopper can land there.'

In spite of everything I was impressed. She was going to get us out of here. I'd be safe. I could rest. We could work it all out. Or maybe I'd let someone else do it. Maybe I didn't really care too much any more.

We heard the chopper when we were still about a quarter-mile from the pub and I had to fight an urge to run and hide.

'Helen, what if it's not your people? What if it's them? What if they tracked your phone call?'

'Calm down. If that sort of technology even exists outside the movies, it's certainly not in common use.'

The noise of the chopper was getting louder. Helen took my arm and frogmarched me across the street and into the car park. The helicopter was overhead now. It started to circle.

I looked round. There was no one in sight but it was only a matter of minutes before the noise of the helicopter's engines would draw the curious. Someone would phone the local police. They would come and check.

Slowly, the helicopter began its descent. It continued to circle around the car park, getting lower with each circuit. In the street a delivery van had pulled over. A woman walking two lurchers approached. The dogs started to bark but instead of moving them away from the noise she stopped and watched, shading her eyes against the early sun.

The helicopter – small, black and yellow, not unlike the one the medical team used to get around the islands in emergencies – was about fifty feet above us now and the wind from the blades whipped my hair up around my head. Helen's, still plaited, stayed put. A car had pulled over now and two men jumped out to watch. One of them was speaking into a mobile.

Come on.

Finally the chopper touched down. The pilot signalled to Helen, she took my arm and we ran towards it. Helen opened the door, I jumped into the back seat and she followed, closing the door behind her. We were in the air before either of us could even locate our seatbelts, let alone fasten them.

Helen yelled something at the pilot that I didn't catch; he shouted back and then swung the chopper round. We were heading south, back over Shetland. I really didn't care, just as long as when we put down again we were off the islands.

Helen smiled at me, patted my hand and then raised her eyebrows and nodded her head in an *everything all right?* sort of gesture. Speech was just about impossible so I nodded. She settled back in her seat and closed her eyes.

The helicopter bounced around as it sped south. Neither Helen nor I had been offered headphones and the engines were painfully loud. I started to feel nauseous and looked around for a sick-bag. Saliva gathered in my mouth and I closed my eyes.

Helen had said nothing but I guessed we were going to Dundee, where she was based. On her own patch she would have the best use of resources and be better able to look after me if (or rather when) Dunn and his gang came after me.

After a while the nausea faded and I risked opening my eyes again. Another ten, fifteen minutes passed and I was feeling well enough to watch the coastline go by. In the early sun the sea sparkled and the white of the foam had turned to silver.

The first time I saw Duncan had been at the coast. He'd been surfing and was walking out of the water, board tucked under one arm, his wet hair gleaming black, eyes bluer than the sky. I hadn't dared approach, thinking him way out of my league, but later that night he'd found me. I'd thought myself the luckiest girl in the world. So what did that make me now? There were a dozen questions that I really didn't want answers to, but I just couldn't get them out of my head. How deep did Duncan's involvement go? Had he known about Melissa? Had we bought the house so that he could keep an eye on the place, make sure nothing disturbed the anonymous grave on the hillside? I couldn't believe it, would not believe it, but . . .

Soon Dundee drew nearer and I prepared myself for the stomach-sinking, ear-popping descent. Instead, the pilot banked sharp right and headed west. We left Dundee behind us and started to gain altitude. A minute later I glanced down and realized why. The Grampian mountains were directly below.

I've probably made it clear already that I'm not a great fan of Scotland, particularly the north-eastern corner of it. But even I have to admit that if there's anywhere on earth more beautiful than the Scottish Highlands, I have yet to see it. I watched those peaks sail below us, some capped with snow, some with heather, I saw glinting sapphires of lochs, and forests so deep and thick you might expect to find dragons in them, and I started to feel better. The pain between my shoulders became an ache and when I looked down my hands were no longer shaking. When we could see the sea again the helicopter at last started to go down.

Helen opened her eyes when we were twenty feet from the ground. We put down on a football field. Fifty yards away sat a blue and white police car. My heart started to thud but Helen didn't bat an eyelid. She yelled something at the pilot and then jumped out. I followed and we ran to the police car. The constable in the driving seat started the engine.

'Morning, Nigel,' said Helen.

'Morning, ma'am,' he replied. 'Where to first?'

'The harbour, please,' replied Helen.

We drove through a small, grey-stone town that looked vaguely familiar. When we arrived at the harbour I realized where we were. A few years ago Duncan and I had taken part in a flotilla cruise of the Highlands' whisky distilleries. The week-long junket had begun in this town and I remembered a drunken, wonderful evening. It felt like a very long time ago.

Helen gave the driver some directions and we drove along the harbour front, stopping just short of the pier, for no reason I could see. We got out. Helen led me to one of the small stalls that line the front of most seaside towns.

'Do you like seafood?' she asked.

'Not usually for breakfast,' I replied.

'Trust me. Do you like seafood?'

'I guess,' I said, thinking what the hell, a good chuck-up will at least get rid of the nausea.

Helen pointed out a bench overlooking the sea and I sat down. I could smell the sour, slightly rancid aroma of sun-dried seaweed and the leftovers of yesterday's catch. And something wonderful. Helen sat down beside me, handing me a large cardboard mug of coffee, several white paper napkins and a grease-stained paper bag.

'Lobster bap,' she said smugly. 'Fresh caught this morning.'

It was an incredible breakfast: the bitter, rich strength of the coffee worked like medicine; the softness of the fresh white bread, dripping with salty, warm butter and coating my lips with flour like fine talcum powder. And the lobster, rich and sweet, every mouthful a feast in itself. Helen and I ate as though we were racing, and by a fraction of a second I won.

I'd have given anything to have stayed there, drinking coffee as the sun rose in the sky and the sea turned from silver to a rich, deep blue; watching the tide go out and the fishing boats come in. But the clock was ticking. The world was waking up and I knew Helen hadn't brought me to Oban just for breakfast.

As though reading my mind, she looked at her watch. 'Seven forty-five,' she said. 'I'd say that's a respectable enough time for house-calls.' She stood up, brushed herself down and held out her hand for my empties.

Back in the car she turned to me. 'OK, listen good, because we'll be there in a minute. While you were in the land of nod last night, I had another look at Gair, Carter, Gow's bank accounts, to see if I could find anything else out of the ordinary. There are six client accounts in total. I found references to your husband's firm, to the hospital where you work and to Tronal. But Dana hadn't cross-referenced anything else and there was nothing to compare with the amounts of money supposedly being moved around by Shiller Drilling. Are you with me?'

'Yep. So far.' We'd left the harbour and were winding our way through Oban's residential streets. Nigel, the driver, pulled over to check a street-map.

'That's not to say there's nothing there. Just that it needs more digging than I had time for last night.'

'OK.' We were on the move again.

'Then I started going through the commercial account statements. Again, nothing really stood out. Cheques and cash are banked most days, but there's no real detail on where the money is coming from.

We'd need to go through their books to find that. There's a fairly large payroll that goes out monthly and various direct debits to the utility companies. Money also comes in monthly from a few clients who have the firm on retainer.'

'All things you might expect?' The car had slowed down. We turned into a cul de sac of newish detached houses. Nigel was peering at house numbers.

'Right. But when I was going through Gair, Carter, Gow's Oban account – which I left till last, by the way – something did stand out.'

'Here we are, ma'am,' said Nigel. 'Number fourteen.'

'Thanks, give us a minute,' said Helen. 'Three payments from the Oban commercial account to something called the Cathy Morton Trust. I noticed them partly because of their size – they amounted to half a million in sterling in total. And this wasn't a client account, remember, this was coming from Gair, Carter, Gow's own money. The other thing that got my attention was the timing.'

Over Helen's shoulder I could see curtains moving. A small face was watching us from a downstairs window of number fourteen.

'Three payments, in September and October 2004. The second of them on the sixth of October 2004.'

I said nothing, just looked back at her, waiting for the punch line. Helen looked disappointed; I'd obviously missed something. 'So then I got back on the Internet and called up a national police register. Only one record of a Cathy Morton in Oban and this was her last known address. Come on, they've seen us. You too, Nigel, please. You'll need your notebook.'

We got out of the car and walked up the drive to the front door. Helen knocked. The door was opened quickly by a man in his late thirties, dressed in a suit that needed pressing and a blue shirt open at the neck. A small boy in Spider-Man pyjamas peered at us from around the door frame.

Helen flashed her badge and introduced Nigel and me. The man glared at us both.

'Mr Mark Salter?' asked Helen.

His head jerked forwards.

'We need to talk to you and your wife. May we come in?'

Salter didn't move. 'She's in bed,' he said. Another child, a girl this time, had joined her brother. They watched us with the unabashed curiosity of the extremely young.

'Please ask her to join us,' said Helen, moving forward. Salter had a choice: step back or go nose to nose with a senior police officer. He made the sensible decision and we were inside.

Salter muttered something about getting his wife up and disappeared upstairs. We went into the living room. The TV was tuned into CBeebies. The kids, aged about seven and three, seemed mesmerized by us.

'Hi!' said Helen, addressing the boy. 'You must be Jamie.' The boy said nothing. Helen tried the girl. 'Hello, Kirsty.'

Kirsty, a cute little thing with porcelain skin and bright red hair, turned and ran from the room. We heard footsteps on the stairs as Mark Salter and his wife returned. Kirsty ran in behind them. The woman had obviously dressed in a hurry, pulling on jogging pants and a crumpled T-shirt. Over one shoulder she held a small baby, about four weeks old.

'I'm Caroline Salter,' she said, as Kirsty clung to her legs.

'I have to be at work in fifteen minutes,' said Mark Salter.

'You'll find being questioned by the police counts as a pretty good excuse,' said Helen. She glanced at the children and lowered her voice as she looked at Caroline Salter. 'I need to talk to you about your sister.'

The woman reached down and pulled Kirsty firmly away from her legs. She spoke to the boy and her voice brooked no argument. 'Come on, you two, breakfast.' She looked at her husband and he led the children from the room, switching off the TV as he went and closing the door behind him.

Caroline adjusted the baby and wrapped her hands more closely around him.

'My sister is dead,' she said, lowering herself on to one of the sofas.

Helen had been expecting that. She nodded. 'I know, I'm very sorry.' She looked round at the other sofa behind us and raised her arm in a *may we?*

gesture. The Salter woman nodded and Helen and I sat down. Nigel perched on a chair by the window. There was no sign of his notebook.

'How are the children doing?' asked Helen.

Something in the woman's face softened. 'OK,' she said. 'They still have their bad days. It's harder for Jamie. Kirsty barely remembers her mum.'

Helen gestured towards the baby. 'This one is yours,' she said.

Caroline nodded.

'He's gorgeous,' said Helen. Then she turned to me. 'Miss Hamilton here is an obstetrician. Brings little ones like that into the world all the time.'

Caroline sat up straighter in the chair and the wariness in her face gave way, just a fraction, to interest.

I made myself smile. 'How are you getting on?' I asked.

She shrugged. 'OK, I guess. It's tough. I mean, I'm used to kids, but babies are a whole new ball game.'

'Tell me about it,' I said, a tick of impatience starting to build in my head.

The door opened. Mark Salter came back into the room and sat next to his wife. Beside me, Helen straightened herself up. Female empathy time was over.

'When did your sister become ill?' asked Helen. Over at the window, Nigel had started scribbling. Caroline looked at her husband. He made a thinking face.

'She had a breast tumour removed about five years ago,' he said. 'Christmas time. Jamie was just a toddler. Then she was OK for a while.'

'But the cancer came back?'

Mark nodded. 'Doesn't it always?'

'When, exactly?'

'Early in 2004,' said Caroline. 'Cathy was pregnant with Kirsty so she wouldn't have chemotherapy. By the time Kirsty was born it had spread too much.'

'The doctors weren't able to remove it?' I asked.

Caroline's eyes were looking moist. 'They tried,' she said. 'She had an operation but it wasn't successful.' *An open-and-shut case.* 'She had chemo and radiotherapy, but in the end just pain relief.'

'She lived here with you?' asked Helen.

Caroline nodded. 'She couldn't manage the children. She couldn't do anything at the end. She was just in so much pain . . .'

Caroline started to cry and the baby squawked in protest. Mark Salter took the opportunity to play the annoyed husband.

'Oh great! We really don't need this right now. Are you through yet?' He didn't do it terribly well. He looked more afraid than angry.

'Not quite, sir,' said Helen, who hadn't been convinced either. 'I want to ask you about the Cathy Morton Trust. I assume you're both trustees.'

Mark nodded. 'Yes, us two and our solicitor,' he replied.

'And that would be Mr Gair?'

'Yes, that's right. Should I be speaking to him about this?'

'I doubt you'd be able to get hold of him right now. When did Cathy meet Stephen Gair?'

Husband and wife looked at each other.

'I want to know what this is about,' he began.

'I think you know already, Mr Salter. It's about the money your sister-in-law received from Mr Gair.'

'It's not our money,' said Caroline. 'We can't spend any of it. It's for the kids.'

Mark Salter stood up. Behind him, Nigel did too.

'We've got nothing more to say. I'd like you to leave, please.'

Helen stood up. Assuming we were going, I did too.

'Mr Salter, at this moment I have no reason to suspect you or your wife of any wrongdoing. But I can and will arrest you for obstruction of justice if you don't start cooperating.'

There was silence for a moment. Then Helen sat down again. Feeling a bit daft, I did too. Salter hovered for a second, then lowered himself back down beside his frightened wife. Baby Salter was seriously creating now. Caroline fumbled under her sweatshirt and released a large breast. She lowered the baby and he started rooting towards the large, cracked nipple.

Salter shot a black look at his wife. 'You tell them,' he spat. 'You were there.'

Caroline looked down at the baby. Her lip started to shake.

'Did Cathy make a will?' asked Helen.

Caroline nodded, still staring down at the sucking baby. 'In June. She knew by then she wasn't going to be around for too long.'

'And Stephen Gair drew it up for her?'

'Yes. She'd met him about a year earlier. When she sold her house. He wasn't based in Oban but he agreed to act for her. I think they even went out for a while. When she was still well. You know, dinner when he was in town, a couple of weekends away. She didn't tell us much about it because he . . . well . . .'

'He was married,' said Helen.

Caroline looked up quickly, guiltily, as though she were the one who'd been dating a married man. She nodded.

'Then what happened?'

She dropped her head again. The baby had detached itself and was sleeping. Christ, it was like pulling teeth. I wanted to scream at her to get on with it, tell us what she knew.

'What happened in September 2004? He came to see her, didn't he?'

'She was very ill. In bed all the time.' Caroline looked at her husband and there was precious little affection in her face. 'Mark thought she needed to be in a hospice.'

He stiffened. 'It was bad for the kids, seeing their mum like that.'

'They knocked on the door one day. Asked to see her. They said they knew she was ill but it was important.'

'They?' asked Helen.

'Stephen Gair and the other man. He talked like a doctor.'

'What was his name?' asked Helen, as my heartbeat went into overdrive.

Caroline shook her head. 'I never knew.'

'What did he look like?' I asked. Helen shot me a *will you let me handle this?* look.

Caroline turned to me. 'Tall,' she said. 'Very tall; big shoulders, fair hair. Apart from that . . .'

'It's OK,' said Helen. 'We can come back to that. Tell me what happened.'

'I took them up to see her. It was hard for her, talking to anyone, but she made a big effort.'

'What did they talk about?'

'They made her an offer.' This time Mark was talking. 'It was between them. We told her she didn't need to do it, that we would take care of the kids.'

Oh, for God's sake, how could Helen stay so patient?

'What was the offer?'

'That she would take part in some trials of a new cancer drug. She would have to go away, to a hospital on the Shetlands where the trial was taking place. They said there was no guarantee that she'd respond to the drug but that it had been developed for the advanced stages of cancer and there was always a chance.'

'And in return?'

'In return the drug company would set up a trust

fund for the children. Entirely for their benefit. The money is completely controlled. It's released monthly for things like school uniforms for Jamie and childcare for Kirsty. We get none of it.'

I looked around the room, at the immaculate leather sofas, the stereo equipment, the widescreen TV. I remembered the new people-carrier in the driveway.

'And Cathy agreed to this?'

'She didn't have to,' insisted Mark.

'Yes,' said Caroline, 'she agreed. It was the worst thing for her, worrying about the kids, about what would happen to them. They had no one, apart from us, and she knew we didn't have a lot of money. She felt it was the only thing she could still do for them.'

'I do understand,' said Helen. 'What happened next?'

'Stephen Gair set up the trust fund, making Mark and me trustees. We signed the papers the next day and the first instalment of money was paid. They came for her a couple of days later.'

'Who came?'

'That man, the doctor, in an ambulance. And a nurse. They told her she was going in a helicopter. He said we could visit once she was settled.'

'When did you see her again?'

Caroline shook her head. 'We didn't. She died just over a week later. I had to tell Jamie. He thought his mummy was going away to get better.'

'Where was the funeral?'

Caroline's face took on an angry look.

'There wasn't one,' said Mark. 'Gair came to see us; said it had been part of the arrangement. Cathy's body would be used for research, donated to medical science, he said.'

'So you never saw her again?'

'No. She was just gone.'

'Did you talk to her?'

'We didn't even have a number,' said Mark. 'Stephen Gair phoned us most evenings with a report. Kept saying she was comfortable but very drowsy with the drugs. Not able to talk on the phone.'

'Can you remember the date she died?' asked Helen.

'The sixth of October,' said Caroline.

Helen was looking at me, to see if I'd finally got it. I had. The sixth of October was the day Melissa – Melissa number one, that is – was supposed to have died.

'We weren't happy,' said Mark. 'We weren't happy at all that she could just disappear like that. We wanted to talk to her doctors, find out about her last days. We kept phoning Stephen Gair but he wouldn't take our calls.'

'Did you try calling the hospital?' I asked.

'Yes,' said Caroline. 'I rang the Franklin Stone in Lerwick but they had no record of a Cathy Morton. I panicked a bit then, went down to Stephen Gair's offices in town. He wasn't there, but I made quite a fuss. Then, the next day, that doctor bloke came round. At least, the one we'd thought was a doctor.'

'Go on.'

'Well, I was on my own in the house and he pretty much threatened me. Said we had to stop pestering Mr Gair, Cathy hadn't been harmed by the drugs and would have died anyway, that she was taken very good care of and that we should let it rest now. He implied that if we wanted to keep the money we'd have to keep quiet.'

'We had to think about the kids,' said Mark. 'Nothing was going to bring Cathy back. We had to think about their future.'

'I wasn't happy, though,' repeated Caroline. 'I threatened to call the police.'

'What did he say?'

'He said he was the police.'

No one spoke for a few moments. Helen appeared to be thinking hard. Then she turned once more to Caroline. 'Do you have a photograph of your sister, Mrs Salter?'

Caroline got up with the baby still clutched to her chest. She crossed the room and opened the top drawer of a dresser. As she fumbled inside, the rest of us looked at the carpet. Then Caroline returned to Helen and gave her something. Helen looked at it for just a second and then handed the photograph to me. It had been taken at a beach on a bright, windy day. Stephen Gair, a couple of years younger and a whole lot happier than when I'd seen him, laughed at the camera. His arms were round a very pretty young woman in a green sweater. They say men often go for the same physical type and it was certainly true in Gair's case. You'd never have mistaken the two women for twins but the likeness between Melissa and Cathy was close enough: similar age and build; long red hair, although Cathy's had been straight; fair skin, fine, small features.

There'd been a semblance after all.

32

I SPENT THE NEXT TEN HOURS AS A GUEST OF THE Tayside Constabulary.

Helen and I flew to Dundee; she sat up front with the pilot, headphones on, talking continually on the radio. I sat in the back, cocooned by noise. After twenty minutes of watching the scenery I dug into my bag and pulled out, once more, Dana's copy of *The Woman in White*. I still hadn't had a chance to look at the Post-it markers she'd attached to several of the pages. They were probably just remnants of A-level notes, but as long as we were still in the air, I had little else to do.

I opened the book at the first marker. Page fifty. Dana had been at work with her pink highlighter again:

> *There stood Miss Fairlie, a white figure, alone in the moonlight; in her attitude, in the turn of her head, in her complexion, in the shape of her face, the living image of the woman in white.*

On page 391 I found another highlighted piece:

The outward changes wrought by the suffering and the terror of the past fearfully, almost hopelessly, strengthened the fatal resemblances between Anne Catherick and herself.

Living image. Fatal resemblances. Stephen Gair had had an incredible stroke of luck. Needing to get rid of his wife, he'd known a terminally sick woman who bore a strong resemblance to her. Terrified for the future of her young children, Cathy Morton had allowed herself to be moved to a new hospital where, spaced out with painkillers, she wouldn't have known what was going on around her. And who was there to suspect she wasn't who a respected local solicitor said she was? None of the medical staff who had treated Cathy had known Melissa; Cathy's sister and brother-in-law hadn't been allowed to visit, Melissa's parents hadn't been told she was in hospital and it was a safe bet that none of her friends had known either.

Even if someone had met Melissa once or twice, it was still possible he or she would have been fooled by the sight of a cancer-ridden Cathy in a hospital bed. Both Cathy and Melissa had been pretty women, but a second photograph Caroline had shown us, of a barely recognizable Cathy towards the end of her illness, showed the devastating effect cancer can have.

Cathy had died just days after being admitted to

hospital. There'd been a post-mortem, the report of which I'd seen in Gifford's office, and then she'd been cremated. I imagined the funeral, the church full of Melissa's friends and relatives, deeply shocked by her sudden death, struggling to even begin the process of grief. Which of them could have dreamed the body in the coffin heading for the furnace wasn't Melissa at all? That Melissa, still very much alive, was . . . somewhere else? How had he done that? How had Gair arranged for his wife to disappear so effectively? Where had she been for the nine months between Cathy's death and her own? And what the hell had happened to her in that time?

I closed *The Woman in White* and put it away. At the time I knew nothing of the story but I read it some months later. It's about a man who fakes his wife's death – for money, of course – by spiriting her away and substituting a dying woman in her place. Dana had known the story and had been well on her way to working it out. Whether she'd made contact with the Salters, whether that was the final trigger that made her killers act, I'd probably never know.

When we landed at Dundee Helen gave me a quick smile and disappeared into a waiting car. Another car took me to the station, where I was given coffee and left to wait in an interview room. I waited almost an hour, nearly going nuts in the process, and then a member of Helen's team, an inspector, came to interview me. A constable sat in the corner of the room and the whole thing was tape-recorded. I wasn't read my rights, I wasn't offered a lawyer, but in all other respects it was an interrogation and he was taking nothing at face value.

I told him the whole story, from finding the body to meeting the Salters. I told him about Kirsten Hawick who'd been killed in a riding accident and about my finding the ring that had every appearance of being hers; about someone breaking in to my house and my office; about the pig's heart on my kitchen table; about my suspicions that I'd been drugged and that someone had tampered with my computer. I told him about my sabotaged boat and useless life jacket; about my belief that Dana had been murdered because she'd found out too much. I described the evidence of financial irregularities that Dana had unearthed and about my escape with Helen through the dark Shetland landscape. Then I went through it all again. And again. He pulled me up time after time, making me repeat myself, clarify myself, until I really wasn't sure what I'd said and what I hadn't. After five minutes I was very glad I wasn't a suspect in the case; after twenty minutes I was starting to think that perhaps I was.

An hour and a half later we stopped. I was brought lunch. Then he came back. More questions. Another hour and he leaned back in his chair.

'Who knew you planned to go sailing that morning, Miss Hamilton?'

'We didn't plan it,' I replied, knowing I was stalling. 'We hadn't even planned spending that weekend on Unst. It was a last-minute thing. But lots of people know we keep a boat there.'

'Do you keep your life jackets there too?'

I couldn't look at him. 'No,' I said. 'We keep them at home. In the attic. Duncan would have picked them up from home before we set off. They were locked in the boot of his car till we used them on Sunday morning.'

He frowned, stared down at his notes for a while. Then looked back up at me.

'Whose idea was it to go sailing? Who thought of it?'

'Duncan's,' I said. 'It was Duncan.'

I was taken to a cell, given more food and a note from Helen telling me to eat and rest. When I woke, it was nearly seven in the evening and Helen was standing in the doorway. She'd changed into a tailored black trouser suit and an emerald-green silk vest. Her hair had been washed and wound up on the top of her head. She looked nothing like the woman I'd ridden across country with the night before.

'Feeling better?'

I managed a smile. 'I guess.'

'Ready to go back?'

Back? Back to the islands? Early that morning, I'd watched them disappear over the horizon and told myself it was over; that that part of my life was finished with. Now, it appeared, it was not.

'Do I have a choice?' I asked, knowing what the answer was going to be.

'Not really. You can eat on the way.'

* * *

On the way to the helipad she was silent. I had a hundred questions but I didn't know where to start and, if I'm honest, I was a little afraid to. Helen wasn't my fellow fugitive any more; she was a senior police officer, probably in charge of a very serious investigation. And I was a principal witness. Having got this far, I didn't want to do anything to screw things up.

When the driver was parking she said, 'Stephen Gair has confessed.'

I'd been leaning back in the seat but at that I sat bolt upright. 'You're kidding me? He just admitted it?'

She nodded. 'He's been in custody since midday. It took two hours and then he cracked.'

'What? I mean, what exactly has he confessed to?' Stephen Gair had not struck me as the type to give in that easily.

'Well, everything. Selling babies to the highest bidder, for one thing. He says he worked with several of the less scrupulous adoption agencies overseas. Whenever a wealthy couple appeared they were told about a way of short-cutting the system for a price. It was all done by a sort of blind auction on the Internet. When a baby became available it went to the highest bidder. Up to a million dollars in some cases.'

Our driver got out of the car. He waved to the pilot, who nodded back, and the chopper's blades started to turn.

'George Reynolds, the director of social services,

is in Lerwick nick, helping us with our inquiries. He's denying all knowledge, but if the babies went overseas with adoption papers, his department must be involved.'

'Who actually took them overseas?'

'A nursing agency. We're talking to them but so far they claim they didn't know anything was illegal.'

'And Gair admits substituting Cathy for his wife at the hospital?' The noise of the helicopter's engines was increasing and I had to raise my voice. Once we got out of the car, speech would become impossible again.

'Yep. Insists she was very well treated, that her illness followed its natural course and that in no way can he be held responsible for her death. He also says no one at the hospital knew anything about it.'

'So who helped him? Who arranged the ambulance?'

'Claims he did it himself. Chartered it privately. The nurse was hired for the occasion.'

I was thinking as fast as I'd ever done. Was it feasible? That no one from the hospital was involved?

'What about the doctor, the one who later claimed to be a policeman? The one who Caroline met?'

'He insists there was no accomplice. Says Caroline was confused.'

'She didn't sound confused to me.'

'No. She's at Lerwick now. We've got an identity parade lined up.'

'So you know who it was?'

'Let's just say we have some ideas.' Her face closed

up. She was saying no more on that one. I tried another tack.

'And Melissa?'

Helen held up one finger at the pilot. 'Gair admits killing her. She found out about the adoptions and threatened to go to the police. You're not going to like this, but he says he kept her in your cellar. A forensic team's been there for the last few hours.'

'You're kidding me,' I whispered, remembering Dana's insistence on looking round my cellar – her instincts right on the button, as usual.

'He'd handled the probate for the last owner and knew the house was empty. He even had a set of keys. He says he kept Melissa tied up and heavily drugged and once she'd given birth he killed her. He claims he acted alone.'

'Bullshit! He couldn't have done that without help. Kept a pregnant woman prisoner for months, delivered a baby. He's covering for someone.'

'Probably. He says he carved the symbols on her back. Got the idea from some markings around your fireplace. Apparently, he wanted to make it look like some sort of cult slaying, to draw attention away from him if she was ever found. Same with cutting out the heart. He can't remember what he did with the heart. Says he was under a great deal of stress at the time and that huge chunks of his memory are missing.'

'Bullshit! Bull-double-shit!'

'Thank you. But we worked that out ourselves. He is also admitting that Connor, the little boy he calls his stepson, is his own child. And Melissa, not Alison his new wife, was his mother.'

'Dana was right about that too.'

Beside me, Helen took a sharp breath. 'Well, we can DNA test, prove it conclusively, one way or another. Look, don't worry. A few more hours, maybe days and he'll tell us everything. Right now, we need to move.'

It took us just over an hour to get back. Helen spent the time reading and making notes, her body language giving very definite *don't ask me now* signals and I didn't want to push her. But shit . . .

First thing that occurred to me, as the helicopter took off, was that we'd never have made it to this point if Stephen Gair hadn't agreed to have his wife's dental records examined. Just days ago, Saturday morning, he'd been cooperation itself. Far from complaining – as he'd have had every right to – about my unethical behaviour, he'd allowed the confirmation that the body in my field was that of his wife. Of course, we were still, at that stage, a long way from working out how the switch had taken place, but even so, Stephen Gair had effectively given himself up that morning.

The helicopter banked and we were heading back over the North Sea to the islands. The sun was low in the sky, spreading its golden warmth over the waves.

Why the hell had he done that? Had he been tired of living with the guilt? I'd heard criminals often secretly want to be caught. Or had he deliberately played along, knowing the system was in place to protect him; that he had friends who could get him off the hook?

Were Dana and I being played that morning; encouraged to reveal just exactly what we knew before being . . . well, neutralized? Put out of harm's way before we could tell someone who might actually take us seriously? Three days later, Dana was dead and I'd narrowly escaped drowning.

Melissa had found out too much and she'd been dealt with; she'd suffered a protracted and terrifying death. I wondered what had roused Melissa's suspicions in the first place, what path she'd followed to discover more, at what point she'd become seriously afraid, whether she'd tried to escape. First Melissa, then Dana had paid the price for knowing too much. And it wasn't over. In spite of what Helen had just told me about Gair's confession, I knew it wasn't. Why the hell was I going back to Shetland?

We landed in a field close to Lerwick police station and the noise dimmed enough for Helen and me to be able to talk. She looked up from her notes.

'There's a car here, waiting to take you home to collect whatever you need. Then we'll put you in a hotel for the night. I'm not sure when we'll need you at the station so just sit tight.'

'Are you in charge now?'

'No, Detective Superintendent Harris is. But I'm officially advising and observing. We're going by the book from now on, I promise you.' She looked round. Several police cars were waiting for us. Then she turned back to me and there was a look on her face I couldn't identify. 'There is something you need to know. A lot of people are in custody tonight, and will stay that way until we're convinced they had nothing to do with all this. I'm afraid your husband is one of them.'

I nodded. I'd expected that. I even welcomed the news. The last thing I could deal with just then was a confrontation with Duncan.

'Also, your father-in-law and your boss from the hospital. You may well be needed at work over the next few days.'

She was right. The hospital couldn't afford to lose me and Gifford. And I'd thought I was getting away.

We climbed down. Helen squeezed my shoulder and stepped into one of the waiting cars. A woman constable introduced herself and led me to a second car. A male constable was driving. We set off on the twenty-minute drive that would take me home. I wondered what I was going to do with my evening, stuck in a strange hotel somewhere in Lerwick.

The car pulled up at the front of the house.

'Do you want me to come in with you?' asked the WPC – Jane, I think she'd said her name was.

'No, thank you. I'll be fine. It won't take long.'

I walked to the front door of the house and found my key. The hall was in darkness and the house had that still, cold feel that houses assume when they've been empty for a while. I walked down the hall to the kitchen, registering but not appreciating the significance of the beam of light shining out from under the door. I pushed the door open.

Duncan and Kenn Gifford were sitting together at the kitchen table, our bottle of Talisker standing open and nearly empty between them.

33

I ALMOST YELLED BUT KNEW THE OFFICERS OUTSIDE would never hear me. I considered making a run for it, but Duncan was too close and he can move like lightning when he wants to. Kenn was staring at me, his eyes so narrow I could barely see beyond the lashes. Duncan moved towards me, the picture of a distraught husband, overwhelmed with relief at seeing his wife again.

'Tor, thank God . . .'

I took a sharp step back and held up both hands in front of me. Duncan looked confused, but he stopped.

'Are you OK?'

'No, I am not OK.' I started to move, edging further round the kitchen, away from the door, but closer to what I'd spotted on the worktop. 'I am a very long way from being OK.' I grabbed out and reached the knife that had been lying on the kitchen counter. It was an all-purpose knife, one I used for just about everything: chopping, slicing, peeling. It was small but sharp. It would serve the purpose. Duncan was looking horrified, Kenn vaguely amused.

'I want you both out of here. Right now. If either of you tries to touch me, I will slice you up. Got that?'

'Tor . . .' Duncan moved forward again.

'Have you got that?' I yelled, shoving the knife in his direction. He was still two feet away but I'd made my point. He stepped back.

'I've got it,' said Gifford, who hadn't moved. He picked up his drink and raised it to his lips. 'How about you, Dunc?'

Dunc? Since when were these two on pet-name terms?

'Why don't you get Tora a glass?' said Gifford.

'There are two police officers outside,' I said.

'Well, they can't drink on duty,' said Gifford. I swear, if the knife had been a gun, I'd have shot him.

'I think you should both sit down,' said Gifford. 'Tora, if it makes you feel better, invite your two friends outside to come in.'

I looked from one to the other: my tall, handsome husband, almost shaking with anxiety; my ugly, compelling boss, the picture of calm. 'I was told you two were in custody.'

'We were,' said Gifford. 'Interesting experience. Got released about an hour ago.'

An hour ago, Helen and I were taking off from Dundee. A lot can happen in an hour. 'Don't tell me, because you and DI Dunn go way back.'

Duncan and Kenn glanced at each other. 'Not exactly,' said Gifford, almost to himself. Then he looked at me. 'Our friends at the station found no charges for us to answer. Can't help but feel you have a few, though.'

For a second, I thought about walking out. Just for a second.

'You helped Stephen Gair substitute a terminally sick woman for his wife,' I said to Gifford. For some reason it was easier to talk to him, accuse him, than speak to Duncan. 'You helped him keep Melissa Gair prisoner – here, in our bloody cellar – for eight months. You kept her alive and delivered her baby and then you killed her.' I stopped and took a deep breath. 'I cannot begin to imagine what she went through, you inhuman bastard!'

Gifford flinched. Then his eyes narrowed even more. 'When Cathy Morton died at our hospital I was in New Zealand,' he said. 'I told you that already and I told the police that today. They checked my flight details and people I stayed with in Auckland. So, unlike you, they happen to believe me. I never saw Caroline Salter in my life until I took part in an identity parade this afternoon. Had she picked me out, I wouldn't be here now.'

I wasn't having it. 'Somebody helped Gair. He couldn't have done it alone.'

'No, I don't think he could. But he wasn't helped by us. Neither of us had anything to do with what's being going on up on Tronal. We had no reason to want Melissa Gair dead.' Gifford had lowered his voice almost to a whisper. I found myself staring into his eyes, wanting to believe him. I made myself look away.

'You wanted me dead, though,' I said to Duncan.

'The idiot at the boatyard got it wrong, Tor.' Duncan was still hovering, wanting to come towards me, not quite daring to. 'I know what you think, but it's bollocks. The mast collapsed while we were out but it didn't break clean off. After I was picked up the boat got caught around some salmon cages. The salvage team had to saw through the rest of the mast to get it clean away. McGill's boy didn't know that. He just jumped to conclusions.'

I thought about it. It wasn't impossible. A mast doesn't always break clean away, sometimes it just buckles under the force of the wind. Still attached to the boat, it flies around in every direction. It's a messy and highly dangerous situation and most sailors carry bolt-croppers in case it happens to them.

'No one's trying to kill you,' said Duncan, in what was almost a whisper.

'Although House Officer Donaldson is pretty pissed off that you yelled at him the other day,' said Gifford. 'He's considering an official complaint.'

'Will you fucking well pack it in? Half the islands were out looking for me last night. You had a chopper searching the moors, for God's sake. You don't do that unless you want someone pretty badly.'

'We were worried about you. You bailed out of hospital with a whole load of Diazepam in your system. For all we knew you'd convinced yourself you could fly and were heading for the nearest cliff-top to boogie with the puffins.'

'Someone killed Dana. She found out too much. About Stephen Gair. About all of you.'

'Dana's post-mortem was carried out today. Do you want to know what they found?'

Suddenly, I wanted to sit down after all. I even caught myself looking at the Talisker. Gifford pushed his glass over towards me. Duncan glared at him. I saw that, behind them, the door to the cellar was sealed off with red and white police tape. I made myself look away; I didn't want to start thinking about what might have happened down there. I nodded to Gifford to start talking.

'Death occurred due to extensive blood loss when the radial and ulnar arteries were severed on both wrists. The angle of the wounds and the weakness of the cut on the right wrist suggest the wounds were self-administered. There was no trace of drugs in her bloodstream and no bruises to indicate she was held down. The conclusion is death by suicide.'

I shook my head.

'You can read the report yourself.'

'Dana did not commit suicide.' I wasn't sure any more about Gifford's involvement, I could no longer swear that Duncan had tried to kill me, but if I had just one thing, one truth to hold on to, it was that Dana did not kill herself. If I'd been wrong about Dana, I could have been wrong about everything. And I wasn't. I bloody well wasn't.

And then Gifford took my breath away.

'Probably not. But – listen now – you may never be able to prove otherwise.'

His pupils were enormous and the irises of his eyes had no colour. I had to blink hard and shake myself to look away. I turned to Duncan. He'd resumed his seat and he reached out across the table towards me. I looked at his tanned, calloused hand and shook my head, putting my own hands firmly together in front of me. Gifford glanced at Duncan, who nodded his head forward just once. Then Gifford spoke.

'Caroline Salter identified Andrew Dunn as the man who accompanied Gair when he visited Cathy. Dunn was involved in the adoption scam, has made thousands from it over the years. He almost certainly conspired with Gair to kill Melissa and he may well have killed Dana Tulloch too. But Tora, in all likelihood, you'll never be able to prove it.'

I leaned back in my chair, hands pressed to my mouth, because I knew that any second now I was going to start sobbing. I didn't doubt what he was saying for a second. I picked up Gifford's glass and drained it. The Scotch hit the back of my throat like a blow but it helped. I wasn't going to cry just yet.

'How . . . how did he . . . ?'

Gifford poured another drink. Same glass. 'DI Dunn leaves a lot to be desired as a police officer but he does have – how shall I put it? – a few unusual skills.'

And something clicked into place. 'He hypnotized her. He made her slash her own wrists.'

Gifford nodded. 'Probably,' he said.

I looked at Duncan. He gave me a sympathetic twitch of the lips. I turned back to Gifford. 'You can do it too.'

He waited for a second before inclining his head forward in acknowledgement.

'Oh Jesus!' I stood up, panic building. I looked round for my knife but it was by Duncan's elbow. When the hell had he done that? I looked at the door.

'Tora, it's a party trick.' Gifford was out of his seat. 'How do you think Duncan got you to marry him?'

I looked, horrified, at Duncan, praying he was going to look outraged and deny it. He just stared back at me.

'You think Up Helly Aa lasts all winter?' continued Gifford, resuming his seat. 'We make our own fun up here.'

'Take it easy, Kenn, it's not funny,' said Duncan.

'No, you're right. I'm sorry.' Gifford reached out and took hold of my hand. It didn't occur to me to stop him but Duncan loudly cleared his throat and Kenn let go. I sat down again.

'So what are you telling me? You can all do it up here? It's on the high-school curriculum?'

'Course not,' said Duncan. 'Just a couple of the older families. It's a sort of passed-down-through-the-generations thing. Bit of a game, really. Although it can give us an edge in business meetings, you know, get people on side more quickly. All harmless.'

'Andy was always better at it than most. I think

he enjoyed the sense of power it gave him,' said Gifford.

'You'll tell them. You'll tell the police about this.'

Duncan and Gifford looked at each other again and I really wished they'd stop doing it. I could not get used to these two as co-conspirators.

'If you want us to,' said Gifford. 'But against considerable evidence of suicide, how seriously do you think people are going to take us?'

At that moment, we all jumped as a sudden noise rang out through the quiet of the house. Someone was banging on the front door, and at the same time the telephone started ringing. We looked at each other, not really sure what to do, what to respond to first. Then I got up and left the room. Behind me I could hear Duncan answering the phone. I walked quickly to the front door and opened it. The WPC was on the doorstep, her colleague immediately behind her.

'Are you all right?' She was trying to see over my shoulder. 'We've been told to check on you, not leave you alone.'

I nodded. 'I'm fine. Come on in.'

I led the officers to our living room. 'Can you wait here for a bit? There's something I need to finish.'

As I returned to the kitchen, Duncan was holding out the phone. I took it.

'Tora, I've only just been told.' Helen was speaking fast. 'About your husband being released. Are you OK?'

'I'm fine, really, don't worry.'

'Are the constables with you?'

‘In the next room.’

‘Well, for God’s sake keep them there. I’m really not happy about this, but I can’t get away right now. Gair has admitted that Andy Dunn was working with him and helped him kill Melissa.’

Duncan and Kenn were both watching me. ‘Andy Dunn killed Dana,’ I said.

The line was silent for a few seconds. ‘I can’t deal with that right now. I’ll get back to you.’ She hung up and I replaced the receiver. I closed the kitchen door so the two officers in the living room couldn’t hear us and sat down again.

‘Dunn hasn’t been seen since about eleven p.m. last night,’ said Gifford. ‘The Salter woman had to identify his photograph. They think he’s left the islands. Until he’s found, you need to be careful.’

Duncan made an exasperated noise. He picked up the bottle, emptied it into his glass and sat glowering at the amber-coloured liquid.

‘Take it easy, Duncan,’ said Kenn, with something like a warning in his voice. There were emotions in the room that were threatening to sizzle out of control. It was no longer just me, venting my righteous anger on these two. There was more at stake and I couldn’t figure it out. Then I remembered something.

‘You two are receiving money from Tronal,’ I said, turning to Duncan. ‘The place even paid for this god-damned house. If neither of you are involved with the maternity clinic, why are you on its payroll?’

‘Looks like we’ve no secrets left, buddy,’ said Kenn, looking round the room. ‘Will you tell her or shall I? By the way, I'm starving. Is anyone planning on eating tonight?'

As Kenn got up and crossed the room, I waited for Duncan to tell me the last big secret.

'Eight people get a monthly income from Tronal,' he said eventually. 'In addition to the staff, of course. Kenn and I, Dad, Gair and Dunn. And three others you probably don't know.'

'Why?' I demanded, leaning back in my chair. Kenn had moved out of my line of sight and I didn't like it.

'We own it. We bought shares around ten years ago. It was in financial trouble, about to go under, and we bailed it out. It was long before I met you and I never thought to mention it. My trust fund was part of the loan. It was paid back in December, in time to buy the house.'

They owned the clinic? And knew nothing about what had been going on up there? Was I seriously expected to believe this?

'The Tronal clinic has been around for a long time,' continued Duncan. 'This business with Gair, it's just like . . . the rotten branch of a tree. Tronal has helped a lot of women in its time, a lot of local families.'

Gifford had opened our fridge door. Finding nothing in there, he turned back. 'Most babies born there are adopted normally and legally,' he said. 'Most people who work at the clinic probably knew nothing about what Gair and Dunn were up to. I'm pretty certain Richard didn't.' He opened a cupboard, closed it again.

'I still don't understand why you bailed it out. Why did you care?'

Kenn opened another cupboard. 'Christ, have you two even heard of supermarkets?' He gave up and came back to the table.

'Because we were born there,' said Duncan. He waited a while, giving me time to take it in. 'We were both Tronal babies. Adopted by island families. So was Dunn. I'm not sure about the others.'

I stared at Duncan. 'Elspeth and Richard aren't your parents?'

'Elspeth couldn't have children,' said Duncan. A shadow crossed his face. 'Richard could,' he added, looking at Kenn.

'Richard is my father,' said Kenn.

I found I had nothing to say.

'Richard and Elspeth tried for several years to have a family,' explained Kenn. 'During that time, when I guess their relationship was under some strain, Richard had an affair with a house officer at the hospital. She had her baby in the maternity unit on Tronal and put me up for adoption by the Giffords. Three years later, Elspeth finally admitted defeat and agreed to adopt too. Duncan was four months old and, I'm led to believe, a very appealing infant.'

'You two are brothers?' I asked, looking from one to the other.

Gifford shrugged. 'Well, not biologically, but yes, I've always felt we're family.'

Duncan's face darkened.

'Why didn't they adopt you?' I asked Kenn.

'Elspeth doesn't know about me. I didn't know who my genetic father was myself till I was sixteen. I wasn't surprised though.'

No, I bet he hadn't been. I couldn't imagine why I hadn't thought of it before. I'd seen the strong likeness between Richard and Kenn, the antipathy between Duncan and Kenn, the cool formality that was Duncan's relationship with his parents, but I hadn't put all the pieces together. Kenn, the doctor, the blood son, the spiritual son; Duncan, the poor foundling, taken in to keep Elspeth happy. Poor Duncan. Poor Kenn, come to think of it. What a mess.

An hour later, I was still at home. I'd found I really couldn't cope with a night in a strange hotel. WPC Jane, at Helen's insistence, was sleeping in one of our spare rooms. Duncan was firmly consigned to another. It wasn't that I didn't believe everything he'd told me. Actually, I did; I wanted to talk to Helen about it, get it all checked out, but the more I thought about it the more convinced I became that the lies were over, that I finally had most of the answers.

I took a long shower, shampooed my hair twice and then cleaned my teeth. It felt good to be back in a bathroom. In spite of my nap in the Dundee police cell I could feel my eyelids drooping. Then I caught sight of Duncan's toilet bag on the bathroom shelf and was suddenly wide awake again. No, I didn't have all the answers yet, after all.

I walked across the corridor and pushed open the

door of the spare room. Duncan was lying on the bed, headphones on, face downcast. He pulled them off, brightening at the sight of me, until he saw the look on my face. I held up the packet I'd extracted from his washbag.

'Anything you want to say?'

He took off his headphones, stood up. 'How about I'm sorry?'

I shook my head. 'Not nearly good enough.' I stepped into the room, wondering how much damage I could inflict on him before either a) he overpowered me or b) we were interrupted by Constable Jane. 'Do you have any idea what it's been like for me this past year?'

Duncan, to his credit, could no longer look me in the eye.

'I have to see, talk to, touch pregnant women every working day of my life. I have to listen to them moaning about nausea, tiredness, backache, groin-strain until I have to sit on my hands to stop myself from slapping them, from yelling at them to stop moaning, you silly bitch, be grateful for what you have. I have to touch every newborn baby, feel its solid little body between my hands, and each time I'm torn between wanting to run away with it or hurl it out of the goddamned window. Each time I hand one over to its mother, I feel like my heart has been ripped in two. I want to collapse on the delivery-room floor and sob, why, why, why isn't it me? Why is it that every other bloody woman in the world can do this and I can't?'

By the time I finished I was yelling and I thought

I could hear movement along the corridor. Duncan still couldn't look at me but what I saw on his face looked like fear. I think I surprised, even alarmed, myself. Months of misery, of bewilderment at being unable to conceive, crystallized for me that evening and, for the first time, I put everything into words. Duncan had turned away from me and was leaning on the ledge of the window. I followed him round the bed and forced myself to lower my voice. It no longer sounded like my voice, though; it sounded evil.

'Except I can, can't I? I can have babies. All this pain has been totally unnecessary. You didn't need to saw through the mast, Duncan, you've been killing me for over a year.'

I threw the packet at him. It seemed ridiculously inadequate and I looked round the room for a bigger missile. Fortunately for both of us there was nothing to hand. The bedside lamp was pretty sturdy but when I realized I'd have to unplug it first the urge left me.

I walked to the door. Then turned back.

'That shit isn't even licensed in the UK. Who got them for you? Daddy or Big Brother? You know what? I don't give a toss any more. And by the way, I know you're planning to leave me and thank bloody Christ for that.'

I walked out, slamming the door behind me, and caught sight of Jane at the top of the stairs. I went back into my room and closed the door.

Well, sleep didn't seem like a possibility any more. I wondered how I was going to get through the rest of the night. I discovered I was hungry but, as Kenn had learned earlier, the cupboards were bare. The bedroom door opened.

'I don't want to hear it,' I said, realizing I'd feel pretty daft if I turned round and found Constable Jane in the doorway.

'There's a reason my birth mother put me up for adoption,' said Duncan.

'You're confusing me with someone who gives a damn,' I replied, still not turning round.

'She had multiple sclerosis,' continued Duncan. 'She was already ill when she had me. She knew she would deteriorate quickly.'

I said nothing but my posture must have betrayed that I was listening.

'I know I carry the gene,' said Duncan. 'There's a good chance I'll get ill myself, although I'm already older than she was when she died. There's a fifty per cent risk I'll pass the gene on to any children.'

I turned. The skin around Duncan's eyes had turned red and blotchy. His eyes were shining. I'd never seen him cry before. How little we really know the people around us. He risked coming further into the room.

'I know I should have told you. I'm really sorry I didn't.'

'Why? Why didn't you tell me? When did you find out?'

'I've known since I was a child. I have no excuse. Except that when I met you you showed no interest in having a family. When you weren't working you were riding, risking your neck on cross-country courses every weekend. You were going to be a consultant by the time you were thirty-five and win the Badminton Horse Trials. I couldn't see how children could fit into that lifestyle.'

What he was saying was true, but he was describing the person I'd been eight years ago.

'I changed. The lifestyle changed.'

'I know that. But when was I supposed to tell you? When we were engaged?'

'Yes,' I interrupted. 'That would have been appropriate.'

'I was terrified you'd change your mind. And you never said, "By the way, Dunc, I want six kids in the first six years."'

'We talked about this. Ad nauseam. You said you wanted kids too.'

'I do. They just can't be mine.'

'I should have known this. I came off the Pill. I had all those tests. We shagged ourselves silly. And all that time—'

'I knew that if we moved up here we could adopt. A newborn. Maybe more than one.'

'Those tests. Your sperm tests. They were all normal. How did you do it?'

'Oh Christ, is it really important?'

'Yes, it's important. How?'

'It was just a matter of timing. Desogestrel wears off pretty quickly if you stop taking it. When I knew I had a sperm count, I just avoided going near you when you were ovulating.'

He moved closer, sat down on the bed next to me.

'Women can love adopted babies. The maternal bond doesn't rely upon a blood link. Neither does the paternal one.'

'Oh, because you and your folks are just so close.'

He shook his head. 'Not a good example. I know a lot of adoptees. They're adored, precious children. They bring huge happiness.'

'You still don't get it, do you? It wasn't just any baby, it was your baby. A little boy with dark-blue eyes and long limbs and hair that will never lie flat, no matter how much I comb it. I used to talk to that baby, tell him stories about his parents, his cousins, what we would all do together when he was born. He even had a name.' There was a lot more I needed to say but it just wasn't possible.

'What was his name?'

'It doesn't matter.'

'It matters. What was his name?'

'Duncaroony,' I managed.

For a moment I thought Duncan was laughing. Then I realized he wasn't. We sat together, side by side, as the night got darker.

34

THE NEXT DAY I WENT TO WORK. BEFORE LEAVING the night before, Kenn had asked me to come in if I felt up to it, my suspension having expired with the knowledge that the hospital was in the clear. I was still smarting from the indignity of it all but, when it came down to it, I didn't have anything I'd rather do that morning.

Some time in the night, Duncan and I had declared a truce. There remained a lot of unfinished business but neither of us had the energy to resume hostilities just yet. We were having some time out.

As to the future, I wasn't sure. Duncan had told me that the fight I'd overheard on Unst had been about his desire to leave Shetland, that Elspeth had been referring to me when she'd said he was in love. He'd declared that no power on earth would make him leave me. The jury was still out, though, on whether I was staying – with him, in the job, on the islands; I didn't know. I was taking it one day at a time.

Because, in spite of all the lies, in spite of everything he'd kept from me, I still loved him.

I did the ward-round, ignoring the curious looks I was getting from the staff. When I'd been forced to admit (but only to myself) that the unit had been functioning perfectly well without me, I went upstairs to prepare for afternoon clinic.

I phoned my friend in Voe and learned that Charles and Henry were fine. I thanked her for taking care of them and fielded her few curious questions as to how and why they were there. I made arrangements to collect them that evening.

I wondered about what was happening at home. As Duncan and I were leaving that morning, the police had arrived in force. As Helen had promised, they were carrying out another sweep of our fields but I no longer believed they'd find anything. Maybe one day I'd have another look at the islands' female mortality statistics, get someone else's opinion. One day at a time. But there was one thing I really had to do that day. I picked up the phone, dialled a London number and asked to be put through to a woman I'd worked with at my last hospital; the consultant anaesthetist.

'Diane?' I said when we were finally connected. 'It's Tora.'

'My goodness, stranger, how are you?'

Well, there was no truthful short answer to that so I gave the usual lie. 'Fine. You?'

'Great. Will we see you in September?'

'Of course, we're looking forward to it,' I said,

having not thought about it in weeks. A wedding in a picture-book Buckinghamshire village; I'd forgotten that normal life was still going on, somewhere out there. 'Look, I'm sorry about this, but I need some information and I don't have much time. Is that OK?'

'Fire away.'

'What do you know about untraceable drugs?'

Diane wasn't easily fazed. She paused only a second before replying. 'Well, ultimately, there aren't any. If you know what to look for, you can find anything.'

'Thought so. But if you were trying to knock someone out, not necessarily kill them, just incapacitate them, just for a short while, is there anything you could use that a pathologist wouldn't normally test for?'

'Has Duncan been playing you up again?' There was an edge to her voice now but I could hardly blame her. It wasn't exactly a run-of-the-mill question.

'I'm sorry, I wish I had time to explain. I'll call you soon, I promise. Can you think of anything? Something unusual, that they wouldn't test for unless they were specifically asked.'

'Well, I'd need to check, but I'm pretty certain they don't routinely check for things like Benzodiazepines – you know, Nitrazepam or Temazepam. Does that help?'

'Yes, it does. I promise I'm not planning anything illegal.'

'I believe you. Oh, by the way, I got the dress.'

She named a hideously expensive London bridal

designer and wittered away happily for a few more minutes. I was happy to let her, but I wasn't really listening.

Dunn might be a dab hand with the old hypnosis, but it still didn't seem likely that someone as sensible and smart as Dana could be hypnotized into killing herself. Hypnotized for long enough to allow herself to be drugged, maybe. Once unconscious, it would be a relatively simple matter to carry her to the bath and cut through both wrists, probably using her own hands to do it. If Stephen Renney hadn't found anything in Dana's system, it was because he hadn't known what to look for. I wasn't going to accept what Gifford had said last night. Dana was not going to her grave a suicide; not if I had anything to do with it.

'Hey!'

I looked up. 'Hey yourself!'

Helen stood in the doorway. She was wearing the same suit as last night but had changed her blouse for a ruby-red one. She still looked great. I wondered if Dana had taken her shopping, supervised her wardrobe. Or maybe it had been the other way round. Maybe Dana owed her sense of style to this lady. I'd probably never know. I felt a pang of regret that I'd never be able to know them as a couple.

She came in. I realized I was ridiculously pleased to see her.

'Coffee?' I offered. She nodded and I got up to pour it out. We sat together for a while.

'Are you OK?' she asked, and from the way she

was looking at me, just a little too intently, I started to think that she might have something to tell me.

'I'm fine,' I said, stalling for time, because I wasn't sure I wanted to hear whatever it was. 'Better than fine, actually. Duncan and I sorted a few things out and here I am, back at work.'

'Things that seemed impossible just twenty-four hours ago?'

I nodded. 'Is Duncan . . . I mean . . .'

'Is he in the clear? I think so. His story about being a shareholder checks out and he doesn't seem to have set foot on Tronal for years. The Franklin Stone and Mr Gifford seem out of it as well. You heard about Dunn, I take it.'

'I did. Is that bad?'

'Bad as it gets. When a copper's your villain, there's no happy ending.'

'Is he still missing?'

She finished her coffee and got up to pour a refill. 'Yep. He was seen catching a ferry to the mainland on Tuesday evening. We've alerted all the air and ferry ports but . . .'

'Could be well away by now?'

She nodded. 'Right, the good news is, your fields have been thoroughly swept this morning. You won't be uncovering any more nasty surprises should you decide to plant a few spring bulbs.'

'And it was all properly done? The instruments were switched on and everything?' Well, I had to ask.

Helen didn't take offence. She almost laughed.

'OK, let me tell you what they did, as far as I understand it. First of all, they flew over in the chopper this morning and took a whole load of aerial photographs. Apparently – and I admit I didn't know this – when soil has been disturbed at any depth, it shows up on the surface: either as marks on the soil or as crop marks. Also, you might get an increase in vegetation – a rush of spring flowers, for example. Aerial photographs can pick that up.'

'Did they see anything?'

'Nothing. But apparently they didn't really expect to. The method works best for larger sites, such as prehistoric burial grounds. Individual graves rarely show up; but it has been known, so they were being thorough to check.'

'So what then?'

'The next step was to use ground-penetrating radar. They have instruments that send electromagnetic pulses into the ground. When the pulses hit a soil surface that differs in water content from that around it, the signals bounce back. The team plot all these signals on a graph and, if anything has been buried, the pattern of reflections will show it up on the graph. It's even possible to estimate how deep a burial might be, based on the time delay for the reflections to come back. We've done that across the length and breadth of the field.'

'Clever stuff.'

'Oh it's amazing. Course, it's not foolproof. It works best, apparently, on sandy, high-resistivity soil, of which there's very little in your field. So they did one further sweep. This time using soil analysis. Want me to go on?'

'Please.'

'Soil analysis depends upon measuring the amount of phosphate in the soil. Phosphate is present in all soils, but where a body – human or large animal – is buried, the phosphate levels increase quite considerably.'

That certainly made sense to me. Bodies are particularly rich in phosphorus which, along with calcium, gives bone its strength and hardness. It's also found in other tissues of the body.

'Decomposition of human bodies after burial enriches the phosphorus content of the surrounding soil,' continued Helen. 'The team took hundreds of soil samples from your field. If any strong pockets of phosphorus are found, that could indicate more burials.'

'How long will it take to test them all?'

'A few more days. But they're already well under way and nothing has been found so far. I really don't think there's anything down there, Tora.'

I said nothing for a moment.

'So, no more worries about little grey men with a silver fixation?' said Helen.

I had the grace to look bashful. 'Guess the stress was getting to me the other night.'

She smiled back. I looked at her carefully. The slightly wary, nervous look was still there.

'There's something else, isn't there? Something not so good?'

'I'm afraid so. It looks like Stephen Gair isn't going to be facing justice after all. Not in this life anyway.'

Helen broke eye contact first. She stood up and walked to the window.

'What happened?' I managed, wondering why I was feeling so cold. It wasn't as if he'd got away or anything.

'He hanged himself,' she replied, still enjoying my view of the staff car park. 'He was found shortly after five this morning.'

She gave me time to think about it. I thought about it. I would never have the chance to face him in court, to say *I know what you did* and have people believe me. I would never be able to look him in the eyes and say *Got you, you bastard; I bloody well got you!* How did I feel about that? Pretty damned pissed off, to be frank. I stood up.

'How could that have happened? What did you do, give him some rope to practise tying knots with?'

At last she turned round. She held up her hand. 'Take it easy. It will be fully investigated. I can't give you details, I'm afraid. These things happen. I know they shouldn't, but they do. He just wasn't considered a suicide risk.'

'Unlike Dana, of course, who you dismissed as a suicide without a shred of evidence.'

As soon as I said it, I knew I'd gone too far. Helen's face had hardened. She started to move. I stepped in front of her.

'I'm sorry, that was totally uncalled for.'

She relaxed a little.

'I guess it's really over then?' I said.

'You're kidding, aren't you? This Tronal business will keep us going for years.'

I found myself wanting to sit down again. 'What do you mean?'

'That place is an unholy hotchpotch of medical work, social services, legitimate business and the illegal trading of infants. A few dozen people are connected with it; they all need to be checked out. And, of course, we obviously have to trace all the babies that have been adopted from Tronal.'

'All that could take a while.'

'Quite. Trouble is, we can see the money coming in but they're all cash transfers that will be hellishly hard to trace to source. We may suspect which adoption agencies were involved, but without proof they're hardly going to admit it.'

'What about at this end? There would be birth records, adoption papers, passports prepared.'

'Maybe, but we can't find them yet. Well, apart from the half-dozen or so a year that get adopted locally, but they seem to be completely in order. Everyone we've spoken to so far, including George Reynolds at social services and his team, are denying any knowledge of overseas adoptions – whether for money or not.'

'Well, they would, wouldn't they?'

'Yes, but the fact is, there's no evidence of any significant number of babies being born there – less than a dozen a year by all accounts. On the surface, it seems a pretty low-key operation; which, when you come to think of it, you'd expect. How many babies are put up for adoption these days?'

She had a point. 'But he admitted it. He said he was selling babies over the Internet.'

'True, but apart from the money and the word of a now-dead man, we really have no evidence.'

She walked over to the coffee table, put her mug down. 'I'm on my way up there now.'

'Long trip,' said a voice from the doorway. We both turned. Kenn Gifford stood there. Neither of us had heard him approach. 'No helicopter pad on Tronal,' he explained. 'You need to go by road and boat.'

'I'll call you later, Tora,' said Helen. She nodded at Gifford and left the room.

'DCI Rowley?' he asked me. I nodded.

'Every bit as gorgeous as they say.'

I felt the need for something to do. I picked up Helen's mug and my own and took them over to the sink. 'Take it from me, you're wasting your time.'

He laughed. 'I'd heard. How you doing?' He came closer, looked carefully at me. It's so bloody unfair, this ability big men have to intimidate others; they don't have to be smart, they don't have to threaten, they just have to be there. I side-stepped round him and walked over to the window.

'Fine,' I answered for what felt like the tenth time that morning.

'Good to have you back.' He glanced at the coffee pot, noticed it was empty and helped himself to a digestive biscuit.

'Says the man who suspended me in the first place.'

'Says the woman who's never going to let me forget it.' He moved towards me again and I retreated behind the desk.

He made an exasperated face. 'Will you keep still? I'm not about to hypnotize you. I never really managed it anyway; you're a particularly tricky subject.'

And yes, as I was meant to, I felt a surge of pride at that. I also felt a bit daft. I decided to risk looking him in the eyes – green, they were, a deep, mossy green this morning – but if he put his hands on my shoulders I was yelling.

'I didn't get a chance to congratulate you last night,' he said.

I searched his face for sarcasm, but didn't see any.

'I'd be tempted to say you picked the wrong profession but I really don't want to lose you from this one.'

'You're only saying that because the hospital has come up smelling of lavender. If there were any dirt still clinging to you and yours you'd be patting me on the head, making worried noises and murmuring about sedatives.'

He fixed me with a stare. 'Richard is still in custody.'

Shit, I'd walked right into that one. Would I ever learn to engage my brain before my mouth opened?

'Sorry. I should have thought of that.'

And then that big warm hand was on my upper arm and I wasn't making a sound.

'You've dealt with more this past week than most do in a lifetime. Richard can look after himself.' He turned to leave and there was a cold space on my arm.

'Kenn . . .'

He turned in the doorway.

'I'm sorry.'

He raised one eyebrow.

'About suspecting you,' I added.

'Accepted. And I'm still thinking about it.'

'About what?'

'About what I'm going to do with you.' He grinned at me and left the room.

I sat down. 'Shit!' I said out loud. And there I'd been thinking all my problems were solving themselves.

I went downstairs. A couple of my third-trimester ladies were kind enough to say they'd missed me at the last clinic. But the Tronal business was still preying on my mind, so as soon as we broke for lunch, I grabbed a sandwich and went back up to my room. From my bag I dug out the pieces of paper that had started it all: the record of deliveries for the Shetland District Health Authority.

Let it go, Tora, said a voice in the back of my head; the faint, slightly wistful voice that speaks for the sensible, grown-up part of me. Unfortunately, I'd never really learned to pay attention to that voice and I wasn't about to start now. Once again, I counted up the Tronal deliveries. Four. Four in a six-month period meant around six to ten a year. If around half a dozen were adopted locally, that just didn't leave enough to sell overseas and make any sort of money.

Where the hell had Stephen Gair been getting his babies from? And how on earth could the sort of state-of-the-art maternity facility that had been described to me be feasible for just eight births per annum? The equipment and the staff would be standing around doing nothing for most of the year. There must be more babies being born at Tronal than were recorded on my stats. But how could a birth not be registered?

Dana had also mentioned terminations, but that made little sense. Terminations are available everywhere in the UK; why on earth would significant numbers of women travel all the way to Tronal for what they could get in their hometown?

If only I could go with Helen to Tronal. I'd know the questions to ask, be able to spot anything that didn't fit, far better than she could. But it was impossible; if any sort of trial came out of all this, I would be a key witness. I couldn't keep interfering in the official investigation.

I started going through the list one more time.

The first thing that jumped out at me were those blessed initials. KT. Keloid Trauma: problems arising from previous perineum scarring. I flicked to another screen and typed 'Keloid Trauma' into the Google search engine. Nothing, but the term had been coined to describe a condition particular to Shetland so maybe it hadn't yet made it on to the world wide web. I went into the hospital archives and ran a similar search. Nothing. I started checking all the KT entries again. First of April, a baby boy, born on Papa Stour. Then, on 8 May, another boy, born here at the Franklin Stone. On 19 May, a third boy – of course, they were all boys. But the sex of the baby couldn't possibly have an impact upon perineum scarring, could it? On 6 June, Alison Jenner had had a little boy on Bressay; later in June another delivery at the Franklin Stone.

Hang on a minute. That name meant something. Alison Jenner. Where had I heard that before? Jenner, Jenner, Jenner. Shit, it had gone.

Stephen Renney was in his windowless office, eating a sandwich and drinking Fanta from a can. He sensed me standing in his doorway, looked up and then started making those slightly embarrassed, fidgety movements we all make when we've been caught eating alone. As though eating were some sort of not-quite-respectable indulgence instead of the most natural thing in the world.

'Sorry,' I said, giving the time-honoured response, and looking slightly embarrassed myself, as though I'd caught him on the loo.

'Not at all,' he responded, ridiculously forgiving me. He stood up, motioned to a chair. I took it.

'I wanted to ask you something. About Dana Tulloch.'

His forearms were on the desk and he leaned forward. I could smell tuna fish on his breath.

'Mr Gifford said you'd found no traces of any sort of drug in her system and—'

'Miss Hamilton . . .' He leaned forward some more and I tried not to back away; it smelled as though he'd been eating cat food.

'I know you can't discuss specifics with me and I really don't want to put you in a difficult position, but—'

'Miss Hamilton—'

'Please, just give me a second. I've been speaking to an anaesthetist friend of mine this morning. She mentioned some drugs that would incapacitate someone but that wouldn't normally be tested for in a post-mortem. I just wondered if you—'

'Miss Hamilton.' Stephen Renney had raised his voice. 'I didn't carry out Miss Tulloch's post-mortem.'

'Oh!' I said. Had Gifford mentioned Stephen Renney or had I just assumed?

'I'll get a copy of the report, of course, but I don't think it's come through just yet. I can check for you.'

'So who did?' I demanded, manners out the window.

He frowned at me. 'I never actually saw Miss Tulloch. She was only here for a couple of hours and I was in meetings. She was taken to Dundee. I understand her next of kin, a policewoman, requested the transfer. The PM was carried out in Dundee.'

'Of course, I'm sorry.' Helen hadn't mentioned it, but there was no real reason why she should. It certainly made sense that she'd want Dana's post-mortem to be carried out by people she knew and trusted.

'Is there anything else I can help you with?'

Well, I know a dismissal when I hear one. I shook my head, thanked him again and left.

Back in my office there was an email from Gifford asking for my help in theatre that afternoon. He had a full list himself and a patient with a ruptured appendix had been admitted that morning. It would save him rearranging his list if I could do it. I'm not qualified for general surgery but the appendix was well within my region of expertise. I checked my messages – one from Duncan, the rest all non-urgent – and went down to theatre.

The patient was a thirty-year-old male, fit and healthy. I opened him up, fumbled around for a few minutes and removed the offending piece; swollen like a drum, no wonder he was in pain. Just as I finished closing and the patient was being wheeled out to recovery, Gifford came in. He was still gowned up and his gloves were covered in blood. I glanced down. So were mine. The other staff had left theatre and we were alone. He unhooked his mask from one ear.

'Will you have dinner with me?'

I left my mask in place. 'When?'

He shrugged. 'Tonight?'

I managed to look him straight in the eye. 'How kind. I'll see if Duncan's free.'

He reached out and took the mask from my face.

As he did so, his gloved fingers brushed my cheek and I couldn't help the shudder. He saw it, of course.

'I'll ask again.'

I wondered if I had blood on my face. 'I'll email you the hospital's policy on sexual harassment.'

He laughed. 'Don't bother. I wrote it.'

He stood still for a moment, looking at me, and from beneath the harsh, antiseptic smells of theatre came a scent so warm and familiar it made me want to step closer, breathe it in, catch hold of his clothes and press them to my face. Then he turned and left and the scent was gone. I found I was shaking. The scrub nurse came back into the room and started collecting up instruments. I thanked her and left, praying I wouldn't bump into Gifford on the way back to my room.

I spent an hour on the wards, then decided to check on my appendix patient. He was awake but drowsy. His wife sat by his side, his young son, about fifteen months old, perched on the edge of the bed. His mother held him with one hand, his father with the other, and he bounced gleefully. It can't have been comfortable but if my patient wasn't objecting, neither was I. I checked him out, aware that something at the back of my mind was nagging me, and agreed he could go home the next day if he got plenty of rest.

I stopped by the canteen, bought a chocolate muffin and carried it back to my room. I made fresh coffee, sat down at my desk – and remembered.

The family group: the appendix patient, his wife

and baby son. I knew who Alison Jenner was. She was Stephen Gair's second wife, the woman who was step-mum to his son by Melissa.

So why the hell was her name on the list of Shetland births? She hadn't given birth; Melissa had. Stephen Gair had admitted that his son, Connor, was Melissa's child. How could Alison's name be included on a list of women who had delivered that summer? And why did her entry include the KT reference?

I found the list and checked, just in case I'd been mistaken. There she was. Alison Jenner, aged forty, gave birth to a little boy, 8lbs 2oz, on 6 June. Surely that couldn't be coincidence, it had to be the same woman. OK, think! The Gairs only had one child. So, either Stephen Gair had been lying about Connor being Melissa's – and why the hell would he? – or the entry must be referring to Melissa's son.

I double-checked the number of entries with the KT initials after them. There were seven that summer. I pulled up the corresponding list for the subsequent period, from September 2005 through February 2006. Couldn't see anything. Then I went back, to the previous winter. Nothing. I went back again, to the summer of 2004. No KT entries. I kept on going back until I spotted them again. In summer 2002 there were five entries with KT after them, born in various centres around the islands, all baby boys.

A tightness was forming in my chest as I went further back, examining whole years at a time. 2001 was clear; so was 2000. In the summer of 1999 there were six KT entries. Boys.

I wanted to switch off the computer, get into my car and drive home, collect the horses and ride for miles along the beach. Better still, run up to Kenn Gifford's office, lock the door and take off every stitch I was wearing. Anything to take my mind off what was now staring me in the face.

I stayed where I was and I brought up more screens.

I went back to 1980 and that was enough. The pattern was unmistakeable. Every three years, between four and eight baby boys had their deliveries recorded as KT.

Every three years, the female death rate on Shetland made a modest but unmistakeable blip. The following summer, some unusual little boys were born. KT; it had nothing to do with Keloid Trauma, that was a smokescreen, the condition probably didn't even exist. KT stood for Kunal Trow.

I flicked back, faster and faster, to the earliest year the computerized records showed. They began in 1975. I needed to go further back.

I stood up, on legs that felt none too steady, and walked as fast as I dared along the corridor to the service lift. It arrived within two minutes and – by some miracle – was empty. I pressed B for basement and went down.

The floor seemed empty. I followed the signs and walked down a corridor lit by occasional electric bulbs. Several had blown. As I walked, I looked out for switches on the walls. I did not want to find myself trapped in pitch-blackness down here, scrambling around for switches that didn't exist.

I reached the end of the corridor. Most hospital archives are a mess and these were no exception. They were housed in three basement rooms. I pushed the door of the first. Darkness. I felt around on the wall for a light switch. The room sprang into a grimy light. I could feel the dust in my throat. Everything was in large, brown cardboard boxes, stacked several high on steel shelving. The labels were mostly turned to the front. I walked along the shelves, keeping one eye firmly on the open door. I doubted these rooms were visited more than a couple of times a year. If a door slammed shut, locked from the outside, Tora could say hi to a pleasant few days of starvation and terror.

I didn't find obstetrics and opened the door to the second room. Same layout as the first. This time I wedged the door open. In the third row I found them. It took a few minutes to locate the box I needed and pull it down. Inside were ledgers, handwritten records of births; the manual equivalent of the lists I'd been looking at on my computer. I found the year I was looking for, 1972, and flicked to July. On the twenty-fifth of the month, there it was. Elspeth Guthrie, aged thirty-five, on the island of Unst, a baby boy, 7lbs 15oz. KT.

I'd been crouching down over the box and I sank to the floor. I sat amidst years of accumulated dust and debris, getting filthy and not caring.

I could think of only one reason why birth records should be falsified to the extent of recording the adopting mother as the birth mother: something was so badly wrong with the real birth that it would bear no investigating. Duncan's birth mother had been killed. Just like Melissa had been; just like all the others had been.

Every three years island women were being bred in captivity like farm animals and then slaughtered. I wondered whether the legends of the Trows had given some maniac the idea in the first place, or whether the stories had sprung from real events taking place in the islands over the years; known about but never discussed, never openly acknowledged, because to do so would be tantamount to admitting you lived among monsters.

I'd intended to find the record of Kenn's birth too, but I couldn't bring myself to do it. Enough was enough.

I pushed myself to my feet, put the lid back on the box and lifted it back on to the shelf. I tucked the ledger under my arm and left the room, willing myself not to run; I switched off the lights and made for the lift. Then I changed my mind and went in the opposite direction, heading for the stairs, telling myself all the while to stay calm, act calm; no one knew what I'd found out, I was safe for a while. I just had to keep my head.

How the hell were they doing it? How do you spirit away a live woman, at the same time convincing all her relatives that she's dead? How do you hold a funeral with an empty coffin? Had no one ever taken a last peek and found a pink-lined casket of bricks?

I'd made the ground floor. I was ridiculously out of breath. I stopped for a second.

They couldn't use semblances – the equivalent of the dying Cathy Morton – for all of them. It just wasn't feasible that enough seriously ill women would be found. The Cathy/Melissa switch had to have been a special case. I was back to hypnosis and drugs, to the involvement of enough people to make sure the procedures were never questioned: the doctor would administer the drugs, pronounce death, comfort the family; the pathologist would fill in the forms, make out reports for corpses that didn't exist; relatives would be discouraged – under any number of pretexts – from viewing the bodies.

I was back on my floor.

Kirsten. Poor Kirsten, my fellow equestrian. I'd knelt by her grave, tidying the spring flowers and feeling a close empathy because of the way she'd died. But she hadn't been down there. She was still in my field, the real grave site, she had to be. The instrument sweeps had been a sham – even the most recent, carried out that very day. If Detective Superintendent Harris had been present . . . well, I'd be interested in finding out where and when he'd been born.

I wondered, briefly, if I'd found out where Stephen Gair had been getting his babies from. Except it still didn't add up. The numbers involved – an average of just two per annum – still seemed far too few to attract the sort of revenues Helen and I had found. Plus, the babies I could name – Duncan, Kenn, Andy

Dunn, Connor Gair – had all been adopted locally. The chances were others had been too. Money might have changed hands but it couldn't explain the massive amounts – several millions each year – that were coming in from overseas. And it would be too big a risk, surely, to abduct women, keep them prisoner and murder them, just to be able to sell their babies to the highest bidder. No, whatever motive was driving these people, it had to be more than money. The babies being sold were coming from another source.

My office appeared as I'd left it. The coffee had brewed and I poured myself a mug, spilling a good quarter of it in the process. I had to get a grip or the first person who saw me would know something was up. I think the desk phone must have been ringing for some time before I reached out and picked up the receiver.

'I was just about to try you at home.' It was Helen. I couldn't tell her yet. I needed to get my head together first. If I opened my mouth I'd probably babble like an idiot.

'Where are you?' I managed.

'Just leaving Tronal. Boy, the wind's getting up. Can you hear me?'

A flash of panic so sharp it was painful. I'd forgotten Helen was going to Tronal. 'Are you OK? Who's with you?'

'Tora, I'm fine. What's wrong? What's happened?'

'Nothing, nothing, just tired,' I managed, telling

myself to calm down, to take it easy. Big, deep breaths. 'How was it?'

'Quiet sort of place. Only a few women, most of them asleep. Couple of babies in the nursery. We're going back in the morning. I'll be staying on Unst for a few days.'

'Will I see you soon?'

She was quiet for a second. I could hear the boat's engine in the background and the whistling of the wind. 'Are you sure you're OK?' she said at last.

'I'm fine,' I said, then because it didn't seem enough, 'I'm on my way home. Dunc and I are going out to dinner.'

'Great, cos look, I wanted to ask you something. Something personal and I didn't really get chance this morning. Is now a good time?'

'Of course,' I said. Now was a great time. I was ready for just about anything; anything that didn't require thinking, moving, speaking.

She lowered her voice. 'Thing is, I have to start thinking about Dana's funeral. I'm her next of kin, you know.'

I knew that; my friendly local pathologist had told me so. Dana's funeral. I closed my eyes and found myself in the midst of a sad, solemn gathering. We were in an ancient church, cathedral-like in its dimensions, softly lit by tall white candles. I could smell the candle smoke and the incense that drifted down from the high altar.

'I know you hadn't known her very long,' came Helen's voice from a distance, 'but . . . I think . . .

well, I think you made quite an impression. On me too, come to that. It would mean a lot if you could be there.'

Dana's flowers would be white: roses, orchids and lilies; stylish and beautiful, like the woman herself. Six young constables, uniforms gleaming, would carry her to the altar. The back of my throat started to hurt. Tears were rolling down my cheeks and I could no longer see the room around me. 'Of course,' I said. 'Of course I will. Thank you.'

'No, thank *you*.' Helen's voice had deepened.

'Will it be in Dundee? Do you have a date in mind?'

'No. I'm still waiting to hear from your place about when they can let her go. They need to keep her for a while. I can understand that, of course, I'd just like to get things moving.'

And the vision froze, the uniformed pall-bearers stopped moving, the candles flickered and went out. 'She's still here? In the hospital?'

I didn't expect her to hear me, I could barely hear myself, but the wind must have died at just the right moment because she did.

'Just for a little while. I have to go. I'll see you.'

She was gone. I blinked hard. My face was wet but my eyes were clear. The room that had been swimming just a second ago was thrown into sharp focus. I could see again. I stood up. I could move again. And, praise the Lord, I could think again.

I grasped, in that moment, the true and complete meaning of the word epiphany. Because I'd just had one. There was much I still didn't get, but I understood one thing with perfect and absolute clarity. Sorry, Helen, couldn't oblige after all. I was not going to be one of Dana's mourners, biting lips and dabbing eyes as we watched her elegant, weightless coffin carried to the grave. I would have no part in the age-old ritual of committing her body to the earth or the flames. This was one funeral I was going nowhere near.

Because Dana wasn't dead.

35

AN HOUR AND A HALF LATER, I DROVE ON TO THE Yell ferry. It wasn't quite eight o'clock but it was going to be the last crossing of the evening: there were dark clouds overhead and a storm was threatening. I sat in my car, shivering in spite of my jacket, and tried not to think about the waves that were beating against the ferry as it pushed its way across the Yell Sound. When the ferryman came to collect my fare I asked him what he thought the wind speed was. It was a force five gusting six, he said, and forecast to increase before the night was out.

And I didn't want to dwell on what other storms might break before the sun came up. I was filled with a sense of my every action being for the last time. Just before leaving the hospital I'd phoned home. Duncan hadn't answered and I couldn't face trying his mobile. I left a message that there'd been an emergency at the hospital and I would be working late. I added that I loved him; partly because it was true and partly because I wasn't sure I was ever going to be able to say it to him again.

Small creatures were dancing a samba in my stomach as the ferry docked and I was off again. I had further to drive but that was all to the good. I needed darkness for what I was planning and a bit more time to drum up enough courage. On the other hand, if I thought about it too much I'd definitely chicken out.

I'd taken out one small insurance policy. I'd put the ledger from the basement, several computer print-outs and a hastily scribbled note in a brown envelope. On my way out of Lerwick, I'd dropped by Dana's house and left it conspicuously on the fridge in her kitchen. Some time in the next few days, Helen would find it. If I didn't come back, she'd know where I'd gone and why. Whatever happened, I was not going to disappear without trace.

Helen and her team had spent most of the day on Tronal and were staying on nearby Unst that night. The Tronal people would be wary. Anything they had to hide would be well hidden. They'd be watching the north and north-eastern approaches to the island; any boats setting off from Unst would be spotted in good time and plenty of warning given. I could not hope to approach the island stealthily from that direction.

So I wasn't going to try.

At Gutcher on Yell there is a small sailing club close to the pier. It has about twenty Yell-based members and is affiliated to its neighbouring club on

Unst. I had a key that I knew would get me into the shed that passed as a clubhouse. Once in there, I'd break into the cupboard that held spare boat keys. That was the easy bit.

After that, I'd have to rig up an unfamiliar boat in the dark, sail it single-handed in winds that were verging on storm conditions, in waters I barely knew, towards an area of notoriously treacherous navigation. Even that wasn't the hard bit.

Jesus, what the hell was I thinking?

I parked. To my relief and disappointment (in equal parts) the car park was empty and the clubhouse in darkness. Anything getting in my way at this stage I'd have taken as a sign not to go on. It took just a few seconds to break into the cupboard and find the keys I was looking for. I took some waterproofs and a life jacket and made my way down to the jetty.

Duncan and Richard had a friend on Yell who was a keen sailor. He'd recently bought one of the new sport boats and he'd taken Duncan and me out in it several times. It was a sailing boat, built for speed, but with a deep keel giving it greater stability than the average dinghy. It had an engine, for when the wind wasn't on your side; a small covered cabin, for when the weather wasn't; and an anchor, so you could park at sea.

I was about to add grand larceny to the list of complaints the police and other island authorities had against me, but, hell, maybe I wouldn't live to face the music.

The jetty, fifty years old if it was a day, rocked

beneath me. The wind whipped my hair up and I guessed it had risen to a force six. Any greater and I would be taking a stupid risk with my own life. I was probably doing that anyway.

Marinas are never silent places and when strong winds whistle through them the noise can really jar on the nerves. Several boats were moored against the jetty and their riggings were twanging and humming like so many high-pitched discordant guitars. Several of them clanged together and even in the relative shelter of the marina small waves were banging aggressively against hulls. It did not augur well for conditions out at sea.

I found the boat, climbed aboard and unlocked the cabin. Only to have a debilitating attack of nerves. I made myself focus on getting the boat ready, one step at a time. If there was anything I couldn't do, that would be the sign to give up. I fixed the jib in place and threaded the sheets. I attached the main sail and released the kicker. I checked fuel and the instruments. Expecting every second to hear a yell of outrage, I finished faster than expected. And I'd calmed down. A little.

Our friend had local charts on board and I studied them for some time. From the marina at Gutcher I would sail directly south-east for about a mile, hidden behind a small, uninhabited island called Linga. Once I cleared Linga, I could alter my course and head directly west towards Tronal. There were cliffs on its western edge but also an area of sloping beach. I'd be able to anchor. If I got that far.

Telling myself it was now or never, I released the stern line, made a slip knot on the bow and started the engine. I put the boat into reverse and pulled slowly out of the marina. No one saw me; or if they did, no one called or raised the alarm.

As I left the harbour a wave came crashing over the starboard bow, hitting me full in the face. I had not imagined it would be so cold. I pulled my hood up and fastened the strings tight.

The sky was thick with cloud and darkness was falling fast. I'd put the chart into a plastic cover and hung it from the instrument panel; pretty soon, with visibility down to virtually zero, I'd need to check it every few minutes. I turned the boat sharply to starboard and I was in the channel between Linga and Yell. Now the waves were hitting me head on. Every couple of seconds – wham – we slammed into another and its freezing particles came hurtling over the bow. I was soon soaked.

I was leaving the lights of Gutcher behind me. On either side land rose up like dark shadows. The engine was a small one, struggling to make four knots, and far too noisy. If I were to get to Tronal in less than an hour and not be heard, I'd have to sail. I started to haul up the mainsail. Immediately the boat began to heel.

It took every ounce of courage I had to unfurl the jib but I knew I wouldn't have enough stability without it. I pulled it out halfway. The sail filled, the boat accelerated away and I switched off the engine.

Within minutes the speed was up to seven knots

and the boat was heeling at a thirty-degree angle. I was braced against the side of the boat to stay upright as we slammed into waves that felt like brick walls. But I was making progress; and I was in control. Just.

I hunkered down in the cockpit. Every strong gust of wind threatened to pitch the boat on to its side. With one hand, I held tightly on to the stick; the other held the main sheet. Every time I felt the tiller pushing out of control, I released the tension in the main and clung on for dear life until the boat righted itself again.

All too soon, I'd reached the southernmost tip of Linga and had to leave the shelter of the channel. I turned the boat to port and altered the sails. The wind was now coming over the port stern and the boat stopped heeling and came upright again. The sails filled and my speed picked up. Seven and a half, eight, eight and a half knots. At this rate, as long as I didn't jibe, I'd be at Tronal in no time.

And what the hell was I going to find there?

Helen had been wrong. Helen was a fine police officer and she'd done what she'd been trained to do; she'd stuck to the facts. But the facts only took us so far. They took us to Tronal being the centre of a scheme involving the illegal sale of babies, to Stephen Gair being head of the operation, assisted by Dunn and several others, identities still to be determined.

They took us to Melissa being murdered to protect the operation; brilliantly dispatched in a way that in the normal course of events would never have been suspected, even if her body had been discovered.

But the facts didn't explain her strange, ritualistic burial on my land, instead of being conveniently dumped at sea. They didn't – paternal bonding aside – explain Gair taking the enormous risk of holding her prisoner for long enough for their baby to be born. They didn't explain Kirsten's wedding ring being found in my field.

Nor could the facts explain the regular rise in the female death rate, followed a year later by a batch of baby boys, incorrectly and illegally registered as the birth children of their adoptive mothers.

To explain all that, you had to take a giant leap of faith; which Helen had been unable to do, but which Dana had been veering towards and at which I, finally, had arrived. Here, on Shetland, legend lived. The Trows of so many island stories were real, dwelling among humans, passing for human.

Of course, I knew that if you were to dissect the bodies of these Trows, carry out every known medical test on their blood, their DNA, their bone structure, they'd be no different, anatomically, from any other human male. But – crucial point here – they believed themselves to be different from the rest of the human race, to have different rights, different responsibilities; to be subject not to ordinary human laws but to a code of their own that was self-determined, self-administered and self-monitored.

The boat sped along as total darkness fell. The compass told me I was on track, the chart told me there were no immediate hazards ahead, but otherwise, I was running blind. A few twinkling beacons aside, I was sailing in a thick black void. Vague shadows on the almost invisible horizon suggested islands or large rocks around me, but none was close yet. The depth gauge had given up, unable to calculate a depth too immense to measure. Logically that was reassuring, but I really didn't like to think of the black fathoms beneath me. I sailed on, thinking instead about what would be waiting for me on Tronal.

History offers countless examples of the self-proclaimed master race. That had to be what I was dealing with now: a group of men who believed themselves to be intrinsically superior to the rest of us. Up in this remote corner of the world, a few dozen island men were operating their own private kingdom. Running the police, the local government, the health service, the schools, the chamber of commerce, they had control over every aspect of island life; automatically assuming the best jobs, the plum contracts, entry to the best clubs, making themselves rich with a complex mix of legal and illegal trading. Since the discovery of the North Sea oil fields, the Shetland Islands had enjoyed unprecedented economic prosperity and a group of local men were taking full advantage. It was the Masons meets the Mafia. With an extra bit of nastiness thrown in.

Of course, as evening became night-time, I asked myself why these men couldn't just leave it at that; marry and mate like other men and enjoy the fruits of their little fiefdom. Why did they have to kidnap, rape and murder the mothers of their sons? That dreadful process, I guessed – and the very small number of boys born out of it – would go to the very heart of their distinctness. Their rarity made them – in their eyes at least – immeasurably special.

Boys born into the Trow community would face a stark choice – accept what they were, enjoy the enormous advantages and deal with the horrific reality of how they were made; or leave and risk the destruction of everything and everyone they'd been taught to value. I knew now that Duncan had no desire to leave me; it was the life he wanted out of. I knew why he'd been so depressed about the move back to Shetland, in spite of the huge advantages it had offered him; why our relationship had been under such strain. Duncan was fighting the forces that had drawn him back to the islands. My heart went out to him, but it was a battle he'd have to fight alone for now. I had problems of my own to deal with and, in any event, I sensed he wasn't winning.

A mass of darkness ahead of me was growing blacker, taking a shape more solid than the night around it. I thought I could even see small lights. I was nearing Tronal. I furled the jib and the boat slowed by a couple of knots. I could make out bumps and ridges in the cliffs and see a lighter area that must be the sand of the beach. The depth gauge was working now. Fifteen metres, fourteen, thirteen . . .

Waves were breaking on the shore. Ten metres,

nine . . . I was about to turn the boat so that it was heading directly into wind to allow me to drop the sails when I spotted rocks off the port side. The starboard side looked clear but I'd have to turn the boat round nearly 300 degrees and I wasn't sure I had the speed any more. I looked again to port: more rocks. I was in five metres of water, four, three . . . As fast as I could, I reached forward, pulled up the keel and released the mainsail. Then I closed my eyes and held on tight to the stick. The wind was behind us and the boat continued forward until a scraping sound under the hull and a massive jerk forward told me we'd hit the beach. We travelled another yard or so, then stopped.

I collected what I needed from the cabin and then came up top again. I stood on the narrow deck, staring at Tronal, the geographical fortress I was about to storm. Since the dawn of time, people have surrounded themselves by water to protect against invasion. But it wasn't just the island I was facing; it was the fortress of the Trows – an invisible but complex structure run by very powerful men. They were strong, they could hypnotize people. It was little use telling myself that they were, after all, only men. For generations past they'd convinced themselves that they were different.

At the end of the day, if you believe something deeply enough, it becomes a kind of truth.

36

THE BEACH WAS NARROW, SLOPING UPWARDS, scattered with boulders that gleamed black in the darkness. On all sides, low jagged cliffs reared above me. They seemed to be moving and I almost cried out, then relaxed. The cliffs were home to hundreds of nesting sea birds – gulls or fulmars, I couldn't tell – white bellies squirming, wings fluttering, heads nodding against the black of the granite cliffs.

I pulled the anchor from its locker and walked several paces up the beach until I could wedge it behind a small rock. Assuming I made it back to the beach, the boat would be waiting for me. I tugged on a small backpack I'd brought with me and set off.

I started towards the lowest point on the cliff. It was far too dark to see clearly and every few seconds I tripped or slid. At the edge of the beach I began to climb. After a few yards the pebbles gave way to thin soil, some scattered clumps of grass and coarse, springy heather. It wasn't steep but I was breathing heavily when I reached the top. A barbed-wire fence ringed the upper part of the island but I was prepared for it. With the aid of a small pair of pliers from the boat I'd soon cut a way through. After that there was a stone wall, about waist high. I climbed over, taking care not to dislodge any of the loose stones. I looked round, found a stone that had fallen and placed it on top of the wall as a rough marker of where I'd cut the wire.

Keeping low, I looked around me. Tronal is a small island, oval in shape, roughly a mile long and a third of a mile wide, with three stubby promontories at its south-eastern edge. It is fifty metres above sea level at its highest point, pretty much the place where I was crouching. Looking north I could see the lights of Uyeasound on Unst and also several down on Tronal's tiny marina. A single pier, new and solidly built, jutted out from the small natural harbour. Several boats, including a large white cruiser, were moored there. A Land-Rover was parked near the jetty. I thought I could see movement around it.

From the harbour a rough, single-track road led across the island to the only buildings that were visible. Almost in the centre of the island, the terrain rose and then dipped, forming a natural hollow in which the buildings nestled. I dropped lower and started making my way towards them.

Instinct told me to stay close to the hillside, to move as quickly as the rough ground allowed. At one point I thought I heard voices, ten minutes later the sound of a boat engine, but the wind was still strong and I couldn't be sure.

After about fifteen minutes of ducking and scrambling, I could see lights not too far away from me. I climbed the hill to its summit and lay down on the coarse, prickly grass. Below me, not fifteen metres away, was the clinic.

It was a one-storey building, made of local stone with a high slate roof, built around a square and with a central courtyard. A gated archway in the north-western elevation permitted vehicular access to the courtyard. The gates stood open. Dormer windows appeared at regular intervals along the roof, six to a side. Only a few lights shone from the building itself, but the area surrounding it was dimly lit by a series of small lights set along the gravel pathways. I set off again, keeping a good distance away, to inspect the building from all angles before deciding whether it was safe to approach.

Moving south away from the gate I found a whole row of dark rooms. Blinds weren't drawn but I could make out nothing inside them.

The south-eastern side was busy. Several windows had blinds up and lights on. I sank back into the shadows and watched. There were men inside. I managed to count half a dozen, but couldn't be sure there weren't more. Three, maybe four, were in some sort of common room; I could see easy chairs and a TV on the wall. Another two were in a large kitchen that gleamed with stainless steel. Some of the men wore jeans and sweaters; a couple were dressed in white surgical scrubs. They stood around, chatting, drinking from mugs. One of the men in the kitchen was smoking, his cigarette held out of an open window. My watch told me it was just after ten o'clock. A normal hospital would be quietening down for the night. No sign of that here.

I crouched low, thinking about video surveillance, security lights, alarms. If this building were the prison I believed it to be, it would surely have all of those. Turning another corner, I found a row of eight windows, all of which had blinds drawn. I moved on. There was a row of outbuildings about ten metres away from the house. I planned to hide behind them.

I must have been about six metres away from the sheds when there came a terrifying explosion of sound: the manic barking of several large dogs. I dropped to the ground, curling instinctively into the tightest ball I could manage, tucking my hands into my chest.

The barking grew in intensity, claws scratched against wood, animals yelped, hurting each other in their urgency to reach me, to be the first to tear me apart.

Nothing happened: I didn't hear the pounding of large paws, jagged teeth didn't clamp down on to my flesh. But the cacophonous din continued, the dogs getting more and more furious with themselves, with me, with the situation. With a relief that almost made me pass out, I realized they couldn't reach me. They were locked up.

I forced myself to uncurl and start crawling. I went back the way I'd come, back towards the common room and kitchen. As my scent faded, the dogs began to calm. After a few more seconds I heard a male voice talking to them, soothing them.

The television in the common room was turned on and several of the men were gathered around it, watching with interest. With any luck it might distract them for a while. Also, whilst my recent encounter with the canine world had left me shaking violently, I realized the presence of dogs was good news; just so long as they remained locked up. If guard dogs provided the island's security, they might rely less on devices like alarms and cameras. Of course, once the dogs were loose, my life expectancy stood at around ten minutes.

The kitchen was empty, the smoker's window still open.

It was a stupid, ridiculous risk to even think about taking with most of the clinic's staff in the next room. Far better to creep back across the island, climb on to my boat and sail to Unst; try and convince Helen to come back here sooner than planned, to take Tronal by surprise. That way, I might just be alive when the sun came up. But would Dana?

Glancing round, I saw a tall bush and ran for it. Behind it, I unhooked my backpack and pulled off my waterproofs. Underneath were the scrubs I'd been wearing all day. I pulled a cap on to my head and tucked my hair up inside it. Seen quickly and at a distance, it was just possible I wouldn't set alarm bells ringing. I ran forward, paused to check the kitchen was still empty and climbed in.

The volume of the TV next door was turned up loud and I was pretty certain no one had heard me come in. I clambered over a steel worktop, dropped to the floor and listened hard: nothing but the low chanting of a sports crowd on the TV and an occasional expletive from the next room. I leaned over and pulled the window down until it was almost but not quite closed. With luck, anyone glancing at it would think it shut and locked. I crossed the kitchen and gently opened the door. The corridor was empty and I set off left, away from the common room. Looking up, I could see cameras tucked away in the corner between wall and ceiling. I just had to hope they weren't being monitored.

I walked slowly, silently, alert every second for the slightest noise that would tell me someone was approaching. Along the wall on my right-hand side were occasional windows showing a dim view of the internal courtyard. Across the courtyard was another lit and windowed corridor. It would not be easy to remain unseen. From the outside, the building had looked old, but once inside I didn't think it could be. It was just too regular, too clean and modern in its construction, the windows large and frequent. On my left were rooms. Most had closed doors, one with light shining under that I passed by quickly. Two had open doors and I glanced inside. The first was an office: desk, computer terminal, glass-fronted book-case; the second was some sort of meeting room.

I came to the end of the corridor and found a door to my right leading out into the courtyard. On my left were the steel double doors of a large lift and a flight of stairs. I started to climb.

Seven steps up and the stairs made a 180-degree turn. There was a fire-door at the top. I opened it and glanced through. The corridor was narrow and windowless. Dim spotlights were evenly spaced along the low ceiling. I counted six doors along my right-hand side. Each had a small shuttered window. I slid back the first shutter.

The room beyond was dark but I could make out a narrow, hospital-style bed with tubular framing and a pale-coloured cabinet by its side. Also an easy chair and a small TV, mounted on the wall. Someone lay in the bed but the covers were pulled up high and I had no way of telling whether the someone was young or old, male or female, dead or alive.

I moved on to the next window. Same set-up. Except this time, as I watched, the figure in the bed moved, turning over and stretching before settling down again.

The next room was empty; so was the fourth.

There was light in the fifth room. A woman sat in the armchair, reading a magazine. She looked up and we made eye contact. Then she dropped her magazine, put both hands on the arms of her chair and pushed herself up. She was wearing pyjamas and a dressing gown. She was pregnant.

She came towards the door. Every nerve ending I had was on fire, but I knew if I ran now the game would be up. She opened the door and tilted her head slightly to one side.

'Hello,' she said.

All I could do was stare back. Creases appeared on her forehead and her eyes narrowed.

'Sorry,' I managed. 'Long day, four hours in theatre, brain not really functioning any more. How are you feeling?'

She relaxed and stepped back, inviting me into her room. I went in, closing the door behind me and making sure the window shutter was pulled across.

'I'm OK,' she said. 'Bit nervous. Mr Mortensen said he would give me something to help me sleep but I guess he's been busy.' She leaned back against the bed. 'We're still OK for tomorrow, aren't we?'

I forced myself to smile at her. 'Haven't heard anything to the contrary.'

'Thank Christ. I just want to get it over with now. I really need to get back to work.'

A termination. Dana had told me the clinic carried them out. This woman, at least, was here voluntarily.

'Have I seen you before?' she was asking me.

I shook my head. 'Don't think so. How long have you been here?'

'Five days now. I really need to get home. I thought it would just take twenty-four hours.'

'I've been away for a week,' I said. 'Just back on duty this afternoon. I haven't managed to look at your notes yet. Have there been complications?'

She sighed and pushed herself up so that she

was sitting on the bed. 'Just about everything you can think of. Blood pressure sky-high, apparently, although it's never been a problem in the past. Sugar and protein in my urine. Traces of a viral infection in my blood, although why that should stop you going ahead is beyond me.'

It was beyond me too. It all sounded like complete nonsense. Something was starting to feel very wrong. I glanced at the notes pinned to the foot of her bed, found her name.

'Emma, can I have a quick look at your tummy?'

She lay back on the bed and pulled her dressing gown open. She was a striking-looking woman: probably in her late twenties, tall with vivid blonde hair showing just a fraction of dark roots. Her eyes were large and light brown in colour, her lips plump and very red, her teeth white and perfect.

I started to press my hands very gently on her abdomen. Immediately something kicked back. I glanced up at Emma but her face had tightened. She wouldn't make eye contact.

'What do you do for a living, Emma?' I asked her, as my hands travelled upwards.

She smiled. 'I'm an actress,' she said, with the air of someone who'd waited a long time to say those words and who hadn't quite got used to the thrill of doing so. 'I've just got a lead in the West End.' She named a musical I'd vaguely heard of. 'My understudy has been filling in but if I'm not back soon they might give her the job permanently.'

I finished my examination and thanked her. I was

far from happy. I went back to the foot of the bed and picked up her notes again. On the second page I found what I was looking for. LMP: 3 November 2006. I stared at the tubular frame of the bedpost while I tried to do the calculation in my head. Then I flicked through the rest of the notes. I looked up. Emma was sitting up now and had been watching me. Her eyes looked cautious, her lips set straight.

'Emma, it says here your last menstrual period was on the third of November. Does that sound about right?'

She nodded.

'Which would make you . . . about twenty-seven, twenty-eight weeks?'

She nodded again, more slowly. For a second, all I could do was stare at her. Then I went back to her notes, checking and re-checking everything I found there. She started to push herself forward on the bed.

'Don't tell me now this is going to be a problem. I've been promised—'

'No, no . . .' I held up both hands. 'Please don't be concerned. As I said, I'm just catching up. I'll let you get some rest now.'

I glanced at her notes once more and then moved towards the door. She sat on the bed, watching me the way a cat watches someone moving around a room. At the door I stopped and turned.

'How did you hear about Tronal, Emma? If you work in the West End you must live in London. You've come a long way.'

She nodded slowly, still wary of me. 'I'll say,' she agreed. 'I went to a clinic in London. They said they couldn't help me, but they had some leaflets.'

'Leaflets about Tronal?'

A small shake of the head. 'Tronal wasn't mentioned. I had no idea I'd have to come to Shetland. The leaflet said something about advice and counselling for pregnant women in their second and third trimesters. There was a phone number.'

'And you called it?' Somewhere in the building a sound rang out. I tried not to let Emma see me stiffen.

'I didn't have anything to lose. I met a doctor in a room just off Harley Street. He referred me here.'

I had to move on. I forced a smile at Emma and looked at my watch. 'I'll be seeing Mr Mortensen in about an hour,' I said. 'I can check with him then about giving you something to help you sleep. Will you be OK till then?'

She nodded and seemed to relax a little. I gave her a last smile and left the room. With luck, she'd wait an hour before following up on my promise. I had an hour. At best.

Back in the corridor I leaned against the wall, needing a moment to get my breath, to clear my head.

Like most obstetricians, I'm trained to carry out terminations and since being on Shetland I'd performed three. I don't enjoy it, don't particularly approve of it as a general rule, but I respect the law of the land and a woman's right to be the ultimate determiner of what happens to her own body.

Under no circumstances, though, would I have agreed to carry out Emma's termination.

Compared to the rest of Europe, the UK's laws on abortion are fairly relaxed; too relaxed, many would argue. Here, up to the twenty-fourth week of pregnancy, an abortion can be legally carried out providing that two doctors agree the risk to a woman's health (or the risk to her children's health) will be greater if she continues with the pregnancy than if she ends it. This usually amounts to doctors supporting a woman's decision to terminate and has become known as 'social abortion', a practice many deplore.

After the twenty-fourth week, termination is only permitted if there's medical evidence that the woman's life or health would be seriously threatened by continuing with the pregnancy, or if the child is expected to be born severely handicapped. Looking carefully through Emma's notes, I'd found no valid reason why the procedure was being carried out so late. Nothing in her notes suggested either a serious deformity in the foetus or a significant threat to Emma's own life. The pregnancy was normal; inconvenient, obviously, but otherwise quite normal.

I wondered how much Emma had paid for her illegal operation, why on earth they'd kept her here for five days on ridiculous pretences instead of performing the operation straight away and how many other desperate women arrived here every year, seeking a procedure unavailable to them anywhere else in Europe.

I moved on. I pulled the next window back an inch and looked through. This time the woman inside was sitting up in bed watching television. The woman (no – girl – she couldn't have been more than sixteen) looked pregnant too, although it was impossible to be sure. If I had time to watch her, she'd undoubtedly give herself away. Pregnant women instinctively adapt both their usual pattern of movement and their posture in order to protect the growing foetus. Sooner or later, she'd rest her hands on her abdomen, raise herself up without putting pressure on stomach muscles, rub her back gently. I moved on and turned the corner.

I passed six rooms, all of them empty, and turned another corner. The first room on the next corridor was empty. The bed was bare, pillows without pillow-cases piled up, a folded yellow blanket but no sheets. The next room was a twin of the first.

The third was empty but looked ready to receive a patient. I stepped inside. The bed was neatly made. White towels were folded on the armchair. A flower-patterned nightdress – clean, perfectly ironed and folded – lay at the foot of the bed. On the walls hung several prints of wild flowers. It looked exactly like a neat, clean, comfortable room in an exclusive private hospital. Except for the four metal shackles chained to each corner of the bed.

I backed out and pulled the door towards me, careful to leave it slightly ajar, exactly as I'd found it. As I'd discovered two days ago, the death rate among young Shetland females peaked every three years. The last peak had occurred in 2004, the year Melissa and Kirsten were believed to have died. It was now May 2007, three years later.

Three more rooms. I wasn't sure I wanted to see what was inside. The handle of the next room moved under my fingers and the door opened. A small bedside lamp gave just enough light.

The woman on the bed looked around twenty. She had dark-brown hair and thick dark eyelashes, the willowy slenderness of the very young and perfect white skin. She lay as if sleeping, breathing deeply and evenly, but flat on her back, her legs straight and close together, her arms by her side. People rarely sleep naturally in such a posture and I guessed she'd been sedated. The blanket over her lay taut across her stomach. I wandered to the foot of the bed but there were no notes, just a single name: Freya. There were shackles on her bed but they hung loose, reaching nearly to the floor. I tiptoed out.

The woman in the fifth room looked older, but like the girl in the previous room she lay in an unnaturally still state of sleep on the narrow bed. Her name was Odel and her feet, though not her arms, were manacled. Odel? Freya? Who were these two women? How had they arrived here? Did they have families somewhere, grieving for them, believing them dead? I wondered if I'd seen either of them before, whether they'd passed through the hospital. Neither looked familiar. Neither showed any sign of being already pregnant. I wondered where they'd been that day, during Helen's visit. Where they'd be hidden when she returned tomorrow.

I pushed open the last door, noticing, as I did so, the pyjamas folded neatly on the armchair. They were white linen, with an embroidered scallop pattern around the collar, cuffs and ankles. They were laundered, pristine, showing no trace of the blood that had turned them a soft pink the last time I'd seen them. I turned to the bed, knowing that I'd stopped breathing but seemingly unable to start again. Someone lay in it. I walked over and stared down at the face on the pillow. I know that I cried out: part yelp, part sob. In spite of everything I'd been through, in spite of the immense danger I was still in, such a wave of joy hit me that it was all I could do not to dance round the room, punching the air and yelling. I forced myself to be calm and reached under the covers.

Two days ago I'd arrived at Dana's house, exhausted and scared, already dreading that something terrible had happened to her. I would have been putty in the hands of a skilled hypnotist. Planting ideas in my head – ideas already there in a half-formed state – must have been child's play for Andy Dunn. I couldn't believe how arrogantly stupid I'd been not to think of it before.

The wrist I held had been dressed with fine white bandages. I leaned over and found the other. Just the same. I was glad I hadn't imagined the ugly, bleeding gashes I'd seen in Dana's bathroom. Her wrists had been cut, but probably only superficially. She would have lost blood, but not so much it couldn't be replaced once she arrived on Tronal. I hadn't felt a pulse in Dana's bathroom – whatever drug she'd been given had made her peripheral pulse undetectable. But I could feel one – strong and regular – now.

As I'd sat trembling and close to fainting in Andy Dunn's car, I'd heard the sirens of an ambulance approaching. Dunn had driven me straight to the hospital and I'd assumed the ambulance was following with Dana. But it wasn't. Instead, Dana had been brought here. For what? To be part of this summer's breeding programme?

I bent down. 'Dana. Can you hear me? It's Tora. Dana, can you wake up?'

I stroked her forehead, risked giving her shoulders a shake.

Nothing, not even a flicker. This was not a normal sleep.

A door slammed and footsteps were coming down the corridor. Voices were talking, softly but urgently. I had seconds. I looked at the narrow, upright cupboard. Wasn't sure I'd fit inside. The bathroom. I crossed the room and pulled open the door.

There was a lavatory, wash-basin and shower cubicle. No window. I pulled open the door of the cubicle, jumped in and crouched down. If someone entered the room, they couldn't help but see me. I would just have to hope. Maybe they weren't even heading for Dana's room. Maybe my luck would hold a bit longer.

The footsteps stopped. The door to Dana's room

opened, the draught it caused blew the bathroom door open another inch. For a moment there was silence. Then . . .

'What do you think?' asked a voice that sounded remarkably like that of my father-in-law. I realized my luck had run out.

'Well . . . she's bright, healthy, good-looking,' answered the voice I knew better than any other in the whole world. 'Seems like . . . like a bit of a waste,' he continued, and I didn't know whether I was going to scream or be sick.

'Exactly,' said the voice of Detective Inspector Andrew Dunn. 'Why the hell go to the risk of getting another one?'

I sat in the shower cubicle, shivering so violently it hurt and thinking, *Why . . . why did I come here?*

'This was an unforgivable risk,' came another voice, one that sounded vaguely familiar but that I couldn't quite place. 'You were told to get rid of her, not bring her here.'

'Yeah, well, sorry about the reality check,' snapped Dunn, 'but even I can't hypnotize someone into slashing their own wrists. And haven't we learned by now that if we rush an accident we mess it up?'

'She's half-Indian,' said the man whose voice I couldn't put my finger on. 'We don't pollute the bloodstream.'

'Oh, for God's sake,' spat Dunn. 'What is this – the Middle Ages?'

'Robert is right,' said my father-in-law. 'She isn't suitable.'

Robert? Did I know a Robert? Oh God, I did. I'd met him just over a week ago. Robert Tully and his wife Sarah had come to see me about their inability to conceive a child. The bastard had sat in my office, pretending to need my help, knowing his wife wanted a baby so much that she was close to breaking point. Was she, then, intended to be the adopting mother of one of the latest batch of Trow babies?

'All right,' my husband was saying. 'What do we do with Ms Tulloch then?'

'We'll take her in the boat with the other two,' answered Richard. 'When we're far enough out, I'll give her another dose and slip her over the side. She won't know anything about it.'

'I need a leak,' said Duncan. 'Won't be a sec.'

The bathroom door opened and Duncan came into the room. He was still wearing the charcoal-grey business suit I'd watched him put on that morning. He walked to the basin and leaned over it.

'And what do we tell the girlfriend?' asked Dunn.

'We send her a coffin,' said Richard. 'Leave it till the last minute, day of the funeral if we can. Someone goes with it in case she wants to view the body. No big deal, we've done it before.'

'OK then, settled. Now, what else do we have to do?'

Duncan turned on one of the taps and splashed water over his face. He sighed deeply and straightened up. In the mirror above the basin I had time to notice the tie that I'd given him at Christmas, tiny pink elephants on navy-blue silk. A second later we made eye contact.

'Patients in one and two we don't have to worry about,' replied Richard. 'Standard adoptions, both likely to deliver in the next couple of weeks. The Rowley woman spoke to both of them today, shouldn't think she'll want to bother again.'

'What about Emma Lennard? Aren't you due to deliver her tomorrow?'

Duncan had turned to face me. I braced myself for him to shout out, alert the others or, even worse, to laugh. I wondered what they were going to do to me, how much it would hurt, whether it would be quick. Whether Duncan would be the one who . . .

'We're going ahead,' said Richard. 'Once the operation's over, I'll keep her sedated. We can't risk her talking.'

I tried to get up. I didn't want to be caught crouched, damp-assed, in a shower cubicle. But I couldn't move. All I could do was stare at Duncan. All he did was stare back.

'Isn't Emma safer on the boat?' In the outer room they were still talking, oblivious to the silent drama being played out in the bathroom.

'She would be, if we could be sure the police will only be here one more day. We can't hold on to her much longer, she's getting very edgy. Better to get it over with and get her out of here.'

'And the woman in room six?'

'I think we'll be OK. She's only twenty-six weeks anyway, plus she's insisting to everyone who'll listen that all the scans are wrong and she's just twenty weeks. I've already changed her notes.'

'It's risky.'

'Tell me something I don't know.'

One of us had to break the deadlock, one of us had to move, say something, shout out loud. I would do it. Anything was better than this unbearable tension. Then Duncan put one finger to his mouth. He glared at me as he left the room, pulling the door firmly closed behind him.

'A cargo of three then, Richard. Sure you'll be OK on your own? Don't want to leave it till dawn?'

'No, I want to be well away before there's any chance of the police coming back. Right, I'm going downstairs to get that TV switched off. There's work to do.'

Footsteps faded away down the corridor. Had they all gone? Could I risk moving? What the hell was Duncan going to do? Dana's room was silent. I started to push myself up—

'Sorry, mate,' said Duncan, as though commiserating a friend on losing a tennis match. 'It really doesn't do to get involved.'

'Oh, and you didn't with Tora?' shot back Dunn, his voice thick with bitterness. Did he actually care for Dana? Was that why'd he'd saved her life against orders, why he'd been arguing to keep her alive for a few months longer?

'You look like shit. Been here all day?'

'In the basement,' replied Dunn. 'With three sedated women. Felt like the house of horrors. Police nearly found the door at one point. Probably will tomorrow.'

'We'll sort it. Have it looking like a dusty old storeroom by morning. Right, we need a trolley. Can you get one from downstairs? There's something—'

A furious, terrified yell broke through the night, just as the door of the bathroom started to move inwards.

'Next door,' sighed Dunn. Footsteps ran from Dana's room and I heard a struggle in the next room along. There was banging and then a low, terrified whimpering, a noise I might have thought came from an animal; except I knew it wasn't an animal they were keeping chained up in there. Then the bathroom door opened and Duncan reappeared.

'What the hell are you doing here?' he hissed at me. 'Jesus, you idiot, you fucking idiot!' He opened the door of the cubicle, reached in and pulled me up. 'How the hell did you get here?'

I couldn't reply. Couldn't do anything but stare at him. He waited a split second before shaking me. 'Boat?' he said. 'Did you come by boat?'

I was able to nod.

'Where is it?'

'Beach,' I managed. What did it matter if they found the boat? There was no way I was going to get away now.

'We need to get you back to it. Now.' He took my arm and started to drag me out of the room. I found the strength to pull back. No, not that easy, Duncan; I wasn't going to be that easy. Then Duncan grasped me close, wrapped both arms around me and put one hand over my mouth.

I could hear something. A clanging, whirring sound. Then footsteps returning along the corridor. They were coming back. Creaking, sliding noises told me they were bringing trolleys with them. I wanted to struggle against Duncan but he pressed his mouth against my ear and whispered, 'Ssshhh.' The door to Dana's room slammed open. A trolley was wheeled inside. I heard footsteps moving around the room, the sound of covers being pulled back. A voice I didn't know muttered a countdown, 'Three, two, one, lift . . .' and there was a soft thud.

'Strip the bed, bring the chains,' said another voice. Then I heard the trolley being pushed out of the room. Beside me Duncan let out a noisy breath.

From the next room along the corridor came similar, if fainter, sounds. I thought I heard someone cry out, but couldn't be sure. For a few seconds the corridor outside was as noisy as that of any normal hospital. Then the footsteps and the sound of the wheels faded. I heard the clanging noise of the lift's mechanism and then nothing. Silence.

Duncan spun me round to face him. He was white, except for red blotches around his eyes. I'd never seen him so angry. Except it wasn't anger. He was afraid.

'Tora, you have got to get a hold of yourself or you are going to die. Do you understand what I'm . . . no, don't you dare cry.' He pulled me close again. 'Listen, baby, listen,' he whispered, as he swayed gently, the way a mother might rock a child. 'I can get you out of the clinic but then you have to get back to the boat. Can you do that?' He didn't wait for a reply. 'Head for Uyeasound. Get as far from the island as possible then get on the radio to your policewoman friend. Can you do that?'

I didn't know. But I think I nodded. Duncan opened the bathroom door and we slipped out. Dana's room was empty. The bed had been stripped back to the mattress and her pyjamas were gone. If I'd been fifteen minutes later I'd never even have seen her. Duncan walked to the door and looked out. Then he beckoned me forward, grabbed my hand and pulled me into the deserted corridor. I wasn't sure my legs would carry me but they worked fine. We rounded a corner, ran down a short, fourth corridor and made it to the stairs. Duncan paused at the top. We could hear nothing below so risked running down to the mid section. A camera fastened high on the wall glared down at us.

We listened again. Nothing. We ran to the bottom of the stairs and found ourselves in a short corridor, twin to the one above. One door stood open on our left. I glanced inside. It was an operating suite: a small room where the anaesthetics would be administered, then an open door into theatre. Duncan pulled me onwards.

We were now in the wing of the building I'd been watching when I'd disturbed the dogs. The rooms had been occupied; I'd seen light and movement behind them; we had to move quickly, someone could appear at any time. We walked forward, reached the first door. The glass window showed only darkness. We moved on. Another door, another window, light beyond. Duncan stopped and I was able to peer through. The room was well lit, about twenty metres long by eight wide. As far as I could make out there was no one inside. At least . . .

Duncan tugged again but this time I held firm. 'Come on,' he mouthed at me, but I shook my head. A sign on the door read: STERILE AREA, STRICTLY NO UNAUTHORIZED ADMITTANCE. Pulling my hand out of Duncan's grasp, I pushed open the door and went inside.

I was in a neonatal intensive-care unit. The air temperature was several degrees warmer than that of the corridor and heavy with the continuous humming of electronic equipment. Around me I saw ultrasound scanners, a Retcam, paediatric ventilators, a transcutaneous oxygen monitor. Several of the machines emitted soft beeping sounds every few seconds. Dana had been right. It was state-of-the-art. I'd worked in some very modern, well-equipped facilities in my time, but I'd never seen such a concentration of the very latest equipment.

'Tora, we don't have time.' Duncan had followed me into the room, was tugging at my shoulder.

There were ten incubators. Eight of them were empty. I walked across the room, no longer caring if someone found us. I had to see.

The infant in the incubator was female. She was about eleven inches long and, I guessed, would weigh around 3lbs. Her skin was red, her eyes tightly closed and her head, tucked inside a knitted pink cap, seemed unnaturally large for her tiny, emaciated body. A thin, transparent tube ran into both nostrils, connected by sticking plaster to her face. Another tube ran into a vein on her wrist.

I found myself wanting to reach in through the hand access, to touch her softly. I wondered how little human touch she'd known in her short life. The longer I looked, the more I wanted to scoop her up, hold her to me and run, although I knew that to do such a thing would be to kill her.

I moved on, towards the next cot. Duncan followed, no longer trying to stop me. This baby was male, even smaller than the girl. He looked as though he'd be lucky to make 2lbs, but his skin was the same dark, blotchy red. A ventilator was breathing for him, a monitor by the cot gave a continual reading of his heartbeat and a tiny blue mask covered his eyes to protect them from the light. As I watched, he kicked one of his legs and gave a tiny, mewling cry.

I felt like someone had stuck a dagger in my heart.

We stood there, staring down at him, for what felt like a long time. Neonatal units should never be left unattended, it could only be a matter of minutes before someone would return, but I simply couldn't move, except, every few seconds, to look up and glance across towards the baby girl. I wondered if they too had spent the day in the basement with Andy Dunn and three sedated women. Or maybe the people in charge had taken the risk of leaving them where they were, gambling that Helen and her team wouldn't insist upon a closer look around a sterile neonatal unit, and that, even if they did, they wouldn't recognize the significance of what they were seeing.

I knew now where Stephen Gair had been getting his babies from. I knew why Helen had been able to find no paper trail of the babies that had been adopted overseas.

George Reynolds, the head of social services, had protested his innocence, claiming that he and his team had been involved in no overseas adoptions, had given no approval, prepared no papers. He could well have been telling the truth. The babies Duncan and I were looking at would need no formal approval, no paperwork to be adopted overseas, because – officially and legally – these babies did not exist.

Their gestation had been terminated prematurely, some time between twenty-six and twenty-eight weeks. They were aborted foetuses – that were still alive.

37

IN RECENT YEARS ENORMOUS PROGRESS HAS BEEN made in the care of babies born extremely prematurely. Not so very long ago, a baby born at twenty-four weeks would have been expected to die within minutes of birth or, if it survived at all, to be severely handicapped. Now, such a child has a good chance of survival, and babies born at this stage of development have been known to grow into normal and healthy children. Yet twenty-four-week foetuses are still routinely aborted.

Every day that a foetus remains inside its mother's uterus, it is growing stronger and more viable. At twenty-six weeks, the possibilities of its survival are considerably better than at twenty-four. By twenty-eight weeks, its chances are getting quite good.

The next day, Emma's twenty-eight-week foetus would be delivered and rushed into one of these incubators. Emma would go back to her stage career, relieved and thankful, believing a termination had taken place. The infant would remain here, receiving a high level of care, for several months. If its brain, lungs and other essential organs remained healthy and normal it would, no doubt, command a high price at an Internet auction. Emma's 'termination' had been delayed by five days. I guessed that was standard practice with all the women who came here seeking late terminations. It would allow a little more time for the foetus to grow and develop; it would also enable the team to administer steroid drugs to encourage foetal lung development.

Twenty-four hours ago, I'd have said it was the most vile thing I'd ever heard of. Now, knowing what these guys had planned for Dana and the others, what they'd done to so many women already, I couldn't say I was exactly surprised.

I turned to Duncan. 'How long have you known?'

His eyes held mine steadily, without so much as a flicker. 'About this? The premature babies? Only a few weeks.'

'And the rest?'

'Since I was sixteen,' he said. 'We get told on our sixteenth birthdays.' He swept his hand up through his hair. 'But I didn't believe it, Tora.' He stopped, looked away, then back again. 'Or maybe I just told myself I didn't believe it. That's why I left Shetland. I went away to university and not once, in all those years, did I ever come back, not even for a weekend. I've never set foot on this island before tonight, I swear.'

Duncan was a good liar. I'd learned that in the last few days. But somehow, I didn't think he was lying now.

'But we did come back. You wanted to come back. Why?'

'I did not want to come back,' he spat back at me. 'They threatened to kill you if I didn't come back. To kill any child you and I had. I had to take those fucking pills. If I'd got you pregnant they'd have c—'

He couldn't finish. But he didn't have to. 'Cut out my heart?' I asked.

He nodded. I could see the bones beneath his face, the huge purple shadows under his eyes. For the first time, I understood what Duncan had been going through during the past few months. What he'd had to deal with for most of his life.

'Your mother didn't have MS?'

'My mother was perfectly healthy. Until they got their hands on her.'

I reached out for his hand, afraid at how cold it was. 'What the hell are we going to do?'

He glanced round at the door, as though even now someone could be watching us. 'You are going to get back on your boat, just as I told you.'

'You too. Come with me.'

For a second I thought he was going to agree. Then he shook his head. 'If I come with you, those women are going to die. As soon as we raise the alarm Richard will drop them all over the side. He'll claim he was out on an all-night fishing trip, and who's going to prove otherwise?'

'We will. We've seen everything.' I'm not proud to admit it, but I think I was too scared at that moment to really care about Dana and the other two women. All I wanted was Duncan and me off the island.

'Tor, you have no idea what we're dealing with. These people have influence you can't imagine. Even if we're allowed to live, no one will believe us. We need Dana and the others alive.'

He was right, of course. 'What are you going to do?'

'I'm going down to the harbour to get on that boat. Richard is taking it out alone. I can deal with him. I'll wait until we're out at sea and whack him on the back of the head. Then I'll drive the boat back to Uyeasound. With a bit of luck, your friend Helen will be there to meet me.'

'I love you so much,' I said.

Somehow, he managed to smile. Then he pulled me across the room and through a door at the far end. The room beyond lay in shadow. We slipped inside and closed the door behind us. We were in a nursery. Six white-painted, wooden cots stood around the edges of the room. Cartoon characters had been painted on to the whitewashed walls, mobiles swayed gently as they hung from the ceiling, soft toys – overstuffed teddy bears and floppy-eared rabbits – stared down at us from shelves. There were changing tables, sterilizing equipment, a baby bath. It was all so creepily, terrifyingly normal.

The cots, unnecessary for the time being, were all stripped bare to their mattresses. As I stared at them, so much fell into place. Since hearing about Tronal, I'd been puzzling how a maternity clinic could exist, given how few babies were supposedly born here each year. Now I knew the officially recorded babies were merely the 'cover' for the island's more sinister activities.

The clinic had been built to facilitate the births of the Trows' own baby sons. The rooms upstairs would house the abducted women – often drugged or restrained – during the whole of their pregnancies. When containment wasn't necessary, when no outsiders were on the island, the women might even be allowed a certain level of freedom: because Tronal was as impenetrable a prison as any I could imagine. How many pregnant women would risk swimming half a mile of rough ocean? Of course, if they knew that shortly after giving birth they'd have weird Nordic symbols hacked into their flesh, that their hearts would be cut from their living bodies, I imagine one or two might just risk it.

The six or so babies born from these women would be adopted by Trow men and their wives, previously discouraged, as Duncan and I had been, from having children of their own. To legalize these babies, their adoptive mother would be registered as their birth mother and would appear as such on their birth certificate. Did that mean these adoptive mothers, the men's wives, were colluding in what was going on? Did Elspeth know the truth about Duncan's birth? Not a question I really wanted to dwell on.

Duncan and I ran across the room towards a door at the far end and stood listening. Nothing. We opened the door and went into a storeroom.

More wooden cots had been dismantled and were propped against a wall. Folded buggies leaned against another. Two other doors: one opened on to the corridor, the other led outside. Duncan crossed to the external door and pushed it open. A rush of cold air came in as he leaned out and looked all around. From somewhere in the clinic I could hear voices but none of them seemed close.

But the Trows only made babies in every third year. The babies offered legally for adoption were few and far between. The rest of the time, the facilities on Tronal would sit empty and unused. So the enterprising Trows had come up with yet another use for the clinic: a facility for illegal late abortions. Finding desperate women through a network of hospitals, family-planning centres and abortion clinics around Europe, and dressing up the service as 'counselling and advice', they'd probably found plenty of women happy to pay over the odds for their operations. A few days on the island and these women would resume their normal lives, oblivious to what they'd really left behind on Tronal.

They'd never know that their own flesh and blood was still alive; growing and developing in the clinic's intensive-care unit until well enough to be sold to the highest bidder. It was brilliant. Monstrous, but brilliant.

Duncan came back into the room. 'OK, the dogs are locked up and most of the staff here will be moving the women down to the boat. But you still have to be careful. Go as fast as you can and don't be seen.'

I've never performed a parachute jump, but I imagine the moment of standing at the open plane door, waiting to jump, must feel exactly as I did then. I knew I had to go, leave Duncan and make my way across the island alone, but couldn't quite bring myself to do it that second. Then Duncan pushed me, not remotely gently, out of the clinic and I ran.

Stopping for just a second to get my bearings, I made for the ridge of rock that would shelter me from anyone searching the immediate grounds. I reached it and dropped low, giving myself a second to get my breath back and make sure I hadn't been spotted. Looking back at the clinic, I saw the door had been closed. There was no sign of Duncan. When I had enough courage I set off again, retracing my footsteps. I found the rucksack I'd left earlier and pulled on my waterproofs, then followed the cliff path until I reached the marker stone I'd left on the wall. I climbed over, squeezed through the gap in the barbed wire and ran to the cliff top. I was about to start the scramble down when I stopped. Something was moving on the beach.

It was the cliff birds. They'd scared the hell out of me earlier; they were just doing it again, that's all. I had to get down there. Duncan was going to need help. Whatever it was moved again. I froze. No bird could be that big. I crept down the cliff path. A loose rock went tumbling beneath me and I froze again. Below, where I guessed the boat would be, a light flashed on. A beam of light started to creep around the rocks. I flattened myself against the cliff and kept as still as I could. At one point the torch's beam touched my foot but didn't linger and after a minute or two it was switched off.

Slowly, carefully, I started to climb back up the cliff, praying I would disturb no more loose rocks. I reached the top and paused for breath. My boat had been discovered. They would be looking for me, would search the island until they found me. I might manage to hold them off until dawn, but once daylight came there'd be nowhere to hide. And they had dogs. If they set the dogs loose . . .

One way or another I was getting off that island; and there was only one other way I could think of. Richard was about to get another passenger. I set off again, running almost due north. Once I reached the track I kept as close to it as I dared for the half-mile or so that took me to the other side of the island. At one point I had to dive for cover when the sound of a diesel engine came roaring up from the harbour. It was a large four-wheel-drive vehicle, similar to the one Dunn drove. It might even be his car. Several men were inside it. They were travelling at considerable speed, given how rough and potholed the road was.

I ran on, getting more and more out of breath. I reached the highest ridge I had to cross and began to stumble down the other side. The water of Skuda Sound was ahead of me and, tantalizingly close, the lights of Uyeasound. The motor launch was still moored to the pier. Its cabin lights were on and, from the bubble of water at its stern, I knew its engines were running.

The wind was still pretty ferocious, masking any sounds that might be coming from the boat, but several of the dark clouds had blown away, allowing a small moon and a few stars to shine through. Visibility was better than when I'd arrived on the island and I could make out the figures on my watch. Eleven-thirty. I ran down to the pier and crouched low, by the side of the launch. It was fastened, port side to, by lines at the bow and the stern. I crept to the nearest cabin hatch and peered through. It was the main cabin. There was a helm, control panel and radio, a small teak-fitted living area with tiny galley, a chart table and three further doors leading off. No sign of Richard. I moved on and looked through the hatch of a small sleeping cabin. Dana lay on the bunk, motionless, but she wasn't alone in the cabin. I could see the tip of a polished black brogue and a few inches of charcoal-grey trouser fabric. Thank God, Duncan was already on board. As gently as I could, I pulled myself up and swung my leg over the guardrail. The boat rocked only a fraction.

'Someone up there?' called my father-in-law from below.

Small boats aren't exactly blessed with hiding places. Frantically looking round, I could see only one way out – jumping over the side and swimming for Unst. Someone was moving below, climbing the steps.

On the cabin roof was a folded awning, used to protect the cockpit from spray in poor weather conditions. I climbed up, lay down and burrowed into its folds.

The boat rocked as Richard climbed the companionway steps. I could see nothing, but knew Richard would be at the top of the steps, looking around, puzzled to see no one on board. He'd be less than two feet away from me. I held my breath, praying the canvas awning covered all of me and that he wouldn't notice it looking bulkier than normal.

Below, the boat's radio burst into crackling, static life. '*Arctic Skua*, come in, *Arctic Skua*. Base here.' Richard climbed back down the steps. I prayed the wind would die down a little, just enough for me to hear what was going on.

The radio crackled again; I thought I heard the word 'basement' and a couple of expletives but I couldn't be sure. Then Richard spoke.

'Right, I understand. I'll be careful. I'm setting off now. *Arctic Skua* out.'

Below me, Richard was moving again. A cabin door opened and shut, then I heard him heading up top. I counted seven footsteps and then he was in the cockpit. He climbed heavily on to the seat and then the deck. I heard him walk forwards and then the sliding sound of the bow-line being released. At once the boat swung round, the current taking it away from the pier. Then Richard walked back down the deck towards the stern. I waited for him to stop and then I risked peering out over the top of the canvas. He was bent almost double, his back to me, unfastening the stern-line from the cleat. Once released, the boat would drift swiftly away from the pier and he would have to rush back to the cabin to steer us away from Tronal. This was my best chance. Creep up behind him, give one almighty shove and he'd go overboard. It would be the easiest thing in the world then for Duncan and me to drive the boat to Uyeasound.

Too late. Richard began to turn. I crouched back down.

The boat was drifting fast from the marina. Richard strode through the cockpit and down the steps. Then I heard the engines revving and the boat swung round to starboard. I looked up, trying to get my bearings. Nothing but blackness ahead. Behind me the lights of Uyeasound were shrinking. We were heading east down the Skuda Sound, out into the North Sea.

Richard wasn't sparing the engines. We sped along at seven or eight knots. Rhythmically, like hammers striking the seconds on a giant clock, waves thudded against the hull. The bow of the boat rose and dipped and spray came hurtling over the deck like an intermittent and very cold shower. It was extremely uncomfortable and I knew the longer I stayed where I was, the colder and stiffer I'd become. When was Duncan going to make his move? I got up. The cabin roof was slippery with sea water and I gripped the rail before lowering myself on to the deck. The rucksack on my back was making me clumsy. I pulled it off and fastened it to a cleat. Then I reached inside. I found what I was looking for and tucked it into the front pocket of my waterproofs.

Then Richard cut down the revs and the boat slowed by several knots. We were heading south; Tronal was about two hundred yards away on the starboard side and around us loomed huge, dark shapes, as menacing as they were unexpected. I'd never been this far east of the islands and I didn't know that some of the oldest rocks in Shetland can be found exactly here. Stacks of granite, echoes of the majestic cliffs that towered here millions of years ago, were all around us. Some were massive, soaring above us in archways and monoliths, others crouched low in the water like fell beasts waiting to pounce. They'd be beneath us too, making navigation treacherous and explaining Richard's drop in speed. Like black-cowled monks, frozen in prayer, they stood in silence and watched us passing.

And something weird had got into my head that night, because it seemed to me these rocks were sentient, that the human drama taking place before them was hardly new, and that they watched, coldly curious, waiting to see how the act would be played out this time.

After ten minutes or so we left them behind and Richard picked up speed again. Still no sign of Duncan, but we were travelling away from help. We had to move soon. I wondered if Duncan, down in the cabin, might not realize which direction we were going in. In any case, we couldn't wait much longer. I moved along the deck until I could step into the cockpit. Glancing down the companion-way, I could see Richard at the helm, chart at his elbow.

If he turned, he would see me. I just had to hope he wouldn't. I raised the lid of the portside locker and looked inside: several coils of rope. I chose the shortest and closed the lid. Then I moved across the cockpit to the steps. I wasn't going to hide again. When he turned, he would see me. So be it.

I stepped into the companion-way, put my foot on the top step.

Richard didn't move.

Holding the guard-rail with my free hand, I lowered myself on to the next step down. Then the next.

The third step was damp and my trainer slipped a fraction. It made a faint squelching sound.

'Good evening, Tora,' said Richard quietly.

All the wind went out of me and I sat down, hard, on the steps. He turned and we looked into each other's eyes. I'd expected anger, exasperation, maybe even a cruel sort of triumph. What I saw was sadness.

We stared at each other for a long time. Then his eyes flickered over my shoulder to the port-side cabin. Did he know already that Duncan was on board too? I glanced to one side. The door was closed tight. I turned back to Richard. He pulled back the throttle and the boat slowed almost to a halt. He reached over and switched on the auto-pilot. Then he stood and took a step towards me.

'I wish you hadn't,' he said.

I felt my eyes sting and my jaw start to tremble. *Please let me not be about to cry, not now.*

'I suppose Emma gave me away?' I asked, praying that was the case. If Emma had told them, they might not know I'd met up with Duncan. Richard might not know he was on board. And where the hell was he, anyway? I pressed my right hand against my chest, felt the reassuring hardness beneath my waterproofs.

'Yes, she mentioned your visit. And then it was a simple matter of checking video footage to confirm it was you. Not that any of us had any doubt. You've been very brave, my dear.'

I pushed myself up and jumped down into the cabin. Richard took a step back. Again his eyes flickered to the door behind me, but I wasn't about to be distracted.

'OK, less of the "my dears"; you and I have never been close, nor are we likely to be in future, given where you're going. I think the GMC might have a few questions about the services you offer at that clinic of yours. That's when the police have finished with you.'

Richard stiffened. 'Please don't presume to preach at me. Those babies would have died before birth – would have been murdered before birth – without us. Because of us they will have a good life, with parents who love and want them.'

I was close to speechless. 'It's totally illegal.'

'The law is a complete mess, Tora. The law allows us to inject potassium chloride into an infant's heart, right up until the moment of birth. Up to twenty-four weeks we can do it for no other reason than that the pregnancy is inconvenient to the mother. Yet if a child of twenty-four weeks is actually born, we have to do everything in our power to preserve its life. Where's the sense in any of that?'

'We don't make the law,' I said, knowing I was sounding lame. 'And we certainly don't exploit its weaknesses for commercial—'

'Do you have any idea how many terminations go wrong every year, when the babies come out alive, often severely handicapped?' Richard came back at me angrily. 'Because I've come across several in my time; babies whose mothers abandoned them even before birth. What kind of life are they going to have? Surely our way is better than that.'

'You're trading in human beings,' I almost hissed at him.

'We help women out of difficult situations. We provide childless couples with hope for the future. And we save dozens of babies who would otherwise be murdered for social expediency. We are preservers of life.'

I couldn't believe he was seriously trying to take the moral high ground. 'And Dana? Are you planning on preserving her life?'

He seemed to shrink a little into himself. 'Sadly, no. That's out of my hands. I hear she was a fine young woman. I'm sorry she had to get involved.' Then he pulled himself up again. 'Although, frankly, if anyone's responsible for Miss Tulloch's death, it's you. If you hadn't been so determined to meddle in the police investigation, she'd never have learned enough to put her life in danger.'

'Out of your hands, you sick shit? It's your hands that will be weighting her down and throwing her overboard.'

Richard shook his head, as though dealing with an unreasonable child. I began to wonder if he was mad. Or if I was.

'This is so typical of you, Tora. You can't reason your way out of an argument, so you resort to abuse. Is it any wonder we've never been close?'

'Shut up! This is not family therapy time. I can't believe you're preaching to me about saving lives. You tried to kill me last Sunday. You sabotaged my boat and my life jacket.'

'Actually I knew nothing about that.'

'Stop lying to me. You're about to kill me: the least you can do is tell me the truth.'

'He isn't lying. I sawed though the mast.'

I whipped round. Stephen Gair stood in the doorway of the port cabin. His face was crumpled, slightly red. My eyes dropped to his feet. Black brogues.

'Jesus,' he said. 'What do you have to do to get some decent kip around here?'

38

I DROPPED THE ROPE AND BACKED UP OUT OF GAIR'S reach, and came up sharply against the chart table. Gair stepped to one side and leaned against the steps. No way out. 'You look like you've seen a ghost, Tora,' he said, smiling sleepily.

I took hold of the zip on the pocket of my waterproofs and started to inch it down. 'Don't tell me,' I said, 'reports of your death have been exaggerated. Where's Duncan?'

'Duncan had a change of heart. He won't be joining us tonight.'

I risked taking my eyes off Gair to look at Richard.

'What have you done with Duncan?' I demanded.

Richard leaned over and fumbled on the shelf that ran around the cabin's interior. He straightened up again and I thought I saw the wrapping of a hypodermic concealed in his large hand.

'And no one's about to kill you,' said Gair, his arms stretching high above his head. 'At least, not any more,' he continued when he'd done yawning. 'You're going back to Tronal.'

I stared at him, not sure what he meant. Then I got it; as a strong, cold hand took a grip on my heart, I got it.

'Not this time,' I managed. 'I think one or two people might just notice I'm gone.'

Gair shook his head, seemingly unable to take the grin off his face. 'That boat you stole will be found drifting some time in the next couple of days,' he said. 'Some of your things will be discovered in the cabin, traces of your blood on the deck. People will assume you had an accident and went overboard. They'll look for your body, of course. Hold a very tasteful memorial service when they don't find it.'

I bit my tongue to keep from blurting out about the note I'd left for Helen. If they knew about that, they'd break into Dana's house before dawn and destroy it. Without the note, without Duncan, who would doubt that I'd taken out a boat in storm conditions – for unfathomable reasons of my own, but I had been pretty disturbed of late – and hadn't made it back? Without the note, the bastards might just get away with it. I couldn't let them know about the note.

'If it's all the same to you,' I said, glaring at Gair, 'I'd just as soon you drowned me now.'

Without my noticing, Richard had moved closer. 'She has a weapon, Stephen. Something tucked down the front of her suit.'

Gair glanced at Richard, then back at me. His eyes

dropped to my stomach. 'I'll say she has. Sorry, love, you and your little friend are far too valuable.'

My right hand was ready to slip inside my waterproofs. 'What are you talking about?'

'You're pregnant, Tora. Congratulations.' His grin got even wider. He looked like a wolf.

'What?' For a second I was so amazed I forgot to feel afraid.

'In the club, up the duff, bun in the oven.'

'You're insane.'

'Richard, is she pregnant?'

I risked a glance at Richard. 'I'm afraid you are, Tora,' he said. 'I took a blood sample last Sunday while you were sedated. There were significant levels of hCG. I guess Duncan got careless with his medication.'

hCG, or human chorionic gonadotropin, is the hormone produced by the body of a pregnant woman. It is hCG that home-testing kits are designed to detect, but a blood test can pick it up a matter of days after conception.

Gair was still smiling at me but I could hardly see him. It didn't occur to me to doubt what they were saying. I'd felt like shit for days: nausea and exhaustion are classic symptoms of early pregnancy, but I'd put them down to stress. I was pregnant. After two years of trying and failing, I was finally pregnant. I was carrying Duncan's child and these guys – these monsters – thought they were going to take it away from me.

'How did you get into my office?' I said, feeling a

surge of hatred for Gair as I remembered the drugs I'd unwittingly taken the night I'd discovered Melissa's identity. Drugs can do any amount of damage to a young foetus. 'I know how you got into the house; how did you get into my office?' Even as I spoke, I realized how he'd done it. My office keys had gone missing. Gair had stolen them the night he left the strawberries and the pig's heart in our house. He was a petty thief as well as everything else.

'Pick up that rope and tie up Richard,' I said, gesturing to the rope I'd dropped minutes before. 'Do it quickly and properly and he won't get hurt.'

Gair looked back and the emptiness in his eyes was perhaps the most terrifying thing I've ever seen.

'And why would I do that?' he asked.

I pulled my hand out from my pocket. 'Because a two-inch iron bolt ramming into your brain is going to hurt a bit.'

Gair glanced down, looking, to my immense satisfaction, slightly less sure of himself.

'What the hell is that?'

'My grandfather's humane horse-killer. Except you're not going to think it very humane when it's pressed up against your temple.'

Out of the corner of my eye I saw Richard drop his head into his hands, rub his face and then straighten up. As a gesture it was so completely Kenn I wondered why I hadn't guessed immediately the two of them were father and son.

'Tora, please put that down,' Richard said. 'Someone's going to get hurt.'

'You are so right,' I said. 'And it isn't going to be me.'

Gair moved towards me. I jerked my hand up. He danced back and came at me the other way. I jabbed the weapon at him and he jumped back again. He moved, left then right, feinting attacks, always diving back at the last second. He was taunting me, trying to unnerve me, and it was working. He was also gradually moving round the cabin, away from the steps and closer to me, forcing me to turn my back on Richard.

I spun, jumping round and away from him, to Richard's other side. Richard reached for me and I ducked. Then I grabbed Richard by the neck of his pullover and pushed the gun up against the side of his face. If I pulled the trigger now I would miss his brain but still make a hell of a mess.

'Don't move. Don't move a fucking inch. Either of you.'

Gair froze. He held his hands in the air and stood poised, ready to leap, eyes glinting with excitement.

'Tora,' gasped Richard. 'Others are coming – they'll be here any second.'

'Good,' I spat, although I was still thinking coherently enough to know the news was anything but good. 'There are one or two things I'd like to say to Andy Dunn, not to mention my favourite boss.'

Gair frowned. Richard twitched his head in my direction.

'Do you mean Kenn?' he asked.

'Richard, can we just—'

'Kenn isn't coming,' said Richard.

I released the pressure I'd been applying to Richard's face, allowing him to turn his head and face me. Gair tensed, as if ready to spring.

'Don't try it, Stephen. I can pull this trigger before you get here.' I hadn't taken my eyes off Richard. 'What do you mean?' I asked.

Richard's eyes narrowed, as though searching for something in my face. For a moment or two he said nothing and I held my breath. Then, 'Kenn isn't one of us,' he said softly, as though breaking bad news. 'I can see why you might think so – he certainly looks the part – but he isn't.'

'How come?' I demanded, unwilling to let myself believe something that logic told me couldn't possibly be true. 'How come Duncan is . . . was . . . but Kenn isn't?'

'Richard, do we really have time for this crap?'

'I loved his mother,' said Richard. 'When it came to it, I couldn't hurt her. I helped her escape. She's lived in New Zealand for the past forty years.'

'Kenn knows nothing about this?'

Richard shook his head. 'He knows his mother. I helped them make contact a few years ago. But no, he's not one of us. It's a great shame in many ways. He is an exceptional man, very gifted. What he would have achieved if . . . Well, it doesn't do to dwell on these things. My fault, of course. I let myself get involved. It won't happen again.'

I could see Gair making impatient movements.

'You were never intended to be part of this, you

know,' continued Richard. 'Elspeth and I are fond of you. We know Duncan loves you.' His eyes left me and his gaze seemed to turn inwards; I wondered if he was remembering Kenn's mother. 'A year from now you could have adopted a newborn baby. It could even have been Duncan's baby. You weren't supposed to be harmed.'

'Unlike the poor child's mother, of course. Did I meet her tonight? Which one was it to be? Odel or Freya?'

'This is getting us nowhere . . .'

'I wish you'd put that thing down,' said Gair, taking a step forward.

'And I wish you'd slit your wrists and jump over the side.'

A sudden movement, a noise – that none of us had made. Richard and I both turned as one to the port cabin. Gair leaped at us. Too late, I swung the gun up, just as his full weight came crashing down on me. I pulled the trigger, felt the bolt connect and then the gun was knocked from my hand as we both fell.

For a second I lay stunned on the cabin floor. Gair lay over me, pinning me down.

'Be careful with her, for heaven's sake,' said Richard. 'We don't want to lose that baby.'

'Richard, will you take care of the boat? God knows where we are right now.'

I heard Richard move, then the revs of the boat increased and we turned sharply to port. I heard the crackle of the ship's radio and him speaking into it, trying to make contact with another boat.

Gair was wearing a crumpled grey business suit, no doubt the same one he'd been wearing when he'd been arrested, questioned and charged with murder. He probably hadn't been allowed to change before spending the night in the cell. He'd have been wearing it that morning when he'd swallowed the sedatives that reduced his peripheral pulse, when he'd pretended to hang himself and had been carted off: not to the morgue, of course, but to Tronal. A dark stain on his right shoulder was spreading slowly, but if he felt any pain he wasn't showing it.

I think a thousand different ways of pleading with him came into my head that moment. I was all out of bravado. I didn't want to fight any more. I just wanted to live a bit longer.

I think I even got as far as opening my mouth, forming the first words, but I never got the chance to utter them. Because Gair's eyes left mine and searched along the cabin floor until he spotted the gun. His weight shifted as he raised himself up and reached out. Then he leaned back over me, pushed the humane killer against my left thigh and looked into my eyes. He smiled as he pulled the trigger and my world exploded in a mass of white-hot pain.

39

I COULDN'T SEE, COULDN'T HEAR, COULDN'T BREATHE. The boat swerved again.

'. . . the hell are you doing?' I heard Richard calling out from some great distance away. 'She'll bleed to death before we can get her back.'

'Then fix it, Doctor. I'll drive the boat.'

Marginally, the pain was receding, leaving my head, my chest, my abdomen, and concentrating in one spot, the fleshy part of my upper thigh. The blackness in my head faded a little and I could see again. And hear again: a terrifying noise filled the cabin and I realized it was me – screaming. Richard pushed his hands under my shoulders and dragged me across the floor, into the starboard cabin. With a strength I'd never have believed he possessed, he picked me up and lay me on the bunk, beside the still form of a woman. Freya. Even through the pain I recognized her. Then he took hold of both my hands and pressed them against the wound.

'Push hard,' he instructed. 'Stem the bleeding. You know what will happen if you don't.'

Only too well. Crimson fluid was pumping from my leg. Gair had most likely hit an artery and I was in big trouble. I pressed hard but I could feel the strength draining from me. I felt like I do when I'm falling asleep, when keeping the mind focused on even the simplest thing becomes impossible. Except I could not sleep. I had to stay conscious. I could hear Gair on the radio and the crackle of someone responding to him.

Richard was back. He pushed my hands away and started wrapping something around my leg. He pulled tight, then tighter. I looked down – the white of the bandages was already soaked scarlet. I can never see fresh blood without admiring it. Such an amazing substance, rich and strong and vibrant; such a beautiful colour; so sad to see it leaking away, dripping down through the floorboards, into the bilges and out, to disappear without trace, amidst the cold salt waters of the North Sea.

Gair was giving the coordinates of our position. Reinforcements were on their way. I had lost. I was going back to Tronal, to spend the next eight months chained and drugged, while a new life grew inside me. A life I had planned for, longed for, prayed for. And now that it was here, it was to be my death. I wondered what they'd do with Duncan, whether he would be allowed to live, be given one last chance to come back to the fold. Or whether he was already dead.

Richard twisted me so that my head rested on Freya's shoulder and then propped my left leg against the wall, allowing gravity to do its job.

Then he leaned forward, put his hands on my shoulders and looked into my eyes. The room seemed to darken around him.

'Relax now,' he said. 'The pain will go.'

I struggled hard and forced my eyes shut. 'You're hypnotizing me?'

'No.' He stroked my forehead and my eyes opened. 'Just calming you, helping you with the pain.'

He continued stroking my forehead and, remarkably, the pain did seem to ease. But with it went what was left of my focus; I was starting to drift. Didn't want that to happen.

I reached out and caught his hand.

'Why?' I managed. 'Why do you kill us? Why do you hate your mothers so much?'

He held my hand in both of his. 'We have no choice,' he said. 'It's what makes us who we are.' He leaned closer. 'But never think we hate the women who bear our children. We don't. We mourn our mothers, honour their memories, miss them all our lives. We are not a religious people, but if we were, our mothers would be our saints. They made the ultimate sacrifice for their sons.'

'Their lives,' I whispered.

'Their hearts,' he said.

I tore my eyes away from his, back to the poppy-stained bandages around my leg. And knew what he was about to tell me.

Oh God, please God, no.

Richard sat down on the bunk beside me. He was still holding my hand. 'When I was nine days old,' he said, 'I drank the blood of my mother's heart.'

He paused, giving me a moment to understand what he was saying. I couldn't speak, I could only stare at him.

'It was given to me in a bottle,' he went on, 'along with the last of her milk.'

Bile rose in my throat. 'Stop. I don't want . . .'

He hushed me, stroking a finger gently across my cheek. I swallowed hard; concentrated on taking deep breaths.

'Of course, I knew nothing about it at the time; it was much later, on my sixteenth birthday, that I learned of . . . shall we say . . . my extraordinary heritage?'

Breathe in, breathe out. It was all I could think of. I heard his words but I don't think I was really registering them. Not then, not till much later.

'You can imagine the shock. I'd grown up with my father and his wife, a woman I loved very much. I had no idea she wasn't my biological parent. And the horror of what they were telling me, of what had been done to the woman who . . . I think it was just about the darkest day of my life.'

A derisory phrase sprang into my head, was on the tip of my tongue: *my heart bleeds,* I nearly said. Jesus, who on earth came up with that one?

'But at the same time, it was the start of my life, of understanding who I really was. I already knew I was special, brighter by far than any other child in the class. I was a gifted musician and I could speak four languages, two of which I'd taught myself. I was stronger, faster and more able in just about everything I did. Every sport I attempted I mastered. And I was never ill. Not once in all my sixteen years had I ever had a day off school because of sickness. When I was twelve, I broke my ankle playing soccer. It healed in two weeks.'

I found my voice. 'You were just lucky; a fortunate combination of genes. It had nothing to do with . . .'

'And I had other powers too, stranger powers. I'd discovered I could make people do what I wanted, just by suggestion.'

'Hypnosis.'

'Yes, that's what some of the younger ones like to call it.'

I shook my head. I wasn't buying it, but I couldn't find words to argue.

'I was introduced to two other boys who'd already turned sixteen. One was from the main island, the other from Bressay. They were just like me, just as strong, just as clever. I was told about four others, a few months younger, who were the rest of my peer group. And I met six older boys who had just turned nineteen. They knew what we were going through, had been through it themselves three years previously.'

'Every three years,' I said. He nodded.

'Every three years, between five and eight boys are born. We have just one son, in our lifetimes, one son who will become one of us.'

'Trows?' I wanted to scoff, tried to scoff, but it was hard.

He frowned. 'Kunal Trows,' he corrected. Then he relaxed, even half smiled. 'So many stories, so much nonsense: little grey men who live in caves and fear iron. Yet tucked away inside all legends, a kernel of truth can be found.'

'All those women. All those deaths. How do you do it?'

He smiled again. I think he was even starting to show off.

'The practicalities are remarkably simple. The key is having people in the right places. Once a woman has been identified, we watch her very closely. We may stage an accident, or her GP might discover an illness. Not all GPs on the islands are with us, of course, so it depends. Once she's in hospital it becomes very straightforward, although obviously every case has to be handled differently. Typically, a high dosage of something like Midazolam is given to slow the metabolism right down so the life-support machines automatically sound the alarm. If relatives are present, the medical team make a great show of trying to save the patient, but fail. The unconscious woman is taken to the morgue, where our people are on standby to take her to Tronal. The pathologist produces a report and a weighted coffin is either buried or incinerated. Naturally, we encourage cremation.'

'Naturally. What about Melissa?'

He sighed. 'Melissa was a special case. Like you,

never intended to be part of all this.' He glanced towards the open door of the cabin, glaring in Gair's direction. 'We do not use our own wives.'

'She found out?'

He nodded. 'She learned Stephen's passwords and went through his computer files one night.' He stretched out a hand, stroked my forehead again. 'Melissa was a very clever, very stubborn woman,' he continued. 'She was like you in so many ways. It struck me as the deepest irony that you should be the one to find her. Her mistake, of course, was in confronting Stephen, telling him what she knew. We had to act fast. At first, we planned to eliminate her, but she'd told Stephen she was pregnant and he didn't want to lose the child. It was his idea to substitute the other woman, the one from Oban. I was against it. Too many complications. But we'd pretty much run out of time.'

'And Kirsten Hawick. I know she's in my field too. Did you stage that accident? Did one of you drive the lorry?'

He shook his head. 'No, Kirsten's accident was genuine. We just exaggerated the extent of her injuries. She had a son. He lives on Yell now, a fine boy.'

Kirsten might have recovered. The almost unbearable grief I'd seen Joss Hawick enduring could have been totally unnecessary. I wanted to scream, but knew that if I did, I wouldn't be able to stop.

'Why do you bury the women? Why not just dump them at sea? Or burn them? If you'd done that, I'd never have found Melissa.'

'No, but we can't. It's against our beliefs. Our mothers lie in what is for us sacred ground. It's part of the way we honour them.'

'And I suppose it was just too great a risk to bury them all on Tronal. So you've created burial grounds all over the islands?'

He inclined his head, acknowledging the truth of what I was saying.

'And Duncan? Duncan did this too? Drank . . .'

Richard nodded. 'He did. So did his father and his grandfather before him, and my father and grandfather and great-grandfather. We are the Kunal Trows, stronger and more powerful than any other men on earth.' He stood up, ready to return to the main cabin. I was so tired. I wanted nothing more than to slip into unconsciousness. And I knew that if I did so I would die. I had to keep talking.

'How many? How many of you are there?'

He paused at the door.

'Around the world, between four and five hundred. Most live here, but about a hundred years ago we started to colonize. We prefer islands, remote but with a strong local economy.'

My body was trembling and I felt a strong urge to vomit. I was going into shock but I was no longer in danger of losing consciousness. The pain was hell but I could deal with it.

'You're not special,' I said. 'It's all in your head.'

Richard's voice had fallen, as though he was trying to comfort a distressed child. 'You have no idea of the powers we have. Influence you couldn't even dream of. These islands, and many others around the world, belong to us. We do not flaunt our wealth but we possess it in immeasurable terms.'

'You're just ordinary men.'

'I'm eighty-five years old, Tora, and yet I have the strength of a man in his fifties. How ordinary is that?'

'Richard,' called Gair, 'I think I can hear an engine. I need to go up top and signal. Can you take the helm?'

Richard started to turn. 'Believe me if you can, my dear. It will make the next few months easier.'

He turned and left the cabin, closing the door and shutting me inside with the motionless Freya. I felt a moment of surprise that he hadn't sedated me. Maybe all that showing off about his so-called special powers had made him forget. Or more likely he figured the pain and blood loss would be enough to keep me immobile. I looked up at my leg. Blood was no longer pumping out and it was possible the artery wasn't severed after all. I risked lowering it and then raised myself up so that I was sitting on the bunk. The bleeding increased but not alarmingly. I looked at Freya. Still breathing, possibly not as heavily as before, but otherwise no real signs of life. I could expect no help from that quarter.

I sat on the bunk, thinking. It would be just about impossible to get the better of Richard and Gair, injured as I was, but I had to try. While they were separated, Gair on deck, Richard driving the boat and with his back to me, I had the best chance. Once the other boat arrived, Dana would go overboard and I'd be guarded, possibly drugged, until the police operation was over and I was safely back on Tronal.

I tried standing up. A stab of pain shot up through my leg. I took deep breaths, counted to ten, waited for the pain to subside. Then I stepped forward. Another stab of pain, not so bad this time.

Clinging to the shelf around the cabin I inched forwards until I reached the door handle. Motor launches have terrifically loud engines, but Richard had reduced the speed and I thought I caught the sound of another engine somewhere in the distance. I turned the handle and pulled at the door. It opened silently.

Richard was alone in the main cabin, standing at the wheel, peering forwards as though struggling to see ahead. We'd reached another offshore mass of stacks and the navigation was tricky. If I knocked him out – which was basically the plan – we could easily hit one of the huge granite rocks around us. Once the hull was breached, the launch would sink quickly and I'd have to launch a life-raft (always assuming there was one on board), get three unconscious women on to it and deal with a strong and violent psychopath. All this with only one good leg. Like I said, I didn't fancy my odds.

On the other hand . . . I really didn't like what was on the other hand.

I needed a weapon. Grandad's horse gun lay on a shelf at the far side of the cabin but I'd never be able to reach it without Richard seeing me. I looked all around. The floor was still slick with blood – my blood – and my stomach churned. I forced myself to look away. I checked the shelves that ran around the cabin and found where the boat tools were kept. I slipped my hand down. It was like a life-or-death game of jackstraws – dislodge one from the heap without moving the others or making a sound. Amazingly, I managed it. I raised my hand and examined my find. Some sort of pliers, thick steel, about twelve inches long. They would do. No point hanging about. I limped forwards, arm above my head.

Of course, Richard saw my reflection in the cabin windows. He spun round, catching my arm, pushing it down, behind my back. With my free hand, I pushed at his chest then, in desperation, clawed at his eyes. He hit me, just once, a heavy blow across the temples. Blood shot from my mouth and flew across the cabin as my legs gave way under me. I grabbed the lapel of Richard's jacket and clung on. As I toppled I took him with me.

We landed heavily, he on top of me. He pushed himself up. For a second, I could only stare at him, wait for him to act. Then I grabbed his earlobe and he yelled with pain. He hit my arm hard and I had to let go, but with my other hand I went for his eyes again. He sat up, straddled across me, pinning me down. With one hand, he grabbed my right wrist and held fast. With the other, he reached for my throat.

Knowing it could be the last sound I ever made, I screamed.

Richard's hand wrapped around my neck and squeezed. I thrashed my head from side to side but his grip wasn't budging. He was incredibly strong; I'd been a fool to imagine I could overpower him. With my left hand I struck out at his face but his arms were longer than mine and I couldn't reach him.

I tore at the hand holding my throat, dug my nails into skin, tried to wrench it away. The instinctive panic that goes hand in hand with oxygen deprivation had set in, giving me strength I wouldn't otherwise have had, but it still wasn't enough. Richard was no longer looking at me, but at a point over my head. He wasn't capable of looking me in the eyes as he throttled me. I think I took a small measure of comfort from that as the darkness began to grow.

Then he convulsed – just once – and his grip relaxed, releasing the pressure on my throat. My lungs started pumping, desperate for air, but my throat had been damaged by the pressure of Richard's strong hand. Like a dented pipe, it couldn't let enough air flow through and the darkness in my head continued to grow.

Richard fell forwards towards me; his eyes met mine but were expressionless. His weight shifted, my lungs made a gigantic effort and air flooded in once more. I managed to raise both hands to fend him off and as he collapsed I shoved hard.

He rolled to one side and I pushed against him,

without a clue what was happening but grasping at any chance to be free. He fell face-down on the floor of the cabin. A circle of blackness stained the thick white hair on the back of his head and, as I watched, a small bubble of blood rose from the wound and burst as it reached the air. Tearing my eyes away, I looked at the figure kneeling above him. Eyes met mine and I thought I saw a brief glimmer of recognition before they glazed over. There was a heavy thud as the humane killer, the thick iron-bolt stained dark with Richard's blood, fell to the floor.

Pushing myself up, I reached over and felt for a pulse in Richard's neck. There was nothing. I pulled myself to my feet, stepped over him and peered up the companionway steps. Gair was nowhere in sight but I could make out flickers of light as he signalled to another boat.

I bent down, picked up the weapon and reloaded the bolt. Then, at last, I reached out and touched the face of Richard's killer. Eyes dazed with drugs looked back emptily into mine. Then I saw a gleam of intelligence and Dana's lips stretched into a smile.

'Can you understand me?' I whispered, feeling myself smile in response. She nodded, but didn't seem able to speak.

'Stephen Gair is up there,' I said, gesturing towards the cockpit. 'He is very dangerous.' No surprise in her eyes. 'Can you watch the steps? When he appears, let me know?'

She nodded again and I stood up and limped over to the helm. I could see no immediate hazards ahead; the depth gauge was unable to read the depth – always a reassuring sign – and I flicked the boat on to auto-pilot. Then, I picked up the radio and switched to channel 16.

'Mayday, mayday, mayday,' I said as loudly as I dared, knowing Gair would hear the crackle of the response and hoping he would think it was the other boat talking to Richard.

'Mayday, mayday, mayday,' I repeated. 'This is motor launch *Arctic Skua*, *Arctic Skua*. We are in Shetland waters, travelling south down the eastern coast of Tronal island. We require urgent medical and police assistance.'

There was a crackle of static. No response.

I glanced round. Dana's eyes hadn't left the companionway steps. I could hear footsteps above us.

'There are six people on board,' I said into the mouthpiece. 'Two of us are injured. Three have been drugged. Only one is able-bodied and he is a danger to the rest of us. We need help urgently. Repeat, urgently.'

Another crackle. Still no response.

It was close to hopeless. Even if anyone were listening – which the Shetland coastguard, at least, certainly should be – they would never get to us in time. The second Tronal boat would be here any second and the other women and I were going overboard. All I could do was make sure we didn't disappear without a trace.

'We are Tora Hamilton, Richard Guthrie, Stephen

Gair and Dana Tulloch. Repeat Dana Tulloch, who is alive and well.' Not for much longer, though – I could definitely hear another engine getting closer. 'Also two other women whose real names I don't know. We have been abducted and held prisoner by Richard Guthrie and Stephen Gair. Both men are extremely dangerous.'

That was stretching it a bit. Richard hadn't moved and looked anything but dangerous. Gair was another matter. If he came below he would kill me. He would have no choice. Without Richard, he would be unable to administer the drugs that would keep me insensible until we got back to Tronal. The baby would have to be sacrificed. He would kill me and throw me overboard. Dana too. The other two women might survive the trip, but for what? Another eight months of imprisonment and a violent death. I could not let Gair come below. I had to go up and tackle him head on.

Except I couldn't do it. I was weak from loss of blood and dizzy from pain. I'd spent most of the night running on adrenalin and the tank was empty. I couldn't fight him; couldn't even climb the steps. I would wait, hide inside one of the sleeping cabins, jump on him when he came back down. It was the only possible way.

A noise above. Someone had leaped on the roof of the cabin.

'Hey, ladies!'

Gair's face hung upside-down in the companionway. He was lying on the cabin roof staring down at us. Veins bulged on his forehead and I could see his large white teeth. I realized that he and sanity had parted company. His eyes darted to Richard's body and narrowed. Then he looked back at me.

'Get up here, Tora,' he said.

40

Unable to tear my eyes from Gair's face, I shook my head. I wasn't going anywhere near him. He terrified me.

His head disappeared. I heard him striding along the roof and I stepped closer to Dana. She reached out and held my ankle as I gripped the gun tight.

Then Gair's face appeared again.

'I'm opening the seacocks, Tora,' he sneered. 'You'll have about ten minutes before the boat sinks like a stone. If you want to save your three friends, you come up top now.'

He strode off towards the bow of the boat. I staggered to the companionway and pulled myself up the steps. Gair was bent over the anchor locker. He saw me, straightened up and moved towards me.

I stood my ground. He was wounded too, although not as badly as I, and I still had the gun. I wasn't giving in just yet. He climbed on to the cabin roof and stood there, legs apart for balance, towering above me. The wind whipped his clothes against him, showing the lean, strong lines of his body. His face gleamed white against the night sky and his teeth were bared in a hideous attempt at a smile. He no longer looked like a wolf. He looked like a demon.

I backed away until I came up against the cockpit steering wheel. The contents of my bowels turned to mush and the muscles were no longer able to hold them in place. Evil-smelling warmth started to pour down my legs. Legs that had turned to straw and would hold me no longer. I sank to the cockpit floor.

Gair held something in one hand; a short length of chain. He swung it round and it crashed against the cabin roof. Then he caught hold of the other end with his left hand and pulled it tight. It was about three feet long and the links must have been a quarter of an inch thick. He stood at the edge of the cabin roof, poised to leap down. The boat rocked and he steadied himself. Below, I thought I could hear Dana's voice, repeating the mayday call I'd given earlier. I even thought I heard a faint crackle of response. It was too late, though – too late for me, at any rate.

Just off the port bow loomed a massive shape, for a split second almost as terrifying as the man about to leap at me. Another granite stack, dangerously close. I dropped the gun and reached my right hand back through the spokes of the steering wheel, stretching up and back, towards the centre of the wheel where I knew the instruments must be. My fingers felt buttons and I began pressing. The buttons beeped at me in response. I had no idea what they were, I just had to hope.

Gair raised himself on tiptoe. I reached high again, grabbed a spoke at the top of the wheel and pulled down as hard as I could.

The boat responded; one of the buttons I'd pressed had disengaged the auto-pilot and I was in control of the helm. Travelling at speed, the launch almost tipped over under the force of the abrupt turn. Below, objects rolled across the cabin floor and I heard Dana cry out. Gair staggered, almost slipped, grasped for something to steady himself and then miraculously regained his balance.

Just as we hit the twenty-foot-high granite stack.

As the boat swerved, I'd fallen to the floor of the cockpit; the force of the impact threw me back against the wheel, jarring my shoulders and nearly knocking me out. Through eyes that could barely see I watched Stephen Gair fly towards me. His eyes held mine and in that split second I saw fury, then fear, as he sailed through the air and crashed hard against the steering wheel. I heard a crack that I knew must be bone breaking and made myself turn to face him as he collapsed over the wheel. Then the freewheeling motion of the boat sent him over again, to land slumped in the stern of the boat.

I took hold of the wheel and dragged myself up. I pulled myself around it, close to Gair. He was starting to move, to lift his head up from the deck. Bracing myself against the wheel I kicked out; my foot connected and he slid backwards. His hand shot out and grabbed my ankle. I held the wheel with both hands, lifted my other foot and jumped on his wrist. He let go and I kicked again. He slid further back and I kicked him again, this time connecting with his face, sickened that I was capable of such violence but unable to stop. I pushed one last time with both feet. I fell down into the stern as he slid overboard.

I don't know how long I knelt there, staring down at the wash. I think I even considered rolling overboard myself. Realistically, it could only have been a few seconds before I realized the boat was spinning out of control. I crawled back into the cockpit and reached for the button that would switch the engines off. The engines died and their sound faded into the night. The boat was still moving with the wind and the tide, but no longer careering around madly. And that was it, absolutely it, nothing more I could do. I collapsed down, leaning against the steering wheel, wondering where help might come from. Whether there was any real possibility of it doing so.

Then Dana's face appeared in the companionway. She saw me, but still didn't seem able to speak. Then she disappeared and I wondered if she'd fallen. I wanted to go and help her; I think I even tried to stand up, but I couldn't do it. I wanted to cry, too, but I didn't even have the energy for that.

Then something appeared over the top of the companionway steps. A tangle of canvas straps and metal. It was a life jacket – they'd been stored on one of the shelves around the main cabin. I watched and another appeared. Then a third.

'Tora, come on. Get one of these things on yourself.' I could barely hear Dana's voice, so feeble did it sound against the wind. Reaching up, I took hold of the wheel and managed to pull myself up on to all fours. I crawled round the wheel and across the cockpit floor. My leg was throbbing again and I tried not to think about it; to concentrate only on getting to the steps.

A hand appeared, a woman's arm. I reached out and grabbed it. I had no strength but I held on as I fell backwards and a woman collapsed over the top of the steps. Her dark hair fell forward, covering her face. I pulled again and heard Dana grunt as she pushed from below. The dark-haired woman came up over the steps and landed on top of me. I pushed her to one side. It was Freya, the younger of the two. Her eyes opened briefly, she stared at me then closed them again and sank back against the cockpit seat.

I heard Dana's voice calling 'Tora', saw a movement at the steps, more hands on the rails. Odel was climbing up by herself. She looked weak, barely able to focus, and I guessed Dana was pushing her up. I reached out for her hand as she staggered up, over the steps and into the cockpit. She gasped at the cold and almost fell against me.

Somehow I managed to stand up and stumble to the steps. I reached out and took hold of Dana's arm. She came up surprisingly easily and I helped her climb over the last step. As the wind hit her she started shivering violently. Below, I could see the cabin floor was underwater and it was rising fast. Gair had said we would have ten minutes once water started to flood the boat.

Dana's eyes met mine. 'Life jackets,' I gasped, looking at Freya and Odel. Dana – sensible, practical Dana – was already wearing hers. She nodded and passed one to me. I managed to pull it over my head and fasten the metal buckle. Dana helped me pull jackets over the other two and then I inflated all of them and switched on the small lights that would give anyone searching for us just the ghost of a chance.

Water was breaking over the stern now and all four of us were sitting in an icy pool. Spray was soaking us, filling the cockpit every few seconds, hastening our descent. There was no time for the life raft, even if I could find it. I grabbed four harnesses and clipped our life jackets together at the waist. Sink or swim, we were doing it together.

'Can you stand up?' I yelled at Dana.

'I think so,' she managed, and together we struggled to our feet. Odel was able to stand with us and between us we supported Freya. Her eyes were darkening – she was sinking again. I climbed on to the seat and then the side deck. Dana followed, then Odel, and we dragged up Freya. Stumbling, grasping at anything that looked firm, we made our way to the stern of the rocking boat until we were all standing, looking down at the motionless propeller. I unclipped the rail and held tight to one of the stanchions.

'We have to jump,' I shouted, wrapping my other

arm tightly around Freya's waist and looking at Dana and Odel to make sure they understood. 'I'll give the signal.'

Dana nodded. Odel was struggling to keep her eyes open but Dana wrapped one arm tightly round her and grasped a stanchion with the other.

I lowered myself on to the top step. We'd left Tronal far behind and there was no land close enough for swimming to be an option. Waves were now washing over my feet. I turned back, almost lost my balance and nodded to Dana.

'After three,' she gasped. 'One, two, three, go!'

We leaped through the air and hit the silky smooth welcome of the ocean. Stars sparkled all around us as we sank lower and the blackness below reached up its arms and carried us down. I felt no cold, no pain, no fear, had no sense of the women around me, although I knew they were there.

I was filled with a sense of peace, of finality; it wasn't so bad after all, this dying business, just sinking into silent, velvet-soft darkness.

But the will to live is wonderfully tenacious and I felt my legs moving, making swimming motions. Then the ancient laws of physics kicked in and the air in our jackets began to rise upwards, taking us with it. The surface broke around our faces like shattering glass and the salty night air leaped into my lungs. I reached out for Dana, found her hand and thought I saw the glint of her eyes as they met mine. Odel and Freya were just dark shapes in the water.

I could hear an engine again and knew that

someone was close. I tried to summon up fury that we'd been through so much, only to be picked up by the second Tronal boat, but couldn't do it. I didn't care.

The sound of the engine grew loud, almost deafening, but I had no sense of where it was coming from. I looked across at Dana and thought I saw her gazing upwards, a second before we were bathed in light.

When I opened my eyes again, I started screaming.

41

I WAS IN A SMALL, CREAM-PAINTED ROOM, WITH flower-prints on the walls and a door opening on to a private bathroom. I was back on Tronal, chained to a narrow hospital bed. My screams echoed through the building.

The door to the corridor slammed open and a nurse ran in, followed by an orderly and then a young doctor. They clustered round my bed, making soothing noises, trying to settle me back down again. I'd been sitting up. I looked down at my wrists. No shackles encircled them. I tried to move my legs. One of them moved easily, the other was too stiffly wrapped in bandages. No sign of chains. There was another bed in the room, but I couldn't see who was in it; the nurse was standing in the way.

The doctor was holding my arm, a syringe in his hand. I tugged free and hit him. He swore and dropped the syringe.

'No drugs. Don't you dare drug me!' I yelled.

'Sounds like she means it,' said a voice I knew. We all turned.

Kenn Gifford stood in the doorway. The others stepped back, away from the bed, unsure what to do next.

'Where am I?' I said.

'The Balfour,' replied Kenn. 'On Orkney. DCI Rowley and I thought you might all prefer to be off Shetland for a while.'

'Duncan,' I gasped, ready to start screaming again.

Kenn gestured across the room, a small smile on his face. The nurse had moved and I could see the man in the bed next to my own. Ignoring the pain, I pushed my legs over the side of the bed until I was standing.

Kenn put an arm round my waist and half steered, half carried me to Duncan's bed. My husband's eyes were open but dull. I didn't think he could see me too well. I reached out to stroke the side of his face. His entire head was bandaged. I didn't take my eyes off him as Kenn and the nurse settled me back down on my own bed.

'He took a nasty blow to the head,' said Kenn. 'We did a CT scan when you all came in this morning. The middle meningeal artery had been ruptured, causing an epidural haematoma.'

I watched as Duncan's eyes slowly closed. He'd suffered a fairly common form of head injury. The middle meningeal artery runs just above the temple on either side of the head; the skull is thin at this point, making the artery vulnerable to injury. An epidural haematoma, or build-up of blood between the skull and the brain, can compress the delicate brain tissue and, if not treated, lead to brain damage, even death.

'Will he be OK?' I asked.

'We think so. The blood had time to clot so he needed a craniotomy, but it was all fairly straightforward. They'll keep him sedated for another twelve hours or so.'

The younger doctor had picked up the syringe and was hovering.

'Don't even think about it,' I spat at him.

He and Kenn exchanged a look. Then he left the room. The nurse and the orderly followed and the door closed behind them.

Kenn sat down on the bed.

'Dana and the others? They're here?'

He nodded. 'Dana discharged herself a couple of hours ago. Alison and Collette are still here. Both doing fine.'

For a second I wasn't with him. Then I had it. Freya and Odel: of course, those hadn't been their real names.

'Alison and Collette,' I repeated. 'Tell me about them.'

'You need to rest.'

'No, tell me who they are,' I said, trying to push myself up and not managing it. Duncan's eyes were still closed but the steady rise and fall of his chest was reassuring.

Kenn got up and propped up the bed.

'Collette McNeil is thirty-three,' he said, sitting down again. 'She's married with two young children and lives just outside Sumburgh. Every morning she takes the kids to school and then walks the family dog along the cliff top, over on the west coast. A month ago she was doing exactly that when she was approached by some men. Next thing she can remember is waking up on Tronal. The dog found its way home and raised the alarm. Everyone assumed she fell over the cliff.'

'Her family. They know?'

Kenn nodded. 'Her husband's with her now.'

'And the other one? Alison?'

'Alison was a tourist. Came up here with some friends but split up from them to explore the islands on her own. She can't remember what happened, she's pretty traumatized, but she was apparently seen getting on the ferry from Fair Isle three weeks ago. No one saw her arrive back on the mainland. She was presumed drowned.'

'They couldn't afford bodies to be found this summer,' I said. Kenn frowned at me. 'Stephen Renney isn't one of them,' I explained. 'He's only been at the hospital a few months; he isn't even from Shetland. They couldn't risk faking a death at the hospital this year. They would all have been accidents, with the bodies never recovered.'

Kenn fell silent. We listened to the sounds in the corridor outside, to Duncan's breathing. 'I guess,' he said eventually. 'Look, that's enough now.' He stood up. 'You need to rest.' As he made to leave the room I felt panic rising again.

'No drugs, no sedatives, not even painkillers. Promise me,' I said.

Kenn held up both hands. 'I promise,' he said.

'You're not one of them, are you? They said you're not one of them.'

'Take it easy. No, I'm not one of them.'

'Richard, he's . . . I'm so sorry.'

He walked back and took hold of both my hands. 'Don't be.'

'Between four and five hundred, he said. They're everywhere. They could be in this hospital.'

'Calm down. You're both perfectly safe. I won't leave you.'

'I'm so tired,' I said.

He nodded and wheeled the bed back down again. Then he bent over and kissed me on the forehead. I managed to smile at him as he sat down in the chair beside me, but it was Duncan's face I was looking at as my eyes slowly closed.

Epilogue

A skylark had woken us, just as the silvery light of early dawn was beginning to soften and turn gold. Before breakfast we walked along the cliff tops, watching the waves break on the rocks below and hordes of seabirds bustle about building nests, preparing for the imminent arrival of parenthood. The day was unseasonably warm for late May. Sea pinks and the tiny, blue, bell-shaped flowers of the spring squill were scattered over the cliffs like confetti. Walking home along the roadside, we could hardly see the grass beneath the thick rug of primroses. Shetland was at its best and most beautiful. And a small army of English police officers were searching our land for the remains of Kirsten Hawick.

Duncan and I sat on the flagged area at the back of the house. Even from a distance we could see they meant business this time. The soil samples they'd taken previously had all tested negative for phosphate. Further analysis, on Helen's orders, had indicated the samples hadn't come from our land at all. Big surprise! So the process had begun again. More samples taken, tested at a different lab; and this time, several positive results.

Now, our entire field had been divided up into a grid. Metres of tape criss-crossed the length and breadth of it, held in place by tiny metal pegs. The officers, working in teams of three, were systematically checking square after square after square: measuring, probing, digging, paying particular attention to the areas where phosphate had been found. They'd been at it for four hours and had covered a good quarter of the field. They'd found nothing so far. But the world's media, who'd been camped on our doorstep for the past week, seemed to have swollen in ranks this morning. A sense of grim expectation hung in the air.

Two weeks had passed since our adventures on Tronal. My leg was healing well, Duncan had made a near complete recovery. We'd been incredibly lucky. My detour to Dana's house that night had saved our lives. Helen had instructed one of her constables to collect something she'd left behind there. He found the envelope I'd addressed to Helen and, on her instructions, opened it. Hearing what I was up to (and, I'm told, cursing non-stop for the following two hours), Helen had sent a dozen officers back to Tronal. They rescued Duncan from the basement and my stolen dinghy from the beach. Helen herself directed the operation from on board a police helicopter, the same one that picked us out of the water after the boat went down.

And then the fun really began.

Twelve island men, including the staff of the Tronal clinic, several hospital personnel, Dentist McDouglas, DI Andy Dunn and two members of the local police force, are being held in custody on various charges, including murder, conspiracy to murder, kidnapping and actual bodily harm, to name just a few. Superintendent Harris of the Northern Constabulary has been suspended from duties pending an internal inquiry. Duncan tells me that these men are the tip of the iceberg and I don't doubt him for a second. Of course, believing is one thing; actual hard evidence is proving as elusive as the Trowie folk of legend. These thirteen may be all we ever get.

Stephen Gair is still missing. Whether he's alive or dead we have no idea. We can only hope.

Richard's funeral is to be held on Unst tomorrow. We sank, that night, in relatively shallow water and the launch, with his body on board, was easily recovered. Half of Shetland are expected to turn up to honour Richard's memory, but Duncan and I will not be among them. We've talked about it at length but neither of us can face it. There are still faint bruises around my neck; I can't pretend to grieve for the man who put them there. Neither can I look into the faces of the congregation and wonder . . .

Duncan's motivation is more complex. He is struggling to deal with how close he came to becoming one of them.

So Kenn will be our proxy tomorrow. We've seen

quite a lot of him the last couple of weeks. He's formed a habit of turning up unannounced, usually at mealtimes. He still flirts disgracefully, but only when Duncan is in the room. Other times, he avoids being alone with me so that problem, at least, has been shelved for the time being. I still haven't got to the bottom of who stole whose girlfriend and I suspect I never will; I'm not sure either of them really cares any more. It was Kenn, we discovered, who performed the surgery that removed a clot from Duncan's brain. At the end of the day, I guess, it's difficult to continue hating someone who has saved your life. Besides, they both enjoy bitching about the seemingly endless police investigation.

So far, no charges have been brought against either Duncan or Kenn, but we don't feel we can breathe easily just yet. The strongest point in Duncan's favour is that when Helen's team raided the island that night he was found locked in the basement, bleeding profusely from a head wound and not too far from death. The fact that he didn't set foot on Shetland for nearly twenty years will help too. As far as Kenn is concerned, he was conveniently out of the country during just about every summer when the female death rate peaked. I think Richard went to great lengths over the years to protect his favourite son.

The Tronal maternity clinic has closed for good. The two infants I saw that night have been transferred to a neonatal unit in Edinburgh and are both doing well. Their birth mothers will be traced; as will all the women who attended Tronal for a late termination in recent years. What their legal relationship will be to the babies they thought they'd aborted, who can say. Just another of the many unholy messes to come out of Tronal.

The land around the clinic is being extensively searched. Some human remains have already been found but, from what I can learn, it's going to be a long job. In one area, close to the beach where I landed that night, several tiny skeletons have been unearthed. Of all the babies born at Tronal over the years, these are the ones for whom my heart cries the most. The ones who didn't make it.

Collette McNeil and Alison Rogers are both pregnant as a result of their stay on Tronal. No intercourse had taken place; the pregnancies were achieved by doctors opening the women's cervixes and inserting sperm directly into their uterine cavities. Lawyers are currently arguing over whether, technically, that constitutes rape. Collette is planning a termination. She and her family are leaving Shetland. Alison, a twenty-year-old single girl, is thinking of keeping the baby.

I turned at the sound of footsteps on gravel. Dana had made it through the press barricade and was walking towards us. She was wearing jeans and a large shapeless sweater, her hair scraped back in a ponytail. I hadn't seen her since the night we all leaped into the ocean together and she looked smaller and thinner than I remembered. When she reached us, she didn't seem to know what to say.

‘Thought you were in Dundee. On sick leave,’ I said, because she looked as though she might start crying and I wasn’t sure I could handle that. There had been too many tears over the last couple of weeks.

She pulled a wooden folding chair forward and opened it. ‘Supposed to be,’ she agreed. ‘Bored to death. Flew back this morning.’ She sat down next to me.

‘I think you might be in trouble,’ said Duncan, who was looking towards the top of the field. We both followed his eye line. Helen, in a white jumpsuit, had stopped bustling about like a mother hen and was staring down at us.

I turned back to Dana, risked a smile, saw its pale reflection on her face.

‘How are you feeling?’ she asked, her eyes dropping to my stomach.

‘Dreadful,’ I replied, because that was close enough, but there really aren’t words to describe what a woman goes through in the first trimester. Just as soon as I could talk on the phone without vomiting over it, I was going to contact all my past patients and apologize for not being sufficiently sympathetic.

‘And is that . . . good?’

‘No, but it’s normal,’ I said. We fell silent, watching Helen torn between wanting to come down and lay into Dana for coming back to work and needing to stay where she was and get on with the job. All the while I was thinking that the only remotely normal thing about my pregnancy was the little creature at the centre of it. Jenny had scanned me yesterday. Duncan and I had held hands, tears streaming down both our faces, as we watched a shapeless little blob with a very strong heartbeat, totally oblivious to what had been going on around it.

'And I suppose we're hoping for . . . a girl?' said Dana tentatively. I heard Duncan give a soft laugh and it seemed like a very good sign.

A sudden noise grabbed my attention. On the fence that ran the length of the field were a group of pale-grey birds with forked tails, black heads and red beaks. They were Arctic terns, come back from their long winter in the southern hemisphere. Hoping to nest in our field, as was their usual custom, they were frustrated at the sudden human invasion. Terns are not placid birds. They jumped around on the fence, circled overhead, yelling down at the police officers to be off and find somewhere else to dig. Didn't they know this was breeding ground?

'I think they've found something,' said Dana.

My attention snapped away from the birds. 'Where?'

'That group near Helen. Tall man with sandy hair. Woman with thick-rimmed glasses. Near the reed bed.'

I watched. The small group Dana was talking about was no longer one team among many, it had become the focus of activity up on the field. One by one, other white-clad officers were stepping closer.

'Oh, they've been doing that for the last hour,' said

Duncan. 'I think that team's just more excitable than the rest.'

'They're very close to where I found Melissa,' I said, in a voice I wasn't sure would carry. Nobody spoke. Up in the field four men started digging in earnest.

'We should go inside,' said Duncan. Nobody moved.

The digging went on. Activity around the rest of the field had stopped. All eyes were on the four men with spades. Even the terns seemed to have quietened down.

Clouds began to roll in from the voe. The land, so rich in colour just moments earlier, fell into shadow. No one, either in the field or on the back terrace of the house, seemed able to talk. We listened to the regular thud of spades against damp earth and waited.

When I didn't think I could bear it any longer, the digging stopped. The men with spades stepped back and others strode forward. Cameras began clicking, people were talking into radios, equipment was unloaded from the vans parked in our yard and a surge of excitement ran through the press ranks. Helen started to walk down the hill towards us.

The perfectly preserved, peat-stained bodies of four women were eventually found on our land. The first they dug out of the ground that day was Rachel Gibb; the others have since been identified as Heather Paterson, Caitlin Corrigan and Kirsten

Hawick. All were names I knew: I'd seen them on my computer screen the night I met Helen. In the days that followed I learned more about them, where they'd lived, who they'd been, how they were believed to have died. And I spent more time than was good for me imagining their final year. Torn from their lives, cut off from everyone they loved, these women had to face the long, painful drudge of pregnancy and the terrifying ordeal of childbirth alone and in fear. They'd had the best medical attention possible, but no one to hold their hand, give them a reassuring hug, tell them it would all be worth it in the end. Prisoners of their own bodies as much as of the men of Tronal, these women had sat in their pens like pregnant cattle, biding their time until their purpose was served and they were needed no more. And if thinking of this makes you want to howl with rage, then join the club, my friend, join the bloody club.

Each woman brought out of the earth that week had had her heart cut out, just as Melissa's had been. Each had three runic symbols carved into the flesh of her back: Othila, meaning Fertility; Dagaz, the rune for Harvest; and Nauthiz: Sacrifice.

The search has been called off now, much to my dismay, because I know there must be two more bodies buried somewhere; seven KT boys were born a year after these women supposedly died. The police team insist, though, that the fields behind our house have been thoroughly searched; even Duncan and Dana are telling me to leave it now. So these women will stay out there. They may lie in the Shetland earth for all time, along with all the other women who have disappeared without trace on these islands over the centuries. Or they may turn up out of the blue one day when someone, too ignorant to know better, dares to disturb the ground.

The terns have found somewhere else to build their nests now. We don't blame them: we're going to do the same.

Afterword

The stories on which *Sacrifice* is based are documented, but not extensively; largely because for many years Shetlanders felt no need to write them down. The remote location of the land kept its population stable and for a long time word of mouth was considered enough. I have learned that there was even a certain reluctance amongst the islanders to talk about these strange and supernatural events.

But gradually, over the years, people from outside the islands became interested, then intrigued, and books about Shetland lore began to appear in our bookshops. It was my discovery of the chilling legend of the Kunal Trows (in Aylesbury Public Library of all places) that gave rise to the idea for *Sacrifice*. I wrote this in the English home counties, not venturing north until it was all but complete.

And so my first real glimpse of Shetland was on a clear, crisp morning in late November. The huge expectations I'd built up over several years of writing about the land were not remotely disappointed; I thought it easily the most beautiful place I'd ever seen.

From Sumburgh airport I drove north up the main island, unable to stop smiling as each bend in the road offered a view more stunning than the last; across Yell, the colour of an autumn leaf, and on to Unst, which truly must be the loveliest and loneliest place on earth.

Throughout the day the people I met were warm and friendly, effortlessly helpful and entirely normal (what, I asked myself, had I really expected?), and I wondered that these marvellous islands could be so little understood, so rarely visited. I began to have misgivings: could I really have written such a grim story about such a warm and wonderful land? And yet . . .

Later that evening, Lerwick seemed unnaturally quiet and uncomfortably dark as I followed my map to the small church of St Magnus. Try as I might, I couldn't bring myself to walk down the shadowy, silent street with the weird trees and the empty, brooding buildings. I decided to come back in daylight, and walked instead towards the sea. Dark, damp fishing nets were strewn across every driveway: quite what or who they were destined to catch I didn't like to dwell on. I reached the beach, only to find a group gathered silently around a massive bonfire on the sand. Was it a delayed Guy Fawkes celebration (it was long past November 5), or something else entirely? I remembered all the stories I'd read, of women disappearing, of prisons on remote islands, of shadowy grey men who preyed on their human neighbours, and Richard's words crept, unwanted, into my head. 'So many stories, so much nonsense: little grey men who live in caves and fear iron. Yet, tucked away inside all legends, a kernel of truth can be found.'

I headed quickly back to my hotel, reflecting that, whilst I might technically still be in Britain, I was a long way from home . . .

THE END

Acknowledgements

Up front, a very special thank-you to Kerry and Louise, my two first readers, for proving that true honesty is something you will only ever hear from true friends (and younger sisters).

For patiently checking the medical detail, I am sincerely grateful to Dr Denise Stott and Drs Jacqui and Nick Socrates. Any remaining mistakes are entirely my own.

On the subject of mistakes, I tried very hard to make my portrayal of Shetland as accurate as possible, but there were a few occasions when its geography just didn't fit the demands of the story. I hope the islanders will forgive the occasional liberty I've taken with their wonderful landscape.

I relied a great deal on reference material and would like to acknowledge the following works: *The Book of Runes* by Ralph Blum, *Shetland Folklore* by James R. Nicholson, *British Folklore, Myths and Legends* by Marc Alexander, *Exploring Scotland's Heritage*, HMSO Books, *Northern Scotland and the Isles* by Francis Thompson, *Encyclopaedia of World*

Mythology by Arthur Cotterell, *Shetland: Land of the Ocean* by Colin Baxter and Jim Crumley, *Around Shetland: A Picture Guide*, published by the Shetland Times Ltd, *British Regional Geology: Orkney and Shetland* from the Natural Environment Research Council, *Grammar and Usage of the Shetland Dialect* by T. A. Robertson and John J. Graham, *Bodies from the Bog* by James M. Deem, *Human Remains: Interpreting the Past* by Andrew Chamberlain, *Modern Mummies: The Preservation of the Human Body in the Twentieth Century* by Christine Quigley, *The Scientific Study of Mummies* by Arthur C. Aufderheide, *Conception, Pregnancy and Birth* by Dr Miriam Stoppard and *Natural Solutions to Infertility* by Marilyn Glenville. For procuring most of these books for me, and never once batting an eyelid at my ever more peculiar requests, I am grateful to Sheila and her colleagues at my local library.

'There are nights when the wolves are silent and only the moon howls' is taken from the book *Brain Droppings* by George Carlin. Copyright © 1997 Comedy Concepts Inc. Reprinted by permission of Hyperion. All rights reserved.

I would like to thank Sarah Turner at Transworld for her confidence in the book and for her hard work in polishing away its rough edges; and also the rest of the Transworld team, especially Patsy Irwin, Nick Robinson and Kate Samano.

Last, and by no means least, my heartfelt thanks to Anne Marie Doulton of the Ampersand Agency and to the wonderful Buckman family: the best agents any author could wish for.

DC LACEY FLINT'S
FIRST PULSE-POUNDING INVESTIGATION

IS JACK BACK?

A savage murder on London's streets, 120 years to the day since Jack the Ripper claimed his first victim. A crime with all the hallmarks of a copycat killer. Detective Constable Lacey Flint must outwit a brilliant psychopath whose infamous role model has never been found...

Prologue

THE DARKEST HOUR I'VE EVER KNOWN BEGAN LAST Thursday, a heartbeat before the sun came up.

It was going to be a beautiful morning, I remember thinking, as I left the house; soft and close, bursting with whispered promises, as only a daybreak in early summer can be. The air was still cool but an iridescence on the horizon warned of baking heat to come. Birds were singing as though every note might be their last and even the insects had risen early. Making the most of the early-morning bounty, swallows dived all around me, close enough to make me blink.

As I approached the drive leading to Matt's house the fragrance of wild camomile swirled up from the verge. His favourite scent. I stood there for a moment, staring at the gravel track that disappeared around laurel bushes, kicking my feet to stir up the scent and thinking that camomile smelled of ripe apples and of the first hint of wood-smoke on an autumn breeze. And I couldn't help but wonder what it might be like to walk up the drive, steal into the house and wake the man by rubbing camomile on his pillow.

I carried on walking.

When I reached the top of Carters Lane I saw the door to Violet's cottage was slightly open; which it shouldn't have been, not at this hour. I drew closer and stood on the threshold, looking at the peeling paintwork, the darkness of the hall beyond. She was probably an early riser, old people usually are; but at the sight of that open doorway, something began to tense inside me.

The doorstep was damp. Someone with wet shoes had stood here minutes earlier. It didn't necessarily mean anything; it could easily be coincidence, but none of the reassurances I could summon up seemed to soothe away a growing sense of disquiet. I pushed at the door. It opened a further six inches and hit an obstacle.

'Violet?' I called. No reply. The silent house waited to see what I would do next. I pushed the door again. It moved a few more inches, revealing a damp trail on the floor. I squeezed round it and stepped into the hall.

The sack behind the door was hessian, with a string-tie pulling the opening tight. It looked like the sandbags the Environment Agency produces when floods are imminent. But I didn't think this sack had sand inside. It wasn't heavy enough, for one thing. Nor did it have the solid, regular shape of a sandbag, especially a damp one. And this one wasn't damp, it was soaking.

'Violet,' I called again. If Violet could hear me she wasn't letting on.

The door at the end of the hallway was open and I

could see the room beyond was empty. There was no sign of Violet's dog, Bennie.

And that's the point at which I stepped from anxiety to fear. Because a dog, even one that's elderly and far from well, won't normally allow someone to enter its house without a response of some sort. Violet could still be asleep; she might not have heard me call. Bennie would have heard.

Knowing it was the last thing in the world I wanted to do, I turned and bent down beside the sack. Wet, solid, but not sand; definitely not sand. I pulled out the small penknife I keep in my pocket, cut through the string and allowed the sack to fall open. Then I took hold of the bottom corners and tipped the damp, dead contents on to the worn linoleum of Violet's hall floor.

Bennie, looking even smaller than he had in life, lay before me. I didn't need to touch him to know that he was dead, but I bent and stroked his coarse fur even so. There were a few shallow wounds around his face and neck where he'd injured himself, scrambling to be free as he'd sunk deeper into whatever pond or river he'd been flung. But the sack still wasn't empty. I moved my fingers and something else fell out. Terribly injured, its body badly mauled and just about torn apart in places, the snake convulsed once before falling still.

For a moment I thought I'd be sick. I sank down on to the cold floor, knowing I had to find Violet, but unable to summon up the courage. And the strangest thought was going through my head.

Because it seemed that something was missing. I was remembering history lessons from school, when we'd studied Ancient Rome and hung on the teacher's every word as he'd entertained us with stories of Roman justice, torture and executions. One particular mode of death had caught our imagination: the convicted prisoner – who, I think now, must have committed just the worst sort of crime – was tied into a sack with a dog, a snake and something else; was it an ape – or some sort of farmyard animal? And then flung into the river Tiber. Most of the class had laughed. It was all so long ago, after all, and there was a touch of the comic about that particular collection of animals. Even I could see that. But I'd never really thought before what it must be like to be tied up in a sack with an animal – any animal – and flung into water. You would fight – frenziedly, hysterically – there'd be teeth and claws everywhere and water flooding into your lungs. And the pain would be beyond . . .

I had to find Violet.

I made my way along the hall and through the living room. A door at the far end led to the stairs. I found a light-switch and flicked it on. It wasn't a long flight of stairs but climbing it seemed to take for ever.

There were two open doors at the top. To the left, a small room: twin beds, dresser, fireplace, and a window looking out over woodland. I took a deep breath and turned to the right.

Part One

1

Six days earlier

HOW DID IT ALL BEGIN? WELL, I SUPPOSE IT WOULD be the day I rescued a newborn baby from a poisonous snake, heard the news of my mother's death and encountered my first ghost. Thinking about it, I could even pinpoint the time. A few minutes before six on a Friday morning and my quiet, orderly life went into meltdown.

Seven minutes to six. I'd run hard. Panting, dripping with sweat, I found my key and pushed open the back door. The moment I did so my young charges started screeching.

Rubbing a towel across the back of my neck I crossed the kitchen, lifted the lid of the incubator and looked down. There were three of them, hardly more than a handful apiece, hungry, grumpy balls of feathery fluff. Barn-owl chicks: two weeks old and orphaned just days after birth when their mother hit a large truck. A local birdwatcher had seen the dead owl and knew where to find the nest. He'd brought the chicks to the wildlife hospital where I'm the resident veterinary surgeon. They'd been close to death, cold and starving.

They'd been starving ever since. I took a tray from the fridge, found a pair of tweezers and dangled a tiny, dead mouse into the incubator. It didn't last long. The chicks were thriving but, worryingly, getting far too used to me. Hand-rearing wild birds is tricky. Without some sort of human intervention, orphaned chicks will die; at the same time, they mustn't become dependent on humans. In a couple more weeks I was hoping to introduce them to avian foster-parents who would teach them the skills they needed to hunt and feed themselves. Until then I had to be careful. It was probably time to move them to an enclosed nesting box and start using a barn-owl-shaped glove puppet at mealtimes.

Three minutes to six. I was heading upstairs for a shower when the phone rang, and I braced myself to be called in to deal with yet another roe deer run over on the A35.

'Miss Benning? Is that Miss Benning, the vet?' A young woman's voice. A very distressed young woman's voice.

'Yes, speaking,' I answered, wondering if I was going to get my shower after all.

'It's Lynsey Huston here. I live just up the road from you. Number 2. There's a snake in my baby's cot. I don't know what to do. I don't know what the hell to do.' Her voice was rising with every word; she seemed verging on hysteria.

'Are you sure?' Silly question, I know, but be fair,

a snake in a cot isn't something you see every day.

'Of course I'm sure. I'm looking at it now. What the hell do I do?'

She was too loud.

'Stay quiet and don't make any sudden movements.' I, on the other hand, was moving fast, out of the house, grabbing my car keys as I went, bleeping open the boot, reaching inside. 'Do you think it's bitten her?' I asked. Surprising myself, I remembered that the baby was a girl. I'd seen pink balloons outside the house a few weeks ago.

'I don't know. She looks like she's asleep. Oh God, what if she's not asleep?'

'Is her colour normal? Can you see her breathing?' I grabbed a couple of things from the back of the car and set off up the hill. I could see the Hustons' house, a sweet, whitewashed cottage at the top of the lane. The family was new to the village, had only lived there a few weeks, but I thought I could picture the mother, about my age, tallish, with shoulder-length fair hair. She and I had never spoken before.

'Yes, I think so; yes, she's pink. Can you come? Please say you can come.'

'I'm nearly there. The important thing is not to frighten the snake. Don't do anything to alarm it.' I pushed open the gate and ran up the path to the front door. It was locked. I ran round the back. The phone I was carrying was too far from its base station and began to beep at me. I switched it off and pushed at the back door.

I was inside a brightly coloured, modern kitchen. For

a house with a newborn baby it seemed remarkably tidy and clean. I put the phone down on the table and walked along the hall in the direction of the voice I could hear gabbling upstairs. As I approached the stairs I noticed damp patches and traces of mud on the otherwise spotless tiled floor. A familiar sound caught my attention. Glancing to the right I saw an incubator of newborn chicks in a small utility room. The family kept chickens.

'I'm in the house,' I called out softly. When I reached the top of the stairs I saw a scared, white face peering at me from behind a door at the far end of the corridor. The woman beckoned and I walked towards her. She stepped back and allowed me into the room.

I was in a small, pink and cream bedroom tucked under the eaves. Supporting beams stood out dark against the white plaster of the walls. Pink fabric, printed with fairies and toadstools, lined the small, deep-set window. Stuffed animals, mainly pink, were everywhere I looked. Against the longest wall stood the crib, a baby princess's cradle from a fairy tale: all cream lace and pink flounces. I stepped closer, still nourishing the hope that had sprung up when I answered the phone, that the snake would be a toy one, a practical joke played on the mother by an older child.

The baby, tiny and perfect, panted softly in a white baby-gro embroidered with pink rabbits. Her mouth was slightly open, I could see the perfect raised pores above her upper lip, long dark eyelashes and the faint traces of a milk rash on her cheeks. Her fists were clenched and her arms thrown above her head in the classic newborn-baby sleeping pose. She looked absolutely fine.

Apart from the fact that she was sharing her bed with a venomous snake that would strike the moment she moved.

Now read the complete book . . .
Awakening is out now